*Alarmingly correct at pred[icting]
the physical realities of glob[al]
warming...but predictions [of]
society's reactions have bee[n]
utterly wrong*

*Loss of Arctic ice will
exacerbate global warming,
taking the future out of
our hands with dreadful
consequences*

*I don't understand why
everyone thinks the loss of
Arctic ice is unimportant*

*The young will recognise
that the old generation have
knowingly ruined the planet*

*Keep climate change
conversations for
consenting adults*

*Many will fight to the last drop of
oil to destroy themselves and the
rest of the globe*

*There's still not a branch
of society that's started to
address the issues or even
ask the right questions*

*Spending time saving one's
soul is more worthwhile
than saving lives*

*We are already
starting to
see the rise of
protectionism and
nationalism*

*Over-population
and global warming
together...*

*Progenicide:
the acceptance that our
lifestyle will mean the death of
descendants or progeny*

Greenhush

A novel

Kendra

Thank you for
the support
Robert

R THORNILEY #11

A CIP catalogue record for this book is available from the British Library.

ISBN 978-0-9542599-2-1

Book layout and cover design by Clare Brayshaw

Artwork Front Cover – 'The Turl, Oxford' by Jane Thorniley-Walker
         Rear Cover – 'Seven Sisters' by Jane Thorniley-Walker

Prepared and printed by:

York Publishing Services Ltd
64 Hallfield Road
Layerthorpe
York YO31 7ZQ

Tel: 01904 431213

Website: www.yps-publishing.co.uk

Author's Notes 2021

This book has been written by an environmental and civil/structural engineer who spoke for the World Federation of Engineering Organizations at COP21 in Paris 2015. After preparing several technical papers and journals on risks and low carbon, the author intended this novel to provide an easy method for readers to hear the harsh details of what the future holds and how we have reached that crisis. It has been developed up to 2018 and the inspirational intervention of Greta Thunberg and other activists.

Some will find aspects of the story controversial:

- A male author has imagined life and the future through the eyes of a young, female outsider who sees truths that others reject.
- The risks from global warming have not been downplayed.
- The author has resisted removal of regional accents in characters.

Other aspects of the plot have been overtaken by events:

- Strife in Syria was originally intended to be just a theoretical risk.

- Global warming is now already at around 1.3 degrees Celsius and rising.
- From 2019, discussion of climate change is now more acceptable, yet this has not yet resulted in effective action, leaving responsibility to the young.
- Scientists predict that current promises of cuts to emissions will still leave the young generation facing devastating temperature rises.

This book is a work of fiction. Opinions on climate have been collected, but are not intended to represent the views of any individuals or institutions.

R Thorniley
MA(Oxon) CEng CEnv FICE FISructE MIHT IHBC FRSA

Acknowledgements

Thank you to Jane and Esther; my editor Sarah Speight; and readers Dan, Aliya, Eloise, Anwar, Miriam and Issy.

Greenhush

Dedicated to the next generation.

Sorry!

"When I consider the magnitude of the subject which I am to bring before you – a subject in which the interests, not of the Country, nor of Europe alone, but the whole World and of posterity are involved …. it is impossible for me not to feel both terrified and concerned at my own inadequacies for such a task."

William Wilberforce, 1789 abolition speech at the start
of his campaign against slavery

"The eyes of all future generations are upon you.
And if you choose to fail us, I say –
we will never forgive you."

Greta Thunberg, UN Climate Summit, New York,
23 September 2019

Contents

With the broad subjects of chapters

PART ONE

Prologue

The stone gargoyles and statues, carved on the spires and towers had been reshaped by hundreds of years of weathering, but they still watched as after months of sleepy summer quiet, the streets of Oxford once again started to come alive.

Each individual wandered or marched with their own ambitions, yet when combined with friends or unknown strangers, as viewed from the roof tops, they created a pattern. First there was a discernible trickle, then a flood fed by trains, taxis, coaches, buses and cars. These discharged their hesitant or confident occupants into the roads and alleyways where they soon learnt to dodge the ever-growing frenzy of cyclists. The flow continued to build, yet only from on high was it possible to see this human flow pond and drain into the ubiquitous quadrangles and stately buildings that made up the individual college fortresses. A new university year was about to begin.

CHAPTER ONE

Dreaming Spires

The ungainly, old-fashioned suitcase caught on the elevated threshold of the small entrance. The dull thud indicated the weight of the luggage and explained why the young woman was having difficulty manoeuvring it through the awkward opening.

The main oak gates were vast and ancient. It was difficult to imagine that the heavy black timbers could ever swing back on their hinges, built into the stone walls of the seventeenth-century gatehouse tower. The new student struggled to get through the smaller, inset doorway. Standing astride the high threshold, with one leg inside to hold the door open, she ducked her covered head and stood balanced – half in, half out of this new college world. She eased her smaller case past the doorframe with her left hand, leaned in and dropped it onto the worn stone flags with relief. Using both hands, she now swung the larger case through the doorway and up against the red sandstone wall that supported the carved vault of the gatehouse above her head.

The young woman let a rusty-red kilim backpack fall from her back, and stood clear of the door, which immediately yielded to a hidden closing force. It slammed shut. The narrow city street running between high stone frontiers of opposing colleges was sealed out, disappointing two tourists trying to peer through the opening. It banished the swarms of bicycles weaving their way between pedestrians, as well as the stacks of bikes propped carelessly against the college walls. The surprise, however, was the truncation of noise. The roar of an accelerating taxi and the calling of a tour guide were immediately muted, no longer able to infiltrate this enclosed fortress.

She had left the outside world. She was in.

A trickle of sweat ran down her neck, hidden by her headscarf. It had been further than she expected from the bus stop and the bus system had hardly been designed for use by strangers, but she could relax now. The occasion was not to be missed, so she ignored the other students who were reading the notices, and turned away from the advancing college porter, pulling her headscarf down over her forehead. People rarely dared attempt communication with an unapproachable woman. After three heartbeats, she heard the porter's confident, steel-heeled steps hesitate, and then retreat.

Rhan knew that her appearance would single her out. Despite the relatively fine weather, she was wearing her long black skirt that covered her feet, her black coat buttoned to the neck, and her burgundy-coloured headscarf. With her ridiculous height and her stooped stance, she knew that she offended, but she was used to that and it had its advantages.

'I have made it!' she whispered slowly and emphatically to herself. 'Yes!' Then for good measure, she repeated it in a few other languages. The porter looked up in surprise and heard strange mumblings echoing off the masonry stone walls, funnelled back past the post lockers to his open window in the lodge.

The warm flush and ache from her exertions soon subsided, and she mentally pocketed the money that her uncle had urged her to spend on a taxi from the station. It was a good start, but now was not the time to think about that mountain of student debt.

~

Two or three steps took her clear of the gatehouse vault and she was standing in the bright autumn sunlight, which illuminated the main quadrangle. This was her college now, and hopefully her refuge. How and why she had been selected, despite her stilted and stuttering interview, was a matter of conjecture. She had arrived here because she had dared to try, because of her hidden, tenacious stubbornness at school and her refusal to fit the mould of her new family. Now was the moment of triumph. There might never be another occasion when she had a dream come true, and this was the college of dreams. Since her acceptance, she had immersed herself in the fantasy worlds that took flight from these buildings and this city.

The front quad had a range of different buildings on its four sides. Most of these worked together in a harmony that spanned several centuries, but to her left, dwarfing the medieval tower in the corner, lay the problematic and ill-fitting chapel, which was the pride and joy of the college because it had been designed by Giles Gilbert Scott and housed Pre-Raphaelite artwork. There, in front of the chapel door and just twenty metres away, Inspector Morse had fallen onto the dusty paving slabs with a fatal heart attack. To Rhan, he had been the epitome of British charm, fair play and sympathy in a believable, yet fictional world.

As a student, Tolkien must have stepped through that awkward door behind her as a matter of routine. Would he have appeared to the porters to be deep in thought about his next tutorial? What would they have thought if they could have read his mind when he was a professor, filled with the ways of hobbits, the mystique of woodland elves on Middle Earth and an evil that would ruin the lives of all, even in the most tranquil parts of the Shire?

Another of Rhan's favourite characters, Lyra, had also lived here in a different universe or two created by Pullman. Lyra had been brought up here as an orphan of the college, eating with the college masters, learning from the scholars and yet enjoying the company of staff and the city kids. She had played on the rooftops of that three-storey range of buildings opposite and had run through the high-windowed dining hall to the right. Rhan studied the stone steps up to the hall intently, knowing that she had hardly glanced at them at her interview, but was now aware that she would be eating there later that evening just like Lyra. In the rooms over in the corner of the quad, at the far end of the dining hall, Lyra had saved Lord Asriel from being poisoned by the college master.

The scene was indeed magical and unworldly. The buildings opposite were completely covered with ageing leaves and the hoary, horizontal vines of Virginia creeper. Even at the beginning of October, the thick branches still clung to their glossy red leaves.

The noise of approaching voices and laughter reached Rhan. It dawned on her with a selfish thrill how quiet it had been since the door to the street had closed. There were no clues to the existence of the throngs of tourists from around the world who populated the street outside, beyond the "College Closed" sign. She was within the college fortress. It was just a shame that the rowdy voices she could hear also seemed to be on the inside.

The young men who were searching the noticeboards for anything of interest were clearly also new, and wandered off sheepishly when the porter began to draw bolts that would allow the unfeasible gates to swing wide open.

The porter had a square, short frame, and was probably ex-military. His official bowler hat and horizontal bushy moustache would make him look strange anywhere else, but here he was part of the furniture. Rhan smiled to herself when he tried to move her case to let the big door swing open; he could not know that it was laden with books. Her moment of isolation was broken, however, and she felt obliged to mumble apologies into the ground, collect up her cases, and seek directions and a key for her room.

A few minutes later, armed with directions to her third-floor room on Staircase 6, her way was barred by the noisy party, which had moved into the front quad and was growing as old friends were reunited. The loudest and heartiest voice belonged to a sandy-haired, stocky girl who was addressed as Alice as she received welcomes with copious and affected kissing of cheeks.

So the world of *Brideshead Revisited* really exists, Rhan thought to herself. A plastic smile appeared on Alice's face.

Self-consciously Rhan attempted a smile, but suspected she was failing, so she adjusted her headscarf instead. The popular young woman confronting Rhan was so much more real than the fantasy worlds Rhan had been imagining.

'Ah – welcome to the college,' Alice announced in a shrill voice that made the new arrival the centre of unwanted attention. 'I hope you enjoy your first year as much as I did.'

Rhan's tongue failed her as she took in this confident girl. The most she could muster in response was an uncertain 'Oh, thank you,' mumbled to the flagstone path. Not that it mattered much as Alice continued and Rhan couldn't help wonder if she spoke this loudly with the other newcomers.

'My goodness, you are so tall! You should definitely sign up for the rowing trial. It's one of the college's main sports and the boat club guarantees a good social summer. Have you rowed before? It doesn't matter but, where did you go to school?'

Rhan felt totally out of her depth and felt she had to escape from this barrage, but Alice was flanked by two young men, effectively barring her way. She had limited experience of interacting socially in public, but knew she was making a complete fool of herself.

'I am going to find my room.' Rhan managed to say as she walked around them, her eyes intently staring downward.

There were several seconds of shocked silence.

'Odd character!' a man's low voice pronounced. The scarcely whispered comments were clearly intended to reach the ears of the disobliging first-year.

'She could be just shy,' added another voice, followed by an unmistakable comment from Alice.

'Well, I used to feel sorry for shy people, but I'm afraid now I just find them rude.'

'No loss, Alice – she's far too round-shouldered for rowing. And I don't think she was sold by your summer Pimms parties either. Not the ideal candidate.'

The laughter resumed, leaving Rhan to fume as she walked away.

~

Her garret room overlooked the quaint city streets, which teemed with outsiders, yet it failed to excite Rhan as it should have done. It had a washbasin, a bed, a desk, two chairs and a boarded-up fireplace. The unpacking was soon accomplished and hardly changed the character of the room. But then – nothing.

She felt uneasy at the idea of having to share a bathroom on the next floor up with four or five strangers, especially if they were going to be like Alice and her male sidekicks. All the unheeded warnings against a mixed college came to mind.

The enthusiasm of her arrival was already expended, and was starting to be replaced by anxiety and loneliness. She now thought of Alan Bennett, another predecessor, whose gritty reality was perhaps more appropriate than the magical fantasies she'd been looking for.

She took to swearing at herself in Armenian, never a sign that things were going well. She should be used to being lonely, and even her parents would have been no help now.

She had left home and was at university, so she just had to make the most of it.

It now became her turn to scan the noticeboards and collect the deluge of junk mail already filling her pigeonhole. Going through the circulars amused her for half an hour. She shoved the blue educational book on sex in a drawer for perusal much later, if ever, but she carefully placed on the mantelpiece a letter from her tutors asking her to "drinks" at eight-thirty after dinner the next night.

She phoned Sunderland, but it was an ordeal. There was so much she could not say to her family, even to her sister who had never been to university. She must not mention that there were only four students starting Engineering in her college and she appeared to be the only girl. She must not mention how mixed everything was and, above all, she must not let her sister hear her cry. Thankfully, her sister was very easy to distract and only really wanted to discuss that day's developments regarding her engagement. Rhan, for the first time, felt pleased to hear of her sister's new life, even if it now allowed little place for the gawky little sister, who remained unmarried and an "infidel". Rhan ended the call feeling that there were still advantages to being away.

~

In the throng waiting for dinner, there was general excitement: a hundred and fifty young people, all wanting to know one another – except her. The girls were enjoying being at the centre of small circles of boys, and clearly felt no need to saddle themselves with such an unapproachable creature as Rhan. She sat alone on the crowded benches, sandwiched between two boys, who ignored her. With her head down throughout the meal, she hardly noticed the dining hall that she had expected to enjoy so much.

At school in Sunderland, she had not minded about being a loner, but it had been different. The local boys all seemed small and immature; they would never think of talking to the foreign girl. The Muslim boys knew better than to even look at her. The Muslim Asian girls had, however, accepted her, mainly because of the popularity of her older sister. They appreciated that she rarely spoke, but let her tag along with them, even if she never really joined in. Here, in these new surroundings, where everyone was out to make new friends, she was ashamed of her social ineptitude.

She thought of talking to the boy on her left who looked even more homesick and miserable than her. That made her smile – her, homesick? The boy was probably away for the first time, while she had left home years ago. Yet Rhan imagined that the boy still had a home, whereas her lovely house and secluded courtyards were now just a pile of broken rubble after the shelling. It didn't stop her feeling inadequate for failing to make the boy feel better.

She returned to her room and read *Pride and Prejudice* for the umpteenth time. Thankfully, Jane Austen had absolutely no interest in Oxford, one way or the other.

CHAPTER TWO

The Partner

At breakfast, there was little conversation in the hall, so Rhan enjoyed the sociable silence, interrupted by the chattering calls of the catering staff. She felt sufficiently at ease to gaze upwards at the extraordinary roof trusses, wondering if she would ever achieve the engineering knowledge to design such structures.

That day, Thursday, was the Freshers' Fair. She wandered alone through endless corridors with groups on all sides offering all sorts of fun, politics or relative danger, none of which appealed to Rhan. There was so much to choose from that she chose nothing.

Back in the quad, everyone appeared to be wearing various college sport kits. Groups were assembling, chatting excitedly to new team members. She spotted Alice gathering her rowers and as Rhan crossed to her staircase, she could hear Alice loudly recounting Rhan's deficiencies. It hadn't taken long, she thought, for her to feel like an outsider. An aching loneliness seemed to be enveloping her and she knew only one solution that could numb these feelings of dejection: a run that would get her as far away from this place as possible.

It was good to be out of the college and running free, but she was aware that she must present a strange sight: a weirdly tall girl in bright white trainers, black leggings and headscarf. She had felt less conspicuous in Sunderland – she had known the places on the windswept coast where she would meet no one but a few isolated fishermen.

~

At breakfast the following morning, she was forced to listen with both interest and disgust to tales about the night's drinking exploits. Two of her fellow freshers were already in trouble with the sub-rector. One of them, a character called Danny, was apparently a Cornish wrestling champion. They had been caught peeing in the main quad.

The prospect of meeting her tutors and the beginning of serious study became a beacon to renew her purpose in university life. Despite having done nothing all day, she arrived later than she intended. She eventually found where she was meant to be and was met at an elaborately carved oak door by Dr Field, the enthusiastic, chubby engineering Fellow of the college who had interviewed her almost a year ago. He brushed aside her apologies and Rhan got the strange impression that he was more nervous than she was. There was a tray containing two sherry glasses with different-coloured contents, and a glass of orange juice. He offered her the juice without asking which she wanted. She glimpsed just four people in the room beyond.

Dr Field led her into the wood-panelled room. It smelt of beeswax, cigars and a sweet odour that Rhan later identified as port. He introduced her to two young men whom she had noted previously in college. They stood holding empty sherry glasses and were introduced as Chi Tang from Nanjing and Coch Wei from Singapore. It was awkward as she stood towering over them, even with her head bent low. She knew that she should speak, but they were awkward too and only nodded their heads in greeting. Fortunately, Dr Field filled in the conversation gallantly, explaining that Chi Tang and Coch Wei had asked if they could have tutorials together.

'This leads me to introduce your maths tutor, Dr Oliver, and George Blackledge, the fourth engineering student in your year.' Dr Field escorted Rhan across the cosy room towards them. 'We had intended to have six new students reading Engineering, but one chap fell seriously ill travelling in his gap year and will have to drop back. I hope he makes a full recovery from whatever dreadful parasite he picked up and that he doesn't lose all capacity to carry out academic work in his two years away from it.

'The other regrettable loss…is, erm…a young lady who was meant to be joining us. She's decided against Engineering…to pursue Architecture.'

The slow awkward advance to the waiting pair presented plenty of time for Rhan to study the fine rug, which she decided was eastern Anatolian. One of the men, whom she took to be Dr Oliver, was wearing brown shoes, brown trousers and a matching brown jacket that made up a suit, worn by a short, weak-featured man who must have been close to retirement age. Returning her gaze downwards, she observed that the other pair of legs displayed a pair of neat brown suede boots, burgundy cords, and a brown-and-green tweed jacket with a blue tie. Rhan had to stifle a laugh at what she was beginning to recognise as an Oxford uniform. With a quick upward glance, she noticed that he was tall enough to be looking down at her bowed head.

'So, this presents you with a choice,' Dr Field continued, without needing much input from the students. 'You can either have your tutorials alone, or with George here. It's entirely your choice.'

There was an awkward pause before Dr Field remembered to introduce Rhan to the two men. Rhan smiled politely, not quite managing to meet their eyes.

'Usually we give tutorials to pairs of students. It works well. We would generally recommend that approach. Three is too many, and one-to-one can be awkward and create other complications. So, would you two mind having tutorials together?'

Rhan cast another glance upwards at George and found his green eyes looking at her with amused interest. He made no attempt to speak.

She nodded her assent, vaguely wondering what it meant, but found herself standing slightly taller. George must also have nodded because Dr Field suddenly relaxed. 'Good, good. Your first engineering tutorial would normally be with me on Tuesday, but at the beginning of this term, you will have ten days to prepare. Dr Oliver will tell you about tomorrow's maths tutorial with him.

'Here, in the meantime, are your lists of maths and engineering lectures.' He passed four sets of papers around the students. 'You will note that you generally have maths followed by engineering each weekday, with technical drawing or practicals after that.'

Dr Field now seemed positively relaxed, and continued in a semi-mocking, semi-commanding voice.

'Something that has been added for next Friday is a special lecture on Sustainability. The examination moderators have expressed concern that we, the Engineering School, were not adequately covering that subject. Sustainability is meant to permeate all areas of study. The head of Engineering has therefore asked me to notify all students that a guest speaker from the concrete industry is coming in to talk to all years. I am sure that you will all want to attend!'

Dr Field then passed over to Dr Oliver who told them at length how to find his office for the next day's maths tutorial.

Rhan was acutely aware that she was hardly making a good impression, so as the lecturers were finishing, she made up her mind to talk to her new tutorial partner, and possibly the other two. She steeled herself to ask George where he was from. She looked up, but he was leaving the room, followed by Chi Tang and Coch Wei. Surprised at being left alone, she turned to the two tutors who were helping themselves to an extra sherry.

Tentatively Rhan asked, 'What a lovely Turkish carpet. Is it as old as it looks?'

That was sufficient to launch the dons into discussions on wall panelling and carpets. Ten minutes later, she was able to slip away without having to say much else.

CHAPTER THREE

The Girl from Aleppo

Dr Oliver, the intense, dry-mouthed maths tutor, seemed to enjoy the challenge of the first tutorial with the unusual students. Rhan sat on one side of him, while George sat on the other.

They listened with interest to the slight man's instructions, musings and jokes over the Oxford system of tutoring, aware that Coch Wei and Chi Tang had presumably heard the exact soliloquy an hour ago in their tutorial.

'All our terms have eight full weeks numbered logically one to eight. Now you started two days early to settle in, so we are still in noughth week, ha-ha! Your lectures in maths are shared with the physics students and will be at nine each morning in the Natural Science Museum. If you get lost in there, you could find yourselves with shrunken heads in the Pit Rivers section of the museum, ha-ha! Your engineering lectures and practicals follow on afterwards and Dr Field will tell you about those.

'Now back to today and this week's maths. I would like you to read this book on matrices and sets. Please answer the marked questions at the end of each section. Concentrate in particular on the use of determinants. The booklet is of course available at Blackwell's or you might find a copy in the college library. Now normally in tutorials such as this I would go through any questions you had difficulties with, if any, ha-ha! For what is left of today I will help you with the first few questions, and you may recognise the first chapter from A-Level Further Maths.' He paused, before asking, 'Did you do Further Maths A-Level?'

There was a slight pause as he glanced at the silent students. 'Yes and no,' he said, interpreting Rhan's slight shake of the head and George's nod.

George asked some polite questions as Dr Oliver filled a sheet or two with numbers, while Rhan simply looked on, understanding only snippets of what he was explaining as he neatly manipulated the large bracketed sets of numbers. She felt a deepening dismay that she was only taking in a fraction of what her tutor was trying to teach her.

It was a relief when the hour ended and she and George could each head off to hunt down the book *Matrices and Sets,* so she could report back next Thursday afternoon, as instructed. George and Rhan parted without a word to each other. She frowned at George's brusque departure, disappointed. He just gave her a slight smile, pulling just one side of his mouth – or was it a grimace? For the first time since she had arrived, she had actually wanted to have a conservation. She was anxious to know if he had taken in anything during the last half-hour discussion of vectors and determinants. She was disappointed that her supposed partner had just headed straight off as though she was not worth the slightest effort.

As she searched the books in the college library, Rhan wondered about George. She had noted how he appeared to get on with so many in the college – except her. Her hope that study would restore balance to this frightening, surreal world now looked unpromising.

Rhan had to buy the textbook from a bookshop across the road. She entered the quaint little shop doubtfully and began to search for the obscure maths book. Once again she felt her senses overcome; it was like Dr Who's Tardis. From the cramped domestic-sized front parlour visible from the street, she passed into book-lined larger rooms, then stepped down into a more spacious sales floor before emerging into a space that felt like an underground warehouse, crammed with more books than she had ever imagined in one place.

Later, with *Matrices and Sets* open on the desk in her room, she felt ready to tackle the subject. The first two sentences appeared innocuous, but then each line of subsequent text and each progressing mathematical formula quickly evolved into a frightening new domain of mathematical jargon and symbols. The words gave only minimal hints to the derivation and direction of the logic.

After reading the first page three times, she turned to the next page, then the next, and flicked through the first few chapters with a sinking heart. This book was the worst of the nightmares that she had discovered since arriving in this illusory city. The longing to be back at her old school in Sunderland felt like a physical pressure, pushing against the insides of her body. She guiltily muttered a self-indulgent prayer to her parents – she needed their intervention more now than at any time since their death.

By Wednesday, four days of struggle with the textbook had confirmed her utter sense of failure in maths. Despair in advance of her tutorial had subsumed her previous self-pity about either loneliness or homesickness. She attended lectures in both maths and engineering and these just confirmed her inadequacies. The maths lecturer, performing to a vast hall of mostly young men, lost her within ten minutes. The smaller engineering lecture and the technical drawing made some sense but felt irrelevant as she waded and drowned in the gobbledygook of her maths textbook.

On the Monday afternoon, she made herself go for a second run. This time she noted how people in the streets or in the park reacted to the lone runner in a headscarf. On the Tuesday she simply wandered the streets, enviously watching the tourists who now seemed to have so little to worry about. She wished she could join them and simply move on, to visit the next city.

In vain, she attempted to give herself metaphysical slaps. At eighteen years old, she had already suffered more irreversible losses than most of the population of Oxford. Her early life had been ruined, but she was also lucky – her life was not in peril and she had a future, even if it may not be at Oxford. She had what her friends living in tents in Jordon or Lebanon could not even dream about. Yet such buoyant thoughts did not help for long. Previous hurts and sorrows had been obstacles to overcome for the sake of her sister or parents, but she was on her own now. Despite everything, she had never glimpsed depression before. She was surprised at how easily she could slide into the dark grip of despair. She crossed roads carelessly, almost hoping to be run over – an accident would remove her from this failure and her disappointment.

Her mathematical inadequacies were so unexpected. At school, the real challenge had been to hide how easy she found maths. It now came as a shock to find she could not grasp the subject nor understand the text. The ten main questions required by the tutor remained almost totally unanswered. It was all beyond her.

Her telephone calls home offered no reassurance. Her aunt had never heard of a matrix and repeated her advice – if Rhan had been her daughter she would be doing Islamic Studies rather than Engineering. Her sister could have been sympathetic, but was even more obsessed with her engagement. The outgoing and popular Aisha had settled quickly into Sunderland, but her life was now changing. She had lost interest in doing well at school and was now much more absorbed in her move to Bradford after the wedding. As usual, Rhan felt like the awkward second sister, who never fitted in anywhere.

'Yu'll just 'ave to work harder,' Aisha had said. 'Yu can't 'ave y'bed back – it's covered in engagement presents. Eee, it's all so exciting! You just keep at it – yu always managed to get top grades some'ow at school, so y'can now. Yu've been there nearly a week and ah bet yu've not made friends. Ave you even spoke to anyone yet, or looked at 'em?'

Rhan admitted only to herself that university had been a complete failure. She dreaded the prospect of returning to her uncle's house. It would be really awkward now that she was no longer a child.

That evening she waited in the queue outside the hall for supper, her headscarf cast low over her face, her shoulders hunched, thinking of what job she could do based on her A-Level exams. There was the added complication of where she could live – the prospects felt very lonely. Her contemporaries waiting on the steps around her gave her a wide berth; they had learnt not to try talking to the weird girl.

'Hi Rhan! Sorry to disturb you, but how are you getting on with that matrix tutorial?' She recognised George's voice, although it sounded strained and very different from the confident banter that he used when surrounded by his hearty friends. He was standing directly in front of her on the same step. He just carried on talking, without expecting a reply.

'I'm afraid I've not got far – I am really struggling. I just can't get my head round it or even understand the questions. I've been looking at it for days and it just means nothing to me. Can you help me, please?'

She looked up, pulling back her headscarf slightly to look, almost for the first time, at the troubled face of her tutorial partner. His green eyes no longer indicated detached amusement; she could no longer see the assured arrogance that she had assumed would prevent them from even being acquaintances. She stood up slightly straighter so he was not looking down on her, but then she had to turn away from him and let her scarf obscure her face. She felt ridiculously lightheaded and struggled to prevent herself from laughing like an idiot. *Play it cool*, she told herself angrily. She could tell that he stood ill at ease, watching her to see how his strange engineering associate would react.

'Are you laughing at me?' he asked, slightly amused.

She gained a bit of control and spoke, almost for the first time since her arrival at university.

~

'Sorry George. It is such a relief to hear that you too are struggling. You look like I felt twenty seconds ago.' She fought the urge to ask how someone who had everything needed her help. He was confident, presumably from a good school, with Double Maths A-Levels, probably with top grades – and yet he was asking her, the foreign misfit with just the basic maths background, for help. She bit her lip and cast him another glance. She laughed again, slightly more naturally this time at the sudden reversal of her despair.

He, in turn, this time threw back his head to laugh, but it was short and his expression quickly returned to doubt and anxiety as he looked down at her. Despite all his friends and high life, she felt sorry for him, but she still couldn't help giggling.

'Sorry,' she repeated, studying his face, 'I heard the other two discussing one of the questions and assumed you...I thought it was just me who was stuck. Yet suddenly I find that I am not alone. They can hardly send both of us home, can they?' Her head was down again, trying to hide her smile. 'I can tell you what I have learnt and which questions I understood, but it's only bits and pieces. It won't be much help.'

'Thanks Rhan! That would be great.' He sounded relieved.

There was a crash as the dining room door above them at the top of the steps flew open, and the college steward looked down with interest at the pair of them standing close together on the steps.

Rhan looked around with embarrassment, suddenly mortified at the spectacle that she must be creating, and checked to see if others in the queue were watching. Only a red-headed friend of George, two steps below, was taking any notice, smiling in amusement.

'That's David,' George explained. 'Come on, let's talk over dinner.' She nodded and they walked up together. As they filed through the open half of the hall door, he followed her closely. They were among the first into the hall, so she simply walked to the middle of one of the three aisles of long tables for the students. She looked down, as normal, but she was well aware that she was no longer alone. She forced herself to play it cool, hoping he didn't realise just how giddy she felt.

'Well, pleased to meet you Rhan. Is that what I should call you?'

She nodded at his formal reintroduction. They were standing next to each other, looking at the table, waiting for the dons to take their places at the top table so that they could all sit down after a perfunctory grace by the sub-rector. Other students were filling the benches around them. She felt his shoulder brush against hers, so she moved away just a fraction. Some of the warnings that her aunt had given her about young men came to mind; they no longer seemed quite as ludicrous as Rhan and her sister had thought. Fighting the lightheaded giddiness, she eyed the worn, polished oak bench, desperate to sit. George was now looking closely at her face. He moved his hand to his hip and she felt his elbow behind her back, providing surreptitious support that she could not spurn while the sub-rector said grace. Then while everyone else was taking their seats, George grabbed the water jug and filled two glasses.

'You all right? You're rather pale,' he murmured as he sat close to her, watching her sipping from a glass. Apparently not expecting a response, in a louder voice he announced, 'This is such a relief, Rhan! At least it sounds like we're in the same boat.'

'Thank you,' she responded ambiguously as she sipped her water, wondering at his surprising attention and empathy. She felt even more surprised at his sensitivity for covering up her weakness from those nearby. She looked around, noticing his friend David opposite her, who was talking to a girl Rhan knew was called Fiona.

'I had begun to think my short university career was a complete catastrophe,' she confided. 'I was resigned to going back to Sunderland, a failure.'

George looked up in surprise and immediately responded in a Northeast dialect. 'Sund'lund! Wey, yer n'ver a Mak'em, like?' He grinned and switched to imitating Rhan's slightly stilted English. 'David old chap, have you ever heard such correct and well-pronounced English? One would think that she must be Dutch!'

She laughed easily at herself. 'Well I come from many places, but Sunderland on the North Sea has been my recent home and I was also born near there.'

David smiled. 'Sorry Rhan, but even I don't think you sound like a northerner and I've never even heard of a… Mak'em. Mind you, you don't sound like a southerner either. Sunderland was the place that led the charge to get out of Europe, wasn't it?'

Rhan nodded. 'My English came from my mother who taught me using a series of old books from the 1950s,' Rhan admitted. 'You think I speak strangely? I have been in Sunderland several years, but I have been slow to adapt.'

'No, it's perfect,' George said with emphasis. 'It's only different because it is so perfect. You sound like an émigré princess.' George was obviously fishing for information without asking direct questions. After a week in effective solitary, Rhan didn't mind as she was actually enjoying talking, and had to check herself from ranting. The questions were probably just polite and they didn't expect full answers.

'Well, my sister and I have been living with my mother's brother and family. They took us in and have been exceedingly kind and hospitable. But they have five of their own children, so I was relying on this degree for independence. My sister is taking another approach; she is engaged to be married.'

'So you didn't fall for any of the Sunderland boys?' George asked.

'I was head and shoulders taller than most of the boys in my school.' Rhan found this unusually easy to admit. 'In fact, until I came here I had never come across anyone taller...which makes you a real freak in my eyes.' Both David and George laughed, along with the young man to Rhan's left who was listening to her occasionally. Fiona smiled in a puzzled manner, looking intently at Rhan.

'You don't eat meat?' George asked, looking at Rhan's vegetarian option. 'Is that for ethical or religious reasons?' He asked for the same dish from one of the team of young servers who made good pocket money after school.

'Not really. It is only because the butcher's streets in Syria and Iraq put me off eating meat. I'm Christian, so have no great excuse.'

'Wow, Syria and Iraq, you have been in some interesting places. A bit more exciting than Brighton.' George glanced at David, suspecting he had not heard her response.

'Syria?' David responded from across the table. 'I attended a wedding in Beirut when I was a kid. We went to the Beqaa Valley and travelled up to Aleppo for a few days. This was before the war,' he added for the benefit of several others, who were now listening to the conversation. 'Anyway, I'm glad to find that you can talk after all. We've never actually seen you speak to anyone, so we presumed you were very ... religious or something.'

'You know Aleppo?' she demanded in surprise, ignoring the rest. 'That was my home.'

'The city of Christian cathedrals, it was amazing. There were seven, or nine, within a square mile or something.'

'Yes, I was baptised as a Maronite, although in Aleppo I also used to go to the Armenian cathedral with my father. My grandfather was a Palestinian Christian who met his wife in a refugee camp in southern Lebanon. She was an aid worker from Durham. Each generation kept up the British connection, yet married a range of middle-eastern nationalities and religions. My mother married a

Christian water engineer and we lived in a cosmopolitan area of Aleppo, except for a few months in Iraq and trips to Sunderland. The religious aspects never seemed important until recently. My mother's brother, my uncle, returned to Britain and married a Muslim lady from West Yorkshire.

'Sounds interesting,' David responded, smiling. 'Until you got to the bit about marrying someone from Yorkshire. That's bad.'

'I come from Yorkshire, so David's entire knowledge of that county is based on me,' George explained, before adding quietly, 'Your college nickname, Miss Isil, is rather incorrect then?'

'It says much about the general ignorance of the college,' she retorted. 'Many of my neighbours have probably been killed by extremists…or by Assad, or the Russian bombing, or by the Americans.'

Another young man joined the conversation from across the table. 'So why the headscarf and black coat, if you don't mind me asking?'

She shook her head. 'This is what Christians wear in Syria. It is also a compromise on what my Muslim cousins and aunt would want me to wear in public. Anyway, enough about me; where are you from?'

George responded for them all. 'David and Fiona come from down south, the home counties. I come from North Yorkshire, so I know a bit about Sunderland. I went to a local school – not the private schooling David had. Then I worked on a building site and taught English in China in my year off.'

The conversation flowed easily and even the pauses were comfortable. Her head still swam slightly and she could almost watch herself from above, sitting chatting to a group of strangers. Even more bizarre was that most of them were male. She became acutely aware of the close contact, particularly because her black garb and strange manner had previously isolated her from such proximity. She had difficulty knowing whether moving away from George towards the boy on her left would indicate that she had some hang-up, but she had no idea whether George even noticed the occasional contact with her any more than he presumably had with the bloke on his other side. Rhan was relieved when he had occasional conversations with Fiona; even she managed a few separate words with David and the boy on her left, just to show that George was not special.

'You were in Syria?' David asked. 'Not a good place to be, particularly Aleppo, but you got out before the worst of it, did you?'

'Yes well, my parents were paranoid, or so we thought. They sent my sister and me over here to school early in the civil war. They had previously had to flee Iraq after just a few months and my mother had left southern Lebanon when young, so they knew the signs of trouble.'

'Good grief!' George said. Everyone on the table was trying to catch this conversation so the question from David could not have come at a worse time.

'So where are your parents now?'

There was an awkward pause.

'You don't need to answer that,' George said quietly, seeing the slight shake of her head and her face tighten. A little more loudly, he said, 'So, are you going to make the college football team, David?'

David was able to talk at length about his inadequacies at football to cover his embarrassment.

A bit later, she returned to an easier subject. 'Did David say that you have been watching me?' Rhan asked George quietly. 'How do you know I never speak?'

'I'm afraid we have all been watching you from a distance,' George responded, with a look at David. You and the organ scholar are certainly the most interesting characters in the college.

'Charming! Observe but do not engage.'

'Well you didn't seem to want to talk to anyone, boy or girl. Would you have chatted at that first tutorial meeting if I'd tried?'

'No, I suppose not,' she conceded.

'So, as your tutorial partner for the next three or four years, I decided not to be rejected in the first week, but to tread very carefully. I was also rather scared of you, I suppose!'

'Well where are we going to address these matrices?' she asked, changing to what she thought would be a safer subject. 'How about the library?'

'Sorry, but you underestimate the depths of my ignorance. Would you mind if we avoided having this session in public? Your room or mine?' His eyes dropped, realising that it was placing her in a difficult situation.

A sense of the unreal still carried her along. An image of her extended family, and what they would say, flashed through her mind again. Yet this was a different world.

'Yours? You probably have coffee and milk?'

'Yes, fine' he agreed, smiling.

~

There was nothing of the accidental contact from the slap on the shoulder, which George gave Rhan several hours later in appreciation of her insight into Question 6. It was their third attempt and one of the last major sticking points.

'You're a bloody genius!' he emphasised in relief. 'You're right, that's what that paragraph was looking for. So, the skinny matrix there is the "Eigen vector", which Question 7 is on about. Let's shove it in.'

There were papers and books scattered over the desk and among record sleeves on the floor after their six-hour study session. George had been pleased and surprised at her interest in his vinyl records of David Bowie and Pink Floyd, but they were aware that the college was now silent around them. Rhan's headscarf had slipped; she had given up trying to keep her distance, and up to the breakthrough, they had been sitting with their heads very close together, quietly discussing formula and sentences from each other's book. She found the excitement of the intimacy and his warm, rich breath more effective than coffee at keeping her awake. She wondered what it meant to him, but in the exhilaration of being alone with a young man, she was surprised to find that she was only really worried about the opinion of George's neighbours – especially when she had to creep up to the bathroom upstairs. The whole evening had been a surreal experience.

'Come on, that will have to be enough to get us through,' she sighed.

'Yup,' he grunted, flopping his head onto his arm. 'God, it's been hard work. It's half past three. Time to give in. It will be light in a few hours. Do you think we made sense of most of the questions?'

'Well, perhaps 60 percent. What a book! Let's see how many questions we've answered: 2, 3, not 4, most of 5 and 6, and a bit of 7. Not 8 or 9. We need to tidy up the answers, but will that be enough and do you think Dr Oliver will mind that we worked together?'

They both yawned as she stood up.

'I have no idea,' he responded without concern.

'Well, thanks for all the coffee and everything. See you tomorrow after lunch.'

'Are you skipping lectures?' he asked, surprised.

'No. I am still hoping that one day the lectures will shine some light on some of this maths. I will be there.' She reinstalled her headscarf.

'Well, in that case, I'll see you at breakfast in...well, just a few hours.'

Rhan opened the door to the landing, aware that others were asleep close-by. 'Goodnight,' she whispered with a smile.

She tiptoed down the uncarpeted and resonant wooden stairs, trying in vain to be quiet. With relief, she reached the external door at ground-level and stepped outside, pausing on the path surrounding the grass square. The quad was empty and refreshingly silent. Some oddly shaped clouds could be seen peeking over the roofs of the surrounding buildings, lit up by the city's light pollution beyond the college walls. The still courtyard reminded Rhan of the yard at home in Sunderland, safe from the streets outside, where gymnastics and feats of daring had been the primary preoccupation for her and the young cousins.

After a moment's hesitation, she skipped off the path and ran straight over the grass, past the "Keep off the grass" sign towards her own stairs in the opposite corner of the quad. Enjoying the soft grass and the extra space not available in the yard at home, she adjusted her stride, threw herself into a handstand, took three "steps" with her hands, and sprung back to her feet, her headscarf and black coat still in place as normal.

She had taken only a few self-satisfied paces across the grass to the sanctuary of her staircase when the silence was broken by a clatter of a window opening behind her. There was the quiet but unmistakable sound of clapping. She grinned and without looking round, she raised a finger over her shoulder towards George's window. It was the first time she had ever made that rude gesture and she had no idea whether he could have seen it in that light, but she guessed he would be amused by her defiance and cheek. Her whole body tingled in excitement at the idea that she might have a friend. She'd never felt so alive.

~

There was no return to normality for her at breakfast. George was already seated with friends when she walked in, but he beckoned her over to a seat he had saved. This broke the normal protocol of sitting in the order that students staggered into breakfast, but no one objected and she was greeted by nods and smiles and had to say 'morning' three or four times as she sat down. Being totally withdrawn and silent was no longer going to be an option.

For those sitting around George, their late-night ordeal to prepare for their tutorial had clearly been a topic of general conversation, as far as breakfast chat went. She was relieved to find that it was not a secret.

'Morning, George! Are you still buzzing from all that coffee last night? You clearly look pleased with yourself now that we have something prepared for Dr Oliver.'

'Well that's me – dedicated to the protestant work ethic!' George replied. Rhan had seen George noisily join a contingent heading off to the catholic chaplaincy last Sunday and had heard, but not fully understood, his joking about the excessive Jesuit influence in the college, so she responded with an Irish twist she borrowed from *Father Ted*.

'That'll be you and me excluded then. Anything that was correct from last night's effort could only have come with the help of my prayers to the blessed Virgin Mary.' Several heads from around the quiet breakfast tables shot upwards by this early morning surprise from the quiet girl, previously known as "Miss Isil".

~

Lectures were also very different. 'I usually sit at the front – the benches are less crowed there,' she urged as they walked through the museum between aisles of beetles displayed in trays and past the reconstructed bone structures of a couple of dinosaurs.

'But I have a new paper aeroplane design I want to try out,' George protested. 'Please try the balcony?'

She was pleased to agree and followed him up a spiral stair to the timber gallery. The view of the lecture hall was good, but the rows were ridiculously packed.

'Sorry, bad idea!' he admitted once they were squeezed into a row at the front behind the solid balcony rail. 'It's been fine on previous days, but appears to be getting rather too popular. Cosy isn't it?'

Twenty minutes later, she whispered, 'You are not listening at all, you childish kid.' She watched him create a bat-shaped paper aeroplane. His activities involved his elbows encroaching into Rhan's space far more than necessary, which she observed with interest and even brazenly retaliated. They took in little of the lecture, but managed to keep awake.

The flight of George's paper plane, just as the lecturer concluded, was extremely spectacular involving a complete circle, before crashing to the feet of the retreating don. He ignored several other planes that landed around him, but Rhan was horrified when he suddenly stopped and picked up George's elegant bat-like model, and waited for silence. The packing of pencil cases and files and the rush to the doors all stopped, as everyone wondered if the culprit was in trouble.

'It is always disappointing to see that the engineers and physicists of today...,' there was a pause while the grey-faced mathematician peered at his silent, frozen audience before he pulled George's origami to pieces, '...have no better designs than in my day.'

He was immediately contradicted by the flight of a circular, modern paper creation with an almost triangular tail, launched apparently from the bench to the right of George and Rhan. Everyone watched, including the lecturer, as it dipped and soared twice in a beautifully straight trajectory, hitting the blackboard above the don's head. He snorted, and marched off while everyone, including the relieved George and Rhan, burst out clapping.

Leaving the museum lecture theatre, Rhan and George walked with other students over to the Engineering lecture theatre, which was in the base of a separate six-storey tower. They walked side by side on the footpath, talking occasionally to Coch Wei and Chi Tang ahead of them, or to engineers from another college behind. Rhan was glad of the exercise and fresh air between two lectures after her short night. The occasional touch of George's arm enlivened her more than the fresh air and was surprisingly reassuring.

The next lecture, on electricity, was more civilised without the physics students, and the subject more comprehensible. As soon as it was over, they dashed back to college, promising that they would buy bikes to save time and effort in future. They reconvened in Rhan's room for a final polishing of their input before the afternoon tutorial, but made little extra progress.

'Sorry, but I need food before we go,' George admitted after an hour. 'We're nearly there. Any tea?'

'Sorry, I only have green tea,' Rhan replied, smiling. 'With one mug, one plate, one knife, and a teaspoon. It is silly isn't it?'

'No it's fine. That solves the milk problem. I'll get some food from the lunch bar to share back here, if you can make the brew.'

Ten minutes later, sipping the green tea, George said, a little surprised, 'That's almost nice.' He passed her the cup of tea in exchange for yoghurt. 'And cosy.'

She idly watched him copy the last answers before he put down his pen and finished off the last spoonful of the shared yoghurt.

'Cosy, but crazy!' she agreed, taking her turn for a sip of the tea. She decided not to admit that, less than a day ago, she had hardly spoken to a boy who was not "family".

'Well maybe, but Coch Wei and Chi Tang appear to be totally inseparable already,' was his reasonable, yet illogical response, indicating that he had guessed what she meant.

She said nothing, shaking her head and smiling. It seemed impossible, but he was clearly not finding her repulsive.

~

In a compact room at the top of the medieval tower, they again sat on either side of the tutor, but this time they were not just passive observers. Dr Oliver expressed no surprise at their difficulties, and was unperturbed when George admitted that they had needed to work together. Rhan even ended up speaking when she realised that George would think her a wimp for not admitting to a fair share of the problems that had defeated them. The hour-long ordeal was soon over and they were then receiving the ominous briefing on the next subject, for the following week.

Rhan shut the heavy oak door at the end of their tutorial with great relief and followed George, stomping noisily down two flights of timber stairs, without talking. George stopped on a landing, still a flight above the quad and excitedly grabbed Rhan's file-carrying arm as she emerged.

'Yes!' he exclaimed. 'We did it! You were great.'

'But why the hell did you ask him about Question 5, which we had completed, you numbskull?' She pretended to be angry, forcing his wrist upwards and pushing him backwards with her free hand.

'To keep him off the last question, which we'd hardly touched, of course! Besides, there were aspects I still felt were unclear,' he replied, defending himself physically and verbally.

'That was so stupid!' she retorted, shaking her head and laughing in disbelief as she let him go and lightly slapped his arm.

Back in the quad, they stood for a few moments in the early-evening autumnal sun, watching a troupe of tourists following the pink umbrella of their guide through the college.

'Washing!' he exclaimed, out of the blue. 'Have you found the college basement laundrette yet? I'm running out of shirts.'

'I had no idea that the college had such practical and urbane, or do I mean urban, facilities?' she replied, laughing. 'After all that mental excitement, an exploration of the nether regions of the college would suit me fine. I had thought I would be trailing my washing back up to Sunderland once I was kicked out for failing my first tutorial.'

'OK, let's dump our files, collect our washing, and meet in the back quad.'

CHAPTER FOUR

Hatter's Tea Party

'We have almost an hour to wait before supper and the wash will take that long. Come up to Tom and Danny's room,' George suggested, as they stood in an overheated basement watching their laundry churning in two machines.

'But I don't know them,' Rhan objected.

'Tom's the really lanky, curly-haired PPE student – the Marxist – and he shares a sitting-room with Danny who's also doing PPE. I said I'd see David Booth up there.'

'PPE? Politics, something, and Economics?' she asked, yielding somewhat.

'Philosophy.'

'Sounds interesting. Does David do PPE?'

'No, he does Chemistry.'

She felt swept along, totally out of her depth yet again, but it was exhilarating to relinquish control and follow him up a front-quad stairway.

Even when they tackled their washing, he had suggested swapping clothes and sharing washes to separate the colours and the whites in two machines. Rather than refuse, she had asked him whether such behaviour could be considered normal.

'No way!' he had replied with a self-deprecating smile. 'You're the only one I could imagine asking...or who I would want to ask.' On a lightheaded tide of fun, she had laughingly agreed with his scientific and domestic logic. It was all so unreal and exhilarating. As she followed George up the stairs, they managed to touch twice, almost accidentally. She wondered whether she would regret the excitement of the past twenty-four hours.

~

A confusion of music, smoke and people accosted her as she followed George into a palatial room on the second floor, which had separate bedrooms leading off at each corner. David was there, whom she had seen the previous evening. He theatrically waved an arm at her from the floor; he was seated at a low card table, which was covered in a brightly coloured cloth. She smiled and nodded back, wondering if she was being suitably cool.

Tom, just as described by George, was perched in an armchair, dealing cards. The girl, Fiona, looked up at Rhan curiously, but smiled at George. Tom, however, stood up to greet the newcomers.

'Hi George, did you survive the tutorial?' Laughing, he didn't wait for an answer. 'You're Rhan, I believe? Pleased to meet you. Can I offer you tea? Coffee? Or a taste of this beer?' He gestured at the bottles around the table.

'Just tea, please,' Rhan replied, attempting a polite smile. Then, after a second thought, she added, 'Although after that ordeal a sip or two of beer would be great.'

'I'm afraid you catch us starting early on three-card brag,' Tom continued. 'Do join us; it's very simple and relatively harmless.'

'Harmless? He lies, Rhan! It's expensive,' David complained from his seat at the table. The warning did not stop George, who immediately grabbed a cushion and sank down at the table in anticipation of receiving a hand. He appeared to forget the newly discovered friend he had dragged along, but she saw him looking to see if he needed to look after her.

From the other player at the table, there was a grunt that Rhan recognised from the *Poldark* television series to be a Cornish slur, but she could not catch what he'd said. He had cropped brown hair, broad shoulders and a rough-skinned complexion. As she looked at him with interest, Rhan concluded that he could only be the wild Cornishman that she had heard people talk about. She smiled grimly and Danny nodded to her, starting to move aside to give her space at the table. She raised a hand to decline his offer, but accepted a glass with some of George's beer.

It was time for Rhan to act. After a second glance at Fiona, who was now chatting quietly to George and David, she realised that there was a need to show independence from her tutorial partner, even if this meant engaging in conversation.

'What a wonderful room, Tom. You have windows looking out over both the front and rear quads. Would you mind if I looked at the views and...' she paused here to gesture to the packed bookcases, '...your impressive collection of books and records?'

'Please be my guest,' Tom offered, gesturing with an upturned palm.

'Gosh, aren't Marxists polite?' Rhan said to no one in particular, but to the amusement of all.

The spacious room had doors in each corner, and through one of these she glimpsed a small bedroom. The front windows had a similar view to George's room, looking over the grass and activity of the main quad. The rear window was slightly ajar and she opened it wider, placing her elbows on the sill to look out; she glanced up at the Gothic stone arch, which was shaped nicely above her head. She took in the tranquil lawn of the Fellow's Garden, flanked by the decorated stonework of both the college library and the rear of the Bodleian university library, with all the decorated paraphernalia of the fifteenth century.

Their histories, ranging over past centuries, seemed to whisper a sense of tranquil continuity. The noise of students arguing about a card game over her shoulder seemed to complement, rather than clash with, the scholarly scene.

Looking beyond the libraries, Rhan could see the delicately arched Hertford Bridge. She had seen pictures of this Italianesque copy of Venice's Bridge of Sighs. But Rhan had seen the original on the slow and steady train journey across Europe, away from her father to her uncle's house in Sunderland. She and her sister had stood holding their mother's hands, looking down a canal near St Mark's Square.

Here in Oxford in this dreamy world there was, however, none of the sad connotations associated with the Venetian convicts' sighs as they took their last tragic sight of Venice before entering the prison quarter. This Oxford design had clear and accessible windows, and had no sinister purpose other than carrying a college corridor over the public highway. Feeling slightly disturbed, however, Rhan glanced back over her shoulder and saw George look up at her from his cards.

Reassured, she returned her attention to the bridge, appraising it in her new engineering role, wondering whether the stonework was indeed arching, or whether the stone was fake and merely concealed hidden iron beams. She wondered how the ancient stonework of her childhood city was looking now. She saw the world before her, but imagined how it would look exposed and laid bare from shelling and pecked by bullet holes from snipers. The condition of some of her favourite Aleppo buildings had been imprinted on her mind from images on the internet.

Comments from the players behind her about Arctic drafts and tough northern girls persuaded Rhan to close the window and to browse Tom's bookshelves instead. She received a mug of tea that Tom had poured from an old, chipped teapot. She extracted *Parliamentary Socialism*, which she started to skim through, sitting in the corner, removed from the game and trying hard not to keep checking whether George was noticing her. Good-natured derision was poured equally on both Tom and her, with the suggestion that such reading material was wholly unsuitable for an engineer. Fiona slipped off just before they all thundered down the wooden stairs to the hall for dinner.

Rhan felt there were surprised looks from the assembled throng outside the hall as she walked between Tom and David, with George and Danny behind. Rhan felt as if she was glowing with pride at these fascinating new friends.

As they merged with the crowd before the door, George broke off and approached a large, self-conscious girl in the queue. However, as soon as Rhan joined them, the girl moved off.

'Oh dear, Rhan,' George smirked, 'you've frightened her away! Hattie's pretty different and…this place isn't ideal for such temperaments.'

'Did she think that I wanted you all for myself?' Rhan asked, mortified. 'Goodness, things were so much easier when I was a loner.' George merely frowned as he considered this.

'So…are you just being kind to me?' Rhan continued. 'Is that why you are being so nice?'

George smiled, shaking his head, but stumbled several times when he tried to explain. 'No, I sort of want…I sought your help, remember? You are my partner.' He received no help from her as she looked intently at him with furrowed brow, so he added quietly, 'You are too lovely for me to feel sorry for you, but thanks for the beatification! Unfortunately, I'm not that nice.'

They walked up the steps towards the now open hall door.

'Here, Hattie! Do you want to join us?' Rhan said, waving at the surprised girl as she walked past their seats. Rhan offered her a place next to George.

'Good move,' whispered George, as Rhan walked past him along the bench where she brazenly pushed in to sit between David and Danny and opposite Tom. After initial surprise, they appeared pleased to make way for her.

They continued to mock the book she had been browsing and after that, they got stuck into the politics of the Middle East. She gradually learnt that Tom had Science A-Levels, which helped with the Economics and Philosophy, but he needed no help with Politics. Each time she looked over, she noticed that George was frequently and casually glancing at her, even as he chatted with Hattie.

Rhan was surprised to find that Danny the Cornishman was soft-spoken and very intellectual, yet she struggled to understand him. He mentioned that he had just given his first English lesson to two Libyan schoolboys, which laid him open to ridicule as the others also clearly struggled with his accent.

David, the chemist, had a wide geographical knowledge. He told her more about the wedding in Beirut, his trip into the Bekaa Valley and his visit to Aleppo for three days. Her eyes filled with tears, which she tried to hide with the headscarf. To find that there was someone she could talk to about home was overwhelming.

It was all so easy to speak and argue with these new friends. She mentally pinched herself; she had friends!

'So what is a Marxist?' She threw the question out to the three of them, knowing that she would not have to speak again for quite some time.

CHAPTER FIVE

Sustainability Lecture

The following morning, a Friday, was hot, and this time it was the Engineering lecture theatre where the benches were packed. Rhan and George had already sat through two hours of lectures and they had made the mistake of grabbing some fresh air after the previous lecture. They were jammed together in the second row from the front but were lucky to have found seats as a succession of older students, whom they had never seen before, continued to file in along their bench.

'Sorry about this,' said the mature-looking student clad in a tweed jacket, seated on Rhan's left. He, unlike George, was valiantly trying to give Rhan some space. 'This is the first time in my three years that they've tried to bring all four years together, and this theatre wasn't built for such numbers.'

Rhan turned a little towards him with an ironic smile, which she hoped provided an interested and encouraging expression. It worked because he continued, which allowed Rhan the opportunity to pretend to be oblivious of George.

'I've heard that the department might be forced to mark down exam results if there continues to be no sustainability stuff – hence the incentive for a big turnout from the top two years in search of some easy marks. I presume you're a first-year?'

Rhan was saved from having to answer with anything more than a nod by the call for quiet. The talk began with Dr Bloom from their department, making the introductions to an enthusiastic, middle-aged man in a grey suit from the cement industry. Undaunted by the large audience, the speaker launched into his subject with relish.

'You need to start wearing a jacket instead of a jersey,' she whispered during the change in speakers. George looked at the cool third-year's jacket, and nodded.

'I am pleased to say that concrete is now at the heart of the drive for sustainability within the construction industry, and my organisation sits on and leads several key committees. There are many aspects to sustainability and we will go through some of these after I have introduced the product, concrete – one of the most important materials you are likely to specify.'

Rhan watched a series of slides showing the materials, including coal, involved with the making of cement, then concrete, through its use in roads, buildings and dams. The slides then switched to the demolition of a large factory and the crushing of concrete from both the structure and hard-standing parking area to form a mound of useful rubble. Rhan had worked for her uncle the previous summer, scanning files at his foundry, and had walked past such a derelict site in her lunch break. She had a vague, older recollection of a city centre site in Baghdad that her father had proudly shown his younger daughter – it was the water supply works. Her father had been so enthusiastic about his work, until he gradually became aware of his family's vulnerability once water became a key weapon in the civic conflict. She heard later that some of his colleagues had simply disappeared, which had precipitated her family's rapid move back to Syria.

George sat up, forcing Rhan to pay more attention. The talk had moved on to supply centres and transport but was now focusing on cement substitutes, with photographs of huge mountains of pulverised fuel ash, whatever that was.

'…and we have worked harder than any other industry to reduce the carbon footprint of concrete products, which is down some 20 percent from previous decades. We believe that this is the biggest cut in any construction product and we are very proud of our achievement. This may be relevant for those who believe in climate change and anyone who believes that warming may be partially due to human influence.'

George swore under his breath.

'This slide shows data for three materials: concrete, steel and timber, based on the carbon footprint per tonne over their lifetime, which…' Rhan stopped listening but caught on for the summary.

'You will note that a concrete post or whatever has a lower carbon footprint than the equivalent timber one. This means that you can reduce the carbon footprint of a project by designing in concrete.' The lecturer looked around smugly at his conclusion, clearly waiting for everyone to make a note of this key point.

'Bollocks!' George whispered. He was listening intently.

'This is a new language to me,' Rhan sighed in George's ear, aware and strangely piqued that for the first time since they had met, he did not seem to be acutely aware of her. It was fascinating to note her power over George. She had soon realised that physical contact was not as accidental as it appeared when they were close, and that even when they were deliberately apart with friends, he often glanced in her direction. They both knew it. This was presumably flirting, a subject she had heard so much about. But they were tutorial partners so their relationship could surely go nowhere.

'But what is perhaps relevant is not the "greenness" of the product, but the application. Concrete, with cement as the main ingredient, has qualities such as thermal mass and fire-resistance, which allows for sustainable construction solutions if correctly designed.' George shook his head slightly at the lecturer's explanation.

Rhan felt drowsy and was having real trouble concentrating. After supper the previous evening, she had been persuaded by the enthusiastic Tom to join David, George and the enigmatic Danny on a trip to the Jericho area of town, to a late-night showing of some vintage Marx Brothers films. It had been a strange, magical night, and Rhan's sides had ached with the prolonged infectious laughter, with Tom and David on either side of her. She was now paying the price for two very late nights, yet George, who had hardly listened to a word of the first maths lecture, was now wide-awake.

It was warm in the confined row, and with insufficient room to take notes, she could only let her thoughts wander again. She had determined to go for a run that afternoon but it seemed boring compared with everyone else's college activities. She wondered what other options she had now that she had a term or even four years ahead of her. She needed something removed from the intense college life that she now found too exhilarating.

'...the handout gives you more examples with calculations to show how concrete can be used to store heat in buildings. This reduces the energy required to heat buildings in winter, and more particularly, it reduces the energy needed to cool them in summer. This is vastly superior to timber, which has a much lower specific heat value than concrete. After a century, you will see that the total carbon footprint of concrete is very superior.

'I have already mentioned how concrete materials can be recycled when the structure, whether a building, bridge or other civil engineering infrastructure, comes to the end of its useful life in two hundred or so years' time. I might just mention that once the concrete is ground up to form aggregate, it starts to absorb carbon dioxide from the atmosphere, partially completing the cycle.'

Rhan watched as the lecturer illustrated the impressive cyclical life of concrete, but then frowned as she saw George slowly and almost imperceptibly shaking his head. Was she missing something? She tried harder to listen.

'So again, please compare that with timber, which can decay to methane once it reaches the end of its short life. You probably know that methane is some twenty to thirty times worse than carbon dioxide at causing global warming, if you are concerned about that. I emphasise again that where concrete scores in sustainability is that at the end of its life, it can be recycled to some extent and this can prevent the need for further quarry extraction of natural resources. So, at each stage, concrete scores well on the sustainability tallies and it helps designers achieve the highest ratings now required by many clients, whether using sustainability codes such as BREEAM or the old CEEQUAL code for civil engineering.

'Returning to the need for sustainable materials: gravels and sands obviously need to be extracted in a manner that does not affect the natural environment and such issues are very important for scoring in sustainability.'

As Rhan's concentration wavered again, she became aware that George was shifting around, and getting literally hot under the collar. 'Are you alright?' she whispered.

'This is all bollocks,' he said. She furrowed her brow again and shook her head to indicate that she didn't understand, but it encouraged her to listen more attentively.

Forty minutes later, after going through a few case studies, there was a call for questions. There were a few seconds of silence; questions tended to be few and far between in normal lectures, and the mixture of year groups made it even more nerve-wracking to raise a hand.

Dr Bloom stepped in. 'Can I ask you to say something more about these cement replacement products that are by-products of the steel industry? Would you like to discuss how they affect the concrete product?'

The lecturer reiterated and expanded upon what had been previously mentioned 'The products, such as PFA, are industrial by-products from the steel industry, which have been stored in huge mounds over the past few decades, so it is in everyone's interest that they could be used to reduce the cement content in concrete and hence the carbon footprint. They add other benefits such as better control of temperature and lower water content for the same workability. However, as I mentioned, they are no good on their own and a portion of the cement is still needed, which is fortunate, as otherwise who would pay my salary?' There were polite smiles from the audience.

'Any other questions?'

George reluctantly raised his arm. 'Ah, good, a question from a first-year!' Dr Bloom announced disparagingly.

'You suggested earlier that, err, some people may be interested in keeping carbon levels down, if we…' George stumbled before continuing, '…if we believe in global warming. Surely no aspects of sustainability are more important than the short-term carbon footprint? Isn't concrete production, in particular the cement element, the major problem that we need to avoid? I gather that around 5 percent of all world carbon emissions come from the cement industry.'

'Well, there are a range of views about this,' the guest speaker responded in a dragged out, bored manner that contrasted with the crisply presented lecture. 'We don't like to get involved one way or the other, but most people think the whole-life timescale is more important than the short term. However, we are fully committed to the government target of carbon-emission cuts of 50 percent by 2050, and we are proud to say that we are one of the few industries that are well on programme to achieve those targets. As I mentioned earlier, we are very proud of our whole-life footprint. There are papers that prove that concrete is one of the most sustainable and lowest-carbon materials available for the construction industry over the centuries, so your grandchildren and great-grandchildren will be grateful that you designed concrete structures!'

George now addressed Dr Bloom, rather than the industry spokesman, in a more assured manner that bordered on aggression. 'But in the meantime, is the university advocating that we should be using materials that produce such high levels of carbon emissions? There has been no mention of how current and previous carbon emissions will remain in the atmosphere for many decades and affect us for centuries and do much more damage than any saving and absorption of CO_2 in the distant future. And with the ice caps melting rapidly, fires and flooding affecting us already, surely it is the present rather than the future we need to worry about? Isn't all this talk of sustainability a sham if current carbon footprints and the short timescales are ignored in the expectation that our generation can invent a way to sort it out later?'

Dr Bloom had clearly not anticipated being involved in such discussions, but he recovered quickly.

'Well, the university will be following government guidance and industry standards, which may involve cutting emissions in a few decades' time. We are certainly cutting down our carbon emissions in this department. We are now almost entirely paperless.'

'Yet encouraging each student to use tonnes of concrete in our designs will very quickly wipe out any savings on envelopes and paper,' responded George. There were smirks around the room as well as embarrassed fidgeting by the third-year sitting on the other side of Rhan.

The spokesman took back control. 'Well, this is clearly a very controversial subject – for one of us at least! Perhaps our friend here would like to see the Engineering department shut down and no new developments throughout the world? Concrete and cement are probably the most essential products for the advancement of our society. You live in a wonderful city with fantastic buildings, so would you want to prevent others from enjoying your privileges? No, of course not. So, last question please?'

'Oxford was almost entirely built without concrete or cement!' George interjected, but no one was listening.

'How long can we expect concrete to last?' a deep voice asked.

'Ah a good question,' the spokesman replied. 'It depends on what is required, but most infrastructure is intended to last at least a hundred and twenty years, while some Roman concrete is still in remarkably good condition. So, the more concrete infrastructure we build now, the more the next generation will appreciate our efforts.

'We can't be expected to build offshore wind turbines in stone and timber! What's more, I attend architectural courses and I see their final-year projects. Almost every architectural student is still designing with reinforced concrete and steel as their main structural component; they know little else. So you engineers can be sure that concrete is going to be your key structural material for the foreseeable future. Despite any talk of a climate emergency, your professional institutions are happy for you to carry on using as much concrete as you need. They just suggest you don't use more than you need and ask you to use it wisely, in the manner I have suggested today. Thank you.'

The session was winding up. Rhan kept her distance from George, knowing how hot and bothered he was. She followed him out slowly. He was caught by Dr Bloom at the door and words were exchanged.

'Bloody hell!' George exclaimed. 'Why, why, why did I get involved?' He was angrier still as he unlocked his bike. Wet patches had appeared on his shirt.

He ignored Rhan, who had to pedal hard to catch him up halfway down St Giles.

'You were brilliant!' she called after him.

'No, I was rubbish. I sounded like my father. I don't care what they do or say.' His voice was harsh. 'It's all far too late anyway so why bother?'

'But you think it was a sham? Which bits?'

'All of it! How absolutely stupid! I just got pissed off that they were spouting off with two-faced hypocritical whitewash. So, I ended up making a complete fool of myself and sounding like a crank! Why did I think that anyone needed to hear the truth, or would be at all interested?'

They hurtled recklessly into the back quad, where George flung his bike against a wall and locked it carelessly. 'See you later. I need a shower before lunch. Fucking stupid!'

Rhan flopped on her bed with a sigh and read the handouts and the very few notes that she had taken. She glanced at the various sheets, wondering about the way climate change may have been subtly ridiculed. On her second reading, she searched for differences between sustainability and climate change. She began to have a nasty feeling that there were differences, and that careful wording had been used to confuse rather than clarify the issues. Recalling Dr Bloom's words, she looked again at the statements of sustainability, which had little in the way of policy to minimise climate change, but might have had a different context.

Reading some of the details, it became obvious that the underlying guidance and actions were clearly not intended to tackle global warming anytime soon. The documents seemed to emphasise things like planning, noise, dust, life expectancy, long-term efficiency and other aspects. One aim covered the net long-term carbon footprint, but only after the structure had been used for several decades and even once it was demolished. It all seemed reasonable, but she doubted that George would agree if he was looking for urgent action.

Next, she looked at her handout on the UN Sustainable Development Goals. She shook her head as she read through the seventeen numbered goals and smiled once she found climate action, hidden away at number thirteen. It was a small relief to find that the United Nations gave little concern to fighting climate change. George had made a mountain out of molehill and she could see why he regretted his stance.

Yet, bearing in mind her experience in Syria when she looked down the list again, the leading goals of no poverty, zero hunger, good health, education, equality and clean sanitation and energy, had all immediately failed once the war started after a few years of drought. She filed her papers, but felt dissatisfied that there was no discussion relating to the short-term carbon emissions, which George had considered so important. Even worse, she began to wonder why there had been no discussion at all on the impact of warming that continued use of high-carbon materials would bring.

She headed out for lunch, but felt slightly relieved that George made no appearance. She sat next to Danny in the hall and told him about the lecture and her review.

'At the time, it was alarming to find that George made points that were not being addressed,' she explained. 'So I would be happy to find that the vast majority in the lecture were correct and that George must be an idiot. Yet, I am not convinced there is nothing to worry about. It was disconcerting that George's lonely concerns were so unpalatable, and needed to be quashed without debate.'

Rhan was talking earnestly, and Danny appeared to be listening.

'Then there were the overall hints in the lecture that climate change might not be real or might have a cause beyond human intervention. What else do they think is causing climate change, if not greenhouse gases?'

'Well,' the Cornishman said slowly. 'I thought everything was under control and presumed you engineers would 'ave it all sorted. I seem to recall that temperature rises hadn't been as high as predicted. Then there was that Paris Agreement – temperatures will be pegged at 1.5°C, or is it 2°C?'

Noticing Rhan's disquiet, Danny added, 'I confess, I've 'ardly bothered with the subject recently. I feel stupidly ignorant of such an important subject. Sorry Rhan, but I have to go and get changed for rugby. There's David,' he said, beckoning to their friend. 'He's interested in climate change, so ask him. If you see George, tell him to meet in the back quad at two.'

David sat in Danny's vacated seat, eating a yoghurt, but smiling occasionally as Rhan relayed the subject of the lecture again. She was dismayed to realise that David appeared to have little inclination to comment. He waited until Rhan had finished before he pompously gave his unexpected verdict.

'I'm sorry to say that George was absolutely correct. Sorry, I have to dash off; I'm halfway through a chemistry practical and have to get back to the lab. See you.'

CHAPTER SIX

Novice

Rhan felt strangely lonely after lunch as she prepared for another boring run. Everyone seemed to be occupied by sport, practicals or tutorial work. She shook her head angrily. After years of being alone, how could she be lonely for just an afternoon? It was ridiculous.

She had decided to trust George with so many aspects of this strange, new, dreamlike world, but she could not lean on him for every aspect of her life. Her auntie had warned her that popular men had a girl in every town and although she suspected her aunt of having little direct knowledge, she considered it a useful premise.

She felt no inclination to join in any college activity, but halfway out the door, she turned back and looked up a deleted email. It had been sent to first-year girls at all colleges inviting them to make up numbers for Gloucester Hall's women's rowing novices. It had been useless junk earlier in the week when she thought she had no future. Although she had failed to respond by the requested deadline, candidates were asked to meet at two-thirty that afternoon at Gloucester's boathouse.

Half an hour later, she was inspecting the boathouses while trotting along the opposite bank to her own college boathouse. The third nameplate she came across was Gloucester Hall, which appeared to be sharing with another, larger college. With her heart beating from nerves rather than from the running, she stopped and looked around, aware that she was a quarter of an hour early. She felt so exposed without her headscarf, yet she hated standing out as different.

The building was like a very long garage, with a double door at the top of concrete steps leading down to the river and a steel-and-timber pontoon floating on the water. It was empty so she crept inside. There were racks for boats on both sides, most of which were empty. One boat was designed for eight oars, which had four steel brackets protruding on each side. On a higher rack was a shorter boat with two brackets on the near side, which was clearly designed for four rowers, and beyond that, a short pencil-shaped boat, obviously built for just one rower. All boats looked delicate and ridiculously thin. On one side of the garage, there were racks of oars, which looked enormous. It was almost silent in the boathouse. She stood still, gripped by indecision. She went outside again, relieved to no longer be poking around, and reassured that no one had seen her.

She walked up the river and returned on time, just as a crew was lifting a boat from the water. She approached a tall girl who stood watching, painfully aware that she had never spoken to a stranger without the protection of head cover.

'Are you still looking for rowers – well, novices I mean?'

'Oh great, you want to row with us? Wow. Perfect. You're almost a tall as me! My name is Claire. Those girls are Suzie, Elizabeth, Sarah, Jenny and Shrimpy – they're all Gloucester. I'm hoping that the girl talking to Nick over there is another recruit from outside college. What's your name and what college are you from?'

Rhan felt reluctant to divulge too much – the idea of adopting a parallel life suddenly seemed quite liberating. She turned away, needing time to think. That was rude – she had to say something. She turned back to Claire. 'It is very good of you to let me try rowing for you. It is all very exciting. I have never done anything like this before.'

'You're not British are you? Are you from Israel?'

'No, I am from Sunderland,' Rhan answered with a mischievous smile on her face, which Claire returned. Rhan looked across at Nick hoping for a distraction while she floundered with questions she was not ready to answer. He looked up, saw her, and smiled back. Rhan automatically lifted her hand to her head, but her headscarf was not there. She flushed as he came straight across to her.

'Do I gather you want to row with us?' he said, and then continued conversationally when he detected a slight nod from Claire on behalf of the awkward stranger. 'Delighted you came! I'm Nick and I will be coaching you today and for the first week at least. What's your name?'

'Bar,' muttered Rhan. It was the least offensive nickname she had from the options of Stick, Lanky, or Monkey Bars.

'Well Bar, as I was just saying to Elisha over there, first we'll look at safety, then some theory, a quick session on the bank tub and we have the clinker booked from three. It's all very easy compared with elsewhere. I can get a couple of extra rowers from the men's novice boat to make up numbers for this outing, which is great as I know of others who couldn't make it today.'

There was much to take in from the technical talk. Once they found that she was ambidextrous, "Bar" was given a place as Number 5, which was on the "bow side", although she had no idea what it meant. First, she was made to sit for a few strokes in a "bank tub", where she felt stupid pulling an oar with a hole in it through water while moored to the bank. Nick crouched down, giving instructions. She was surprised when he leaned over and physically moved her hand round on the shaft. She looked up at the crowd of girls watching from above, but they appeared to think nothing of his hand on hers.

Slightly later than planned, they swapped places with a returning crew. A young man was press-ganged by Nick from the returning crew and they were on the river. Nick sat in the back, or "stern", as "cox" – the only one facing forwards – to steer and coach the rowers. Elizabeth came next at Number 8 looking backwards, with the rest sitting one behind the other up to Number 1 in the "bow" at the front end. They all had to follow the movements and speed of Elizabeth, who was "stroke".

It was fun from the start. The unsteady rhythm that they had to follow, combined with trying to take in and apply the shouted instructions from Nick, soon removed all other worries and Rhan was staggered to find herself loving every moment. There was a moment, however, when Jenny sent a spray of river water over the girls in front, including Rhan, to shrieks of annoyance. The boat rocked alarmingly, and with water running down her neck, Rhan almost stopped pulling on her oar. The oar suddenly took on a life of its own and she lost control. She felt helpless as the blade-end dived down, while the end of the oar she was holding shot upwards, almost pulling her off the seat. Nick shouted for all to "hold water" and they came to a sudden halt.

'That's called "catching a crab",' Nick called out. 'Pull right up to your chest, Number 5! That'll keep you in control of your oar.'

'Up to where?' Sarah called out mischievously, making the embarrassment worse.

Moreover, the tourists meandering along the river had all stopped and were laughing at them. Rhan decided that from then on, she was going to pull hard on each stroke as a safety measure. That proved fun but difficult, as every few strokes there were other incidents, and the other newcomer, Elisha, had particular trouble. As far as Rhan was concerned, however, it was going to be the first and last time that she "caught a crab".

~

It was while they retrieved the boat from the water that things nearly went wrong. The boat that the novices used was called the "clinker" and it was notorious for being heavy and difficult to lift from the water. Even with Nick helping to lift, and an extra man from the boathouse, it was a strain to lean over and lift it clear from the water. Once clear, Nick – who was helping from the bow end – instructed the stroke-side rowers to change sides. Every second person was then supposed to let go and cross beneath the boat so that it could be carried between them with equal numbers on each side. Unfortunately, it went very wrong and Rhan was left at one end, with Nick and Claire at the other, holding the weight of the whole boat between them while everyone else let go and scrambled beneath the boat. Rhan felt her face go purple with the strain, and she ignored the shouting around her as she concentrated on not letting the stern touch the ground.

'That was an impressive display of strength, Bar,' said Nick, once the boat was safely laid on its rack. 'I'm sorry for the incompetence. I do more rowing than coxing, so that's my excuse. Your rowing was good towards the end. Combine that with your height and strength and you could be perfect. Will you join us again tomorrow at the same time?'

'Thank you, Nick. Yes please – it was a marvellous experience. Is it OK for me to row with you? I would like to keep my college out of it if possible. You see, I am from the Middle East and should not be seen doing sport in this western dress.'

'No problem,' responded Nick, not even bothering to ask which college. 'No one's going to mind you rowing for us at novice-level. We've a chance to build up a good Women's Second Eight this year. Send me your email and I'll confirm other sessions. We will have to go for pre-breakfast sessions next week if that's OK?'

Rhan was distracted by Sarah winking at her behind Nick's back.

'Great!' responded Rhan, who was not sure what it meant.

Rhan jogged back to her college, replacing her headscarf as she ran. Some of the rugby players were hobbling around the quad in their steel-studded boots while shouting out arrangements for their first round of drinks.

'Ah, the loneliness of the long-distance runner! Did you have a pleasant afternoon Rhan?' George's voice echoed around the quad but was answered by Danny's booming Cornish voice.

'Cos if not, you wanna join the rugby club? We need someone who can jump'n catch at the same time. George has problems with multi-tasking.'

So far so good with the double life, thought Rhan.

Brimming with surreal self-confidence, Rhan set out that evening in the hall to make a new friend and to ease her conscience.

'Gerry isn't it?' she asked of the boy she'd sat next to on her first night in college. She had observed that, although he no longer looked so homesick, he was still usually alone. He looked up, surprised and pleased to be addressed by the striking girl, who was now rapidly becoming one of the college personalities.

'You read Maths and come from Bradford – is that right?' Rhan had prepared her ground. The boy nodded, and Rhan continued confidently. 'My future brother-in-law comes from there. How are you finding your subject? I thought I was good at maths before I started Engineering, but I am barely coping.' That was sufficient for Gerry to take over the subject on the delights and difficulties of maths.

Later that evening in her room, Rhan confided in George. 'Talking to Gerry was easy and quite fun. I was a chatterbox back in Syria but since coming here, I hardly spoke at school, or in my first week here. So it was good to put my new sociable personality to beneficial effect. At least he can count me as one of his acquaintances or friends now, and he has offered to help with my maths. So you may not be so indispensable from now on!'

George pretended to look alarmed, but Rhan could tell he was proud of her.

CHAPTER SEVEN

A Wonderful Life

The second week of term continued to feel like a silky dream, which made Rhan fearful that it was all too good to be true. Morning lectures had become ridiculously enjoyable. It was a revelation for Rhan to find herself on easy terms with a best friend, who happened to be male. They whispered comments and complaints in the large maths lecture room, and amused each other in the engineering lectures with puerile written comments on each other's notes. At technical drawing after lectures, their individual knowledge of the computer package leapt forward as they pooled their discoveries of new techniques and pointed out each other's errors. Rhan was aware that their close collaboration usually involved more physical contact than was necessary. It was all so intoxicating.

At the end of the week, on the Friday following the almost-forgotten sustainability lecture, they started their engineering course practicals. Rhan stood attentively with a dozen first-year students on the concrete floor of a laboratory on one of the upper floors of the engineering tower, surrounded by a range of daunting apparatus. She read through the general instructions and could not hide the irregularity in her breathing as she noted that each experiment was carried out in pairs. Coch Wei and Chi Tang were already heading off to choose their experiment. She had always hated that aspect of school; no one ever wanted her as a partner. The idea of doing three years of practicals on her own loomed. George was bound to strike off with someone cool from another college, yet there he was standing alone watching her.

'Sorry George,' she apologised. 'You seem to be stuck with me again.'

'Just what I was going to say,' was his smiling response, which made her feel at ease again. No wonder she found it a worry that life was so alarmingly good. She woke each morning in eager anticipation, yet the scars from the loneliness and sense of inadequacy were very recent and lay just beneath the surface. Rhan had filed the memories as useful references.

Most interaction with George appeared to revert into an amusing game, yet they both knew that there were dangerous undercurrents in their friendship. She had soon rescued her instruction book about humans from the back of her drawer and, to the amusement of both, they had even reviewed sections that were unclear as though it was part of their coursework. There were fascinating complications and delights with being so close, in all senses of the word, to someone who was neither an indifferent friend, nor an official lover.

Once they found the last unclaimed apparatus for their first practical, they were pushing each other in a childish manner, fighting over the easy task of sitting on a chair and taking the readings. Rhan, aware of other students in the room, suddenly became self-conscious, laughed, and gave in.

'OK George, you need to sit down, so you can get a grip on those complicated creep readings while I will fetch the weights. I have already had a strenuous morning, so lugging a few more loads around will be nothing.' She said this with a hint of sarcasm.

It bothered her slightly that she had told him nothing about her rowing, nor had she checked his assumption that she was spending her time running, yet he had not asked questions about her time away. On the one hand, she wanted to tell him about her successes on the water and describe the exhilaration of gliding through the early morning mists; on the other hand, it helped to have time completely removed from him. Around college, they were just friends who worked and went about together as part of a group, yet they rarely chatted or sat next to each other when others were near. Generally, though, they were only a glance apart.

After collecting a couple of weights, Rhan had nothing to do but wait while George took timed readings, which suited her fine. She could let her thoughts wander.

~

Life was too much fun to go to bed as early as she would have wished. Rhan found that she was surprisingly popular with many young men in the college, who seemed to regard her with some interest and almost as one of them, now that she was no longer too "odd" to communicate with them. She often had invitations to the college bar and calls to visit the pubs in the town with some of the rugby squad.

It crossed her mind that they particularly enjoyed the incongruous scene of a headscarf-covered girl drinking the pints of beer that they insisted on buying her. She managed to resist Danny's now semi-serious invitations that she try out the position of jumper for the rugby lineouts, but the boys still enjoyed speculating how high they could lift or throw a lightweight girl who almost had the height of a second-row forward.

Rhan found it much easier than she would have believed to come up with banter that seemed to amuse, but she preferred the more penetrating, cerebral discussions. She had many new acquaintances, yet she was surprised to admit that her best college friends were also George's early friends. And they all appeared to have a genuine interest in her. Danny, when sober, was always keen to discover Rhan's views and knowledge of a variety of topics, yet he was happy, in turn, to pass on his good knowledge of politics and economic theory. She had been able to indulge in quiet conversations with David, who had knowledge of Syria and Lebanon, and her eyes often swam with nostalgic tears. Tom expanded her limited knowledge of music, books and his brand of politics.

She broke off her reverie sufficiently to answer George's call for another weight to be added to the loaded plastic wire. She watched for a few seconds as he frantically noted down the readings.

Within the college, Rhan could relax with Hattie and her circle, who were happy to include Rhan. Otherwise, her new closest college friends hardly included any girls. George had many female friends, but Rhan felt judged by and shy with them. Intimate conversations with Fiona had not gone brilliantly.

'Rhan, if you start going out with George, then tutorials will be dreadfully awkward when you break up,' Fiona had advised.

'Good advice,' Rhan had responded modestly. 'I have very little experience in this area.' Yet Rhan had then mischievously added, 'But do you really think that George would like me in that way? I thought he was only interested in my engineering expertise.'

'I don't know,' Fiona had responded cautiously, looking up at the tall, austere-looking Syrian. 'I sometimes get the feeling that you are much closer to him than his girlfriend back home would like.'

The conversation had made Rhan pleased to hear that her intimacy with George was not entirely in her own head, but she could see the logic of a taboo against going out with a tutorial partner. In a three-year arts subject, where students had individual study and preparation of essays, it would be bad enough. It was so much more dangerous for students of four-year science degrees; rowing, rugby and bed were the only real periods that Rhan was apart from George. Fiona would be shocked if she knew how close they had become and how they had tried to hide that closeness.

The problem of coping with the maths was still a looming cloud each week, but like every aspect of her life, it was now shared – halving the pain and doubling any gain. They had only panicked a little about preparations for their first engineering tutorial, but it was much easier than maths. Working together, Rhan and George had been content to spend most of the previous weekend reading up about the theory of beams and answering questions about bending moment diagrams. It had almost been fun. Working out deflections and discovering forces in bridge members appeared so much more logical and useful than learning about mathematical transformations and vectors in that week's maths tutorial. It had dawned on them that their time in Oxford was set into an alternating rhythm of maths and engineering tutorials, interspersed with laboratory practicals. It was all set as rigidly as the stone boundary walls to each college.

Gently lowering another weight onto the plastic wire, when instructed by George, Rhan considered the bikes they had bought. Rhan was pleased with her heavy second-hand bike with its three-speed gears, but could not restrain her laughter at the pink girl's bike that George had purchased, which was ridiculously small for him. Annoyingly, though, he managed to beat her in most sprint races, despite the apparent handicap. Looking at maps, they were planning expeditions out from the city to explore surrounding woods, rivers, villages and pubs.

Rhan made her thoughts switch from the future to the crazy Gloucester girls, who were such fun to row with. She turned away to hide her smile. There were real advantages in having a new separate life as a rower.

After three days of rowing in the afternoons, they had settled into a pre-breakfast regime. It provided more time during the day, but it left her feeling sleepy later in the morning, like now.

Their coach Nick had tried out a different member of the Gloucester crew as stroke on each of the initial outings, in an effort to find a suitable rower to take the lead. She could appreciate why he wanted the Number 8 rower, whom the rest of the crew would follow, to be from Gloucester. It had therefore been with apparent reluctance that on Wednesday, Nick had placed Rhan as stroke in front of Shrimpy, the cox, at the back of the boat. She had found it very strange not being able to see other rowers and to have no one to follow; she had nothing to think about other than her own stroke. After a few minutes, she resolved not to try that lonely position again. After a few more minutes, she started to admire the way they were moving through the water.

'Wow!' Shrimpy had called out. 'Keep it up!'

Rhan had to admit that there were advantages in controlling how much energy she expended, particularly at such a cold time of the day, and she enjoyed feeling the boat powering through the water. 'That's brilliant!' called Nick from the bank. Sarah, who tended to keep up a constant dialogue from the forward end of the boat, was also saying something positive, but the words were indistinct.

'What a difference – that was amazing!' Elizabeth said as soon as they were unbuckling their shoes at the landing stage. 'Well done, stroke. Job landed at the Bar.'

'Bar made Nick a happy man, yet again,' Jenny added frivolously.

'Sure! Trying everyone out was just pretence. We all knew from the beginning he was after a stroke from Bar!' Claire contributed.

'Oh, are you and Nick an item?' Elisha asked, while Anna looked round in interest and the others smirked.

'Only in their minds!' Rhan responded, pretending to be angry, but she had felt herself glow, both from the enthusiastic praise of her rowing, as well as the implications of their jokes.

'Elizabeth was dead right, you know,' Claire said more subtly, once the boat had been laid back on its shelf. 'Rowing suddenly became so much easier following your lead. I'm not sure why, but stick with it.' It was rare for Claire to be serious, and Rhan was struck by her praise. She had learnt to admire Claire as both a good friend and as the best rower in the crew. Nick had tried to get Claire to be stroke at Number 8, but Claire had hated swapping hands when she moved from one side of the boat to the other and she soon returned to Number 7 on the bow side of the boat. She was now positioned directly behind Rhan, where they were able to chat when there were dull moments.

That had been their last trip out in the heavy clinker training boat, where the timber planks lapped with each other. Nick had arranged for them to move onto a light shell, which appeared to consist of a single layer of thin, curved plywood. They found the less sturdy shell much more difficult to balance as it wobbled badly from side to side, spoiling their rowing for a while. Yet they were soon accustomed to balancing the lighter, more responsive shell.

~

'Next weight please, if you don't mind!' George's resentful voice cut through Rhan's dreamy state, dragging her back to the present.

'Yes sir!' Rhan retorted. 'May I just remind you that you wanted the role of recorder? I am happy to be the dozy labourer.'

'Can I just point out then that we need lots more weights soon, once this gets to the work-hardening zone? Would it be a good idea to assemble them close-by?'

~

'That is so ungentlemanly!' Rhan complained ten minutes later, after assembling some of the required heavy loads from across the room. The low October sun radiated the glass wall of the centrally heated tower building. 'Your turn for the physical stuff. Let me sit on that chair and cool off while taking the readings,' she complained, slumping into his chair. 'Which way is this gauge reading? What time step are we on?'

He leant over her, pointing out his methodology for taking the readings until she pushed him away.

'Go and get the next weights! It's your turn to do the manual stuff.'

He grunted assent, walked across the lab and opened a window, letting in a stiff breeze. Several of the other students looked up in surprise, smiling at the obvious solution to the overheated room.

'You could have done that earlier!' Rhan suggested as he stood leaning over her again.

'Well you were brought up in the Middle East, so I thought you must be used to working in the heat! Besides, you have the advantage of being fragrant.'

'Not this girl! I am not wasting my money on perfume just for you.'

'You're so much better than any bottled scent,' he said quietly from above her head.

'George, what would your girlfriend say?' Rhan said firmly, but then inwardly, she cringed, wondering why on earth she had said that.

'Next weight in ten seconds,' she demanded, wanting the experiment to move the conversation on.

'She's coming to see me next weekend, which could be awkward,' he said flatly as he threaded another two kilograms onto the cage.

'Oh, why?' she asked, wishing she could put the metaphorical cork back in the bottle.

'Why is she coming to see me, or why awkward?' When Rhan didn't respond, George continued. 'Because we should break up.' There was a long pause while Rhan made notes and sucked her pencil. 'Everyone in our college, both boys and girls, are in a similar position,' he added.

'OK, I got that,' she said. 'Next weight! Quick!' She glanced at him, adding, 'Why do you need to break up?' She hated the idea that anything from the last week or so should change when everything was so exciting. Her heart felt like it kept missing beats, but was that even possible?

'You know why,' he said, but then deflected the answer. 'I couldn't go out with anyone who's not an engineer, could I?' He smiled, but without warmth.

'Creep!' She elbowed him in the ribs in a few spare seconds from the experiment. It was a brief return to their typical behaviour, but George soon reverted to the more serious conversation.

'I don't think I'm being fair to anyone,' he admitted.

'I don't mind. The most important thing is to be friends,' she said while looking at the dial and the clock. 'You and I have to stay friends, somehow or other, for the next four years. Load it in five, four – OK, now!'

They stopped to let Rhan take more measurements before George continued on a different tack.

'I'm not sure what "I don't mind" means, but look, as far as I can make out, any romantically inclined couple have a mystery over who likes each other the most. There's nothing worse than unrequited love.'

'152.4, got it. Right, unload now. Take a weight off! 148.5. Sorry, George, I have no idea. What are you talking about?' Rhan did not want to be having this conversation.

'Well I don't mind admitting that I have a real thing for you,' George whispered. 'So, I'm just hoping you can put up with that, and not mind too much if I…just carry on… Another weight off?'

'No, wait, not yet,' she said, trying to concentrate on the experiment while taking short, sharp, panicky breaths. She had to stay cool. Now was not a good time for the full truth. She managed to control her voice.

'No I don't mind. I suppose I am flattered. I never thought of anyone having a "thing" for me. I just thought that I am conveniently on hand for you. Hang on…time for a reading and take a load off – 143.8 millimetres. Go!'

'Well, wouldn't it be a disaster if you fell for me!' George replied, looking at her with growing confidence. 'It would be stupid for us to…' He stopped to take off another ring of steel and started again once he had at least some of Rhan's attention. 'It's just painful ecstasy. It could ruin our time here. It's been the most electrifying time of my life, but… we have to kill it. You have the upper hand. You need to be indifferent about me.'

'I am not sure if this is a particularly fair proposal,' Rhan sighed with a grim smile and a shake of her head. 'I am no expert, but I don't think that many classic romances have ever covered the subject in that way. So, you want me to…138.1. Remove another weight! You want me to feel sorry for you, and just put up with you having a crush on me? I am then meant to take on policing our relationship. I thought that things might be more equal.'

George's face twisted while he considered this, but he had no answer. She shook her head while she continued. 'I appreciate that girls are supposed to do that anyway, especially those with my upbringing…but I had hoped to escape such a role here. Why should I take responsibility for us both?'

She stopped herself. Rhan certainly had no experience of this. She had been just about to admit that she had chemicals rushing around in her system, which already made her feel empty when they were apart for more than a few hours – never mind the idea of being estranged permanently. She was well aware that their time together had been so precious. Everything was better when he was there: every joke funnier, each building they admired more beautiful, and every evening walk more exciting. Each crisis had even been fun when faced together.

'Oh, blast, you made me miss a reading,' she exclaimed out loud. 'Last reading…119.5. OK, last weight off. All finished.'

'Great. Do you want to tidy these up?' he suggested. 'I'll take that pile of weights back and shut that window before we go.'

'Look George, we are better than good colleagues,' Rhan called out. They were cycling slowly together back to college past the Lamb and Flag pub and St John's College; neither of them were able to enjoy the clear low light of autumn. She pulled up alongside him. 'I really want to be trusting friends. Surely, if we are friends, then we can do, or not do, anything. Isn't that better than being a couple?' Rhan had returned to the subject after a few minutes of silence between them, terrified at the black pit she could see ahead if they fell apart. 'If we were really good friends, we could probably talk through these problems,' she persisted. 'Look how far I…we have come since we met just a few days ago.'

'Maybe. We could be friends in theory, but it never happens that way.' She caught a glimpse of her own despair in him. It frightened her.

They broke off where traffic forced them to separate and she had to brake hard to avoid a car pulling out. Recalling George's grim voice outside the hall during their first conversation, she accelerated with new determination and caught him up in the quieter road beside Balliol College, adjacent to the memorial to the burning of the Oxford

Martyrs, which Rhan tried not to think about each time she went past.

'You should keep your girlfriend!' she pleaded, hoping no one could hear as they cycled slowly, as close as they dared in the cold shadow of a building. 'Even if you really wanted me, I would actually prefer not to be coupled with you in everyone's mind, right from the beginning of our time here. Thank goodness we have been subtle so far. That means we can continue to spend time with each other. Come on, we are together almost every waking hour, so I can hardly be jealous as things stand. I don't mind.

'George, I know you want to be fair and do the right thing, so wouldn't dropping your girlfriend and removing her stability after a week of university be cruel?'

'Maybe,' George replied again doubtfully, as they emerged into the sunshine of the spacious Broad Street. 'She's been at her uni over three weeks and is having a great time without me, but she's keen to see this place. I have a gut feeling she wants to end things, but I'll see. I was more worried about you, yet are you saying that we should, and could, just carry on…as before?'

'Well that would certainly suit me best,' she responded with relief. 'Just carry on, just as before.' They broke off as they swept into the college through the open back gate, clattering over the cobbles and paving setts under the tower and into the back quad. They stopped at adjacent bike stands at the rear of the chapel.

Chris, whom Rhan had got to know from Sundays at the Catholic chaplaincy, was on his way to lunch. He walked towards them as they each locked up their bikes, apparently not noticing him. Rhan squatted down next to George to fiddle with his bike combination lock while she muttered something. Chris assumed it was to do with his lock, as George suddenly looked pleasantly surprised and uttered under his breath in a hoarse whisper that Chris overheard. 'Rhan, you're fantastic!'

'Oh, hi Chris!' Rhan said enthusiastically as she appeared to notice him for the first time. 'George is taking these practical notes up to his room, so he can write them up before his girlfriend arrives this weekend. If you are on your way to lunch, may I join you?'

Apart from a slight nod, there was an uncharacteristic silence from George.

CHAPTER EIGHT

Magisterium Strikes Back

Dr Field was waiting for them on the way past the senior common room after supper the following Monday.

'A word if you don't mind, George!' George went over to Dr Field, while Tom and David carried on. Rhan stopped, waiting and listening, a little way off.

'I have heard from Dr Bloom that you were making very negative contributions to the sustainability lecture and that it was particularly inappropriate as it gave a poor impression to an external lecturer. I gather that you objected to the way sustainability is being addressed?'

'I am very sorry sir. It won't happen again.'

'Good. Let's not argue about petty issues with lecturers again. Please apologise to Dr Bloom.'

'Yes sir.'

'But,' interceded Rhan, 'George was only pointing out that high-carbon materials are likely to cause real trouble.' Dr Field's head shot up at the intervention of the tall, hitherto-shy fresher. 'He just pointed out that there were real risks that needed to be assessed if concrete only yields sustainability benefits in hundreds of years' time. The lecturer was pushing his concrete product and ridiculed George for worrying about climate change.'

'Yes, I have heard all about George's opinions on tipping points and ice melt. Do you think that you are the first to raise such issues? I think you will find that there are senior professors throughout the university who know much more about this and who may take a different line from George here. For that reason, we aim to teach the standard current view on such issues, which only requires moderate cuts rather than giving up all design in concrete and steel. We simply cannot have scaremongering in front of a guest speaker. None of the professional engineering institutions officially warn against the use of cement, concrete or steel, and none of them suggest, as far as I am aware, that the use of these products is dangerous and should be stopped. They only ask that they are designed more efficiently, aiming at cutting materials by a few percent. Bigger cuts might be required in the future, but not now. Universities concentrate on what is wanted.'

There was a pause while Dr Field let his words sink in before he continued.

'You will know that the rector of this college is a leading economist. She had the honour of presenting a lecture to the Royal Academy a few years ago. In that lecture she stated unequivocally that the best way to find solutions to any climate change problem involved keeping the economy strong and vibrant. Drastic attempts to reduce carbon emissions will not be sustainable. That advice was well received and has been effectively adopted by the UK government and the rest of the world. Enough said. Good evening.'

Dr Field returned to the senior common room, leaving the two students standing there in silence. It was Rhan who appeared most upset.

'So was that the Magisterium clamping down? Or is it the Ministry of Magic stating that You-Know-Who can never come back? Or Saruman advising that Sauron, the necromancer, can be left alone because the ring will never be found?'

'It doesn't really matter,' George responded calmly, smiling at Rhan's fury. 'Thanks for trying to help and for standing up for me, but they're not interested in life-and-death issues. Do you always live in a fictional world? Anyway…one of those three didn't come from this college, so doesn't count.'

'So is our life here just a fiction?' Rhan asked, ignoring George's question and looking around the beautiful enclosed front quad, which by chance happened to be empty at that moment. There were only the two of them, reluctant to retreat from the scene on this mild and still evening. George had nonchalantly stepped onto the stone at the corner of the grass and balanced, looking down on his partner who was shouldering the indignation on his behalf.

Artificial light, escaping through windows and from occasional lanterns, merely suggested the veiled secrets of the college buildings which hung back, skulking in the shadow, away from the open lawn and surrounding walkway. Only a distant cacophony of chat, music and laughter, mostly emanating from the undercroft bar beneath the dining hall, confirmed that modern life was continuing around them.

'I no longer feel so sure about reality.' Rhan continued her considerations concerning fact and fiction. 'This whole place is beginning to feel like something from *Alice in*

Wonderland. Now even you want to pretend that your statements in the sustainability lecture were untrue, unreal, or just never happened. No wonder I feel the one around here who is obviously mad! Have we wandered over a line in those graphs we did last week, where vectors indicate directions in the unreal, mathematical i-plane, where imaginary data can suddenly become real again, just by interaction with another imaginary function?'

George listened, fascinated to hear Rhan philosophising so eloquently about a subject that he and she had so recently been cursing in the run-up to their tutorial.

'After that sustainability lecture,' she continued, 'I checked through my notes and decided that they were trying to hide the low-carbon issues. Just as you said, "sustainability" appears to be a term that can mean anything to anyone.' She kicked a pebble along the path beside the grass square as she spoke. 'I was told about climate change at school in both Syria and Sunderland, yet out in the real world, no one talks or thinks about it. How strange is that? But you – you know stuff! You say something sensible, almost for the first time this term, but then just melt back into the crowd with everyone else when challenged. Yet it was you who had the reprimand, not me! So why am I the angry one? You stand perched on that stone, as placid as the caterpillar smoking his hubble-bubble, as though everything you said about climate change was just an academic debate that will affect no one!'

'Come on!' he said, smiling at her, but denying nothing. 'Let's go to your room for one of those weird and wacky teas.'

CHAPTER NINE

History Lessons

George was rather subdued for the next few days, but happy to head up to Tom's room to celebrate after their Thursday tutorial on *Mathematical Sets*, once their two combined laundries were churning through their cycles. Rhan was slightly disappointed that he had not remarked on her new sports outfit, which made up her Gloucester rowing uniform in the approach to the novice regatta. She was dying to tell him all about her progress and new friends and had resolved not to lie, but neither was she going to volunteer information about her other life.

They climbed the stairs and entered Tom and Danny's palatial room where an argument seemed to be in full swing. 'Nah, no one claims to predict the future,' argued Danny, emphasising his points with an almost-empty beer bottle. Rhan tried to decipher Danny's accent. 'History ne'er repeats itself exactly; there's always something different, some change in parameters.'

'But history can lead to predictions of likely outcomes,' Chris responded on behalf of his subject, running his fingers through his dark hair.

'Well that's what economics tries to do as well,' Fiona got in. 'There are well-known principles that can predict what will happen to trade, balance of payments, inflation and the like, if certain measures are taken.'

'I'm not sure that economics has definite rules or laws,' Tom said, laughing. 'We can't pretend economics is a science. History might repeat itself because conditions are the same or because a warlord knows his history of previous victories and knows when and where to strike. Economics, however, has relatively rapid positive and negative feedbacks, so whatever the prediction, the very science of economics ensures that the predictions will never come true in quite the same way.'

'Well if all sides knew their history,' David said, 'the same feedback would apply to larger events, so the parameters would be different, as Danny so succinctly pointed out.' The argument stopped, having completed a circle.

'Look, I'll go and get the source so I can prove my point,' said Chris. 'Hang on a sec, it's just upstairs.' He dashed out and the conversation froze. George asked quietly whether, while they were waiting, anyone wanted him to read from *Theory of Sets and their Applications*, to general snorts of derision. Chris returned, and coughed theatrically, leafing through a small book.

'We are talking about 731AD and the Venerable Bede, who lived in the north of England and expressed a concern for the future. Bede was the eminent historian of his time and made use of his keen historical research…'

'Gerr on wi'it!' Danny heckled. 'What did Bede say?'

Sighing, Chris began to read from the text. '*At the present time, the Picts have a treaty of peace with the English, and are glad to be united in Catholic peace and truth to the universal Church. The Scots, who are living in Britain, are content with their own territories, and do not contemplate any raids or stratagems against the English. The Britons for the most part have a national hatred for the English, but they have also been brought to some extent under subjection to the English.*

'As peace and prosperity prevail in these days, many of the Northumbrians, both noble and simple, together with their children, have laid aside their weapons, preferring to receive the tonsure and take monastic vows rather than study the arts of war. What results from this will be seen in the next generation.'

'So?' Danny asked.

'Vikings!' exclaimed David with excitement. 'Of course. Cool! Seven something or other was just before the Vikings started hitting the coast where Bede hung out. Bede saw that not having the power to resist would create trouble, and the first Norse raids found gold lying around in the churches and monasteries without any protection. Not only that, they got their oats in both senses of the word with the local girls and the grain stores, so this created a raiding culture. Brilliant!'

'Thank God for chemists!' Chris intoned.

George, who was standing against the wall, arms crossed, murmured under his breath to Rhan, 'Cooling of the local climate also came into it.' She raised her eyebrows in partial interest.

Danny went on a bit more cynically. 'Yerr well, the Viking raids and invasions continued for generations and extended south'ards as far as Crete, east'ards towards

Constantinople and west'ard across the Atlantic. So Bede predicted all that did he?'

David answered for Chris, who was pleased to stand back. 'It is interesting – to think that the whole raiding and bragging society might never have begun if the monks had listened to Bede, created a militant order and sent the first raiders home crying to their mothers with bloody noses.'

'The only snippet I can remember about Bede,' George said, 'was that he had no real idea who built Hadrian's Wall, even though he lived at its east end, just – what, two or three hundred years after the Romans left? Not inspiring for a historian!'

Fiona, who had been sitting quietly in the corner, took the conversation off in another direction. 'I have often wondered what the Romanised Britons thought when they heard that they were on their own and the legions were never coming back. Did everyone realise that their cosy, safe lives were doomed sooner or later?'

'Well getting out of Europe might not be that bad!' Tom fired back immediately.

'If you want bad news,' George said, 'you chaps should study what may have happened at the end of the Neolithic age, when the Bronze Age hordes arrived.'

'That's not even history – it's prehistory, George!' Chris was trying to retrieve the subject. 'We know that the people of Roman Britain relied on mercenaries, who eventually brought over their families, settled and took over. But, like Fiona, I sometimes wonder if it was a gradual process that benefited the majority, or whether it was seen as the end of a civilisation.'

The conversation then split into two: one group covering the Romans, with the other returning to the politics and economics of twenty-first century nationalism, until Tom asked, 'What do you think, Rhan?' Everyone else had butted in, but the foreign girl standing at the window had her own slot and spoke slowly and quietly in a rich voice that no one wanted to interrupt.

'In my part of the world, Syria, the Roman Empire ended much more recently. We used to visit houses in the desert that must have been abandoned in a hurry for a few days when the Turks invaded, yet remained in that condition six hundred years later – right up to the recent war.

'So, I wonder how long you fine philosophers think our current society will last in the face of real upheaval?'

There were raised eyebrows at this question, but Rhan carried on.

'Following the industrial revolution led first by Britain and then by its protégé, the United States, your world has so far enjoyed a mere three or four hundred years of western supremacy. With banking, trade, engineering and gunboat diplomacy, the whole world has been forced, without choice, to industrialise as well.'

'Capitalism is unstable and carries its own downfall,' Tom responded, to the usual cries of derision. 'Everyone knows it is only a transition state, as Marx pointed out.'

'Well with the engineers around here I can understand that collapse,' said Chris, looking at George, who was propping up the wall.

'But will collapse be due to the stupid expectation and self-deception that the laws of physics can be bent and set aside by popular consent?' Rhan argued. 'What happens if or when nature hits back, tossing first the outlying reaches of our world into the dustbin, but eventually even the ancient ruins of Oxford?'

'Will this collapse be 'fore or after next week's essay?' Danny asked.

'Are you suggesting that we might be spending three years studying a system that could collapse partway through?' Chris asked. 'If so, I'm going to refuse to repay my student loan.'

'Come on, Rhan. What do you have in mind?' David asked.

'Well, I suppose my parents taught me to see war coming, to recognise the writing on the wall and to listen out for subjects that are too sensitive to be discussed,' she continued. It was the first time that she had mentioned her parents in a gathering and suddenly everyone was listening without interruption.

'I, like Fiona, have also wondered what it would feel like to be living when a civilisation collapses. When Justinian, the emperor of the east, sent an army from Constantinople under Count Belisarius to recapture Rome from the Goths, he found hunger – not because of a lack of wheat, but because the citizens could only grind corn by hand and had lost the know-how to repair the mills. For us it would be much worse after such a long period of specialisation. We probably wouldn't recognise wheat until it's ripe, and wouldn't know how to guard it or grind enough of it to make a loaf. We have been in isolation from the essentials of life and any instability for so long.'

'Apart from the odd world war,' Chris murmured.

'No, they were just capitalist-inspired internal struggles for leadership and never really threatened western society,' Tom responded quickly, with a nod from Rhan.

'You're talking about global warming!' David nailed the issue smugly, not mentioning his prior knowledge of the sustainability talk. He elicited a second nod of the head from Rhan, who was silhouetted against the setting sun.

'So creating a Marxist state of equality of need is an obvious option?' Tom suggested, to more howls of disdain as they dashed off for supper.

'Well that was a surprise from you, Rhan!' George said quietly as they wandered towards the dining hall. 'I'm not sure if that's good or bad.'

CHAPTER TEN

Inappropriate Conversation for a Pub

'I hear you think that the British Empire has yet to come to an end, but you say it will do soon?'

Rhan was taken aback by this question and it showed. She looked at George who, standing next to her, lowered his pint from his lips to exclaim.

'Nothing to do with me! I'm just surprised that Gareth, a second-year historian, needs to seek advice from a first-year engineer on historical philosophy.'

The group were mostly rugby players and second-years, enjoying the glowing timber logs in a brazier within a little courtyard of the Turf Tavern. It was midweek and quiet; the pub was tucked away down twisting alleyways off minor streets, yet close to the city centre. Danny – now the team's regular hooker – was there along with George, who only had an occasional position in the first team. Rhan's role in the group was more obscure.

Once the laughter and ribbing had subsided, it became clear that some of the conversations from Tom and Danny's room several weeks earlier had been relayed.

'It's just I have an essay on that subject, see.' Gareth's Welsh accent became more pronounced after a pint or so.

'What I said,' Rhan explained, 'was that from my point view it has never ended. The British Empire was not just a geographical hegemony, it was based on concepts of banking, trade and technology, and it was spread around the world at the barrel of a gunboat.' Rhan expanded again on her theme. 'It developed and became more invigorated, even if it outgrew Britain. Few in the world now dare question current forms of capitalism.'

'Ah but can you call it a British Empire if it is not controlled by Britain?' Simon, the jovial third-year ex-captain asked. 'You're just changing the definition.'

'Yes, but not by much,' Gareth rejoined. 'But you better not get me into trouble at my next tutorial, Rhan!'

'Anyway, which of you capitalist pigs hasn't bought a round?' said Danny. 'I got the last one.'

As they stood warming themselves at the brazier in a much smaller group, Rhan took the opportunity for some easy research. 'Simon, you are reading Geography, yes? Can you tell me something about climate change?'

'Well there may be something in it,' he replied soberly. 'But there are other causes that would invalidate the assumption that greenhouse gases directly control temperatures.'

'Oh, really?' Rhan persisted.

'Well the biggest one is the natural cycle of the sun,' Simon explained, clearly thinking on his feet. 'Heating depends on the tilt, energy emitted by the sun, the inclination of earth's orbit, its position in the solar system...well, there are many variables and these probably caused the ice ages and perhaps current warming.'

'Have these effects never been calculated for our current position and recent warming?' Rhan cast Danny a look that prevented him mentioning their previous discussion several weeks earlier.

'Well possibly.' Simon was more wary now. 'But we don't know everything that can cause major shifts in climate. In geological timescales, previous eras have warmed and we don't know why, so it may be more complicated than we think. It could be influenced by carbon dioxide levels, but then the measurements are imprecise so extra greenhouse gases could simply follow the warming and the expansion of grass and trees when ice retreats, rather than cause the warming, if you catch my drift. Anyway, I'll just go and help with the scrummage at the bar.'

'Sounds like horse shite!' Danny muttered. 'Least I owned up to ignorance. But I think yo'rl find climate change isn't a subject for the pub, Rhan.'

'Maybe, but I need to know more,' she said, shaking her head thoughtfully. 'Something very strange is happening.'

CHAPTER ELEVEN

Falling

' *In The World at One today: the government announce that planning for expansion at London's airport has cleared another hurdle...*'

The radio clicked off and Rhan sat down at the desk as soon as her laptop screen came to life. She had dabbled for six weeks and needed answers.

She clicked in the Google box, and typed "climate change". She skipped the UK Met Office site and perused a few items about how any warming was fabricated by climate scientists looking for grant money, and how Arctic ice melt could not be significant if Antarctica was still gaining ice mass. She had seen the arguments by the deniers, but she was not sufficiently convinced by their aggressive assertions to cease her investigations. Besides, since the articles had been written, evidence that Antarctica might be gaining ice mass or that the climate was not warming had tended to dry up.

There were a few articles about the 2015 Paris agreement and international efforts to keep temperature rises below either 1.5°C or well below 2°C by promised actions. Rhan wondered at the obscure threats implied by "dangerous" levels above those temperatures, but could see no discussions or further hints of what that could entail. The dates up to 2050 and beyond for removal of greenhouse gas emissions to the atmosphere seemed a long way off if there was any real danger.

She then clicked on an older newspaper article about warming since the 2015 Paris Accord. Noticing that it was by NOAA, an American group, she expected a sceptical article but instead, she saw a graph that shot upwards to around 1.2°C of post-industrial warming. 'Not far from 1.5° then!' she murmured.

Rhan followed other links and was surprised to find that NASA was endorsing similar views. She bit her lip in annoyance that her previous prejudices had stopped her searching those sites before, and that she had been confused by the way different sites were using different starting points. Some sites compared temperatures with pre-industrial temperatures, while others compared temperatures with the 1980s. Most data was based on "anomalies", which was even more confusing. Checking carefully, she printed off a graph that indicated a temperature rise of around 1.3°C in 2016. Clicking back, she found the links to the UK Met Office, which still had only 0.8°C of warming, and which steadfastly agreed with the latest United Nations' IPCC report. 'Half a degree different – what a mess!' she muttered.

Staying on the Met Office site, she skipped on to the subject that she wanted to reach – the Arctic ice – and read that the director was very confident about the computer predictions. These, along with a straight-line graph, indicated that the ice would not disappear for decades according to all the computer models. She furrowed her brow as she read that this was again in accordance with the latest IPCC view. Rhan felt worried. Something was very wrong; how could a straight line represent the previous steady centuries of ice mass prior to 1980 as ever-increasing, never mind fit the straight line to the recent plunging data? Then they were using that line to predict the future! No school kid in a science class would get away with that, Rhan thought, furrowing her brow.

She changed tack and deliberately searched for Arctic ice loss, and this time started in Wikipedia. George had told her that sea ice was the best indicator. She scanned through an article that described why the sea ice was so important to keeping the earth cooler and how its loss would greatly exacerbate temperature rise, allow faster melting of the tundra permafrost, and encourage decay of the peat bogs to methane. She knew that from school, but not the current timescales. She read with interest how for many millions of years the ice had been a permanent fixture, and felt bemused while looking at images of the Arctic Ocean as the view was from above the North Pole; it was so different to the normal view from above the equator in the Atlantic. She tried to concentrate on the dotted lines indicating the location of ice over the past few decades. The area was shrinking, so there was certainly something to worry about, but she had a feeling that this was not the reason why George had been driven into attack mode with the university.

She then read an interesting item on how the rapidly warming Arctic resulted in a reduced difference in temperature between the equator and the Arctic. This meant that the jet stream, which circled the world in northern latitudes, was changed from a stream to a sluggish river, complete with meanders and oxbow lakes. This left pockets of heat or intense rainfall stranded in places like Russia, Pakistan and even the UK, while other places like Rome suffered from blizzards. So that explained the extraordinary snows that she had played in, even in the coastal town of Sunderland in 2012. She recalled walks with her sister and young cousins along a beach covered in frozen seawater and her uncle's assurances that such cold was extraordinary, even for England. She shook her head, resetting her focus to the matter in hand.

She clicked on the graph of ice extents. There again was a definite shrinking of the area of the ice. There was much discussion over the age of the ice and she appraised how thin ice could fluctuate rapidly from season to season depending on the weather.

'Hmm, volume would be more appropriate,' she mused.

Just as she hoped, scrolling further down the Wikipedia page, she saw the ice mass graph and clicked it; the plunging shape filled the screen. Her focus drifted forward, leaving her gazing vacantly at the keyboard. She was unintentionally holding her breath. 'What are you doing?' she demanded of herself. 'It could mean anything!'

Grabbing a dirty coffee cup, she fetched a drink of water from the washbasin and returned unsteadily to the graph.

It was credited to Washington University but there were no discussions. There were some notes but no attached arguments one way or the other to explain the plummeting graphs. It was based on PIOMAS, whatever that was, and had been constructed by deduction from a range of data as far as she could make out. 'So, an example of unreliable data from climate experts?' she said out loud, beginning to calm down. 'Yet no claims or conclusions about the data?' Nonetheless, she printed out the graph. While doing so, she noticed that some of the data was claimed to be consistent with Cryosat2, which meant little to her.

With the paper copy on the desk, she used a ruler to extend the timeline and followed the curve down with a pencil to where the volume would be zero. She reported under her breath, '2025, give or take. Is that some of your data, George? God, that could be not long after we graduate, yet the risk was not even acknowledged. Something must be wrong.'

In a business-like manner, she tried to contort the curve of the graph to extend it to 2050 or to any other dates in decades to come. Yet any such extension to the curve would only be fantasy and relied on a complete change in long-term direction. There was no way that her A-Level Physics teacher would allow such cheating, so she rejected her attempts to find the optimistic view suggested by the Met Office.

'So much for the Paris Agreement if our goose is already cooked,' Rhan muttered crossly.

She found a discussion forum, where climate sceptics were outraged and disgusted by the PIOMAS data, which remained immutable and undefended against the onslaught.

She returned once again to the Met Office and its links to the Hadley Weather Centre. She tracked down Cryosat2 and discovered that it was the European-backed satellite to survey the ice, and particularly the ice depths. It was confusing but she found a discussion which, with controlled dignity and a reassuring lack of alarming information, managed to say little. The news was dry and unexciting. After half an hour, she found an early announcement that the delayed Cryosat2 was functioning as a replacement to the initial Cryosat, which never made it out of the atmosphere. Measurements were surprisingly close to PIOMAS's deduced data, but the article thought it no great issue because loss of the Arctic ice would not be that significant.

'You lot used to work in Syria! No one dares say anything that might be controversial.' Rhan's loud accusation rang round the empty room. 'Your so-called "free press" are happy to print lies if they are more convenient than the truth!' Rhan rehearsed her argument for George later. 'You have the same situation here – playing politics with billions of other people's lives!' Rhan's anger swelled. It was all so unfair and unjust. She knew exactly who would suffer – the younger generation and the poor.

She lay on the bed, the implications swirling around her head in an uncontrolled tornado. She could only grasp snippets of a horrible future that she could now envisage, with seemingly no one prepared to stop it.

CHAPTER TWELVE

The World Between Worlds

She was still on her bed when George stuck his head in at the door.

'You texted, but didn't respond to my reply!' he complained. 'Come on, let's go for a walk; there's still plenty I've yet to see. Let's just try to avoid the Christmas shopping scrummages though.'

He glanced at her laptop screen, which had come to life as she prepared to go out. 'I thought you were looking at *Electrical Properties of Materials* for the next practical? He moved closer and leant towards the desk. 'Oh no, not global warming!'

'What is the point? Why do I need to learn about silicon bloody chips?' Rhan's response was brittle. 'Once the ice is gone, do you think that understanding how electrons move in doped crystals will be a route to the future? We will have more pressing needs, and that stuff won't help me mend a generator once the electronics are fried. As you said, we learn nothing of any use except how to screw things up more and bloody more.'

'Bloody hell, I never heard you swear and now you won't fucking stop!' He looked at her, as it dawned on him that she was not in robust condition. The room was littered with sports gear from her early-morning activity and she was biting her lip as she shut down the computer.

'It never works this way in books or films,' she muttered. 'Someone is supposed to know how to save the world. Yet who is going to prevent this future if it is taboo to even mention it? Is it too late, George?'

'God knows. Everyone, including the UN reports, still seem pretty relaxed about the total Arctic ice melt and everything else, so maybe it's all fine after all. The computer models all say it'll be fine; it's only reality that's on the blink! You could ask my father; he spoke in the Paris climate talks for the engineers, telling them they were all doomed, I imagine. But he's nuts. Come on, you definitely need a walk. It's cold.' He smiled, adding gently, 'You look good in my jumper, but you'll also need a coat.'

~

The cool air was refreshing, but she felt surprised to see her fellow students gathering for activities, laughing and talking around the college gate. She had the strange feeling that the people around her were there just to act out normality, perhaps for her benefit. She must be the Queen of Hearts and they were the playing cards, pretending that everything was correct and normal; the white roses had all been painted red. College rowing was more important than global warming.

She walked slowly and deliberately on the flat paving slabs which formed a path around the grassed quad.

'I feel as though I might miss a stepping stone and the ground of this fantasy world might tip up. I might fall through a gap into reality.'

'Oh, and there was me just thinking that you would be grabbed by the bears!' he mocked. 'Was it A.A. Milne who did the poem about bears grabbing anyone who stepped on the cracks?'

'Maybe. The bears could easily haul me away right now. I no longer feel part of this world.'

'You could take my arm or hand,' he offered awkwardly as they passed into the shadow of the rear gateway arch. 'There's no way I'm going to fall through any cracks.'

She took his hand surreptitiously once they were under the vault.

'This is all so surreal and dreamlike. Do you know the unreal Wood between the Worlds in *The Magician's Nephew*?'

'No, sorry, I don't know that one,' George apologised as he ducked through the doorway into the street after her, still holding her hand.

'From *The Lion, the Witch and the Wardrobe* series – the first of the *Narnia* books! Two children get stuck in a sort of junction world and they need to find their way from there to Narnia. The danger is that the transition world has a soporific atmosphere and the children are in danger of forgetting and neglecting their concerns and purposes; they just want to sit down beside a pond and relax.'

'I don't recall much of that book, but C.S. Lewis used to hang out in that pub there.' George pointed at the tiny, quaint pub opposite their college, his knowledge of pubs making up for his missed literature.

'I never even noticed a pub there before!' she gasped. It is right opposite the college, but it's not noticeable…like the pub in Diagon Alley. This place is just fantasy land, within a dream.' Rhan sighed, and added dejectedly, 'Is anything real, anywhere?'

'Probably not. I heard a tourist guide telling a small group about that lamp-post down Turl Street, the one you may be able to see from your room if you lean out far enough,' George said. 'The guide claimed it could be the one set at the edge of Narnia as there's a Lion Yard next to it.' He smiled at her and at his own small talk. 'But I think there's another in the square just behind our college with a better claim.'

'My God!' Rhan exclaimed unexpectedly. 'I noticed that lamp-post on my first day, just after getting off the bus. I walked past it with all my cases on my way to the college. That explains much – this *is* fantasy land. I entered it as soon as I entered The Turl.' Rhan's eyes were wide. 'Everything, from the architecture to the sport around here, seems to be aimed at providing a distraction – to help us forget things that really matter.' They were walking past the showy architecture of the Sheldonian Theatre.

'We play games while our planet is in real trouble,' she continued. 'We think that we are in a timeless pleasure garden where we never need to worry about the future. People neither know nor care that the planet is on the edge of a precipice that will change their lives completely. Everything we now consider important is actually pretty meaningless. I don't know that much, but George, there must be a relatively high chance that this whole way of life is doomed? It can never survive in its current form with what I have begun to see. Things could start to change by our fourth year!'

'Well, Oxford has institutes that specialise in climate change somewhere, and education's hardly going to stop, is it?' he replied, the voice of reason.

'Education came to a crashing stop for my school mates and at my intended first-choice university, in Aleppo.' Rhan's voice was brittle and sarcastic. 'A few years of drought, a clash of militant ideas and the whole lot has been blown away. What about the First and Second World Wars here? They must have had some impact on Oxford, or did everything just continue as before? What would it take to get lecturers and students to focus on the issues at hand; or even acknowledge the threat or the concept?' She looked at him sadly, but continued again when he said nothing.

'After that pathetic sustainable concrete lecture, I doubt that a single student gave their future a second thought.' She paused, before going on. 'I have a confession. I was just annoyed with you. You were totally engrossed by the lecture. For the first time since we met, I felt irrelevant. The subject seemed hardly relevant. We are all so gullible! I didn't have the sense to question what we were told; and neither did anyone but you.

'Students of Geography don't worry about the world, and we engineers are not being trained to handle hotter and more primitive or hostile environments. The economists think that carbon has no value. So what does it say about most of the other disciplines? Just what is the use of our education?'

'Welcome to Oxford!' he answered sarcastically, stopping in front of a high stone-walled building. 'We're lucky that we don't have our lectures in Latin! My uncle had a compulsory exam in Latin to read Law here. Remember that this wall is part of New College, which dates back to the thirteenth century or something; they are still trying to decide if it should be renamed…OK, I'm joking!'

After a few moments he went on. 'But Rhan, you're missing a trick! Don't you have a reference to anything as cultural as Thomas Hardy's *Jude the Obscure*?' He pulled her arm and stood right in front of her so he could watch her intently. When she shook her head with a puzzled look, he explained.

'Another literary point to me then! You've been in that pub with the hidden courtyard, the Turf Tavern, down that passageway there behind me. Well, *Jude the Obscure* was about someone who wanted to come to university here, and one of the major scenes was set in that pub, the Turf. Jude wanted to be a scholar but had the wrong background for Oxford. He stood up in that pub and recited the creed in Latin to prove to other drinkers that he should be a scholar.' George smiled sympathetically at her troubled face. 'But don't read *Jude* if you value your sanity; as soon as anything starts to go well, there's a dreadful catastrophe.'

Rhan now shook her head, smiling at his advice, but still looked sad. He changed tack.

'Well at least it wasn't a fantasy story!' George tried again. 'But on the subject of disasters, dare I ask what you found in your research? What's going to happen to us?' They remained standing, while Rhan assembled her thoughts. She let go of his hand to concentrate.

'Well, please remember I start with only the basics that I learnt at school in Sunderland and Aleppo. I probably had no more than two or three hour-long lessons and perhaps a bit of reading afterwards.' She spoke slowly. 'The alarming thing is that I discovered there are huge dangers that should have been addressed decades ago and certainly now, yet they – or we – have decided against any action. So timescales could be extremely close, yet we are making it all hush-hush.' She bit her lip, not minding how close he stood. After a brief pause she continued.

'What did I find? Well, temperatures have been shooting up, with almost every year hotter than in previous decades. Within a pretty short time I think I found the ice area and the ice volume charts that you mentioned, and yes, the curve has plummeted, but it lifted for a couple of years around 2012 before being indecisive from 2015. The ice looks doomed. It was very strange though: there was no text to go with it; there were no claims that it indicated a sensational event. In neither the plummeting ice volumes nor the soaring temperatures were there even discussions on how it would affect us. Yet the threat was there – the end of the world as we know it.'

'Things won't remain the same,' he agreed. 'But aren't you being rather melodramatic? Will it really be the end of the world?'

Rhan shrugged. 'It took quite a bit to find, but an article from the Met Office confirmed the curve was "about right" based on recent Cyro, no, I mean Cryosat data from the European satellite. So why all the hush-hush? Why do they then deny it?'

'Well that's what greenhush is all about, as my dad would say,' George sighed as he explained. 'Greenhush is pretending there's nothing to worry about. It's what everyone wants to hear. And anyone suggesting there are dangers and that we need to do something…well, you've seen what happened to me. I bet your old teachers have had to change their science-based lessons too.'

'So it's fine to deny that millions of people may die, or will it be billions?' She looked him full in the face. 'If anyone tries to stop it, will they be condemned?'

'Yes,' George confirmed. 'It's a taboo subject that you can't talk about, apparently. I know it's crazy, but it's stupid to offer resistance. There's no point. I could have been sent home for arguing against the use of concrete or steel. Anyway, there's little that can be done at this stage, so it's no great shakes.' He moved on eagerly. 'What about the other side? Did you find anything convincing or interesting from the sceptics?'

'That was much easier to find,' she said, relieved that she could answer his question. 'There were plenty of websites and I expected complexity because I had heard that the science was not at all clear-cut, yet the arguments I came across were just shapes in the mist – not even footprints in the snow.' Rhan felt smug at her metaphors and felt confident in her subject. 'They were sufficiently forceful and plentiful to be persuasive, but each item melted away when I considered the details, even with my limited common sense and technical knowledge.

'For example,' she went on, counting the points on her fingers, 'one argument is that ice melting at the North Pole is not significant as there has been an increase of snow at the South Pole. Gains on land in Antarctica are supposed to balance out the loss of ice cap at the Arctic. How could anyone believe that?

'There was no attempt to justify how the loss of reflective white cover, the loss of cooling ice in the sea, and the risk of methane releases from clara-whatsit could be balanced by an extra widening of the fringe of ice around the Antarctic continent or a few deeper snowdrifts on the frozen land.

'What I don't understand is why everyone thinks the loss of Arctic ice is unimportant and will soon return to normal after a harsh winter. Nor how thin new ice could match the staying power of the ridges of solid old ice. It is all so irrational, even in the international forum, the IPCC.'

'What did they say would happen next?' George asked.

'Nothing really,' she complained, holding her arms out in condemnation while stepping backwards. 'No one seems to know or want to know. Apparently, once the floating ice is gone, the Greenland ice will follow, and that is apparently inevitable. There are no timescales to suggest when coastal towns can expect waves at their doorsteps, or when huge numbers of refugees from Bangladesh will wash up around the world along with farmers from East Yorkshire!'

He moved closer to Rhan to let a pedestrian pass, standing right in front of her again, looking into her troubled face. She could almost taste his warm breath, anchoring her back to the present in the dark street. He did not appear to notice or mind. She continued, feeling slightly stronger.

'Then there were pathetic assertions I have heard here among students. Even if there is climate change, then it is only natural and not related to mankind's actions. It is apparently normal for the planet's climate to flip about and is hardly affected by the rising concentrations of greenhouse gases. In fact, it is even suggested that the heating of the planet at various times in the geological past caused extra carbon dioxide gases in the atmosphere, rather than the other way round. Carbon dioxide is natural and can therefore do no harm!'

'I've often heard that too,' he confirmed. 'Huge numbers of people cling to the argument that global warming is due to the sun's activity.'

'Well, it took me just a few minutes to work out that the sun can cause fluctuations in the region of 0.6 watts per square metre,' Rhan continued. 'Yet we now have problems with an extra six watts – ten times that value. And temperature rises over the past decade or so have set so many new records, even when the sun has been relatively dormant.'

'People believe what they want,' George repeated. 'There's probably no logic for you to spot,' he smiled before continuing. 'Come on funny face! You're getting cold just standing here.' He moved away from the head-to-head discourse.

'Oh yes!' she began again as soon as they were walking. 'There was stuff that argued we could not afford to do anything and that jobs were too important, give or take Brexit. It was all very depressing. Sceptics emphatically deny science that the Victorians had established a hundred and fifty or so years ago.' George grunted his agreement.

'Arguments against climate concern involve flat denial or just snipping at the facts from the margins,' Rhan complained. 'Yet those margins are so narrow and they fail to address anything meaningful in the science! It is all just based on hope and denial: we cannot afford to address the issues and it is all a left-wing plot to put people out of work.' She stopped suddenly and turned towards her companion.

'How come you have never looked at this yourself?' she asked. 'You have more knowledge than me, so why the lack of interest?'

They had now left the narrow streets and were walking through Magdalene College gardens and park, so they could talk and walk more freely.

'I'm afraid I've never really looked,' he confessed. 'After years of having it forced on me at home, I never felt like looking for answers in textbooks, online, or in the great beyond. You seem to have picked it all up pretty quickly though.' George neatly deflected the questions.

'I had done a bit of research since that lecture, but then it seemed to really click today,' she said, barely aware of their route or surroundings. 'I have just a scattering of the concepts. The bigger problem is then determining meaningful and usually hard-hitting facts from the optimistic predictions of a soft global warming. The soft approach seems to involve sticking the term "sustainable" in the sentence and allowing things to work out in decades or centuries to come. I have a feeling that nearly all of the recommendations are just window-dressing, like that lecture we had here.'

Rhan clasped her hands together and looked down as she vocalised her opinions as she walked.

'On the whole, the emphatic information is from the climate deniers, which is obviously rubbish, as I mentioned. The half-truths appear to be from the governments and scientists who want to remain popular and credible. The more worrying stuff is often in biological studies of birds and animals or is presented as stark facts, with little in the way of supporting opinion. That makes it difficult, so I could have it all wrong.' George nodded his understanding, but Rhan was keen to continue.

'My worry is that what you said in that lecture could be true. It looks like our generation will "cop it", as my grandmother apparently used to say. Reliance on the certainty of the sceptics is as sensible as belief in…oh, I don't know…relying on Father Christmas to make Christmas Day happy. Yet there seems to be enough data to suspect that most climate scientists, with their timescales for heating in hundreds of years with big sea-level rises in thousands of years, are only telling us a fraction of the truth! They say we still have a decade or so to act! Their opinions on the future seem to be tailored to make people happy. It feels wrong to rely on the future.'

She looked up at George's face again. 'I acknowledge… that I am messed up enough to be looking for trouble, war, drought, famine and deceit in my lifetime. But all this could make wars in the Middle East seem petty. We must do something!'

'Oh no, Rhan,' George sighed. 'What have I done?'

'Do you think I could be swayed easily by indoctrination, with my background? I am grateful for your outburst at the concrete lecture and will remain so, even if you run off with a jolly-hockey-stick from Christchurch and never speak to me again.'

'Right. But what happens if I don't do that?' he enquired.

In answer, she grabbed his hand and held his arm tight against her as they walked back in friendly silence through the darkening lanes. She dropped his hand and arm as they neared the bright lights of Broad Street.

CHAPTER THIRTEEN

Selected

While George often wistfully mentioned the rapidly approaching end to their first term, Rhan ignored the issue as much as she could. Each day was so full that she could do little but contemplate the present, leaving little scope to worry about climate change. Returning to life as a dependent in her uncle's family was just inevitable and sometimes appealed to her for a pleasant break from the work deadlines. She and George had three engineering practicals in various states of readiness to hand in, a drawing practical each to complete, and they had to prepare for the last week's tutorials in both engineering and maths.

Fortunately, they had developed a routine that suited the three aspects of their lives. In outward social events and meals with friends, they only exchanged occasional glances. Their individual sporting activities remained completely separate. Yet they managed to spend almost every minute of the rest of their day together at lectures, practicals, or in one another's room, often working late into the evenings.

Rhan was often tired, but still managed to enjoy the early-morning outings on the river several days a week. George was frequently standing at her door ready to escort her down to breakfast as she was caught returning late from a shower. He became used to being recruited for rapid hair drying.

Her early-morning start was offset by relaxing afternoons usually spent working in George's room, listening to his records, and waiting for him to hobble into the room after rugby on several days of the week. As dating a tutorial partner was unthinkable, they conspired to keep their time together secret where possible.

In the last week, things started to change. Rhan had done nothing about getting a job so was aware she faced several weeks ahead where she would be almost restricted to the house or backyard in Sunderland, with just her cousins for company. Each afternoon, she now had the distraction of slipping away to row in the novice regatta. At least the races enforced a rescheduling of the early-morning practices, so she was glad for an extra hour or so in bed.

The novice races took place with bewildering speed. They involved a rapid run down to the river straight after lunch to meet with the rest of the nervous crew. They then rowed down to the start line, spent a few minutes waiting around with the Gloucester boatman who held the stern of the boat until the start, and raced back up the river in two columns. It was fun, and the victories were clocked up without incident. Their coach, Nick, had not been exaggerating when he had said they were a powerful crew. The most stressful aspect occurred when she was late one day after finding her simple Gloucester rowing strip missing. After checking the laundry, she had to sprint into George's room to rescue her kit, which he had picked up with the rest of her washing.

It was a surprise and a delight to the girls to find that the Gloucester novice crew were as good as Nick's prediction. No other female novice crews came near their slick performance through the water. On the last day, Nick was there waiting at the boathouse to congratulate them and to drag them off to a presentation further along the river bank.

'Rhan and Claire!' he called out as they set off through the darkening December afternoon. 'I have someone who wants to meet you from the university's coaching team. I believe you two have especially caught his eye. Well done.'

Poor Nick's attempts to be official were, as usual, destroyed by cheeky ribbing from the girls and, on this occasion, by Sarah. 'Yes Nick, but remember – Bar caught your eye first. Don't lose her! We've already extracted a promise from her, without too much duress, to row with us for Torpids next term. Bar, you won't abandon us will you? Bump after bump, here we come.'

Nick was surrounded by his crew as he walked, and found it a useful chance to talk about the future.

'I've no idea what will happen to Claire and Bar, but it'd be great if they get special coaching from the university. If Bar is available for Torpids…' he said, pausing to look at Rhan, '…then I'd be surprised but pleased. It would be great if Gloucester could borrow both Bar and Elisha again, but you'll have to ask your college captains. As Gloucester II is a completely new boat, you'll start so far down the tables that no one will care. But don't do too well, not like today. Yup, that's a thought – it might be best if Bar and Elisha are at the back in the photographs, if you two don't mind.'

'Yes, that would be fine,' Rhan conceded readily.

'Roger, this is Bar and Claire.' As they entered the presentation venue, Nick introduced the two girls to a tweed-jacketed young man who held a glass of red wine in one hand and a cap in the other. 'Do you want to speak to them now or after the presentation?'

'Well both if that would be possible,' Roger replied in a much more diffident manner than expected, slipping his cap into a pocket so he could shake hands with the two girls. He was obviously a rower himself, judging by his height. He was older than an undergraduate, but was still in his mid-twenties, with short black curly hair.

'It has been a delight watching you row. Nick kindly emailed me last week that you might excel and you certainly did. You have learnt much in just a few weeks and are a real credit to you, Nick.

'I have been given the task of assembling a squad of first-year girls for coaching, with a view to hopefully feeding some into the university squad next year.'

He looked up at a bustle further down the room. 'You need to go for your presentation now, but can you let me know afterwards whether you may be available next week, in ninth week and in noughth week of next term? Speak later.'

'Gloucester, over here please!' An official commanded the girls to join the rest of their crew.

~

'Yes definitely, is the answer,' Rhan declared to Roger some minutes later, once the ceremony was over. 'But I vacate my room on Friday and I have nowhere to live.'

'No problem, Bar!' Roger smiled. 'It is a fully funded residential course a few miles down the river. There are small dormitories and a canteen. You only need to ask your college to stay an extra night, which they should allow. What about you Claire?'

'It is a marvellous opportunity, but I need to speak to my parents first. I think I am expected at a family party on Tuesday, if you don't mind me missing a couple of days?'

'Brilliant,' Roger said, smiling again as Claire shook Rhan's arm excitedly. 'I'm beginning to enjoy this job. You will be with around twenty others who have already signed up.'

'So will we be your only novices?' Claire asked.

'No, there is one other, a girl rowing for Keble who I signed up yesterday after you wiped them out. So, to business, as time and daylight are short and my bike light has packed in. Can I have your email addresses so I can send you the details? It would be helpful if you could leave your baggage somewhere in college and bring a small bag on the minibus.'

'You will love working with Bar,' Nick advised Roger as they split up amid titters from the Gloucester girls. 'And Claire will keep you entertained.'

~

As the girls boarded the small coach a few days later, the atmosphere was subdued for their first meeting. The day before, Rhan had helped George carry his numerous bags down to the railway station and had seen off almost the whole college before spending a friendless last night in college. Few of the girls seemed to know each other and

Rhan was without her cheerful friend Claire, who would be joining late. As the girls quietly discussed their home or school rowing club and their position in their college First Eights, it dawned on Rhan that with so many experienced oarswomen in the squad, her own experience so far would count for very little.

As the most junior rower in the squad, Bar was moved to various positions on successive days. She found that she was ambidextrous and it only took her a few minutes to swap hands and master a change from one side of the boat to the other. There was, however, so much to learn. She enjoyed rowing as Number 1 on the bow side, from where she could watch the seven blades in front of her moving as one when the rhythm was good. Yet she was glad to move back to stroke side so she could sit as Number 2 in front of Claire, who could only row on the bow side.

Roger was an inspiring coach. On the second evening, while Claire was still absent, he caught Rhan working alone at the supper table while most of the girls sat around the stove or TV at the end of the room. He picked up her fluid mechanics textbook and looked at the open chapter.

'What's this, Bar, laminar flow? A good subject to study for a rower. So are you a mathematician, a physicist or an engineer perhaps? My guess is you're an engineer, as your book skimps on the maths and has practical examples.' She smiled and nodded at his deduction.

'This is my subject! I'm doing a PhD on the Martian atmosphere and its effects on spacecraft and landing probes, but I come at it as a physicist. So, you're just beginning fluid mechanics?'

'Yes, this is my first real look at the subject,' Rhan replied, 'although we have had some lectures and we did a couple of experiments on standing waves and hydraulic jumps in the fluids lab, which was great fun. It was horrific to see that a swimmer caught at the base of a weir cannot escape being sucked back under! I am trying to write up the practicals and prepare for the first tutorial next term on the subject.'

Rhan looked up at the slender coach, trying to picture him and his curly dark hair in a context away from rowing and the river. Even as he spoke, she started to wonder whether he had the strength to be a first-class rower.

'Fine idea. It'll also help you appreciate the complex issues for cutting resistance to your boat passing through the water. Each stroke drives the boat through the water against the laminar flow, which acts like a form of friction. Water tends to stick to the boat's surface and has high velocity relative to the rest of the water in the river, even on a polished boat surface. Yet just a few centimetres away from that surface, the water has zero flow. And between those, the flow rates vary with the distance from the boat surface. The friction increases markedly if there is any chaotic, non-laminar flow, if say the cox over-steers and eddies are shed by the rudder.'

Roger pointed at Rhan's book where there was a sketch that indicated the different rates of laminar flow away from an object moving through a liquid. Rhan nodded her appreciation of laminar flow.

'However, at the blade, where you want to maximise the resistance, there are whirlpools of disturbed and separated water. The bigger the whirlpool, the more force in the stroke. It's easy for me to see from the bank who is, and who isn't, pulling their weight!' He smiled before going on.

'The effort at the stroke is no definite measure of the oarsman's contribution to the boat's motion, however. What counts is the net balance between force in the stroke and the contribution of the rower to the Reynolds number, which for laminar flow is effectively proportional to the weight of the rower. Lighter rowers can be effective with a weaker pull than heavier rowers, but that's not often the case.'

'Right,' Rhan responded uncertainly.

'I'll do some sketches and make some notes so you can see what I mean. It'll help your rowing and your understanding of fluid mechanics. Oh, I'm afraid you need to be able to derive those formulas – they are the basis of a whole branch of fluids. I'll test you on them tomorrow if you like. You may as well get double coaching while you are here!'

Rhan was grateful for the help, but relieved that Claire was not present to make the usual inferences that provided such a laugh for the Gloucester girls.

~

Anxious not to be singled out for extra advice among the seasoned rowers, Rhan listened intently to every hint and tip from Roger as he cycled along the towpath in his flat cap. There was much aggressive competitiveness among the other girls, but as novices, Rhan and Claire were beneath their notice and were left alone. Rhan concentrated entirely on acquiring new skills and extra fitness, both on the water and with the rowing machines.

The men, and in particular one called Dumas who generally had a couple of friends as wingmen, turned up at the gym from time to time and delighted in taunting Rhan by changing the settings of her machine to test her stamina. The mucking about by the dark-haired, tanned and chunky Dumas was good-natured and the boys were apparently always impressed. Yet Rhan hated the idea of being beaten by the challenges of these swaggering young men who appeared to be picking on her. On the third occasion towards the end of the week, both Claire and Roger were close by, but Roger only looked on without saying a word, taking notes like a junior technician, and made no effort to intervene as Dumas brazenly taunted Rhan. She felt isolated and could not believe that her friend Claire was just watching, without the usual good-natured banter which might have made keeping up with the boys' challenges more fun.

'Where were you when I needed you?' Rhan gasped angrily once they and Roger had all trooped out.

'Bloody hell Bar, I wasn't going to stop you making a hero of yourself while that lot flirted with you,' Claire said. 'You know who that was, don't you? Dumas is only the bleeding president! There's a female president who seems nice, but that guy's the king around here. I think even the coaches work for either the male or the female president. If the other girls had seen that attention paid to one of us novices, they'd scratch your eyes out.'

Claire slowed her breathless excitement, and went on more slowly. 'I'm not sure, but I think you've recorded some strength and endurance tests in front of a president and a coach, even though you've hardly trained. They must've been good, judging by their comments. Come on, you're too tired to move, aren't you? Let's get to the showers, then bed.'

CHAPTER FOURTEEN

Waves on the Wear

The silent, timber-floored hall of the large Victorian terraced house felt both familiar and strange. The girl who returned to her Sunderland home was acutely aware of an internal metamorphosis that had taken place since she had left. Outwardly, she was still garbed in the same black coat, skirt and headscarf, but within the formerly stooped chrysalis, she felt new energies that she had to fight to control.

She was bursting with fitness, vigour and confidence, especially now she was almost on top of her homework after major help from Roger with her fluid mechanics. She could almost brush off anxiety over the small matter of a maths exam awaiting her at the beginning of next term.

Yet she was finding it difficult to be mindful of the present after several days away from George. She felt as if part of her mind had been cut away – a feeling that was exacerbated now that the distractions of rowing camp were behind her. She was seeing everything anew, as though through George's eyes. What would he think of the impressive but slightly faded nineteenth-century street? Would he like the massive stone steps up to the large front door? What would he say to the carpentry in the doors and windows? How dismissive would he be of the small garden and lower level yard at the rear? How would he get on with her family? Would there be emails from him, despite her warnings that she would be out of touch for the first week?

'Anyone home?' she called to the calm quiet of the house. She walked past the silent main rooms, the best room and the one cluttered with children's toys. As she descended the stairs, the clock chimed a reminder that her aunt and young cousins would be at the school gates at that time, with the older boys not due to be let out for another half-hour. Rhan was uncertain when her sister would be back after work.

Keen to plug in her laptop, Rhan hurried back up to the hall, grabbed her cases and climbed two more storeys to the pair of rooms in the roof-space, where she was relieved to find that her old room was cluttered with only a few of her sister's belongings. She took her laptop from her backpack and switched it on. There were three emails from George.

The first email had been very polite as if to a stranger, signed in an androgynous manner, "Georgie", as agreed. The second was resentful over the lack of response. The third threatened to text or call her if she did not respond quickly. She deleted the last email and quickly typed a holding apology, promising better communications along with as much help as he wanted with questions on the flow of fluids through tubes, hydraulic jumps and tsunami waves. She was pretty certain that her sister would see the email at some point.

It pleased her to hear the hurt in his emails. They had been apart for a week, but it was going to be a long holiday. Her earlier vitality was only a shell; there was an inner need she could only banish for ridiculously short periods of time. She sat, vacantly wondering who held which cards in this relationship. It was exciting and felt so normal, yet surreal. But then, she had so little experience other than through her novels and other media – and none of those seemed to fit her plot.

Rhan could look back and acknowledge that from the beginning, she had enjoyed testing the young man she had been thrown together with, and whom she had found to be a fascinating and addictive study. She tried to determine what he liked about her and vice-versa. She had willingly become not only his workmate, but also his secret tag-along companion – and had even surprised and delighted him by taking the lead on many of their adventures and deceptions, which allowed them to spend so much of their time together. At the same time, she had wanted to discover the extent of his interest in her. It had been an interesting experiment; his declaration of love for her had ironically only been an attempt to scare her off, and even to prevent her from loving him. She knew that had it been the other way around and she had declared her love, then he would have been terrified. On the other hand, she knew she would be seriously worried if she had to commit to being his official girlfriend.

Through genuine affection, excitement and trust, her strange relationship with George seemed to work well without commitments. She felt little concern about losing his respect in the manner her aunt would preach. She felt happy with the way things were, but she wondered at the strange difference in circumstance between herself and her sister. She wondered whether her relationship with George was unusual or relatively typical for the Western culture. It felt special, but…

Rhan heard the kitchen door slam three floors below. She sprang up and rushed downstairs.

'Oh good, you're back!' said her aunt. 'Be an angel and hang up yer' cousins' coats would yer Rhan!' The three children shyly made straight for the TV. As she embraced her aunt, Rhan noted just how small she was beneath the long, traditional robes. She also noticed the soft West Yorkshire accent and the lack of the Sunderland twang that the rest of the family had picked up at school.

While her aunt prepared vegetables and bustled around the kitchen, Rhan made toast for her cousins and called them to the large pine table. As they all sat down, Rhan, sipping a welcome cup of tea, felt the comfort of familiar surroundings and family. Half an hour later, voices in the hall warned them that the teenagers were back, and soon after that her sister returned.

'Hi Sis!' Rhan received a brief embrace from Aisha. 'How come you're home so early? Sund'lund Uni students are still here, so ah thought yu must be wrong when yu said y'term was ending. How was it? Sorry about y'room, but yu should've seen it before ah sorted it out.'

It was great to enjoy and be annoyed by frivolous conversation with her sister, who expected so little from Rhan. Following her engagement, Aisha now thought herself so worldly-wise that Rhan wondered how much she should, or should not, pass on to her naïve older sister from the wealth of experience she now had after a few weeks' socialising, working and almost cohabiting with the opposite sex.

It was relaxing to help her aunt with the younger two girls and the baby boy, who looked at her with large, brown, curious eyes. The girls were fascinated by this familiar stranger and, after their brief shyness, they followed her around, studying her and trying to work out whether she was their old friend or a new adult. They soon discovered that Rhan still enjoyed children's games and was much more fun than her preoccupied sister, Aisha, who had disappeared upstairs to use her phone.

The boys, aged fifteen and thirteen, now stood head and shoulders taller than their mother but also greeted the lanky university student cautiously. Their horseplay in the kitchen, before beginning their evening Islamic Studies, became more and more physical despite the scolding from their mother. Rhan soon decided that their prolonged argument and wrestling was put on to show off their newfound physical dominance in the house.

She ignored the squabbling boys and played the part of a cool university student until the mounting shrieks, followed by threats from their mother, forced Rhan to intervene on her behalf.

'Look, chaps,' Rhan addressed the grappling pair in hearty language borrowed from George. 'You are about to knock over the fridge and I am looking forward to an evening with your father, so would prefer him not to be troubled by bad reports about you. Why don't you finish this fight in the yard?'

'Not until I get m' phone....Ow!' Rhan was suddenly towering over them and was gripping an arm of each in an irresistible clamp. They were being physically forced apart and inexorably directed to the back door.

'Come on you two princes! Let's see how far you've got with the Spikes of Doom. I have been looking forward to being the escaping princess again.'

'We're way too big for that; we can both reach the ground!' The younger cousin dismissed the obstacle course in the yard.

'Well that just makes it harder,' Rhan responded with enthusiasm. 'If you even touch the ground, then you are contaminated by a dreadful disease that within ten seconds will cause you to fall, be impaled on the spikes and killed. I had that problem of being too tall ever since your father fixed the bars. It makes it much harder as you have to keep your legs up.'

'But one of the monkey bars has snapped,' the older brother reported.

'Oh no! Will that stop us escaping?' Rhan feigned fear. 'Can we do a double-reach across the gap? I fear we will lose many lives in that chasm!'

'You're crazy, Monkeybar! I thought they'd lock yu up at Oxford.'

'No way!' she laughed. 'I have not told them you two call me Monkeybar when I leave you standing, but I gave them part of your nickname for me, Bar, which I get called when I row. Look at my blistered hands! You two training me here has paid off – I'm one of the strongest women. And at

129

Oxford, everyone lives in a fantasy world. The proof is that if I lean out of my bedroom window, guess what I can see? The Lamp Post!'

'Eh?'

'What d'yu mean?'

'I can see a lamp-post that might be the one the witch planted in *The Magician's Nephew* and which Lucy and the others see on the edge of Narnia. Come to Oxford in the summer and I will show you. My college is right in the middle of Narnia! But to get there we have to cross the spikes of doom with that gap. Who's going to try to escape first?'

~

The tired boys were busy with their religious studies and the house was infused with appetising spices by the time her uncle returned. He was clearly delighted to see Rhan.

'So tell us about college!' he asked her after the meal as they all sat in the best room, which was rarely used by the family. 'What are you learning and 'ave you made any mates?'

'Well, I have some friends, but most of the girls in my college think that I am rather strange…'

Rhan was interrupted by inevitable laughter and sarcastic comments from her family.

'What d'yu know?'

'No surprises there then!'

'Impossible!'

Rhan continued, smiling at the teasing, but noted her guardians' concern for their awkward niece. 'I still have lots of good college friends, as well as girls in other colleges. I spent most of last term studying structures, which is to do with bridges and buildings. We spent a bit of time on silicon chips and electronics practicals. I am now starting fluid mechanics, which covers streams, rivers and airflows. It explains how boats and aeroplanes behave. We study supersonic flow in the third year.'

Aware that they were likely to ask more about her friends, she launched into one of the subjects that she was most willing to discuss.

'One of the most controversial subjects is climate change. I had not expected engineers and academics to be actively ignoring it.'

'Well, there's nowt gunner happen for thousands of years is there?' her aunt responded, laughing. 'Besides if it means a bit of sun here in Sunderland, well I'm all for it!'

Rhan smiled as she now noted the difference between her uncle's occasional Sunderland twang and her aunt's West Yorkshire accent. She wondered how her sister would get on with her new family.

'Well,' her uncle pondered, 'I used to think that climate was part of a Western plot to disenfranchise the Arab countries of oil. Yet now, America has so much gas from frackin', I'm not so sure anymore. Trump blamed China for inventin' it, which I know is wrong. You think it's important, Rhan?'

'Well the graphs all indicate that countries like Britain will be affected least. Sorry aunt, but warmer is no guarantee of sunshine. Countries like Syria will be baked, and crops will fail so almost everyone will need to leave if they haven't left already, I suppose.'

Turning back to her uncle, she continued. 'There does seem to be a very real conspiracy. But it seems to be the other way around – both developed and developing nations have continued to produce and burn fossil fuels at ever-faster rates, and the shock is that everyone, including engineers, are conspiring with the general public to deny there is a problem. I have discovered that every tonne of carbon dioxide sent into the atmosphere stays up there for ages and adds to the problem. We have known for around a hundred and fifty years that carbon dioxide has these properties, but we are still pretending to be ignorant.'

'But isn't it true that most people believe the whole of society is based on fossil fuels, and that without it, society would collapse?' Rhan's uncle suggested.

'That's right, so we are doing almost nothing; we are not carrying out meaningful research for new materials, and we are not equipping the next generation with the skills to face the obvious major problems. We are just carrying on almost the same as before, as if the future has nothing to do with us.'

This new outspoken undergraduate was a completely different creature from the diffident girl who had left their home. Rhan's aunt and uncle looked at each other to show their surprise.

'But when would this happen, love?' asked her aunt.

'Timescale is difficult. I need to know more: it might be just years away or it may be decades before we find ourselves in real trouble. It will almost certainly affect our generation.' She waved her hand to include her older cousins, who were partially listening by the door.

'So how's that gonna affect ma business?' her uncle asked.

'Well I suppose metal casting is a high-carbon industry,' Rhan considered, but your contracts with the rail industry should really take off, if or when they start to prepare for low-carbon travel. I believe rail is the greenest form of transport so you should be busy in the medium and long term.'

'Well you'd make a great sales rep, Rhan!' said her uncle. 'Hear that boys – keep studyin' and the business will see y're alreet.'

There was a short pause before her uncle turned to Rhan with a serious warning. 'You 'ave a care though, girl. I wonder if your views could get you into trouble. A'fore you know it, you'll find you're on police records and marked down with having "extremist views". So 'ave a care! Gan canny. People like us need to keep our heads down. You know what I mean – the way things are at the moment.'

Climate change, thought Rhan, is great at discouraging further enquiries. Her strange life at university was safe for the time being.

~

She was wrong in some respects. As soon as they reached their attic retreat, Aisha rounded on her.

'Blimey Sis, I never thought of you as a radical. A've always had to nag yu to do 'owt. What are they doing to you at that posh college? What would ower ma and pa have said?'

'They would have said, "You must find out more. Dig deeper!"' Rhan insisted. 'As far as I can make out, the current pretence that there is no danger is only going to make everything so much worse. You and I were always told, "Flee, hide and only fight as a last resort." It was our family mantra, and God knows it has kept us alive enough times in all the wars our family have seen over the last few generations. Yet we may have run as far as we can, you and me.'

Rhan sighed and glanced around the room. 'I need to find out more. Britain might be one of the safest places in the world, but without preparations…well it could be hell, especially for immigrants like us. Things could get very nasty. We need to look at what is ahead, Sis.'

'Look, a'll 'ave a man to look after me,' Aisha responded, getting wound up. The new bride-to-be Aisha sounded so different from her former self. Before she had changed her name from Anna to Aisha, she had just been Rhan's more lively big sister. 'I can't expect you to understand what having a bloke is like, but there's no need for you to start stirring things up. It also gets me out of here. It'll be great. It's what I want!'

'I hope you are right, but from what I've seen and read, men are not always as superior and all-powerful as you think.'

'Well listen to you, Miss-Know-It-All! What would you do? Where would you be safe?'

'Well if we were seriously going to hide up here...' Rhan began smiling to subdue the argument and hesitated, unsure what to say, until she spotted her way out. She then continued in a mocking manner. 'I think you should marry Gary from your old class. You could settle down with him and help look after his father's greyhounds. You would soon be a mainstay of Sunderland and one of you could become a City Councillor, like Gary's dad!'

'So what are yu trying to say?' Aisha asked in an accusatory manner, but then also started to laugh.

'Well I know how close you and Gary were when you first arrived.'

'Ha bloody ha! What about you? What would you do?'

'Well, I suppose I could become a management consultant, buy a London home and sell it for a few million and become the Lady of the Manor in some village somewhere,' Rhan replied loftily. 'Perhaps I should marry a red-faced middle-class pillar of the rural community!' The girls giggled, but Rhan then continued in a more serious tone.

'The trouble is, I would live to regret my inaction whoever I married, and my children would pay the price.' Aisha's head shot up, not at concern for the next generation, but at this astounding new confidence of her lanky sister. It had always been assumed that Rhan was unlikely to marry.

'I always thought yu far too autistic for men. So yu got a boy then?' There was both suspicion and curiosity in her sister's question.

'No. But my friends point out that I have some interesting and interested admirers!' Rhan was not certain herself whether she was lying to her sister. Was George hers or not? Was half of what Claire and the others said about her rowing admirers true?

'You've really got mates then?' her sister persisted, quizzing her.

'Yes. We have some good laughs.' Rhan could not help smiling at the thought of her nutty Gloucester rowing friends, her philosophising college friends and her rugby drinking mates. Thinking of them diluted the ache for George for a while.

'What's it like being all on yu' own? How do you know what to do? Don't you miss us? What happens if yu get ill, without anyone to look after yu?'

'I suppose our tutors tell us what to do when it comes to work. The college seems to run itself by tradition, but there are people pulling the strings of course. My worst times were when I was homesick in the first week, and when I was ill after a birthday party halfway through the term. I ate something that kept me up all night. It was agony and I actually thought I was going to die!' She gave up not thinking of George.

'So were there men at that party?' Aisha asked. 'And alcohol? Was that what made you bad?'

'Yes, yes and no,' Rhan responded, smiling at her sister. 'A large group of us went out for a meal and there were blokes and alcohol, but I hardly had any, as I felt sick really early on, soon after a fish starter.'

Rhan felt slightly ill even at the recollection. She had managed to last through most of the meal, with just one hasty trip to the ladies' to be sick. She had then quietly slipped away to her room, texting George to say she was having an early night. *"Fine but are you OK?"* had been his response.

Half an hour or so later, Rhan had been wishing she was with her family in Sunderland, or even better, back as a little girl in Aleppo with her parents to care for her.

'Just as you say, being ill away from home is not good,' Rhan told Aisha grimly, recalling just how frightened she had felt.

"Help!!!" she had texted George, as her need overcame her humiliation.

'I was sick so many times, and my skin was all blotchy.' Rhan gave a summary report to her sister, who for once was listening intently. 'And every few minutes, I had to keep running to the loo upstairs. Friends had to lend me clean pyjamas and sheets. It was dreadful; you need friends to get by.'

There was no way Rhan was going to admit to her sister that the "friends" that night was just George. She had been so grateful to see him when he'd walked through the door, sooner than expected – breathless, but clearly still sober.

He had looked after her for hours on end, right through the night, sleeping occasionally on the floor beside the bed, but had jumped attentively to her side whenever she needed him. He had fetched bedding so he could take hers to the washing machines, cleaned her up, massaged her back, and had discussed whether and when to call an ambulance. She had felt so relieved having him look after her.

She looked at Aisha before changing tack. 'My point is that you and I, we are free to make new friends.'

Aisha watched her sister intently, wondering what she would say next.

'Most of our old friends are stuck in pitiful conditions as refugees, probably in Lebanon unless they have reached Germany. Some might never have left the warzone, dead or alive. We are so lucky, but we must make sure that we make the best of the chances mother and father gave us.'

Rhan felt guilty for not trying to tell her sister explicitly that global heating would ruin their plans anyway. Instead, she said she was ready for bed.

Aisha waited a few seconds, surprised at the end to the conversation, but knew her sister well enough to realise that Rhan was unlikely to divulge any more of this strange university world that she now inhabited. The moment was gone and they retreated to their separate rooms.

Rhan stood at the attic window, peering into the dark. She knew that tomorrow, if the tide was right, she might be able to glimpse the sea between neighbouring rooftops.

~

Rhan's promise to her coach, Roger, to keep fit seemed to Rhan something worth fighting for, but she avoided any dispute at home by furtively setting off for runs in the early afternoon, when her aunt was not usually at home and the others were at school. To avoid drawing attention to herself, she again resorted to slipping off her headscarf once clear of the streets where she could be recognised.

On her second day, she was following the south bank of a choppy River Wear upstream from the city when she spotted the boathouse of Sunderland Rowing Club. Drawn to inspect the facilities that she had never noticed before, she jogged slowly down to the launching steps where there was a group of four men. Two were crouched by a boat in the water that tried to lurch against the steps with every wave. The other two were looking down from the top step. One of these, whose hair was less grey than the others', was tucking his mobile phone into his jacket while he reported his news.

'Bob's not fuckin' cumin'. He's at the 'ospital. He's broke his foot or summat, the soft bastard. He could've bloody well let us know earlier.' He noticed Rhan, who had walked quietly past him as he swore. 'Oh, sorry pet!'

'How we gonna git the tub out of the watter with just you three?' complained a slight man in a cagoule, who was obviously the cox. 'That's what worries me, na? It was bad enough throwing it in!'

'Can I lend a hand to lift the four out?' Rhan suggested, in an accent that was clearly not *Made in Sunderland*. Her offer elicited a range of conflicting responses.

'No, you're OK, luv.'

'Oh, that would be grand, ta pet.'

'Yu don't want to row with us do yu, luv? Can yu manage bow side?'

'How do yu know she rows?'

They set off onto the river in a most exhilarating outing. The weather conditions were ludicrous. However, the men were clearly experienced and all appeared to know what they were doing, although the timing went slightly out when they hit a patch of alarming waves. Rhan had introduced herself and found out that the rower in front of her was called John.

It was Rhan's first time in a four, and it was thrilling to feel the shorter boat responding more directly to her movements. It was also the first time she had been out in rough water, even if it was several kilometres from the sea.

They first went upstream, where they chased the waves that had built up on a long, straight stretch of river. The waves appeared to be slow and lounged lazily against the shell, adding a whole vertical dimension to rowing that was new to Rhan. She was amazed by the majesty of the A19 road bridge, whose slender, concrete columns sprang up from the river to the steel-and-concrete decks far above their heads. The towering banks and the winding of the river gradually stilled the waves and they were rowing through calmer water.

The conversation in the boat turned rather awkward as the crew debated her rowing skills. Comments along the lines of 'near enough', 'alreet', 'sound' or 'canny' apparently resulted in an early turn and a trip back down-river. She wondered vaguely whether that meant her rowing had passed their requirements or not.

As they rowed past the rowing club again, the waves were fast-moving and with a high frequency that slapped against the prow just behind Rhan. It gave her a real feeling of speed. She noticed that the three rowers before her glanced over their shoulder before planting their blades into the choppy surface. Smiling at the lack of complaint from Nick or Roger, Rhan followed the example of the older rowers.

The next item of interest was soon providing a new distraction as they rowed through a forest of cranes and barges constructing a new bridge. Seeing Rhan's interest in the site, the cox kindly held their strokes. The rower before her, John, half-turned and pointed out the new steel mast for the cable-stay bridge, which had been towed across the North Sea on its barge and was being prepared for winching into its vertical position on the concrete pier. Someone laughed about the previous design that had cost millions and had tried to copy a sketch by an artist.

'I am doing engineering at college,' Rhan told the men. 'I read that the design was unbuildable, yet still won sustainability awards!'

John laughed. 'That figures about the design.'

For the first time, Rhan felt slightly proud of her chosen profession.

The boat trip then became an extraordinary mixture of bizarre rowing and sightseeing as the river took them beneath bridges and alongside giant industries that were no more, yet which were re-summoned from the past by the various members of the crew for Rhan's benefit.

Once they had left the frenzied bridge construction behind, Rhan learnt that the clean steel industrial units on the north bank had been a black swath of coal from shafts and heaps along its bank. On a bend in the river, she was told to imagine massive concrete slipways and huge steel dock gates where ships had been built and launched or floated out onto the river. She felt foolish trying to reconstruct the massive facilities in her mind, as instructed, while looking at the car parks and modern building on the slope where absolutely nothing remained from the recent past.

'I did me apprenticeship there! It was a busy place,' John informed her, much to Rhan's surprise.

Passing the towering piers of the Queen Alexandra Bridge, which once carried a double-decker railway deck immediately above a road bridge, required much less imagination. The perspective was so very different from what she usually viewed from the back seat of her uncle's car, but the towering stone viaducts adjacent to the bridge clearly indicated how the steam trains had managed to climb so high.

'It's some sight, na?' called the cox.

'Aye, but it must've been bleedin' gobsmacking when it were first opened,' the stroke added.

'It's amazing!' Rhan called out into the wind to show appreciation, knowing her words would carry back down the boat – even to the cox in the stern.

'There's a few tens of thousands of rivets in that structure, but it'll outlive even you pet, never mind us oldies.' The guide before her continued with the tour. 'We're back into shipyards again here on this turn in the river. There's nowt there but grass now. Yu'll recognise the stadium where they try to play football.' His words set off several more comments one way or the other from different members of the crew.

On the south bank, Rhan's guide managed to point out hills of ballast, brought up from East Anglia in the sailing collier boats, and dumped before they filled with coal. John also invited her to look for railway tunnels in the rock that lowered coal wagons from the top of the bank, down to the flat riverside below at the base of vertical cliffs that towered over their flimsy rowing boat.

'That's where ah worked as a lad!' the cox shouted, not bothering with the microphone. He was pointing at some trees on the north bank.

'It's the site of the former Wearmouth Colliery,' John explained over his shoulder. 'It 'ad its shaft right by the river, but the roadways extended miles out to sea.'

Rhan once again felt very small as they rowed under both the Wearmouth road bridge and the adjacent rail bridge, far above their heads, leaping from bank to bank. 'There was a cast iron arch 'ere for the road – it was designed by Robert Stephenson if you know him,' the shipyard worker continued to inform her between strokes. 'It was too small, so they built this around the original. You'll see it's got three pins, so it could move with the colliery undermining one side.'

Rhan looked up and started using her new skills at analysis on the massive arching bridge, working out the advantage of the pins. However, the river dictated otherwise. The choppy waves they had rowed through near the rowing club had been just local waves. As they cleared the last bridges, their boat gradually felt the larger waves that had sneaked in past the two protective breakwaters on each side of the river. Rhan leaned out slightly to look back down the boat at the three rowers and the cox. Surely they were going to turn around soon, thought Rhan.

'There were yet more shipyards along both banks,' John continued to explain, apparently oblivious to the swell. 'All that remains is a steel tree and other sculptures. They're by a local artist, Colin Wilbourn and his mates…Look, it's like one of the massive hammerhead cranes that were here all along this quay.'

The closer they rowed to the river-mouth, the more Rhan, in the bow of the boat, felt the wind on her back stiffen. There were ever-increasing waves surging up the river from the open sea.

Beside the boat, the waves steepened, which made rowing difficult, as the surface of the water varied from a trough to a peak, while the bow rose or sank and rocked from side to side, regardless of the crew's attempts to stabilise the craft. It was all so different to the flat surfaces of the Oxford Thames. She would start to pull on her oar, only to find that the water had gone and she was just pulling air, or she would be returning up the slide with the oar in the air when the blade was suddenly grabbed by a passing wave. Rhan lost interest in the guided tour, but fortunately her guide was also thinking more about boatmanship and the conditions.

'It's got up a bit, with the tide,' John calmly informed her. 'Don't yu worry about details pet, or yu' timing, just watch yu' blade. That way, you won't have us all tit over ass. An' just keep an eye on me back, so yu don't ram that oar into me just as I'm shifting backward, alreet?'

It started to dawn on Rhan that almost everything she had learnt on the quiet River Thames needed to be dropped in such conditions of extreme rowing. Errors could be a matter of life or death rather than lost efficiency. Precise following of the stroke was much less important than catching or avoiding the water that rose and fell beside her. It was so very different. She should be terrified, but no else was. It therefore had to be fun.

Rhan felt rather uneasy, however, as the height of the swell increased still further as they rowed along battered stone walls on either side of the river. There were large panels of the massive stones missing from the walls, and these had apparently been hastily replaced with poorly formed concrete. Beyond these inner walls was a large basin of turmoil within the vast encircling piers. These stretched right out to sea on either side and allowed Rhan her first exposure to open water, while still within the basin protected by the sea piers.

It was clear that Roker Pier, on the north side, was taking the brunt of the storm. Concentrating on each swell passing the boat, she hardly dared look up when plumes of spray shot skyward as waves crashed against the outer face of the pier midway along its length, cutting off the lighthouse at its tip from the land. Rhan's uncle had often assured his family on their walks along the pier that a secret tunnel ran from the lighthouse back to the land, but none of the family believed him.

The occasional waves, which managed to throw themselves over the high wall, sometimes with a frightening boom, created a mist of spray which smelt of the sea. This was only a distraction compared with the succession of peaks and troughs that diffused through the gap in the outer piers and sneaked around the corner along the sheltered side of the wall to fill the basin, giving the dainty rowing craft no calm water – only a series of peaks and troughs.

At last, almost out at sea, with waves easily capable of swamping their boat, they slowed as the cox prepared for the turn. They were close to the elegant lighthouse at the end of the pier, majestically defying the brunt of the North Sea. Rhan calculated that each stone in the pier must weigh a tonne, with the top ones weighing twice as much.

'It must have been built by giants,' Rhan suggested to John. 'No one could build that nowadays.'

He nodded but did not respond. His silence and the lack of enthusiastic commentary disconcerted Rhan. She glanced around for ladders or stairs up the pier, with an uneasy feeling that they might need to swim for it. Up until then, her battle had been either to have the oar in the water or lifted well clear of it. Now the crew were instructing her to keep her oar on the water, as they rowed slowly, clearly tense while they waited for the cox to yell out the turn order. A last wave passed down the length of the boat beneath them.

'Let's go for it! Pull bow side. Back stroke side!'

They swung around, quicker than in an eight, but for a few heartbeats they were positioned precariously at right angles to the approaching waves. Rhan noticed that they all swept their blades back on the surface of the water like novice rowers to ensure that the shell remained upright and she followed their lead. As the boat rotated, she glanced seaward, and was horrified to see the next wave steaming towards them. They had to achieve most of the turn before that wave hit them. This was not a good place to be swamped.

'Pull 'ard lass! Git the bow round!' yelled the cox in an even higher-pitched voice than usual, but Rhan had already seen the need. She was almost lifting herself off the slide seat as she pushed her legs straight, forcing her oar to lever the bow of the boat round before that next wave.

'Don't mess up,' she muttered to herself through clenched teeth as she concentrated on not losing her seat, not letting her blade get caught in the rising swell of the next wave, and not rushing back up her slide for the next stroke once she had completed her stroke. 'Now all row!' yelled the cox. 'Follow bow side! Pull 'ard!'

Rhan waited a few seconds, despite the rush, for John in front to give her room to move up her slide. They all took a hard stroke and were moving again. Rhan felt the bow dip alarmingly behind her and saw the next wave lifting the far end of the boat in the stern beyond the cox. Could a boat like this nose-dive? She looked behind and saw with relief that the covered bow part of the boat was emerging from beneath the surface as it surged forward, even as they came up their slides, blades still flat on the water for balance. With their next stroke they shot forward, the bow lifted even higher and they were surfing.

Hardly believing what they were doing, they were soon racing the waves back towards safety. Now they were selectively dropping their blades to hit the dipping and rising water, which now had a frequency so very different from the outward trip. It was tremendous! They shot through the narrow river opening, surfing on wave after wave at a speed that gave Rhan little opportunity to re-examine the sites on their way back. It dawned on Rhan, as they pulled gingerly into the boathouse, that these veterans were seeking thrills that differed somewhat from those expected at larger rowing clubs.

~

'She was alreet, na? Bye, when we were wallowing out there in the North Sea, I were reet glad to see that she can pull better than Bob.'

'Ay, yu near enough, pet.'

'Can you make Thursdie, lass? Same time?'

'Yes, brilliant,' Rhan said, smiling. 'But will I need to join your club or something?'

'Well, I'm Ray, the president,' the man who had been stroke declared. 'And yu can pay the treasurer when he asks. I'll take him round a bottle toneet, but it sounds like yu might not see Bob on the river for a bit, so yu can keep yu money for a while!'

~

With such diversions, the Christmas holiday was more fun than expected. Rhan's previous anxieties about being a burden to her aunt and uncle also abated. She saw that her aunt had missed her and valued her help with the children. Even the boys found a use for their cousin as a companion-cum-protector. With rowing camp eating into the holiday a week at both ends, the vacation was also much shorter than expected.

The trips out on the Wear became regular, and although the swell varied between nothing and too extreme for even the intrepid veterans to venture out, she learned much. She was somewhat concerned that she was picking up bad habits, but was pleased to have won the respect of the senior oarsmen at the Wear club.

There was a steady stream of relatively formal emails from "Georgie", which relayed technical input on the practicals and preparations for their first tutorials. Despite his exciting festive parties, regular family get-togethers and meetings in the pub with old friends, she read between the lines that he was missing her, at least as much as she missed him. He seemed desperate to show her everything and introduce her to everyone at his home.

Conversely, her emails to him nearly always included a climate change question to clarify something she had read, such as, *'What is so special about 2°C of warming?'*

His written answers might not be immediate, but they were much more diligent than any verbal response she would have prised from him during term-time, when he had her there in person. So, two days later she might get a response like, *'Experts such as James Hansen point out that 2°C is a symptom and not the problem, as it is the concentrations of CO_2 in the atmosphere that everyone should be looking at, not the temperature. Nothing is significant about 2° except it is a relatively arbitrary target for a Danger Level. Some countries point out that it will be a genocide temperature, although others suggest 1.5°C should be enough for mass deaths. Strife will really start to kick in long before 2°C. Pa says engineers think that 10 percent of* *the World Population will have to move at that temperature, so God help the Greeks, the Spanish, the Italians – oh and of course the poor old Syrians. We have been close to 1.2°C already by NOOA and NASA, so we may reach the danger level in around 2025!'*

~

Christmas on 25th December meant little to an Eastern Orthodox Christian living in a Muslim household, especially as Aisha was turning sharply away from such Christian feasts. There were, however, no rowing outings on the River Wear over the holiday, so Rhan was forced to go running, both to keep fit and to maintain her regular exercise slot, now acknowledged by the rest of the family.

Shattering the family's hope that she would also convert, she started attending the church at the end of her street, which happened to be Methodist. She found that, unlike her trips to the Catholic chaplaincy with George, Chris and others, the Methodists actually prayed for action against climate change.

At the end of the service, she found herself talking to the minister, Mike, who had been on several climate rallies and protests. As others from the congregation joined them, Rhan found herself surrounded by well-wishers, especially when they discovered not only her concerns over the environment, but that she was more or less a Syrian refugee and her parents were war casualties. All this kindness caused tears to flow down Rhan's cheeks. Embarrassed, she put down her coffee cup and rushed out of the room, head bowed, so that she could sob alone in the empty pews. The hugs she received on her return just made matters worse.

It took some time before she managed to get angry enough with herself to stand aloof from the overwhelming empathy and explain that she had no reason to be pitied. She had the perfect life that no other refugee orphan could even begin to dream about.

~

Rhan gave herself the Christmas present she most wanted, succumbing to the invitation to visit George's home the following Easter. The rational explanation was that she wanted to talk to his father about global warming. The response to her news was as enthusiastic as she could have wanted.

'Brilliant, I am dying to show you the moors and our latest archaeological findings, and to introduce you to my sister Grace, and my Mum. Dad will love having someone to talk to/at!!'

~

There were more storms after Christmas and the veteran crew on the Wear started to tease Rhan about her continuing enthusiasm, no matter what the conditions.

'Why, that college girl's more of a storm junkie than the rest of yu combined!' complained the cox.

Just as the Orthodox Christmas began to loom in early January, Rhan was saying her farewells to a surprisingly wide selection of family and friends. This 'storm junkie' was heading south to quieter waters, or so she thought.

CHAPTER FIFTEEN

Riders of the Storm

'Well Roger,' Bar reported with a hint of mischief, after their first trip out at rowing camp seven days before the beginning of term. 'I trained as instructed, but also sort of joined the Sunderland Rowing club and was out almost three times a week in a four. The crew were all veterans with interesting personalities. I may have picked up some bad habits, but it was good fun and I learnt so much.'

Roger seemed pleased, if a little surprised. 'Well done. Claire got some useful practice too. Where were you rowing?'

'I was rowing Number 1, bow. We were on the Wear,' she laughed, answering both options. 'We were rowing in the tidal reaches of the river most of the time but kept going out to the ends of the piers that separated the river and the sea. We went out in all weathers, so I picked up a whole load of weird techniques to cope with the conditions most of the rowers here would not believe.'

'Why? What do you mean?' Novel rowing techniques was Roger's favourite subject.

'Well we had a really stormy Christmas. I was with a crew that went out just to check that it was too rough for the rest of the club!' Rhan explained, smiling at the absurdity of what she was saying. 'Or that was their excuse. I was taught to flout all your advice, but it meant that we never once swamped the shell. I learnt to cope when rowing into choppy waves or dramatic swells and even breaking waves at one point, although that surprised everyone. There are different techniques for waves when they come astern, or amidships. I'm afraid that our trips out on this millpond of a river will be rather tame!'

'Well, I was going to ask you to row stroke tomorrow in one of the boats if you don't mind? That should liven things up for you!'

'Umm...OK.' Rhan's heart beat faster. 'But I would prefer not,' she added quickly. Her days of laid-back enjoyment, following someone else's lead, might be over. Claire had been cross to discover that she and Rhan were known as the "virgins in the bow", presumably due to their lack of experience, so giving one of them a prime position was going to stir things up.

'Well, we've also had a week or so of rain down here so water levels are rising,' Roger continued, ignoring Rhan's last comment. 'The forecast is looking bad, so you may have some of that northeast weather on our "millpond".'

~

There were gasps and barely concealed comments when the crew lists went up that evening and these continued as they took their new positions in the boat the next morning. Claire had also been moved from the lightweight position at Number 1 into the Number 3 position. Rhan decided that making everyone pull a bit harder, longer and faster would be a good way to shut their mouths and keep warm in the blustery wet conditions.

The camp was at full capacity, although most senior rowers were cycling daily back and forth to Oxford. Claire found the whole set-up fascinating and excitedly fed her findings back to Rhan.

'Have you noticed that everyone is now wary of you, Bar? If you're to be a stroke after your good show today, then everyone suddenly wants to be your friend, which means going through me. Isn't that great?' Claire was delighted at the sudden reversals in their squad. Rhan smiled and raised her eyebrows, both in pleasure and exasperation at Claire, who was not at all daunted.

'That girl, Di, in our boat was making snide remarks earlier at breakfast.' Claire was clearly dying to tell her story. 'She says that the First Eight men are flirting with you and me. Isn't that great too! I thought they messed around with everyone, but in my mind I'm framing that accusation as a press cutting – some of them are really fit and so cool. But I can see why they like us, rather than the women's main squad; they're really frightening!'

Rhan listened with interest and amusement at her friend's foolish chatter.

'Oh and Bar, remember that redheaded girl who asked us to help lift the boat this morning – she's the female president! She was so polite to us, but she's not that popular with the top rowers. I'll have to find out why.'

Rhan was surprised to hear that she knew both the male and female presidents, but had no opportunity to suggest a comment. Claire just continued, waving a finger to emphasise her points.

'Di was bitching about the First Eight ladies too. She says lots of the best rowers are already internationals and are semi-professional. They are just here to pick up a Blue in the London boat race and won't row with their colleges in the Summer Eights, and might not even finish their diploma or whatever soft subject they are allegedly studying. Cool info eh?'

'Well for once Di was not slagging people off for nothing,' Rhan finally got in. 'Last night, when you were away, the senior women, usually with foreign accents – I am not good at identifying which – made it very clear that they wanted us "little girls" to leave any room they enter. They expected us to disappear to our dormitories so they can have the stove or the TV to themselves. We are to be neither heard nor seen!'

'I'm not that surprised. Some of our squad are annoyingly loud!' When Rhan gave her a questioning look to suggest she might be a hypocrite, Claire added, 'What are you trying to say?' They both laughed.

~

At their return for lunch on the second day, the junior squad was addressed in the boathouse by Esther, the women's president.

'It is marvellous to see such a powerful junior women's squad being developed and trained. 'I would like to thank Roger for the huge amount of effort he has expended on this new, and very necessary, initiative. Thank you all for coming back early to start training. I saw both boats on the river this morning and was very impressed. I look forward to meeting you individually when I can. I understand some of you are experienced junior champions and most have rowed for your clubs, while others have only been rowing for a few weeks.' Rhan carried on looking at the plaited rope ends on the wall behind Esther, not wanting to catch anyone's eye.

'I would hope that in eight months' time, the existence of this junior squad will significantly help my successor and provide more options with the selection of the main university squad to replace those of us who will be moving on. Good luck and thank you! Oh, I need to apologise for stealing Roger away from you tomorrow – we need him in London for some important trials.'

~

'I'm not surprised that she doesn't get on with some of the top rowers.' Claire leaned closer to Rhan as they joined the lunch queue.

'Why? You said she seemed really nice, and I agree,' Rhan said, assuming correctly that they were talking about Esther.

'She is really nice. Far too nice. What's more, she was pleased to hear that you are a climate change freak.'

'What! You told her I was some type of freak! But I have hardly even opened my mouth on that subject to any of you Gloucester clowns,' Rhan burst out, not knowing whether or not she should be cross with Claire. Rhan looked around to see if anyone in front or behind was listening.

'Just what I mean – only a real fanatic would mention the subject,' said Claire. 'Remember, I do Geography and have learnt that even those doing Environmental Science aren't allowed to mention global warming outside tutorials.'

'So when did you talk to Esther and what did she say? Tell me!'

'I tried to tell you earlier but you told me to concentrate on rowing, remember? I spoke with her at breakfast after you went early to get ready. She knew of you and me. She had heard about you from both Roger and Dumas and was looking forward to meeting you. She knew that you were trying out stroke.'

'Strange!' Rhan mused, shaking her head thoughtfully. Then, changing the subject, she added, 'So Roger is away tomorrow, which partially explains the lack of crew lists.'

'Yes, I've heard that he has to help the chief coach and the other trainers for the tideway practice with the first and second boats. I don't think they're bothered about us and don't want us out on the river unless the weather improves. We may be stuck on the boring exercise machines all day. Oh God!'

'I thought Roger was our exclusive coach. And what is the tideway?' Rhan asked, also a little aggrieved. They had to stop their conversation while they were being served.

'I think it's the tidal stretches of the Thames in west London.' Claire continued the conversation as they were sitting on the floor against a wall to eat their food, leaving the remaining places at tables for their betters. 'Yeah, it's a pain losing Roger and everyone's grumbling. Esther may be nice, but I keep hearing that a big group in the first boat and a couple of coaches want her out. She and a few others who gained their Blue last year are struggling to keep their position. I've heard there was a mutiny under similar conditions in the men's Blue boat a decade or so ago.' Rhan looked open-mouthed at Claire and then at the three tables of senior women rowers.

'Esther and Peter, her chief coach, are under great pressure to sort it out, but it sometimes happens that the president doesn't make the top eight. This week's crucial so I feel sorry for her. I hope Roger can help.'

With this new insight, Rhan began to appreciate the tensions in the cafeteria around her. The promotion of a novice to stroke in her own junior boat suddenly seemed very petty.

~

With such matters at stake, it came as a surprise later that afternoon to find both Peter and Roger cycling through the rain on the towpath alongside their junior boat. They were on an open stretch of water and the tailwind had raised boisterous waves that occasionally splashed the boat and made balance and rowing difficult. Their cox was nervous and called for a slower pace as she headed for the sheltered bank. Rhan was not surprised at this cautious approach, but felt slightly disappointed not to be reliving her exhilarating days on the Wear.

'Take it up Bar! Let's see what you can do in this!' The authoritative command from Peter reached them clearly through the rain and wind across the water. Rhan had never heard him speak before, so was amazed that he knew her name and was shouting at her personally, rather than the cox or the boat as a whole. The cox looked at her, also surprised and rather intimidated by Peter's attention.

'Tell them to watch their blades going into the water and to shorten their stroke, and keep the blades clear of the water on the return up the slide!' Rhan ordered the cox. The cox looked at Rhan, Peter and the waves, but clearly decided that Peter was the more frightening and complied with Rhan's instruction. She left the calm and headed off through the choppier waves.

'Tell them not to watch me, but to watch their blade at the plunge!' Rhan yelled again. 'Tell them they will enjoy this. Timing is not that important.'

Once the instructions were relayed down the speaker system, Rhan shouted out, 'Come on let's go for it!' She knew her voice would travel down the wind to the crew, who were clearly as apprehensive as the cox about attacking the waves. 'Don't worry about the timing – watch your blade!' Rhan hoped Peter could hear why the rowing would appear scraggy. She knew too little of Peter to be shy, but anticipated what Roger wanted to see.

They were off, flying through spray that leapt from the tops of waves and from splashes that their oars made with the surface of the river. They were all cold and wet already, but at least they were exercising hard again.

'Yahoo!' Rhan heard Claire's voice through the wind in a hark back to the Gloucester days. No one joined in, but no one told her to shut up either, and it certainly boosted the morale of the nervous crew. Rhan noticed that the whirlpools from Claire's position remained to be seen in the muddy, turbulent river longer than most, indicating that she was certainly putting her effort where her mouth was.

As soon as they reached the calm in the lee of the next bend, Peter was shouting at the cox to turn around and run the rough in the other direction. During the third stint, Peter goaded them for a final effort and then disappeared. The crew heard the gentler voice of Roger cut through the wind.

'Brilliant! Well done! It lacked elegance, but Peter and I were delighted. You're cold and wet, so make your way back. Effective rowing Number 3. Well done.'

The crew was buzzing with their achievement. However, no one was more delighted than Rhan, who was just bursting with pride that her friend, Claire had been singled out. She had to admire the way Roger knew how to give an effective compliment.

~

Things at the training centre had completely changed by the time they climbed out of the rain-splashed, rocking pontoon. The boatman, swathed in a full-length oiled Barbour waterproof, yelled at them. 'Come on you lot, everyone else was ordered in an hour or so ago, and you have to help me get that shell dismantled and onto the trailer straight away, ready for the Tideway in London tomorrow.'

Almost an hour later, the soaked and shivering Rhan was dripping her way along the corridor. As Number 8, her rigger had been the last to be undone so the shell could be fed into the trailer alongside the first and second boats. She only had one thought on her mind: a hot shower. Dumas appeared to be hovering by the entrance to the common room before rushing over to her.

'Well done, Bar!'

'Oh, thanks,' she responded automatically and uncertainly as he hurried away. She was slightly annoyed to find her path totally blocked by girls and boys peering at the noticeboard. They weren't just looking and walking away, but hung around chatting and looking again.

'Yes! She's gone!' someone rejoiced in a foreign accent.

'That's almost the crew we wanted!' said another voice, followed by a high-five clap of hands by two very tall girls. Rhan's heart sank as she noticed that celebrations were held in a tight fraternity around the stove with two of the coaches that Rhan had hardly seen. Most, however, saw little to celebrate, and this appeared to include all the boys, who looked on as sullen spectators.

'Cool rowing, Bar!' said one of the now showered and dressed junior crew who had hardly spoken to her before.

'Our rowing has improved so much since you took over as stroke,' said another.

Dumbfounded by this incongruous and creepy behaviour, Rhan looked up to see Claire approaching, obviously excited, but no longer just by her previous commendation from Roger.

'My God, Bar! Where've you been? You're not going to believe this, but have you heard what's on those lists? You and me, we've made the big time! We are only in the President's Eight! I think it means that we are, like, the third boat, and you are stroke. I'm Number 7. It is just unbelievable!'

Rhan shook her head in confusion over the incredible news.

'Bar and Claire, if you would care to step into the presidents' office,' Roger asked in a none-too-gentle manner, leading them away from the throng to a room next to Dumas'. In the cramped office, Rhan stood dripping on the carpet in front of the president's desk, conscious of her wet clothes against Claire's dry ones. Once the door was securely shut, Esther spoke, sitting upright behind the desk. 'Oh, you poor thing! So sorry to keep you from your shower, Bar. The thing is that Roger says you can make sure we win tomorrow. Will you do it? Beat them I mean?'

Roger intervened. 'Sorry Esther but I don't think Bar has seen your crew sheets yet, so she will be struggling to understand. If I may explain? The weather forecast for tomorrow is not good.' He was leaning on an old-fashioned filing cabinet as he spoke, casting a glance through the window at the darkening sky outside. 'But Esther and Peter have constantly stated that this should not affect the trials on the tideway, unless it would be classified as too bad to be rowed on the big day. Cat and several of the big-name rowers are making life very uncomfortable for Esther, so I have suggested that Esther lets them have their way tomorrow. We have given them the rope to hang themselves. They have most of the crew they want as Boat A. They will be in the light boat with the lightweight oars, which I think will give them no advantage at all.' He smiled mischievously. 'Their trainer thinks the conditions will force the trail to be postponed, and Peter is not denying it. He cannot of course predict the conditions, but we know that on the race day with Cambridge, the worse the conditions, the more the TV crews and sponsors will want to see another public sinking. We will therefore have trials tomorrow, if at all possible.'

Roger looked at the still-puzzled Bar and Claire, and continued. 'The Second Eight, who have trained together nicely for the past six weeks, will stay together as Boat B. We have then put together an eclectic crew for the President's Eight. We have four from the bow half, including Esther, who have been training together in the senior squad and are the president's preference for the first boat. They are of course the lighter rowers, which may give the President's Boat a small advantage.

'For the stroke, I knew of Bar's special knowledge and we – Peter and I – saw what you could do in rough water this afternoon.' He addressed Rhan directly. 'You led an inexperienced crew through the roughest water. Claire caught Peter's eye in those conditions, and we figured that courage and confidence in the stroke from time together in your College Eight were possibly more important than fitness, finesse and experience.'

'That's right!' put in Rhan, hoping that she was praising her friend.

'Not to mention beginner's luck!' Claire added. Roger paused and smiled while shaking his head, then continued.

'Well, you've seen that you are Number 7, Claire. You two will be lightweight for a stern pair, but I think it may help in such weather.'

Esther then took up the narrative. 'For 5 and 6, Peter and I know of two strong rowers, both ex-Blues, who want to help. One, Martha, is a fourth-year Chemistry student who

I rowed with last year, and Rebecca is a PhD graduate from two years ago. The cox – well, back to you Roger.'

'The cox is a PhD medic from my college, Chandra Morton,' Roger explained. 'I have just persuaded him to jump on a train from Edinburgh. His interests are sailing and kayaking, so he'll love the conditions tomorrow. He coxed for the college last year and pulled off some clever tricks. I asked him to study the Boat Race rules on the way down. He is another wild card, but…'

Roger raised his hands in a gesture of hope and deliverance.

'You will appreciate that this scratch president's boat has been specifically designed to ride the waves tomorrow.' He repeated his sales pitch to the two girls. 'You will have a distinct advantage, in my opinion, as a relatively lightweight crew in a heavier and stiffer boat with traditional timber oars. Add Chandra and your new skills, Bar, and we have a good chance of pulling something off. It will be an exciting day.'

'Let's hope it goes well,' Esther added nervously. 'We've already explained this to the bow four. I have persuaded three team-mates to join a losing team if we fail! Peter is trying to be seen as standing off from this dispute and has asked Roger to work with me tomorrow. Two trainers have effectively joined the opposition, which…'

'Sorry, would you mind if I went for a shower?' Rhan interrupted, overwhelmed by what was being asked. Esther and Roger nodded, obviously surprised at her reaction.

Rhan reached the door hastily but, wanting to appear keen, turned to ask, 'When can we see the course, and how much practice can we get before the race?'

'High tide is due at two twenty-eight tomorrow afternoon, so I think the start will be around ten past two,' Esther replied. 'I'll show you the course with video footage and Roger will see you later. He has kindly offered to fetch Rebecca and Martha and will then pick up Chandra late tonight.'

~

Back in the common room and corridor, voices were being raised and at least one was American. 'No! You know we wanted Frances and Gabriel in our boat, yet they're in the loser's boat. What's going on? Have they agreed to throw their Blues away?' Peter, a pint of beer in hand, was talking to a group of women rowers, some of whom Rhan recognised as Esther's protagonists in the A Boat. The A team's diminutive and pretty cox stood beside their stroke, Lucy, who looked vicious, thought Rhan, as they waited for Peter' reply.

'Well Cat, if the weather's fit, we'll look forward to seeing how your favourites perform tomorrow,' he said, avoiding the question. 'The superior experience of your crew should give you the chance to shine. You have all the best equipment and most of the crew you want, so you should do well.'

Despite the strain and the complexity of the situation, Rhan could not help liking Esther's simplicity and the confidence she bestowed on those around her, once the die was cast. While they ate supper in her office, Esther showed Rhan maps, printed out and Sellotaped to show the course of the race along with digital views. The boatman, whom Rhan had been working with earlier, joined them and told them about the characteristics and conditions on various sections of the river, which he appeared to know well.

Roger turned up, eating a sandwich, after fetching the two extra rowers. Rhan was relieved to see that Martha and Rebecca would help redress the lack of muscle in their boat. They all moved to a changing room to assemble the whole crew. Rhan, the new stroke, was the exhibit of greatest interest, especially for those who had loyally stuck with Esther, apparently on Peter's firm advice.

'Right,' Roger started when Esther gestured to him. 'Tomorrow is going to be different from anything you've previously experienced. The exception is Bar, our stroke, who has experience and who will explain rowing techniques for the various waves we may encounter. The bends in the river mean we can expect waves from any and all directions in different stretches, and the waves will result from both wind action and from the flow over obstacles that will set up standing waves and mini weirs, so pay attention. This will come as a surprise to all of us.' He looked at his watch. 'I need to leave in five minutes, so I'll just slip out. Over to you, Bar.'

They all listened while Rhan tried to portray herself as a confident expert, instead of a floundering novice. She kept feeling for her headscarf, but it was not there.

~

At around ten that night, Roger returned with Chandra, the curly-haired compact cox, and Rhan and Esther went through the options again with him. From the beginning, Rhan noted that Chandra addressed her as an equal, even though she was feeling like a young girl with these senior students. He must have known of her short experience, yet sought her opinion on how the boat might behave under various conditions, admitting that he had never been in an eight or a four in rough water, although he had frequently sailed or windsurfed in much rougher storms. By the time the whole crew, mostly in pyjamas, reconvened in the changing room, Rhan had been made to feel like she knew what she was doing.

'Before you go to bed, can we just discuss a few tactics?' Chandra asked innocently of the assembled crew and their two reserves after fifteen minutes of general discussions and introductions. 'There is a chance that there will be clashes tomorrow, as these tend to be frequent, even when only two boats compete with the whole width of the Thames to go at! These usually result in the blades of the two boats coming into contact. In dinghy racing, this is very much part of the competition, and the boat on the wrong tack or whatever has to complete two 360-degree turns as a penalty for an infringement.

'In eights, it is less obvious who has right of way, but leave that to me. There are no penalty points other than disqualification, so…' He paused before continuing in a firm voice. 'What I want from you guys is to dish out a severe punishment if I call out the signal "watch your blade". If they encroach on us, use your oar in a subtle manner to make them pay for their trespass. Look, I'll sketch it out.'

'Is that OK?' Frances, a tall black American girl from the bow crew asked, looking at Esther and Roger.

'These are racing conditions,' Roger emphasised. 'Remember, no crew gets a prize for being virtuous yet losing the race. Disqualification is very rare, so retaliation is perhaps a reasonable punishment, especially if the other boat is in the wrong.'

'We have to keep in contention, and we have to win if we get the opportunity,' Esther confirmed. 'I think Chandra has a point – if they encroach on us, we should make them pay for it dearly.'

Before they turned in for bed, Chandra gave an interesting lecture to the amused rowers on how to be vindictive.

~

Although last to bed, the president's crew were up before the others, ready for an early-morning dash down to London with the trailers in an extra minibus, long before the coach departed with the other two crews at the scheduled time.

This allowed Esther's team to arrive in west London and get onto the water for a full dress rehearsal, long before the first and second boats were assembled and before their crew turned up. Conditions, with steady rain and blustery wind, combined with the flood of water down the river, made rowing an interesting challenge, and they were all keen to have the safety boat close at hand. They practised rowing in and out of the current and through some of the more turbulent reaches of the river. Chandra and the rest of the crew had no problems adapting. In the calmer stretches of the river, however, Rhan was painfully aware that she and Claire were by far the least polished rowers.

By the time Rhan stepped through the glass doors into the unfamiliar boathouse, she no longer felt that she was contributing to Esther's cause. They were back in the comfort of the clubhouse two hours before the trials were due to start and were met by the stony glare of the A Boat crew. Rhan could not help smiling at hearing Peter talking to his traitorous colleague in a reasonable manner, which Rhan recognised nonetheless as intended to unsettle the A Boat and its trainer.

'So, the President's Boat has been out to try the conditions on the water already. I'm a bit concerned, Patricia. Don't you and Cat think it'd be a good idea to get some practice before the trials? The race is obviously going to take place, despite the appalling conditions, and the difficulties could really separate the sheep from the goats.'

'You're kidding me? We can't have trials in this!' Cat responded, glancing out of the plate-glass windows at the swirling river below them. There was complete agreement by all the rowers, who were sitting around in the dry.

'Let's be very clear about this, all of you.' Esther's authoritative voice shot firmly across the large room, as she advanced casually, combing water out of her thick red hair with her fingers. 'Today we have trials on the tidal Thames, as planned, and possibly in the same conditions as we will meet Cambridge in a few weeks' time. Rough weather is a new norm, so fair-weather rowers are of no use to us. We have three eights here, which means that by the end of today I will probably be saying goodbye to two out of three of you. Not one person has their name on a place yet – not even me. Let me know if any of you want to leave before the trial.'

There were gratifying exclamations of dismay and disbelief at this announcement from the president who, just a few hours ago, had been written off as a lame duck. Rhan noticed that Lucy, the stroke for the A crew, was staring at her – she had clearly realised, possibly for the first time since she joined the university, that she now had a rival in Bar, the unknown novice. Lucy climbed out of her comfy chair, walked to the window and bit her lip.

Both the A and B Boats went out half an hour later, while the president's crew and Roger tried to relax in the warmth. Each time they looked out of the window they watched as the river waves, with the rising tide, swelled further and further up the concrete ramp and steps in front of the boathouse.

Rhan felt that she was in a surreal tunnel. What was she doing here? This was not her place – it had nothing to do with her. George would testify to that. She had barely learned how to pull an oar with two consecutive strokes the same, yet everyone from Peter and Esther to Claire and Chandra expected her to perform a miracle. The outing of half an hour ago had been a success in the rough water, so they didn't really need her experience anymore. Rhan was just a stupid liability, tossed into the wrong league by Roger. The panic was rising; Rhan forced herself to take a different line of thought.

Why was she caring what these pushy girls wanted? Sport was so irrelevant compared with the important matters. If Cat thought she had a better team, then let her have it. Which of Rhan's old school friends from Aleppo would care about a rowing event? They would not be behind a nice double-glazed window, separating them from the rain or the snow. She imagined having to live day after day in a camp, far from education or progress. She could be trekking for thousands of miles with her poor sister, searching for sanctuary. One of the reasons she had taken up rowing was to avoid having to think such thoughts, yet now she was forcing herself to think about them, rather than feel fazed by some petty practice race.

None of this mattered. One of the teams or a mixture of rowers would be selected or dropped – so what? There were a lot more pressing problems in the world. As her thoughts moved from the war in Syria to global warming, she smiled to herself at the irony. It was partly due to climate change that her unconventional rowing skills were needed here and now by Esther and Roger. Maybe, but even if it was irrelevant, even if sport was simply a distraction, it would be nice to help Esther if she could. Esther seemed to be relying on her, on Roger's recommendation, so she needed to live up to expectations. She could do her best and no more.

~

From the start of the race, the three boats set off more or less abreast. Rhan was impressed by the quality of the rowing in the boats on either side of the President's Boat. She found it extremely difficult not to follow the stroke of crew A and Lucy's confident, strong style and very fast rate style, which was so effective at pulling the A Boat into an immediate lead, ahead of both the B Boat and the President's Boat. After the initial effort, the other boats relaxed in anticipation of a long and gruelling race, but as planned, Chandra said nothing and Rhan kept up a sprinting pace that pulled them ahead of the B Boat and apparently regained some of the lost ground on Boat A.

Despite appearances, they were struggling. While Rhan could see half the B crew on the side nearest the bank, she could only see the slight wake of crew A on the other side. Rhan's legs went to jelly, her muscles felt pathetic and her grasp of the oar in her cold hands felt inadequate, even though the rain had stopped. Yet Esther's crew behind Rhan, including Claire, were still pulling strongly. Rhan wagered that they had warmer hands than those in the other two boats, who'd had little time to thaw out after their practice session.

Rhan could now hear the creek of slides in the A Boat ahead of them and could see "puddles" of flat water from the blades of its crew – still ponds amid the choppy mess elsewhere on the surface of the water. It's so different from the normal whirlpools when rowing in a slow-moving river, she thought, as she strained at each stroke.

'Well done, we have our overlap.' Chandra spoke quietly into the microphone so only his crew could hear. 'Just keep that position until the first bend starts in a hundred metres. Rough winds ahead, but I'll give you warning before anything unusual hits us, so carry on as normal.'

Rhan for the first time felt some hope. Roger, with the elusive Peter behind the scenes, may have known what they were doing in their ad-hoc selection. All she needed to do was keep rowing while the cox, right in front of her, executed his plan.

With their slight overlap, Chandra stayed obstinately in the same position on the river, taking a longer route than he needed round the wide bend. The B Boat took the opportunity to cut the corner in the calmer water and reduced wind on the inside of the river loop. The A Boat, however, was pushed outwards towards the centre of the river, which was now choppy.

Rhan was desperate to slacken the pace, but knew that the boats were exceedingly close together and kept up the sprint in accordance with the plan. As they rounded the first corner, the rowers were warned to look over their shoulders to check their blades entering the water and Rhan could now see the A Boat on the outside of the bend. It had slackened its pace as it hit the ruffled water, but Chandra the sailor had no qualms about using the rules and the weather against the opposition.

'Slow down! We don't want to undertake!' Chandra commanded, to Rhan's great relief. 'Blades on the water for the backsweep – wind coming!'

The rough wind hit the A Boat from an angle, lifting their light oars on the windward side, which then became sails that exacerbated the uplift. Rhan could hear the cries of alarm as individual members stopped rowing, while others were still sliding. Rhan tried not to watch and to concentrate on her own stroke, but she could not help registering that the whole crew overcompensated at the same time, so the boat lurched over to windward, just in time for a wave to hit the lowered side and slosh on-board. The water-laden boat rocked again and was swamped by the next wave. There were more cries of alarm as the rowers reached down frantically to loosen their feet, which were fixed to the boat, to allow escape.

'Stay in your places, boat A! Calm down!' bellowed Peter from the safety boat behind. 'The boat is buoyant and will not sink, but the self-bailers will not cope with that. Race stopped! Raise your hands, coxes!' Chandra's hand shot up while he gave the "hold water" command, and backed up to be close to the wallowing boat. Boat B, ahead by two lengths in more sheltered water, started to spin around.

Within seconds, the boatman skilfully brought the motor safety boat, with Roger, Peter and the coach to the A Boat – life jackets already in their hands – alongside the wallowing boat and they were calming the panic among the girls. To get clear of the waves washing over the sides, the girls were crouching unsteadily on the boat, which was semi-submerged.

'This is awesome!' Rhan heard Claire say quietly. She had been uncharacteristically quiet since joining the president's crew.

'President! Row back with the B crew please,' Peter instructed. 'Stick together and take the safest route. The safety boat will be following once we have this crew on board and have the shell under tow.'

Under instructions from Esther, Boat B disembarked first, and her own crew was just clearing the pontoon when the safety boat came alongside, towing the flooded boat.

'You bastards!' Cat screamed at Esther. 'You cheating, dangerous bastards! You deliberately tried to drown us.' There were intrusive camera flashes from a small crowd of onlookers who braved the weather to watch the drama. 'Oh God, the press,' someone said.

'Calm down, Cat!' called one of Esther's bow team in an American accent. 'You just fell at the first hurdle, that's all.'

'Screw you, Frances!' Cat screamed back.

'Right. I want all crews assembled inside in ten minutes for a briefing and ready to set off again in fifteen minutes!' Peter called out.

There was a range of incredulous responses from crew A along the same lines of disbelief: *'You can't be serious?'*

~

'The president and her coaching staff are delighted with this opportunity to test your mettle in difficult conditions.' Peter was speaking to a bedraggled crowd of rowers, some draped in towels and doing their best to get warm and dry. 'I hope that everyone has learnt several lessons already.'

He delivered his team talk to all three crews in just the no-nonsense way that was needed, Rhan thought. She watched the crew A cox, who had been so humiliated by Chandra, looking icily into space as Peter continued.

'I warned you this morning that strategy was crucial to this race. You cannot expect Cambridge to miss an easy advantage if you are stupid enough to make yourselves vulnerable. There is much more to rowing a race on the Thames than logging results on an exercise machine. The team that seizes the initiative can make the opposition pay a terrible price.' Rhan was watching carefully as the A Boat cox nodded slowly to Lucy, her stroke.

'We were aware that there was misplaced arrogance in the squad,' Peter now said in a resigned voice. 'So, the president introduced potential new crew members to add the skills that we need. Don't think that Cambridge won't be doing the same. This exercise has let us see the squad's weaknesses and useful abilities.'

'You're not going to choose your crew based on that farce, are you?' Cat retorted after several seconds of uncomfortable silence, as the implications of Peter's statement sank in. 'No one thinks that the president or any of her bunch of losers can compete with anyone in our boat.'

'We had your measure!' the cox said in support of Cat, while their stroke, Lucy, nodded. 'You couldn't keep up with us.'

'It is on this river we meet Cambridge in a few weeks' time,' Esther intervened, a harshness in her voice. 'Crew A lost the first race and I'm afraid cannot claim otherwise. My boat was second when the race was stopped, giving Boat B the victory. You are the third boat as things stand, but I am giving some of you another chance. I want you back out there to see who has any credibility left. We start launching in five minutes. Due to the previous farce, we have missed the tide and will row downriver this time. Launch sequence: my crew, then Boat B, then Boat A. See you out there.'

'That's not fair!' Cat complained automatically.

'Look, if you want to get out there first, please go,' Esther responded condescendingly. 'If you mean that it's unfair to race again, sorry but the trials are today. Let your coach know if you want to resign from the squad, as we have reserves for everyone.'

Rhan noticed that Lucy was once again glaring at her.

Esther, Rhan and Chandra were huddled around a table in the mezzanine café area, studying the maps, when Cat and another girl approached, followed by Roger, to see what was afoot.

'We want to swap boats. We think our splash boards are inadequate,' Cat demanded of Esther. Behind their back Roger nodded, but then shook his head as he held and pulled an imaginary oar.

'What about the blades, Cat?' Esther asked in a controlled manner.

'No way, most of us have never used timber oars – you can keep those.'

'Fine, there you are: Bar and Chandra, you have your wish to try the latest lightweight carbon boat. We may have to swap rowing positions as a quicker option to swapping around the shoes and the riggers, but we will manage! You may find Lucy's shoes rather sloppy, Rhan. See you at the new boat in two minutes.'

A shadow passed over Cat's face as she took in the extra displacement of the heavier boat and the complexity of changing the shoes and slide adjustments in the rain out on the pontoon. She stormed away. She had clearly not expected to have her bluff called.

'We'll stick to our own boat!' Cat called out from the other side of the building. 'It's not worth swapping everyone around.'

Esther laughed, shaking her head and stating in a low voice, 'Look I don't know how this will end, but thank you, both of you. I owe you big time.'

~

The rain stayed away, and the wind had reduced, but the turbulent surface was now coupled with a torrent of water flowing down the river with the change in tide. They headed upstream with difficulty towards the start, and then had half an hour experimenting with the fastest flows and stationary waves while waiting for the other boats. Although Chandra had frequently kayaked in such conditions, Rhan had never come across stationary waves before – other than the hydraulic jumps she and George created in flow channels at the university lab. It was strange being able to use an oar to lever the boat off a standing mass of upwelling water that seemed to tower over them, but it required Chandra to keep the wave at oar's length. It was wonderful working with the assured Chandra, who used his canoeing skills to steer the long boat to find the gentlest drops or the quietest water. He even used the wind on their faces to reduce their efforts with the oar. He was continually either talking with Rhan, or calmly instructing the crew on what they needed to do, especially in the midst of the biggest waves that loomed behind the rowers' backs.

Boat B arrived and practised in calmer stretches to keep warm, but kept well clear of the biggest waves. Boat A, very late, gingerly joined them at the starting position in the lee of a wall. Without much ado, Peter casually yelled, 'Go!' giving Boat A the advantage of a staggered start.

This time, Boat A made no attempt to forge ahead but used its position to try to push the President's Boat into the rough in retaliation for the previous race.

'Straighten up, Boat A!' Peter called as umpire from the rescue boat behind.

Chandra played with them and refused to move, keeping his boat in the same position on the river.

'Straighten up Boat A! Straighten up!' yelled Peter through a megaphone. The rowing seemed to be of little significance compared with this duel, and Boat B forged ahead yet again.

'1 and 3, watch your blades!' came the ominous and practised command from Chandra, as he pointed at the encroaching blades. Rhan, sitting immediately in front of him, resisted looking round. She saw him surreptitiously nudge the rudder to ensure a firm clash, while the referees in the boat behind were concentrating on the clashing blades. There was the clatter of oars and swearing as their boat rocked alarmingly.

'Do it!' muttered Chandra. This time, Rhan couldn't resist looking over her shoulder in time to see Frances's blade in the bow lift clear and drop onto Lucy's oar, the last oar in Boat A. Rhan and the rest of their crew adjusted the balance to compensate for the slight extra drag as Frances's streamlined blade stayed in the water. Lucy had not been prepared and her blade was wrenched from her hands by the force of the water. Lucy's boat twisted, swayed and dipped as her oar suddenly become an unpredictable anchor. The A crew, with nerves already frayed, wasted no time in starting to pull their feet from their fixed shoes, just in case of a second sinking.

'You bastards! You did that deliberately again!' Lucy's voice shouted angrily. 'You made me catch that crab!'

'Foul!' screamed their cox, raising her hand.

'Come on Boat A; it is you who would be disqualified!' Peter found his voice again once he saw there was not going to be another nerve-wracking swamping. 'It was your boat that was deliberately changing its position, despite numerous warnings. Cox, on the face of it, that was your second demonstration of total incompetence in racing conditions. Now row on and see if any of you can redeem yourselves.'

'Oh shit!' someone from Boat A muttered, realising the implications.

Laughing inwardly, Rhan watched as Boat A drifted on the flow while Lucy clumsily tried to retrieve the handle of her blade, which danced on the end of her metal outrigger. The rest of the crew watched the alarming steel-coloured waves loom closer while they waited for Lucy to reset to rowing mode. The ominous standing waves appeared to hang heavy and solid, hardly moving in the centre section of the river, while indicating huge forces at play just beneath the surface.

'Concentrate! Row on. Time to leave them behind,' Chandra instructed the President's Boat. 'Boat B is ahead by seven lengths or so, after that fracas. Prepare for rough water.' He sat attentive but unruffled, clearly in the habit of humiliating opposition helmsmen. Rhan watched Boat A set off immediately behind them, but did not follow their course as Chandra headed deliberately and without compunction into the rough water nearer the midstream flood. Rhan adopted the exaggerated lazy return sweep and staggered dip that she had learnt on the Wear in Sunderland, and brought her blade back, skimming it on the water. The rest imitated in almost their own timing. Despite the inefficiency of their rowing, they were shooting the rapids with no effort at all. They left Boat A standing and soon shot past Boat B, which was rowing hard in the margins of the river. There were congratulations among the crew, but Rhan noted with concern how Chandra bit his lip and concentrated on the river ahead.

'Keep talking!' Rhan shouted at Chandra, sensing trouble ahead. 'This is not a time for a crab!' They had practised rough rowing that morning, and again briefly just before the race, but they had seen nothing like the flood of water coming down the river now.

He acknowledged the danger. 'Don't you dare relax! Pull hard through the water to get your oar free and to give me steerage! That's it. Number 5, look where your blade's going, not at stroke. Concentrate, all of you. One mistake and we are sunk. Enjoy the experience but keep thinking and pulling. Well done 2...try not to go deep, keep your blades near the surface if you can. Look at the blade... catch, pull out, no hurry on the slides, look...catch...pull. Let's slow the strokes further, look...catch...pull. We are not racing! You're surfing the weir. Big wave on the bow side – pull hard 1 and 3. Ease off 2 and 4. All pull hard! OK, watch that, 5 and 7...we passed it!'

'Yahoo!' came a cry from behind, as Claire started to enjoy herself, which made Rhan and Chandra smile.

'You are riding the Thames tiger, so stay with it,' Chandra instructed sensibly. 'Number 2, look out for that massive wave – it'll pass you all, so make sure you use it rather than the other way round. Your turn 4 and 6! Follow Number 7, not stroke, 'til we're past!'

They were a few minutes into their return journey, hugging the slack water along the shore as they battled back upstream after completing the course, when they passed the dispirited A Boat trailing miserably six lengths behind the determined B Boat for a distant second place.

There were hugs all round on the pontoon; Esther gave Rhan the biggest hug she had received since her parents had died. Hugs with Chandra were more awkward, as the girls stood a head taller than him in their bare feet.

Rhan was one of the first to leave the hot showers this time, and watched the other shivering and miserable crews, who were coming in from derigging their boats. The cox was in floods of tears, but all of the A crew seemed lost in self-doubt as their pedigree careers faced a sharp dip after months of effort. A drenched reporter, wearing a saturated rain mac, had reappeared and was frantically trying to find people who would explain the story.

'Bar! I'm off,' Chandra called from the entrance. 'We did it! Roger is kindly taking Martha, Rebecca and me back to Oxford. Here's my email.' Chandra handed Rhan a slip of paper, which she stashed in her purse. 'Can we meet up for a drink? I'd love to take you sailing in Edinburgh one day. Which college are you at?'

'That sounds great fun,' Rhan responded vaguely. 'I'll get in touch. It was brilliant having you here. You were just what we needed.' As Roger appeared, she added, 'Well done Roger, good management.' The five of them paused for a few seconds, watching Patricia, the A Boat trainer, walking off towards London with her bags. Esther had obviously given the former coach her marching orders, and was now reoccupied in advance of her report to the press on the team's training. Chandra tarried, no longer looking triumphant.

'Third weekend of the summer holidays?' Rhan suggested to him. 'The North Sea might not look so frightening from a flimsy dinghy by then.'

'Great!' Chandra was clearly taken by surprise at Rhan's enthusiastic response.

~

Back at the training camp, which was nestled on the Thames upstream back towards Oxford and further from the tidal reaches, the wind was no longer a threat. Pools of light on the dark river revealed that it was no longer choppy, yet it was very full. Still slightly stunned by the day's events, Rhan looked out over the river and felt a strong sense of the water's foreboding and resentful power.

Back inside the brightly lit timber clubhouse for the university rowing squads, Claire was very happy. 'Wow, I am now the friend of the girl who can walk on water. You are the young Queen Bee, a new first-team stroke. This is amazing!'

'Congratulations again, Bar and Claire,' a deep voice confirmed. Claire glanced round and fell silent upon seeing Dumas, the men's president. 'I think Esther is great, so you two were bloody marvellous to achieve those stunning victories. I hear you totally humiliated the rebel crew. I gather it's not yet all over, but well done anyway. I will thank Chandra next week when I see him.'

'That is very kind, Dumas,' Rhan managed to say. 'You are quite right – it was good to help Esther.'

'OMG!' Claire mouthed as Dumas moved off after looking at Rhan for a couple of seconds longer than necessary.

At that moment, there was a stampede to the noticeboard and Roger came over, preventing them from needing to join in the excitement.

'We've lost Anna, one of the junior squad coxes – she's on trial for the second boat,' Roger informed them. 'But, I'm back with you again tomorrow, Claire. Bar, you're down as one of the two strokes in tomorrow's seat trials. Two boats are timed over a short course; members of the crew are then swapped and timed again. That way Peter can compare pairs of crew members.'

'But crew members surely try harder for their friends?' Rhan struggled with the concept.

'Anyone who doesn't try their best in each leg might then be swapped and their replacement will show them up,' Roger explained. 'So they stand to lose their own place. Thanks to the fun on the river today, there's not a person who feels secure, even the stroke, Lucy – so Peter and Esther are taking the opportunity for tests without delay.

'Have you noticed how quiet it is?' Roger continued. 'From boat A, Cat's gone and so has the cox. Esther told them before they left London that they were out of the squad.'

'Oh my God, yes!' Claire exclaimed looking round with wide eyes at the Cat-free building. 'This is bad. I'm now the noisiest person around!'

'You'll enjoy that, won't you Claire?' Roger grinned. 'Anyway Bar, good luck tomorrow. If you want to grab a Blue in your first year of rowing, you have a wonderful opportunity.'

'Do you think I should?' Rhan asked, looking directly at Roger.

'Well, that is entirely up to you,' Roger laughed, shaking his head. 'With confidence and ambition, you can finish what you started. You may have to log another formal set of results on the machines, but your strength-to-mass ratio is legendary already, especially among the men!'

'Lucy is better than me on the flat,' Rhan stated simply.

'But in bad weather, you've proved that there is no contest. So you could be a logical safe choice. The tideway is often a rough course.'

Rhan nodded slowly. Claire listened, wide-eyed.

~

For the seat trials, the two boats were timed over a short course rowing upriver and exchanging a member of the crew as they drifted back downriver. Swapping crew members was tricky with both boats out on the river. Esther was the third member to clamber into Rhan's boat.

'OK, we now have the president on board, so look lively,' Rhan called back unashamedly over her shoulder once Esther was settled in at Number 3. After an unenthusiastic start to the trials, Rhan was now in the mood to let fly. Although the stroke rate remained unchanged, the stroke length and effort increased and the crew behind kept up. The cox, whom Rhan had trained with in the junior squad, knew where her interests lay and screamed encouragement.

Rhan was one of the last to make the precarious crossing into the other boat, holding the hands of the B crew cox and Number 7 for balance, while trying not to knock Lucy into the water as she clambered in the other direction. After making the perilous exchange, Rhan could muster little passion for the last two sprints. She realised that her lacklustre effort would show Lucy in a good light, but it would also indicate that Esther was always in the fastest boat. Rhan, recalling her reflections from the previous morning, could see no real benefit in fighting to grab a Blue this year. It just didn't seem worth it.

The results from the seat trials, when stuck up on the board, listed those who were still in contention for a First Eight place and included twelve names in order. The top rower was the president, Esther, who was billed as the most effective rower in the whole squad. Bar's name was not included on the list.

'You fixed that for your crush girl, didn't you Bar?' One of Cat's former colleagues, who had swapped with Esther in the seat trials, rounded on Rhan, almost in tears. 'You sacrificed yourself, but murdered me. I was a junior international, but haven't even made the cut for the reserves! How could that be? You weren't trying, were you?' Everyone heard this outburst, including the coaches, along with Dumas and Esther, who had been chatting on the other side of the room. There was a stunned silence, so Rhan had no choice but to reply.

'I just found it easier to row under an inspiring president,' admitted Rhan quietly but distinctly. 'Others feel the same and it would happen in any race, so the result is fair.'

~

Esther now had the authority to choose the rowers she wanted, although Rhan was dropped and returned to stroking Claire's boat. Yet the junior squad and Roger himself were now welcomed in the clubhouse by the remaining first and second senior crews, reserves and coaches. Bizarrely, Rhan noticed that Esther tended to avoid her and only smiled and nodded at her across the room, but made special efforts to make Claire feel appreciated.

On the coach on the way back to Oxford for the beginning of term, Claire made Rhan listen to some strange opinions that were apparently widely held.

'You're the main candidate for next year's university stroke – unless we get an Olympic champion like Cat,' she added sarcastically. Rhan groaned.

'You could also be a potential future president.' Rhan raised her eyes at this suggestion from Claire, who persisted nonetheless. 'I hope you are; it would be great for me to say, *"must go – my friend Bar, the president, is coming for tea".*'

Rhan smiled but made no attempt to quash Claire's rose-tinted view of the pre-term training week.

'And…' Claire added, knowing that Rhan would find this most interesting. 'Roger has been promoted by Esther to Peter's deputy, above and beyond his roles as selector and coach to the junior squad. He's really gone up in the world, but deserves it, doesn't he?'

Rhan, feeling rather muddled by her friend's extravagant speculations, nodded her agreement, not quite believing what they had actually achieved.

CHAPTER SIXTEEN

Tragedy of the Common World

Rhan was surprised and had to revaluate Claire's comments when, over the first weekend before the beginning of the spring term, she started to receive emails and to find written invitations in her college pigeonhole, addressed to "Bar", often without any surname. They wanted her to join groups and societies that befitted a rising university star. Dumas and Esther were obviously passing on her name.

'So it *is* you, Miss Rhan! I had a feeling that only you could be this Bar character,' exclaimed the chief porter, seeing her retrieving and puzzling over her post. 'You know, I had you down as a rower from the moment you walked through that door with that heavy case. We could do with a university rower or two at this college.'

'Well, I'm not quite there yet. Maybe next year,' Rhan confided without denying the porter's judgement. She turned away, walking from the timber-panelled lodge into the arched gate tower, before she stopped and returned to the porter who was still watching her.

'Everyone will know soon enough, but I would rather not join Alice's boat until after Torpids,' she continued. 'You see, I am currently enjoying rowing with a Gloucester Hall novice boat. You may have gathered that I have been at the university training camp too, but I would be very grateful if this could be kept quiet. Would you mind keeping this – well, under that fine bowler hat of yours? Just for a few more weeks?'

The porter's eyes sparkled at the news and the request.

'I'll help you buy a few more weeks of quiet, Miss Rhan. I can see why.' He looked at her intently before continuing. 'But you must row for the college in the summer, we will really need you. I see that you have some letters from some high-flying friends that could also be good for the college – you know it's been years since we had a member of this college in the Pink Club – so may I suggest that you consider that invitation in your hand? Your rugby friends wouldn't be happy if they discovered that you missed the opportunity.'

'Thanks for the advice,' Rhan smiled. It felt good having the all-knowing porter on her side, although she had no idea what the Pink Club was.

~

It was great watching the college reassemble back to life for the start of term. As soon as George had dumped his bag in his room he was laying on Rhan's bed quizzing her about her time in Sunderland.

At rowing camp, conversations had tended to be exclusively about rowing, and Rhan had missed the lively and wide-ranging debates at university. The first evening in Tom's room, she enjoyed hearing Danny complaining about his essay on the effect that US interest-rate rises and nationalist policies would have around the world in the next five years. Tom was discussing his essay on the stability of the euro and the impact of Brexit over the coming decade for the UK, while Philip, another PPE student, outlined his politics essay on post-war Europe and its effects on current policies. Fiona complained that the textbooks were not keeping up with recent events, which made research into the next decade very difficult.

The mention of timescales into the 2020s goaded Rhan, but she bit her lip and wondered how any subject could look forward without taking into account the physical world. She said nothing, but brought it up on Saturday evening when she, George, David and Danny were sitting comfortably in the bar opposite the college, where George said Lewis Carroll had frequently sat.

'I don't understand the timescales of this university,' complained Rhan. 'We pretend to look to the future, but actually look backwards – or perhaps at best the recent past.'

'Well, try looking backwards,' George suggested inanely. 'You're the one in the window seat with the views of Broad Street and some of Oxford's best architecture behind you!' This raised no more than a snigger from David and rolled eyes from Rhan.

'Well, in economics, two decades can be regarded as pretty soon,' Danny explained more usefully. 'If you think in terms of financial instruments, mortgages and the like, they often have a life of twenty-five years. Yet any economic predictions beyond a few years are just guesswork.'

'But surely,' Rhan finished her question, 'it would not be totally beyond our intellect to take account of physical and social aspects that we know will be taking place, due to global warming for example.'

'It's hard to factor in knowledge or parameters of any economic or political scenarios,' Danny argued. 'I have all this econometric data and graphs of how economies have reacted in the past, but things will have different parameters when looking forward, which makes it bleedin' 'ard.'

Rhan wondered if Danny's Cornish accent had lost its edge, or whether she had now learnt to understand most of what he said.

'Well we know how temperatures have risen over the past century or so, and that they are likely to follow carbon dioxide levels on an exponential rise,' David contributed, yet again aligning himself with Rhan, much to her relief. 'You can bet your life that temperatures are going to carry on rising – the only issue is how steep the curve will get. Anyway, the physics is way more predictable than economic trends for inflation, deflation, stagflation, whatever, which depend on human interventions.'

'No one agrees, so it's not predictable, David,' George contested, but David continued ignoring George's point.

'The one thing we can be certain about is that once it's too hot for wheat in Siberia and Canada, it's time to factor in major inflation in food prices around the world. Wars could presumably break out anywhere after that. So, Danny, any meaningful forecasts should include the toxic mix of migration and harvest failures, which might start any decade from now.'

'Or even just a few years from now,' Rhan added

'Danny can't start adding crap no one believes!' George protested. 'You cretins need to understand that no one wants to hear stuff like that.'

'You can't deny that even California, the fruit bowl of the United States, is in trouble!' David almost shouted back. Rhan looked round and was relieved to see that no one seemed bothered by their discussion.

'By 2030, what will they say about this decade and our selfish destruction of the atmosphere?' Rhan asked more quietly. 'I agree, by 2050, wars will be about famine, civil strife, and culling immigrants rather than the power struggles of the imperialist powers or whatever Tom said. There will be no heroes, medals or gratitude...only shame.'

'What would we do without Tom's perspective?' George muttered, smiling.

'Yeah, the "wreckers" was what the young called the older generation in one book.' David was now clearly trying to provoke George. 'Let's face it – we might even be involved in intergeneration wars. Can you imagine anything worse? We are almost certainly going to have wars between "greens" and "rednecks". There are many states and countries that will fight to the last drop of oil to have the right to destroy themselves and the rest of the world, rather than admit that their oil should not be turned into carbon dioxide.'

'Oh come on,' interjected George. 'I can't and don't want to try to imagine one war, never mind what you have in mind. You're in Oxford. How can you foresee anything worse than even more steel and glass architecture or extra admissions from students like me from state schools?'

'Well we don't want more of your sort, George,' laughed David. 'But there are none like you anyway!'

As if summoned, a peal of bells could be heard from outside the pub, particularly by Rhan, who sat on the sill. She glanced out at the darkening spring evening. Cars had departed from their parking bays, enabling a better view of the wide street, lined by a mix of different buildings – some grand, with intricately carved stonework, others with older, cottage-like simplicity. Yet above the buildings, there hovered Oxford's famous towers and spires, some of which were now awakening for the pre-Sunday bell-ringing practice. A range of peals could be heard breaking out throughout the city. Her grasp of the conversation lapsed as nearby bells, possibly from All Souls, ceased for a second or so. There were others to be heard from further off; notes beyond notes, she thought.

'It's great to be back,' Rhan said contentedly. 'I love this time of the week, with the bells.'

The others smiled and for a few minutes calmed the argument that had continued without her involvement, until Rhan stirred the pot again.

'Is it just because I was brought up expecting the worst that I can imagine chaos and conflict here in Oxford without difficulty? Aleppo's beautiful medieval quarter would have made Oxford look brash, but it doesn't take much to turn tranquil courtyards and towers into defendable hellholes. It would only take a few years of drought or floods. War reduces everything and everyone to the basic struggle to survive, and vice versa. Even here your precious port wine would be drunk to anaesthetise the horror, rather than to finish a good dinner.'

Most of the group chose that moment to take a drink. The conversation had suddenly turned rather personal. However, David soon had a new perspective.

'Ah, exactly, the Middle East wars have already involved either containing and besieging towns or driving people away,' said David. 'With such high populations around the world, we could have a situation where people can be driven from A to B. They in turn push people from B to C, but C then drives them on to D.'

Bells from a nearby college – Trinity or Balliol, thought Rhan – inappropriately chose that moment to strike up a joyful and triumphant cascade of bells.

'Which one of those letters is Calais?' George asked, also trying to keep the subject light-hearted. Yet Rhan was being whimsical and David was needling, while Danny listened but could not help making the logical suggestion that made everyone chuckle.

'You sure C wouldn't be for Calais, by any chance?'

'I thought George was going to ask which pint I was drinking,' David said wistfully, looking at his empty glass.

'Well,' Rhan contributed to the main discussion. 'That is what effectively happened to my family and friends in Syria. My parents and grandparents had already fled from two wars before I was born. My sister and I were pushed out by a relatively internal conflict…could A stand for Aleppo?'

'Ah yes.' David grasped the development of his theme. 'Rhan's former friends have been forced from Aleppo, have crossed into Turkey, paid their last money for a rubber dinghy to Greece and have then had to walk most of the way to Calais. Death appears to mean little if there is a chance to move from C to D, Calais to Dover, the Promised Land!'

'Humph,' Rhan snorted. 'We seem to have lost the sequential displacement of peoples with my more personal exodus. There will be no perfect sanctuary once major displacements kick off. Syria and Brexit are only just the initial ripples, with the rise of protectionism and nationalism. It frightens me. Everyone will blame everyone else and countries which contributed least will be expected to die first.'

David had now warmed to his apocalyptic subject. 'The wars in Africa show how future warfare will be. The aim will be to wipe out a population, just so they don't need food. They'll use armies of children like the Lord's Resistance Army. As I was saying before, there will be civil wars with young fighting the old. The young will recognise that the older generation have knowingly ruined the planet, allowing so many to spend their life in retirement jetting to exotic holiday locations, knowing the irreparable harm it would do. It will be like Mao's Cultural Revolution – intergenerational conflict. Euthanasia here we come.'

'So you're suggesting that those approaching sixty-five will need to cross to Ireland to live out their life?' teased George. 'It'll be like Dignitas in reverse. But Danny, why don't you point out that the older generation have the money and most of the votes, so who's going to suggest killing off the rich, no matter what the cost may be to others? The young are all in debt and the old have their pensions. Nothing will happen soon.'

David rattled his empty glass on the dimpled surface of the oak table at the mention of money and debts.

'Britain is currently the end of the line for migrants,' Rhan said, taking the conversation back a peg. 'There is nowhere else to run to once at D, on our doorstep, in Dover. All around the world fences and defences are already going up against migrants and the stakes are increasing. It's all so horrible.'

'Sorry, but safety and climate change are incompatible,' George sighed, confusing everyone by his inconsistent approach. 'Yet the UK is one of the safest countries, so you two are in a dark place looking for trouble at the beginning of this term. OK, yes, it's my turn for the drinks.' He stood up to extract his wallet.

'But you still think the older generation have the right to ruin the world because they have the money?' demanded David in exasperation. 'Should the rich be allowed to carry on jetting off on Saga holidays, just because they can afford it, have the time and don't give a fuck about anyone else?'

Rhan nodded encouragingly, now seeing where David was going with his generational war. She collected the glasses for George, who delayed heading to the bar to express his worry.

'It's not just the old. Just think of all the tourists in the streets outside. Most are young. How many of them would worry that their flights from across the world will contribute to the death of others? Almost all the carbon from emissions that we put into the atmosphere will be hanging around for hundreds of years, affecting generations to come, but who wants to limit their lifestyle now and take responsibility for their actions…or inaction?'

Rhan and David glanced at each other, wondering why they were struggling to appreciate George's approach, which had been cynical but was changing to fatalistic with each sentence. George was engaged at last, especially as the barman had disappeared from the little counter, so the drinks were on hold.

'The owners of oil wells would need to have them forcibly shut down, as you say,' George continued. 'But young people will also have to make some unwelcome sacrifices themselves to secure their own and their children's future. But would they do it?'

'Not many, no,' Danny replied, minimising his input.

'And to shut the oil fields or to stop the hordes – what about nuclear bombs?' George couldn't help asking, even as he picked up the empty glasses when the barman reappeared. 'Would the moral issue against them still apply in the type of wars that you were talking about earlier?'

'No, not really.' David ploughed on through his nightmare. 'Not if they halt those coming to grab your land for even a few months. Appalling isn't it?'

'Well, if you don't mind,' Danny sighed, 'I may give your fine words of wisdom a miss along with that long-promised drink – but don't worry about it. You owe me, George.'

As Danny headed for the door, his serious tone and broad Cornish accent left them all laughing at themselves and their surreal discussions.

~

At supper one evening in the second week of term, Rhan was surprised to hear Josh, who was doing English, discussing something to do with mass extinction a few places from where she sat on a bench with Tom. She started listening, but then found that Josh was covering a very different subject.

'...whether poetry was affected by knowledge of mankind's ability to forsake moral norms. There is an argument that poetry was changed forever by the Holocaust.'

Josh was using a ponderous tone, even with his friends, which made Rhan think how destined he was for an academic career. She still found the subject vaguely interesting.

'The argument is that that once poets discovered how dreadful man could be to man, then poetry could never be pure and simple again. It's an interesting hypothesis that is substantiated by many collections of work.'

'Can I just ask?' interrupted Rhan. 'Have you ever considered the next mass- extinction and whether that might affect literature?'

'What next extinction?' Josh seemed pleased to have the English debate interrupted by the female engineer, but either could not understand her question or was deliberately being obtuse.

'Well,' Rhan said, looking up at the huge timber trusses above the dining hall, 'there are many scientists who point out that overpopulation and global warming together mean that large parts of the world are already being made effectively uninhabitable. Isn't this a moral issue right now?' There were blank looks, so she felt forced to continue. 'I used to enjoy reading, but fiction and even historical literature seems trite compared with the march of reality here and now. Has anything associated with climate change filtered into literature yet?'

There was a supercilious smile from someone across the table whom Rhan did not know, and whom she decided she did not need to know.

'I suppose one would expect a step change in poetry,' Josh replied. 'I mean, we could wander around picking peaches and grapes and holding debates in the town square, once we reach the climate conditions for Hellenistic paradise in Oxford.' He was clearly trying to wind Rhan up with the delights of global warming.

It dawned on Rhan that her views on climate change were starting to be known around the college and that very few felt inclined to support her concerns. She therefore merely smiled and expected the conversation to end. However, after an awkward pause, Josh continued.

'I presume you're asking about dystopian literature?'

Rhan gave a look that she hoped said 'of course', so that she didn't need to admit she had no idea what he was talking about. It worked, as he continued anyway.

'Then you need look little further than Cormac McCarthy and his book *The Road*. It brilliantly portrays a doomed world and those in it attempting to survive a day at a time.'

'And yet, it may not be global warming,' said the girl who was sitting next to Josh. 'It's made very clear in the narrative that the disaster is not climate change.'

'One can write about something while masking the underlying theme, don't you think?' Josh argued in his pompous manner. 'Then there is Ballard and *The Drowned World*. And Harry Harrison wrote *Make room! Make room!* It was set in a world of excessive population and made into a film in the early seventies, called...*Soylent Green*. The film version was actually set in a world that was suffering from acute climate heating, to the extent that nearly all trees had died. The last surviving populous had been relocated to the remaining over-packed cities to enable the dwindling areas of viable countryside to maximise the production of food. I believe you will find the film particularly relevant, Rhan.'

Rhan was uncertain whether she was being patronised or not, but she had to admit that Josh suddenly appeared to have very appropriate theoretical knowledge of the issues.

'What was that film? *Soy-something Green*?' Rhan asked, aware that almost the entire table was listening to their conversation, give or take minor interruptions for requests to pass water or vegetables.

'*Soylent Green*,' Josh repeated emphatically. 'Charlton Heston played a police cop investigating the murder of a politician who'd lost the will to live. The police investigator's elderly assistant similarly opts for euthanasia. It's one of cinema's most beautiful death scenes.'

'Well, once we move into films, there's James Cameron's *Avatar*,' the girl next to Josh added. 'That was about the mindless stripping of world resources. It had a major impact, but more for the filming than the underlying message.'

'So have such subjects taken over science fiction?' Rhan asked, glancing at Tom, who had so far remained quiet, despite his usual interest in books and films.

'Well something has,' Tom said finally, making the effort to join in. 'The books you mentioned, Josh, were all produced decades ago. Nothing good, in my opinion, has been published recently; it's all science fantasy.'

'We were discussing poetry, not science trash!' Josh exclaimed with an exasperated smile. 'Who let these nerds and political hacks into the conversation?'

Tom stepped into the argument, allowing Rhan to duck the limelight.

~

In her alternative *Looking Glass* world, as she thought of it, "Bar" was again training early in the morning with the Gloucester Hall ladies' Novice Eight, but she now also had two afternoons a week with the university junior squad. She read news articles under headings such as *"Stormy Conditions for Oxford Rowers"*, which covered the rift in the Women's First Eight and the dropping of Cat and another international rower from the squad, but that seemed like another world to Rhan. Her life was nicely full, but global warming was constantly at the front of her mind. Nothing else seemed so real and dominant.

She wandered around both the commercial streets and the more bohemian quarters, searching the second-hand and new bookshops for reading material on climate, but found remarkably little of interest other than the range of fellow browsers. Some were definitely university students or academics, while others were clearly locals or tourists.

In the more general bookshops, the sceptics usually had the shelves to themselves and these were mostly vitriolic books by doctors and non-scientists; they aggressively attacked every single concept of climate change. Rhan puzzled at how bookshops could make money from denial books if there was so little information available about the real problem for them to argue against. She took the plunge and purchased a book entitled *A Farewell to Ice,* since that had been George's initial lead and the decline in Arctic ice had disturbed her the most.

~

Rhan's next attempt to discuss global warming came in the usual setting of Tom and Danny's room, on a wet afternoon after PPE tutorials, with Tom, Philip, Fiona, and two other girls whom Rhan hardly knew. Danny was not there, but George witnessed the event. It was a painful lesson.

There was an economic discussion over the pros and cons of inflation or deflation. In a slight lull in the conversation, Rhan turned the conversation to the theme that she wanted to discuss.

'As far as I can make out, economics is a subjective system that can be altered by changing attitudes or by removing or printing money. On the other hand, economists and politicians feel able to reject the laws of physics, as though nature would respect majority opinion. Which would be easier to deal with in ten years' time – rampant inflation or rampant temperature rise?'

'Well the Stern report was pretty emphatic on that subject,' Tom said, happy to divert the discussion. 'It must have been written a decade or so ago, but Stern pointed out the economic logic of starting to reduce climate change to cut the huge bill in decades to come.'

'But since then, the economic and political consensus has been that it's just not worth it,' Fiona's friend, who was wearing bright yellow Wellington boots, put in. 'After discounting the investment that would be needed now, it works out cheaper to leave any investment until it's absolutely necessary, which may or may not be in decades to come. Future generations tend to be richer, so they should be better able to afford the price of action than us. Besides, future generations may be in a better position to see if any action is really needed, or not.'

George said nothing. There was an awkward silence. Rhan had been startled to hear that the economic arguments were so well rehearsed.

'Well,' Rhan suggested slowly. 'Surely we are the future generation?' There was another pause before Philip came back at her.

'Yet there is no certainty that it will get much worse is there?'

'Yes, who's to say it will happen?' Fiona demanded.

'Because we are adding heat!' Rhan explained, exasperated. 'If you have a body and add more energy that cannot escape, then it heats up. Clear and simple! Just look around at how the temperature is already shooting up. It's not going to stop suddenly – not unless our generation can reverse the problem. And we have no idea how to recapture carbon from the atmosphere in a meaningful way.'

The room was split, four to one against Rhan, with George and Tom trying not to get too involved. George finally felt obliged to support Rhan.

'Well, Rhan has a point. The laws of physics are much more defined and definite than any economic laws.'

'Yet there are scientists who would argue that you're completely wrong,' Fiona's friend with the wellies said, who was clearly not willing to give up. 'So, we may as well ignore the issue until it's sorted one way or the other.'

'An interesting strategy,' Rhan pointed out. 'Surely, the philosophical question of the age is why this generation is not prepared to demand a halt in the mad rush to mass extinction. Why would we prefer to risk destruction rather than go green?'

There was a groan from Philip. 'Come on Rhan, not everything and everybody needs to be involved with bloody climate change. It's not just a black and white issue!'

Rhan caught unspoken exchanges between Fiona and her friends, including the one with short, blonde hair who had so far not spoken.

'Sorry,' Fiona said, grabbing her file. 'We have to go.'

With that, the three girls got up and walked out.

'Sorry Tom. I drove away your fan club,' Rhan said gloomily in the shocked silence. 'I hate to admit it, but George has a point; most people simply do not want to care.'

'It's the Tragedy of the Commons,' Tom explained, smiling.

'What is?' asked Rhan, glad of something to cover up her social ineptitude.

'Take a village that has a common,' Tom explained. 'An area of land that is shared, so that each household is entitled to feed up to three cows on that common. The problem is that if every household has three cows, then the common will become over-grazed. The grass cannot grow and the cattle will trample the turf to mud. If they all cut back to just two cows, then there would be enough grass and they would all manage to survive, even if everyone went slightly hungry. But each villager wants the benefit of grazing a third cow, while hoping that everyone else will see sense and graze only two. The result is that no one is prepared to yield from their perceived rights, all the grass is destroyed and all the cattle die from lack of grass. Everybody has to move away or starve. That is the Tragedy of the Commons.'

'Very apt!' Rhan said, brightening a little, but still aware of how quiet it was in the room. 'But with climate change we can't move to a different village and the atmosphere will be ruined for the foreseeable future.'

'And sorry Tom, but that's so ancient history,' Philip chided. 'It has no relevance to our current world. No one believes in food shortages anymore, except perhaps Rhan, and no one here grazes cattle or has problems with muddy fields. So the fable loses its impact. I have a better version.'

Rhan had been angry at Philip's denial of global warming, but after the drama she felt grateful for his cheerful interjection.

'I had a year off,' he started. 'I worked some of that time in a small office that had a lawn at the back where the staff parked their cars in dry weather. For ten years or so they played badminton on the lawn in the summer and used it as extra parking space when they could. As office junior, one of my tasks was to mow the grass, which I quite enjoyed. Then over the winter, the staff decided that they needed to be able to park on the grass, no matter how wet it was – they were fed up with walking down the street and paying some small sum to park for a day. Within a few weeks, it became a muddy quagmire, complete with an almost full-time puddle just in the entrance. Eventually, they all had to agree that no one could park in wet weather until the grass regrew, and of course, it never really recovered. So, for the sake of a bit of restraint they lost their car park and their badminton court and I had no grass to mow in the spring. That's the real Tragedy of the Commons!'

'Yeah, OK,' Tom conceded. 'You're probably right – in our society parking is of more concern than food. In a communist society, we would educate people away from the selfish approach and people would learn to be happy taking only what they needed, rather than what they wanted.'

'Anyway, I get the point,' Rhan said, sighing. 'Society is capable of being selfishly destructive.'

'But my Yorkshire village is worse than that,' George added, just as they clambered to their feet for supper. 'No landowner will agree to any improvement that will make him a pound a week, if he thinks that his neighbour might be making two pounds a week.' As they clattered down the timber stairs, he completed the relevance of his point. 'It means that no one can drain land or install hydro-electric power on a stream if it's a boundary. There's always a reason not to do something to save the planet.'

CHAPTER SEVENTEEN

Scrums on Water

'Rhan. Do you know anything about rowing?' They had just sat down at the workbench in the electronics laboratory after cycling through a chill morning.

'What's that got to do with this practical, George?' she fired back to delay answering the question. 'Now pass me another diode and hold it while I solder. Oh, come on, pay attention! For this logic gate, we need the yellow one. If you read your brief, we are supposed to complete this old circuit board before we can get onto the second half of the practical, which entails plugging in the silicon chips. What did you say about rowing?'

'Well the rugby season is coming to an end, so they are restarting the Rugby Rowing Eight. I've been invited to try for the crew. I'm going for it – I think I would prefer to be in the Rugby Eight than the first fifteen! We have two coaching sessions this week but we only have a cox for one of them. I offered to sound you out as a temporary cox for the second day.'

'No way!'

'Why not?'

'I have never coxed before, I am too heavy and I have better things to do.' Rhan sniffed and wriggled her nose, holding the solder in one hand and an old soldering iron in the other.

'You should get interested in rowing Rhan; the bump races in Torpids this term and the Eights week in the summer sound really cool. About a dozen boats in a division all set off at the same time, one behind the other with a short space between and if your boat can touch or bump the boat ahead, you swap places. Actually, Torpids and Summer Eights have slightly different rules, but you get the gist. It would be great to be involved. You're really strong and I bet you'd be better at rowing than most of our college women. Go on, please help out as cox this week?'

'OK.' She sniffed again and sucked her top lip, trying not to laugh.

'It doesn't really matter if you have no experience, and Danny's going for it if...'

'I said yes. Now pass a resistor over and hold it steady in the tweezers this time.' She was fully absorbed in the delicate soldering operation as George wiped her nose with his left hand.

'Share!' he muttered in a quieter voice, appropriate to the way they sat soldering with their heads close together. This was the term they used when enjoying their intimate weekly lunches in Rhan's room before their maths tutorial.

'Talk about invasion of personal space! What was that about?' Rhan demanded.

'Sorry,' he replied, embarrassed, looking around to check that no one had noticed. 'Are you really pissed off?'

'Not sure,' she said, looking at him suspiciously. 'Just tell me you don't do that to your girlfriend!'

Her heart beat slightly faster as she recalled a previous conversation in a practical, but that seemed long ago.

He looked shocked, and the turn-up of his nose told her everything, even before his reply.

'No, we snogged and did things that normal couples do.' He looked abashed as he added, 'I wouldn't ever do that with any other girl.'

She laughed, saying, 'OK, it is weird, but I'm not angry.'

It was later in the practical when George returned to the subject of his girlfriend.

'I've never mentioned it, but it was clear from her visit last term that she wanted out,' he reported with a wry smile. 'So it was no surprise that I was effectively dumped when I got home for Christmas. I got off lightly.'

'So why the secrecy?' Rhan asked, unsure of her feelings and also ambivalent on the merits of his discretion. George was so different from David, whose private life Rhan knew all about, and the complete opposite of Danny, who had so much more private life than Rhan cared to know about.

'Well, you wanted to be able to just carry on without people pointing a finger, so she's still a useful shield…isn't she?'

Rhan nodded.

~

The task of coxing the heavy clinker beginners' boat was both fun and dreadful at the same time. The wide boat allowed Rhan to move around, but she got very cold just sitting in the stern. As everyone expected her to know nothing about rowing, she offered no advice. The rugby crew had a coach with a bicycle on the bank who gave all the instructions, leaving Rhan with little to do but steer.

After the first session, George – who had now been on the water twice – and Simon, the captain, who had a few months' experience under his belt from the previous summer, sought to compliment her.

'Thanks for coxing, Rhan,' the captain started. 'You picked it up extremely quickly. Please could you cox again on Saturday afternoon? Torpids is approaching for the other boats and we have been warned that practice on the busy river will get more difficult.'

'You're a natural, partner!' George added, using his new nickname for Rhan.

'I suppose so,' Rhan responded hesitantly, knowing that she was booked to row with her Gloucester friends at lunchtime on Saturday.

~

There was no coach with the Rugby Eight on Saturday. Rhan sat glumly for ten minutes putting up with the appalling rowing. The boat rocked all over, and everyone seemed to be on a different rhythm. The crew kept up a barrage of advice to each other. Rhan surrendered to the inevitable and took charge; she had to shout because the old clinker had no sound system.

'OK, ease the oars! Hold, Number 7! Take two strokes, Number 2! Now try to hold the bank, Number 1!'

Some of the crew turned round to look at each other and to raise an eyebrow. There were smiles, but no comments as Rhan, now dressed in a tracksuit and head scarf, suddenly became a new authoritative referee.

'So this is what I want each of you to concentrate on. Number 1, pull right to your chest! Number 2, reach further forward so your arms are straight for the catch! Number 3, you are not in time with stroke, so speed it up! Number 4, good rowing but keep your eyes and head looking forward in line with the back of the rower in front – I do not want to see your face again, it upsets me and the whole balance.' There were laughs from all at Gareth's expense.

'Take two back strokes, Number 7!' Rhan called out to straighten the boat against the bank before she continued her advice.

'Number 5, you are too fast up the slide and are therefore totally out of sync – there's no point in being early so watch stroke at all times, not the girl crews! Number 6, make sure you twist your hands as you lift out. Number 7, keep your shoulders and head up. Number 8, feather the blade slightly earlier and slow down the stroke so everyone has time to follow you. Now concentrate on those specific items, but learn from what I said to the others.

'Push off, Number 1! OK, two strokes 1 and 2.

'Now, together, take one stroke then hold to get the balance until I tell you to take another stroke! Now go... and hold...now balance the boat...raise your hands a bit Number 7...stroke...and hold! Come on, act together!'

~

'I thought you knew nothing about rowing, Rhan,' Simon asked on behalf of them all, once Rhan had completed the orders and had helped to stow the heavy clinker on its rack. 'I'm beginning to think you're a bit of a dark horse.'

'Well I have seen how to cox on plenty of occasions,' Rhan explained evasively. They were now walking back to college along the riverside. To change the subject, she asked the question she had been dying to ask of the third-year Geography student.

'Can I ask you again about climate change? You said previously that there may be something in it, but there are other causes that would invalidate the common assumptions.'

'That's right,' he replied cautiously. 'I mentioned the natural cycle of the sun, the tilt, energy emitted, the inclination of the earth, and its position in the solar system.'

'You also said that we still don't know everything that caused major shifts in climate in previous epochs on a geological timescale.'

He nodded uneasily.

'I am trying to find out if uncertainty is behind the lack of action. Is everyone waiting until we know all the facts, and isn't that risky?'

'Well most think the risks are less dangerous than the inconvenience and risks of suddenly taking action. I have to head off now. Thanks for coxing.'

~

'Why the hell do you insist on making a complete idiot of yourself, Rhan? No one else wants to know.'

'That's my problem George,' she replied emphatically. 'I am sorry I asked while you were within earshot, but I still need to know why people think differently. The facts indicate the physics, but the perceptions are also important even if I cannot understand views like those. I do not feel able to follow your lead and obediently defer like you did with our tutor – effectively agreeing that climate can be considered a taboo subject. I may get to the stage when I will let the whole climate thing wash over me and what will happen will happen. Yet I have the feeling that it is a critical subject for our generation, even though – or perhaps just because – hardly anyone will admit the impact it will have on their lives. People have now spent decades denying global warming, yet surely it is becoming more real each year.'

The conversation stopped while George and Rhan had to separate as they passed a troupe of tourists. When they could walk together again, Rhan was ready to resume.

'People who carry on denying the laws of thermodynamics and who doubt the obvious risks like Simon – well, they indicate the scale of the problem.' She looked at George until he nodded his reluctant agreement. She then continued her argument.

'If geography students are as stubbornly ignorant as engineering students, then we are running into the problem with our eyes shut. I have a nasty feeling that floods, wars, famine and so much more will have secondary impacts that will hit everyone. Suffering will just harden hearts, cut off aid and exacerbate the slamming of doors and frontiers. I need to know what can be expected and when. I suspect that official advice is just wishful thinking.'

'OK, but can't you keep climate change conversations for consenting adults? And, to change the subject to something even more secretive and dramatic…'

Rhan looked at him in surprise both at his capitulation and in what he might say next.

'…why did you pretend to be running rather than rowing? I presume you learnt with another college?'

She laughed nervously, glad that the ruse had finally run its course.

'Well yes. I needed to be able to let my hair down, literally, so it seemed a good idea to have separate lives. Sorry not to tell you, but I was waiting for you…'

'You thought you needed to get away from me?' he asked, clearly hurt.

'Well you were playing rugby most afternoons so you weren't even there,' she argued. 'And yes, it would have been stupid just basing my whole university life on you and this college.'

'But you've been out in the mornings,' George protested.

'So you can hardly complain. I was hoping that you would just ask or notice, especially when you saw the Gloucester Hall rowing kit that you have been kindly washing for me!'

He rubbed his forehead with both hands before replying with a half-smile.

'So you really wear that skimpy outfit without your track suit over the top? He laughed. 'My God, what have I been missing?'

She laughed again, feeling more relaxed by both his ludicrous reaction and by how unnecessary the deception over her rowing had been.

'Well you can watch us row in the Torpid bumps in a few weeks. You can come and see how it's done.'

The next day after lectures, they were having coffee in his room, and starting to tackle their first maths question. George brought up the subject that was clearly worrying him much more than rowing.

'Look, I'm really regretting getting you wound up about global warming. It was fun to see your reaction, but it's all pointless. You must see that no one wants to know. It's better just to accept it; otherwise, you'll end up like my old man – boring everyone and pouring effort into a void. Please, could you let the subject drop?'

He was close to her at the desk, looking at her anxiously, waiting for her reaction.

'No way!' Rhan stated emphatically. 'I owe it to my parents and grandparents to discover the threat. You can complain all you want, but how can you expect me to turn a blind eye, or even two blind eyes to the biggest event of mankind's history? Does this mean my promised trip to your house and a discussion with your father is off?'

'No! Of course not. If you mean it, I'll confirm it with my parents. They're dying to meet you – when? The end of term, so we can travel together?'

'Not the first or last weeks of the holiday,' Rhan said, relieved that the argument appeared to be over.

'Fine, the second week of the holiday it is.' George now happily booked her, yet continued with his tirade in a serious tone. 'But you're not getting round me so easily. Why have you so quickly latched onto climate change as a major thing to obsess over? I was indoctrinated from an early age, so I know it's a waste of effort.'

'Surely it is obvious why I have an obsession, as you call it,' she explained, waving her hands for emphasis while the coffee cooled and their maths waited. 'Warming appears to be the ultimate elephant in the room – it's the very denial that poses the biggest threat, to us and our families. It is the definitive threat to Syria, much worse than the civil war or any religious or political strife, which are perhaps just symptoms. You know life here in Britain may change drastically, so why not take an interest? The shock is that I never bothered to look before. You can't begin to understand how stupid I feel to have missed the lies that are so blatant once I start to think about them.'

He was looking through the window at the sky above the college and across the quad, shaking his head slightly at her response, but said nothing, so she continued.

'Can I just tell you about the first time I heard about carbon dioxide – at my school in Aleppo when I was around ten years old, before we set off for Iraq. It was a small school, with no real science facilities – not compared with many schools here, but the science teacher was good. Anyway, we were talking of gases in the air, with 20 percent oxygen and 80 percent nitrogen. Is that right?' Hearing no contradiction, she continued.

'We had done that experiment with a lighted candle and a glass bowl over it, set in water. We watched the flame gradually die down while the water was sucked up to around a fifth of the volume of the air in the bowl as the oxygen was used up.' He nodded, not wishing to interrupt her mesmerising, deep and old-fashioned voice.

'Anyway, the teacher then mentioned that a tiny fraction of the atmospheric mix was carbon dioxide – well he may have mentioned water vapour, I don't remember. He burnt a wooden splint to show that the timber had effectively disappeared, but he explained that wood was a hydrocarbon. The burning process involved the hydrogen atoms being oxidised to water vapour, H_2O, and the carbon being oxidised to form CO_2.

'Someone asked – I used to talk in those days and at that school, so it might even have been me – whether the fraction of carbon dioxide would rise if we burnt things. The teacher had categorically replied "no" – that all the carbon dioxide would be absorbed by plants. Even at that age, I remember thinking, *"I doubt it. No system works that well. He must have it slightly wrong!"*

'I now know that the system is far from perfect and cannot possibly cope with the amount of carbon dioxide that we are putting out there. Only around half of the carbon in that splint would have been reabsorbed and recycled, and each year a smaller fraction of any splint burnt will return to the earth. Some of the carbon dioxide from that splint will be hanging about in the atmosphere, helping to trap the heat and ruining our lives and destroying our children's future.' She stopped and waited for George's response.

'There is no point in you being a smart-arse!' he said. 'You may see the problem, but no one else will see it. It does you no good. I don't know why, but no one will believe you – they've never believed scientists.'

'But why not? I found out that more than a hundred years ago, scientists discovered that CO_2 allows high-frequency energy from the sun to pass through the atmosphere to the ground, but stops the low frequency heat waves from escaping back out to space. So why is there such denial now? There are books that refuse to admit that carbon dioxide is even a pollutant!'

'Yes, I know. It's the "inconvenient truth".'

'Yet you will do nothing about it?' she accused.

He sighed and shrugged before explaining.

'There is no desire in any country around the world, apart from low-lying islands, to do anything about global warming. Not even those countries or states that will be turned to sand have any desire to lift a finger to stop it. As David pointed out the other day, most people would prefer to die fighting for the right to turn their country into desert, rather than listen to environmentalists on how to stop it. Hardly anyone cares if we ruin the earth. The vast majority are passionate about not changing their lifestyle. Better dead than green!'

'But wouldn't most people do anything to protect their family and loved ones?' Rhan asked.

'Well clearly not,' he replied slowly. 'Given the choice between driving their children to school or letting them catch a bus or cycle, how many parents think it safer for their little dears to be driven? Nearly all. They aren't going to acknowledge that their children can't survive if the planet takes the plunge over a cliff edge, are they? The role of a parent is to safeguard children today, not in a few decades' time. Parents simply assume that someone, somewhere will do something, sometime. Perhaps parents are programmed not to worry about the future of children more than a few years ahead! I suppose that's why it's all so hush-hush. If we deny that there is a problem, we don't need to worry. That's why winding up our friends is just not worthwhile.'

She nodded slowly, not wanting to disagree.

'Sorry Rhan, but we have to ignore climate change for at least the next few hours. We have to get to grips with partial differential equations, whatever they do. They are clearly more important than climate change!'

~

'Alice, please can I have a word?' Rhan had promised the porter that she would row for the college in the summer, so she had two reasons to approach the college rowing captain. 'I now have some experience at rowing, so if you are still interested in recruiting college rowers for the Summer Eights, then I would welcome a trial. I am rowing with a Gloucester Novice Eight for the Easter Torpids, if you don't mind?'

Rhan was slightly taken aback by Alice's lack of enthusiasm.

'Well Rhan, I am pleased to hear of your interest, but I'm afraid we already have a great crew and could hardly change for Torpids anyway. I don't mind at all you rowing elsewhere. We are in the division above Gloucester's First Eight so your input with them would hardly interest us, never mind their Second or Third Eight, so please carry on. We can discuss a trial once we start thinking of the summer.' Alice's tone suddenly brightened a little. 'Oh, hang on...next Thursday, Jane has an interview, so that would be an opportunity for us to take a look at you. You certainly have the height, and you could be quite strong. Can you row at Number 1? That's on the bow side.'

'No problem; that would be great. Thanks. As you say, you won't want me for Torpids, so please can you sign me off to row for the Gloucester Novice Eight?'

~

'I hear your trial for the college Women's Eight didn't go too well,' George commented on the Friday after Rhan's trial. They were applying horizontal shear forces onto a sand box during a soils practical, to measure the angle of friction of various granular materials while applying vertical loads.

'You can say that again!' Rhan replied, colouring at the humiliation. 'Nothing went right. There would be just so many complications having me in that boat. But Alice gave me permission to row for Gloucester Hall, which was the key item. So actually, it went really well…I suppose.'

CHAPTER EIGHTEEN

Social Debutant

'Rhan is that you? What are you doing here? And without your headscarf! Your hair is shorter than I expected.'

Alice's falsetto voice, exaggerated by alcohol, forced its way through the chorus of blackbirds competing around the spacious lawns of St John's College. Her excitement pierced the relaxed early evening chat of six groups who were smoking or were hardy enough for the March climate. The unwelcome outburst certainly broke Rhan's routine rhythm of filling glass after glass with clear, sparkling liquid.

Rhan, or Bar as she was known here, had previously been behind the drinks tables set up in the warm classical drawing room of this wealthy college. There she had occasionally been able to join Claire talking to the rowing president, Esther, but then Esther had been dragged off to meet a sponsor and Claire had stepped outside to find Nick from her college. Rhan had eventually escaped the bar work and had welcomed the chance to bring four bottles outside so she could check that her friends and other guests were not deprived of refreshment. She had not expected or realised that Alice would be here among the university sporting community.

'Oh, hello Alice!' Rhan swallowed the lie that it was good to see her, and felt herself redden at the recollection of their awkward encounter the previous week. She no longer noticed the exotic plants fringing the darkening lawn that had drawn her attention just a few seconds before. 'What did you ask? Oh, what am I doing here, at the Pink Club drinks? Well I suppose I am a sort of…hostess.'

'So, this is your other life!' Alice declared. Rhan stood rooted, disappointed that it was going to be Alice that ruined her separate lives. 'What fun!' Alice continued. 'Do you make good money?'

Rhan was at a loss for a second or so, but then realised the misunderstanding.

'Oh, as hostess? Well – I would guess it is based on a percentage of how much you paid for your ticket,' Rhan responded obliquely, having the advantage of sobriety, and knowing full well Alice had a free ticket. She hoped to confuse the multiple misunderstandings as much as possible, whether or not it was due to her poor English.

Rhan filled the glasses for Alice and the two blokes she was with and moved onto her two friends, who had turned away to suppress fits of laughter. Rhan perceived that both Nick, the Gloucester representative, and Claire, Rhan's personal guest, were also both well-oiled by drink, yet it was clear that they had comprehended the confused discussion with Alice.

'What are we – I mean, what am I doing here?' she whispered to her friends while trying to ignore Alice, who was now talking loudly in the background about her.

'...came for a trial in our college last week actually, but... so I had to turn her down unf-unfortunately.'

'Well Bar, or should we call you Khan?' Nick asked.

'Rhan not Khan, if you really want to know Nick,' Rhan corrected him crossly.

Claire took another swig and steadied herself on Nick. 'Well I'm here having a lovely time because you had a spare ticket. I'm going to use it by meeting some very fit young men, if you don't mind. Nick is here conscientiously drinking for Gloucester Hall.' She raised her nearly empty glass to Nick and her college, before answering Rhan's question. 'You are here because...because you are now a bigwig and that's presumably why you're so busy waiting on everyone and being a skivvy hostess. Have you even drunk a single glass of the stuff you're shoving round everyone else?'

Nick was disconcertingly more interested in Alice's story than Claire's conversation.

'...practising starts. She started complaining that she had snapped her oar. Hahaha!' Alice's voice was hard to ignore.

'No such luck,' Rhan responded, trying to divert Nick's attention. 'Andrew, the club secretary, jumped on me as soon as I arrived, as you saw. He told me that I was a hostess and to stay off the drink. So I would be pleased to leave this stuck-up party, but I am stuck here to the end.'

'Hey Bar, you can't leave. You're doing a great job as hostess!' Nick showed that he could take in two conversations at once. 'My protégé is really flying high and is now a member of the Pink Club – I'm celebrating your success. You appear not to know about it, but Claire and I know why you're here,' he said soberly and quietly. 'You have been invited into the inner sanctum of a very exclusive sporting club and I am very proud of you.' He raised his glass to her, sipped and continued with his long answer, but stopping every now and then to monitor Alice's monologue.

'You asked why. Well, it might be that everyone, from rowers to boatmen, seem to believe that you're going to be the stroke for the Women's Blues next year, give or take the arrival of a mega superstar.' Claire and Rhan looked at each other in surprise at his insight. After a slight pause, he continued.

'It may be that Esther is also subtly starting to campaign for you to be president, even though at least three existing Blues and several from the second boat are likely to come back for another year.

'It may also be that the university coaches and all the top rowing hierarchy see you as Britain's amateur answer to the arrogant and professional gobshites who think they own the sport here.'

Rhan smiled, acknowledging both her reputation for humbling the mighty, while having an exceedingly amateur status compared with most.

'There are probably more than a few,' Nick continued, looking round to check that no one else was listening, 'who also think it about time that an Arab girl joined the club.'

'Unfortunately, the main reason is probably that half the blokes with Blues, including the president, apparently have a crush on you. Little chance for me then!' He smiled crookedly. Claire sent a "told you so!" glance at Rhan while Nick continued. 'I gather some of the women do too! So, is that reason enough for you?'

'Wow!' Claire enthused. 'It's true! Well, most of it.'

'Wow.' Rhan mimicked Claire, smiling and shaking her head at the heap of compliments. 'Nick, you are very charming, and I would usually have accused you of talking utter rubbish. However, I have just escaped from a growing confusion of complications inside, so I can hardly refute any of your points. If you want a chance, you could help me check the garden and lock up, if you don't mind helping a bit,' Rhan suggested rather sheepishly, holding out a key. Claire smiled knowingly.

'Any more wine Rhan?' Alice called over, and Rhan smiled and dutifully started to obey.

'Fine. But Bar, before you go.' Nick gently held her arm. 'I have some bad news for you. I'm afraid you're losing Claire for Torpids. She's just too powerful and we need her in the First. Your boat is ridiculously strong anyway, even without Claire'.

'Oh no!' Rhan felt all Nick's compliments washed away by the bad news. 'I suppose nothing remains the same, but still…'

'Now putting one and one together, Bar – am I correct?' He glanced across at Alice. 'Your own college has yet to appreciate your usefulness with an oar?'

'Correct. I had a trial for next term's Eights bumps and…well, I was rejected.' Both Nick and Claire gasped and laughed dramatically.

'So that is you?' Nick wanted confirmation. 'You're the incompetent rower who wrecked the balance with your rowing and then pretended to break an oar?' Nick had obviously heard much of Alice's story. 'Did you really break an oar? How?'

'It was a cold day,' Rhan confessed with resignation. 'I was rowing in the bow so any effort I put into a stroke yanked the whole boat over. It was very frustrating. When we were practising starts, I thought the balance would be less critical. I pulled too hard. The composite oar just went bang!'

Claire gave a shriek of surprise. Rhan laughed and finished the story.

'It gave me such a shock; I nearly fell off my seat. It was really loud, but no one else appeared to notice it. After that, it was like rowing with a stick of old rhubarb. I tried to report it, but no one believed me and I don't think anyone else has even noticed since then. I was just marked down as a complainer.'

'Wine please, Rhan!' The second call from Alice could not be denied.

Nick headed off laughing but called back to Rhan, 'I'll enjoy helping you!'

Claire raised her eyebrows without saying anything for a few seconds.

'We'll still row together for the juniors,' Claire said, returning to the previous conversation. 'You could always be sociable and invite me to your room for tea. And you could introduce me to Alice and your other nice college friends.' Claire dissolved into a fit of laughter at her own joke.

'Actually, I would like to introduce you to George, my tutorial partner.'

'Ahhhh.' Claire managed to pour several long, complicated conversations into one prolonged exclamation.

Rhan headed off to attend to her duty and the needs of those in the garden. On the way back to the cooled wine bins, she saw a large group of men spilling out of the building onto the lawn. Nick was leading Dumas out and explaining to the others who could have been cricketers and rugby players.

'…an amazing story about how one of your "hostesses", or should I say, "Bar staff…" He pointed at the retreating Rhan, who ignored him, before continuing. '…failed to get into her college First Eight despite being stroke for the university junior squad. I hear from one of the coaches that she gave Lucy Bishop, the stroke, a run for her Blue after just a few weeks of rowing.'

From the door Rhan looked back and beheld two of her separate lives touching a third. She had to laugh at Alice's expense and at the bizarre nature of the scene.

'So this waitress,' Alice paused her story to point vaguely in Rhan's direction. 'She was in her first ever college trial – she's mad about climate change by the way and believes we're all doomed! She claimed she couldn't row properly, because she had pulled so hard, that she'd broken a brand-new, ultra-light timber and carbon-fibre epoxy oar!'

Alice, in an inebriated heaven, was surrounded by the university's best sportsmen and a growing band of women, all anxious to hear her story. Andrew, the club secretary, had clearly not taken his own advice about holding back, and was one of those who could hardly stand for laughter.

Rhan wondered whether it was kind or cruel. Alice was enjoying herself as the centre of attention, unaware just why everyone wanted her story again and again, or why they all found Alice's story so extraordinarily funny. Either way, Rhan was glad to start clearing up.

~

She was gratefully handing in the key to the party room at the now dimly lit porters' lodge when she realised she was being watched. Her first thought was regret at finishing the clearing up and rejecting Nick's offer to accompany her back to her college at the more reasonable hour of half-past ten. That made her think of her headscarf, buried in one of her bags. However, glancing at the young lady with long, blonde hair standing by the exit, Rhan decided that she appeared to be the more nervous one.

'Hello! Are you waiting for me?' Rhan started the conversation.

'Yu Bar, from Sunderland?' the stranger asked in an accent that was instantly familiar to Rhan.

'Yes I am.' Rhan responded in a rather stilted manner, aware of how she must sound to the northern girl. She wanted to adjust the missing headscarf.

'Oh!' the girl bit her lip, obviously disappointed. 'A'm from Easington Lane, a village just to the west. Ah've heard of yu and just wanted to hear 'ow a Sunderland girl could manage 'ere at Oxford and get to the top. But yu're posh! Yu don't sound like you're from Sund'lund.'

Rhan started to laugh, then just spent several seconds just breathing. It was all such a surprise to see herself through this girl's eyes. She was obviously a first-year, like herself, but things had clearly gone differently.

'Is everything alright Miss Bar?' the young, clean-shaven night porter called out.

'Yes, fine thank you!' Rhan called back, surprised how everyone suddenly seem to know who she was. She was puzzled that the porter was not asking the same of the young lady, who was obviously from the college, judging by the closed gate. Though she was shattered, Rhan decided she could not leave without talking to this fellow northerner.

'Do you fancy a coffee, um...?'

'Annie,' the modest young lady completed the question, but then after a pause she added, 'Yu're welcome to my room, but ah've only instant coffee, sorry.'

Rhan smiled, thinking of her first conversation with George. She wondered whether he would know she was still out.

'That would be great!' she responded. 'I'll follow you!'

~

George was enjoying Rhan's indignation after his initial surprise at her appearance so late at night on a weeknight. He was in his bed with his hands clasped behind his head watching her pacing around the middle of the room.

'It was her very first tutorial,' Rhan raged. 'The smug stuck-up tutor told her straight out, "With an accent like that, you're clearly in the wrong place." Can you imagine it?'

'You're joking!' George sat up, no longer relaxed and amused. 'He refused to teach her, just because she had a northern accent? Not in this millennium, surely? He could lose his job, assuming it was a he and not a she? He should lose his job! That's crazy! So what happened?'

'Nothing!' Rhan replied. 'Annie was forced out. Impossible to imagine, isn't it?'

Rhan was still aghast at the story. 'So she had to change tutors, and has had a miserable time ever since – an effective outcast from the college. I think I was a disappointment to her as I was not raised in Sunderland, but we got on well enough. My family originally came from a village near her home.'

She smiled inwardly at how Annie had been delighted to hear the full facts about herself. The high-flying rower, Bar from Sunderland who Annie had heard about, was actually only a fictitious character. Rhan confessed about the awkward engineer who had failed to even make her women's college team. They laughed at how her only role was temporary cox for the Rugby Eight as they messed around on the water.

'But how and why did you meet? And you still haven't said why you were in that college and why you're wearing your best gear.'

'I was there partying with Gloucester rowers.' Rhan felt guilty at telling George this half-truth. 'And I have no idea how she knew who I was.

'Anyway,' she continued, 'tomorrow you and I are dropping in on Annie on the way back from lectures. But do me a favour and please avoid asking how she knew of me.'

CHAPTER NINETEEN

Torpids

Day One

The first day of the Torpids bumps arrived in the eighth and last week of the spring term and all worries over tutorials, practicals and climate change dispersed with the more immediate rowing nerves and anxiety. Rhan was relieved that she no longer had to pretend to be calm with George. He was aware where her thoughts lay through breakfast, through lectures, and through a practical. He tried to point out that compared with a rugby game, at least Rhan was unlikely to get badly hurt.

During their practical, George insisted on talking of his own newfound interest and enthusiasm for anything to do with rowing. Yet Rhan, feeling rather contrary, was in no mood for a casual chat about rowing and wanted George to concentrate on work, even if her own mind was elsewhere. Aware of how petty and pathetic she was being, she still could not refrain from taking out her worries on the resilient George. She could hardly wait to get herself down to the boathouse to be with her Gloucester crowd, but the practical dragged on, making her think that she was late, despite the evidence of watches and clocks.

Making do with just a Mars Bar for lunch, she jogged down to the Gloucester boathouse but was too early, so she had to wait with growing nerves until the rest of the crew all turned up together. Liz, the captain, came straight up to Rhan.

'Sorry, we're about to mess it up, Bar. I know that all we need to do is follow you, but we won't.' Rhan found it relaxing to be the one reassuring others, who were suffering anxieties mainly due to her rising status. The mood lightened considerably once Rhan pointed out that they were literally all in the same boat and would just have a good time.

While their cox, Shrimpy, looked very white-faced, Sarah was cool. She winked at Rhan. 'All right Bar? After what you've been through with Claire at the university trials, this should be easy! We really aced the time trials last week, so no pressure this week.'

Rhan smiled and nodded, but a reminder from Sarah of previous exploits at the university trials removed none of the tension from the impending race, which the bump rules made so much more physical, even if a "bump" just meant the lightest of touches. She refrained from mentioning how much better she would have felt having Claire rowing behind her.

In a blur of rising tension, Rhan obeyed instructions from the cox and carried the boat, dropping it clumsily onto the water. Once afloat, the first strokes soon relaxed Rhan, and rhythm and concentration took over. She had raced before, but with so many boats of new starters in the fifth division chasing them, this felt so much more intense.

Without really noticing how, they arrived at the end of the course downriver and were soon backing into their starting position. They had the top spot at the head of the line-up, as the fastest in the time trials, so they had to row the length of the course without being caught and bumped by any of the pursuing twelve boats. They were instructed in the starting procedures by the reassuringly competent Gloucester college boatman. Rhan did not know his name, but it was good to see a friendly face. They turned around and waited, the stern of the boat being held in the side of the river by the boatman's long boathook. They were at water level and could see nothing beyond the banks on either side of the river. It all seemed unnaturally quiet. She knew that just down the river, around the corner, there would be a succession of other boats also waiting but they could only occasionally hear or see the second boat tucked into the riverbank. Above their heads, there was a layer of mist, which trapped them in a subdued and water-scented world that consisted of nothing but the steady flow of the river past their craft, and the dragging flow of time towards the race.

Nick the Gloucester captain appeared over the top of the bank above them. Beside him, George slowly and uncertainly emerged from the mist.

'Thanks for coming,' Rhan uttered quietly to both of them, as she sat below them near the back of boat in front of Shrimpy, who was grasping both steering strings and the starting rope very tightly. Rhan was aware that Nick would be racing later, and was surprised that George had discovered where she was rowing. Soon everyone was calling their gratitude that Nick had turned up for them.

'No problem, girls.' Nick spoke enthusiastically once clear of his bike. 'You'll do fine. Just go carefully in the first three strokes and don't overdo the effort in the next power-ten strokes. Things will be frantic, so play safe. Bar – don't try and overdo it; remember that the rest have to keep up. Having you at Number 8 is brilliant, yet not without its problems, so good luck to the rest of you. Keep it simple. All you have to do is stay ahead, in the smooth water. It's much worse for those behind.'

There were shouts and a whistle. Rhan's heart started hammering. The boatman called for strokes from Number 2 and they were away from the bank, anchored only by the rope held by the cox. Twenty metres downstream, there was the next boat pointing directly at them. They were a target. This was terrifying.

At the "get ready" signal, they drew up for the first short stroke. The bang from the gun was enough to make Rhan jump out of her seat in fright, but she channelled her energy into pulling a short, hard half-stroke. Then an even shorter stroke. Then another half. Then she was sliding right up, bending her knees, dropping her blade into the water at full reach and throwing herself back, dragging the oar after her as she forced herself up the slide for the first of the power-ten full strokes. She wondered whether she was alone or whether the rest of the crew were following her lead. She could see no proper vortex puddles in the disturbed water. She hated being stroke. Rhan could only see the cox, who had previously sat like a frightened rabbit, but was now all action, her freckled white face rapidly gaining colour as she screamed encouragement. Rhan felt all alone in a world that consisted of chaos; noise in the air and turbulence in the water. It was all so messy. The water was churned white with badly rushed strokes that flung plumes of spray into the air, so that the distinction between air and water was no longer clear-cut. She dipped her oar into the disturbed water and pulled again.

Shrimpy, their shrinking cox, had turned into a maniac and was screaming into a microphone, yet nothing could be heard from the distorted sound from the speakers under their seats. Even from a metre away, Rhan could hardly hear what she was saying. It was unclear whether the enthusiastic crowd on the bank just above her head were shouting for or against their boat. It was chaos.

She lifted her oar clear and prepared for the next stroke. This was normality. The water started to remain in the river rather than the air, and the strokes improved as they settled into a rhythm of ten powerful strokes. Rhan looked up to see that the boat behind was creating similar spray and choppy water. She was relieved to see that it had not gained on them and her second glance, a few strokes later, convinced her that it had fallen back. By the tenth stroke, her knees felt weak, but she made herself slow and immediately started to enjoy it.

They rowed on and the trailing boat receded, but the third boat behind them was rowing well and from a distance; Rhan saw that both boats eventually stopped. There must have been other bumps behind them, because although they slowed the pace right down to finish the long course with minimal effort, none of the other boats came within sight. The boathouses were still almost deserted as they passed them on the way to the finish. They received a few cheers from the Gloucester boathouse and knowing that Claire would be there, they extravagantly acknowledged the support by dangerously taking a hand off the oar and waving back. They repeated the wave on the way back down to the start after crossing the finish line.

They had confirmed their position at the top of the fifth division and were now the "sandwich" boat between divisions. They now needed to row again at the bottom of the fourth division.

~

'That was a fine display, and you'll note that I waited here at the start, knowing you would pull through.' Nick gave them a second talk from his bike as they waited for the next race. 'There's optimism for you!' he boasted. 'Now I'm afraid that this fourth division will be much more crazy. The fifth division was sorted on merit from the time trial, and the upper divisions with the top College Eights tend to be relatively consistent from year to year. But the quality of second and third crews in divisions three and four varies from year to year, so watch out! Anything can happen. There'll be plenty of bumps and it's rare for anyone to row the whole course. Remember, you need to get a bump to secure your place in this division.'

As Nick finished, George appeared on his bike. He had obviously followed them up and down again for the next race, clearly enjoying observing them.

There was a peaceful wait for the next race and the mist was clearing. Out on a limb at the bottom of the division, it was very quiet, with only the occasional gurgle from the water wrapping around a tree on the riverbank. The rowers talked in quiet voices or just sat and waited in silence. Nick and the boatman chatted at the top of the bank, stamping their feet occasionally while George stood, an isolated yet reassuring sentinel. As minutes ticked away, it was only the temperature that was not perfect; the cold penetrated their sweatshirts. Then with a minute to go, they stripped back to their rowing singlets and passed their tops to a grateful Shrimpy, who laid them over her legs.

Nick had not exaggerated the chaos of the fourth division. The Gloucester crew were relatively relaxed as they had excised most of their nerves in the first race and had no one trying to hit them from behind. Such composure was clearly missing from the crews ahead of them.

They set off relatively smoothly but they were hardly out of their first power-ten strokes when Shrimpy went from shouting at them to row harder to peering anxiously ahead. She suddenly applied the brakes.

'Ease the oars! Hold! Hold! Hold hard! There's a pile-up and the river is blocked.' There was jostling as the stroke-side Numbers 2 and 4 had their oars tangled with the boat ahead.

'Wow, that was easy!' Rhan suggested to Shrimpy, who shook her head in contradiction.

'We hit a boat that had already bumped and were therefore out of the race,' she explained hurriedly into the microphone. 'All back down! Quick! Keep going! Harder, stroke side! Numbers 1 and 3 row on to take us round. Join in, 5. All join in – let's get going!'

As they took a very wide detour across to the far bank, Rhan could see that the two boats in front had not gone far before a bump and were not making much effort to clear the river. As soon as they were round that pair, they came across the next two boats, resting after another short race of only sixty metres or so. It was rather dispiriting, as they had missed the opportunity to bump all four of the boats ahead of them.

They were just getting back into a good rhythm when Shrimpy called out yet again.

'Slow your pace, there are more blockages ahead. Slow rowing!'

'It's a sitting duck, Gloucester!' Nick was there on the path like a fairy godmother. 'There are three boats in that mess, so just touch the last one that's trying to back out. Don't let it escape and you'll have leapt up five places!'

It was as easy as that. They were nearly halfway up the fourth division.

Day Two

The Gloucester crew felt like hardened experts by Day Two. They had achieved more equivalent bumps already than their wildest dreams. However, starting for the first time in the middle of the division, there were very different pressures. There were boats ahead to be chased down, along with boats behind who would be out to bump them. Their experience on the day before as top boat, then bottom boat, had been much more clear-cut.

The start went well enough, despite there being twice as much noise and chaos as before. They had just finished their initial power-ten strokes and had kept away from the boat behind when Shrimpy excitedly called out, 'Another power ten! Let's go for it.'

Rhan immediately sprang from the more languished stroke that she had established, back into maximum effort, wondering at the tactics. There was a jarring as though brakes had suddenly been applied.

'Have we bumped?' Rhan shouted, only to be met by Shrimpy's worried shake of the head, in a repeat of the day before. Yet the day before, there had been no one chasing them.

'Get it out! Clear it! Leave it!' the cox was screaming. Rhan could not refrain from grimacing as she surmised that someone had caught a bad crab and had lost control of their oar. She tried to wait calmly, not taking the next stroke and trying to look over her shoulder at the problem. Motion was not useful if an oar had gone too deep, ripped out of the hands of a rower and left hanging in the gate at the end of the rigging. Rhan made herself breathe deeply, inhaling the stale odour from a disturbed river bottom. She glanced up at George, who was half-off his bike, watching the scene silently. The boat was almost stopped in the water. After an eternity lasting several seconds, she pulled forward and completed a slow, weakened stroke, as directed by the cox.

'OK, now get me out of here!' groaned Shrimpy in despair, looking back over her shoulder at the pointed bow of the boat behind coming straight at her.

'Now row! It's clear!' Shrimpy called, before turning round again to look at what she could do to escape being skewered. Rhan and the rest of the oarsmen were facing backwards so could clearly see an eight with light-blue oars approaching rapidly from behind; it was forging onto them at full speed while they were sitting almost stationary. 'Pull! Just leave it Jenny! Let the others row!' the cox pleaded. 'Concentrate on stroke, everyone!'

Rhan put in another almost tentative stroke and they were moving again. She could see Nick, stopped on the bank behind them, holding his head in anguish, with George in the background still just looking on sorrowfully. The following boat was eating up the gap between them. It would ram them at high speed. Mangled boat and flesh sprang to mind. This would not be the slow-speed bump they had inflicted yesterday. Their boat would be prey to a high-momentum impact. They must start moving.

Another short stroke.

They were off, but it was bewildering, with splashing and shouting both to and from their boat, from the boat behind them, and possibly from boats in front. Amid the chaos, Rhan made herself concentrate on rowing, but it was difficult, knowing that her whole crew were also watching in horror as the prow of the following boat headed towards them. It would be hitting them soon.

Another stroke. That felt better. Rhan flicked a glance backward. An oar was moving a bit, but it was clear of the water. There were only seven rowers. 'Get them out of there, Bar!' Nick's strained voice reached her from the riverbank.

'Pull!' the cox screamed, and Rhan obeyed. The timber shaft of the oar bowed as Rhan straightened her legs and pulled. It did not break.

'For Jenny!' Annie's voice screamed out. Rhan guessed this meant that it was Jenny sitting there, unable to row.

In the next three mighty strokes, they took off. They had bought some time and speed, so the bump, when it came, would be gentler. The chasing boat appeared to loom over them now, while they were still accelerating with only seven rowers; it was just a matter of where they would touch to get the bump. The pursuer gained another half-metre and the projecting bow was ready to touch their trailing stern. 'Steer to port! Now! Turn left!' Rhan yelled as she lifted her blade from the water and shot up the slide. Shrimpy pulled the string that yanked over the rudder. The swerve gave them a few more seconds, but it also slowed them down. There was now an overlap of more than a metre between the two boats and their bow was aiming at Rhan's oar. Rhan noticed that their prow was dancing and twisting erratically as their crew failed to balance their boat. They were rubbish; they didn't deserve a bump. She did not want George to witness this.

'Pull!' screamed Shrimpy. She hardly had to turn around now to see the prow of the chasing eight; it was almost in front and to the side of her. It stayed there, moving backwards and forwards as the two boats made strokes.

'Pull!' The overlap reduced, but it would still be easy for the other boat to achieve its bump. All it had to do was make any contact anywhere.

'Pull!' It was impossible not to watch the dirty white plastic bobble on the end of the chasing boat. It was so close to Rhan's oar that she watched in horror to see if she had the space to complete her stroke. This was like the dodgeball she played in the yard up in Sunderland. She would have to cut her stroke to avoid contact, but they would lose speed again and it would break the rhythm for the crew who were following her every movement. She pulled her blade out slightly earlier than normal, leaving it hovering before sweeping it back out of the contact area. It had not yet touched. She raced back up the slide, reaching forward to dip her oar into the water as far as she could, safe from their touch.

'You shall not pass!' Rhan shouted out dramatically for George's entertainment as she straightened her back and pulled on the oar, noting that the rest of the crew had managed to keep up with her erratic stroking. Their eight was powered by only seven rowers, but they still managed to keep the balance that allowed them to make their strokes count. The boat leaped forward again to the extent that she could this time complete her stroke, clear of the chasing bow. They were getting away. The chasing white bobble was now dancing backwards as the Gloucester boat started to escape, but there was still an overlap.

'Pull!' came the repeated call, echoing in Rhan's head. In another part of her brain, she vaguely noted frantic cries from the bank, with George's shouts of, 'You've almost done it!' She refused to lose in front of him. The overlap of the two boats had reduced still further.

'Pull!' The chasing boat gave up trying to touch Rhan's oar and started to swing over, trying again to make contact with the projecting stern. Shrimpy turned to watch, no longer shouting, but staring in silence.

'Go, Gloucester!' It was Nick's voice again exhorting one last effort from the crew, who could then only watch, even as they completed their stroke and pulled their oars clear of the water. The plastic bobble on the prow of the chasing boat started to swing across and was within the arc of their stern; they would touch and the chasing boat would gain their bump. The Gloucester crew all came up their slides for the next stroke. Their backward momentum of the rowers moving up their seat slides made the rest of the boat suddenly leap forward, allowing the plastic prow of the chasing boat to miss the bump by a hand's width. The Gloucester crew reached the end of the slide and the boats had an overlap again. The next stroke from the seven oarsmen, however, pulled them clear. They were definitely escaping.

Shrimpy immediately lost interest in the boat behind. She was now concentrating on what was ahead.

'Keep going!' she called in a strangled voice. Three strokes later, Rhan watched in disbelief as Shrimpy raised her arm uncertainly. 'OK, ease the oars! Now hold both sides. Brake hard!' Shrimpy ordered, and the whole crew brought their boat to a sudden stop in a manner they had never practised.

'But they missed us!' Rhan panted, totally bewildered. She had continued to row and had only eased off as she felt the rest of the crew no longer following her and holding, as they had been instructed. Rhan, utterly shattered from the brief but frantic efforts, slumped over her oar and continued to watch the drama developing behind the boat, while she regained her breath. They were now an easy target again with Rhan's oar about to be touched.

Shrimpy ignored her. 'Ship your oars stroke side, quick! Let this boat through.'

Gaining strength with each gasp of air, but still confused, Rhan started to pull her oar in, but too late. Two oars from the boat behind hit her blade, just as they'd been trying to do over the past few minutes. Yet their pursuer was now swerving to avoid contact, and the obstructed oars were trying to row again, not slowing down. Their cox didn't look happy, but Shrimpy was now smiling with self-satisfaction. 'Well done! That was bloody magnificent!'

A second boat behind them now came steaming past.

'What happened?' gasped Rhan to the cox, who was peering ahead again.

'Well we bumped the boat in front of us of course. And now…our pursuers have been bumped. Fun eh?'

'You didn't tell us we were about to bump! We had no idea,' Elizabeth complained. 'We thought we were being bumped!'

'Well, you nearly bumped the boat in front straight away at the start. It was too exciting and you screwed up, nearly losing everything to the boat behind. In the meantime, the three boats ahead were caught in a pile-up, so this time I just let you row into the bump while they were trying to escape.'

Rhan twisted round on her seat to look at Anna and the girls behind her, who were smiling or shaking their heads in disbelief.

'What happened to Jenny?' Rhan asked.

'Her seat jammed,' Sarah explained from further up the

boat. 'And she then caught a massive crab that almost lifted her out of the boat. The seat stayed stuck on the slide, so she just moved to allow the rest of us to do all the work.' There was shrieking as a water fight developed.

'That was both awful and impressive!' Nick complained, standing on the bank just above them in the quiet after the storm. 'I could've done without it, before my own race. Now get yourselves free of the dog fight and get back to the boathouse. And Bar, I thought you were going to break yet another oar – you nearly bent it double!'

George, standing next to Nick again, laughed happily, enjoying Rhan's praise. Even so, Rhan noted his puzzled stare, as if he were trying to make sense of all this information about the friend he thought he knew so well.

'Who was that fit guy next to Nick?' Elizabeth asked as they languidly rowed back up the river to the boathouses. Rhan made no response.

Day Three

The third day, Friday, was almost fun. Their cox, Shrimpy, had confidence in their superiority and even avoided making an early bump, just so that they could chase the boats further up the league and gain a double bump.

To Rhan, there was little significance in how far they progressed, but she was starting to enjoy not only the races, but also the social life. This entailed drinking Pimms on the roof of the Gloucester boathouse, followed by further drinks at her own boathouse where she joined George and other college friends, who came down to watch the later top women and the men's races.

Annie had met them on the second afternoon and she and George continued to get on well. Annie reported quietly to Rhan that her college porters seem to report "Bar's" every visit. A handful of the top women rowers from all years, who had never even glanced at Annie before, were now keen to sit next to her at breakfast to discuss their mutual friend. Annie was finding she was no longer a total outsider.

'Well you can repay the favour,' Rhan had suggested. 'Come and meet my family next holidays, and tell them I am not a total recluse.'

~

With one more day to go, Rhan's boat lay second in the fourth division. If they could bump the first boat, they had the prospect of moving into the next division, as sandwich boat again. The atmosphere at Gloucester Hall was, therefore, exuberant. Claire and the crew in the Gloucester Hall Women's First Eight were gradually going up the third division, and Nick's Men's First Eight were doing remarkably well for a small hall.

Drinking at her own boathouse required a more fatalistic perspective. None of her college boats were doing well. There was understandably much less interest in the divisions and the position of the College Eights on a day-to-day basis.

Although it was not widely discussed, Alice's boat had been bumped two or three times and they were rapidly descending the second division. The men's second boat was having mixed results, but the men's first boat was struggling to retain its position in the lower reaches of the first division.

Rhan hardly knew the men's college captain, Richard, and was surprised when he came up to their group; they were standing around drinking when he addressed Rhan directly for the first time.

'How are George and the rugby crew getting on? Do they listen to you?'

'Rhan runs a very tight ship. Everyone's terrified of her!' George intervened on her behalf.

'They are coming on fine,' Rhan took over, with a look at George that told him not to fight her corner. 'They moved into a shell last week and are now fully adjusted. Even after spending the winter running around a square of grass after a distorted ball, it can be seen that there is some really useful power in the boat, which you might want to inspect. I'm afraid there are still a few useless novices who need to be whipped into shape by the Summer Eights!'

There were yells of condemnation and appreciation from the group, especially from Danny and George. The noise spread across the roof as the conversation was relayed to other members of the rugby rowing squad. Richard smiled and then continued his conversation with Rhan more quietly so that fewer could hear.

'It's not right that the rugby crews had so little coaching over the past few weeks, other than from you. After Torpids, I'll see if I can get some tuition from someone in the First Eight or perhaps the exam schools' crew. The schools' crew is where much of the experience lies, but they are very precious with their time in the run-up to exams. If they can't help, perhaps someone from the Second Eight or the Women's Eight could give some advice.'

'Well I think I can manage,' Rhan suggested. 'There are other places where people can pick up rowing skills – other than through the college, you know.' Rhan felt herself turn red at what she was saying.

'Oh yes, I was sorry to hear that your trial to row for the college went poorly. You row for a Novice Eight in another college, don't you? Good idea. We need to resurrect our own Women's Second Eight.'

'I am obviously not ideal as a cox, but I have had excellent coaching myself.' Rhan was both amused at her situation and fuming at the same time. She wondered why she was arguing.

'Yes, thank you for standing, or should I say, sitting in,' Richard said. 'I am at least aware that the Rugby Eight need to find a lightweight cox, as well as a coach. Actually, the college is ridiculously short of experienced coxes, which is one of the reasons I wanted to speak to you. Is there any chance you could help out next week with the Schools' Eight on the Tuesday and the Second Eight on Thursday? I'm trying to get them out every day next week to prepare for the summer, and it only takes an awkward science practical or something, and we are in trouble.'

Rhan did not want to continue the conversation. At the same time, she was conscious that after Saturday and her last day of Torpids with Gloucester Hall, she had no further rowing commitments until university rowing camp at the end of term. She simply nodded to the extra coxing, allowing Richard to walk away, his mission accomplished.

After a few drinks, George reported with great authority the growing concerns that Richard had over the college

Men's First Eight. Richard had been known to drink with the rugby squad following their conversion to water sports.

'The men's first boat might keep their place or drop a position or two in this week's Torpids,' George explained. 'Yet they could drop like a stone in the Summer Eights. You see, other first-division crews will be strengthened in the summer by extra rowers from the university squad after the Boat Race. Our college has no first-class rowers to add strength in either the men's or the women's.'

'Ah, so that's why he wants to train us up!' Simon from the rugby boat suggested, to laughs all round.

'We hold a high position in the men's top division,' George continued. 'But we've not won Head of the River for around a century. Richard's scared he's going to get bumped right down to the second division in his year as captain.'

'I've 'eard Richard's got funds to employ a high-flying professional coach who'll help all boats, but especially Richard's boat,' Danny reported. Rhan knew Danny had joined a college committee that controlled college budgets.

'They need help. They could do as badly as the ladies have done this week. And God help the Women's Eight next term if they're in trouble this week,' Simon suggested quietly.

'The women's crew obviously needed your help after all, Rhan!' George suggested. After three days of watching her, Rhan knew he was probing the ground. However, with the condescending looks around the group, Rhan saw the opportunity to wrap truth in obscurity and irony in sarcasm.

'Well, I thought of insisting that they accept my extraordinary talent. There would be difficulties to be overcome to balance the force from my stroke and that would entail reconfiguring the rigging for most of the boat, and the college would go bust with the cost of all the snapped oars on each outing. I am also afraid that rowing with the first team may affect my style and might jeopardise my chances of stroking the Blue boat against Cambridge next year.'

Everyone laughed politely. But George looked on with a puzzled expression, no longer knowing what to make of his partner.

'Besides,' Rhan concluded to laughter that was now much more raucous, 'Why would any real sportswoman want any position other than cox to the Rugby Eight?' This initiated more opportunity for the full-time oarsmen to rant against muscle-bound rugby players who thought that they could row, and vice-versa.

'I don't understand,' George murmured to Rhan a bit later. 'Why didn't you want me to tell them how good you are?'

'It's complicated,' Rhan replied. 'Every new opportunity looks worse than where I am now, if that makes sense.'

'I can see your point,' he conceded.

~

The arrival of David provided a welcome respite from all the expert rowers and spectators. However, his first question was, 'George tells me you're rowing for another college, as well as coaching those fine specimens from the rugger buggers. How's that?'

Rhan was still feeling far from charitable towards her college. 'Well, after assessing my talents, Alice readily agreed to my free transfer to a new Gloucester second crew for Torpids. The trouble is, I don't think that option will be possible for Summer Eights.'

'So I hope it's going well with your alien team?' David asked politely. 'I don't really understand how these races work, but I get the feeling that our own college is not doing too well, especially with the women. Is that right?'

'I am afraid so,' Rhan confirmed. 'Alice's crew started high and I think they may have dropped almost a division. Whereas my alien college novice crew, as you call it, had to qualify with time trials and started in the bottom-fifth division, and I think we are now close to the top of the fourth division. It is all very petty really, but it can be very intense when you are down there on the water,' Rhan explained.

'So we need to look out for you and cheer you on tomorrow – if no one else is leaping up divisions.'

'That would be kind, but don't hold your breath. Most boats in the lower divisions bump or are bumped very quickly, so don't row up as far as the boathouses. Besides, if you start drinking with the early races, you will be too cross-eyed to see the major action later.'

'Sounds good to me,' David joked as he headed off to the bar.

Day Four

There was no chance of doing useful coursework on Saturday, the last day of Torpids. There was a party atmosphere in college after an exciting final men's race on the previous evening when Richard's boat just managed to escape over the finishing line, hotly pursued by the boat behind.

Rhan was relaxed about the last day. Her crew had nothing more to prove. She sat at her computer and yet again searched for the paper on climate change, written by the rector of the college and presented to some Royal Academy. The rector was an eminent economic journalist who had generally argued for tackling global warming, so Rhan was keen to see what she had actually said, if that was now the basis of her college's justification to ignore the issue. This time, Rhan found the paper.

As she read, Rhan became hot and bothered. Her rector had effectively told leading scientists and engineers that the laws of economics needed to take precedence over taking drastic measures to prevent climate change. The economist had asserted that there would be time later to come up with fixes to the planet and that science would find a way somehow. She suggested that the most important consideration was to keep the economy in good health.

Rhan looked back at the date – it must have been just a few months before the 2008 financial collapse and the years of reduced carbon emissions. So no logic there! It appeared that the economic argument for doing nothing had gone down well with the majority of scientists and engineers. Yet how many people would die because of that policy? The college was clearly proud of the output, as it had reproduced the paper in its alumni magazine. The rector, on the other hand, had gone on to write a book on the need to tackle global warming. Rhan had only seen one paper and just snippets of other papers, and she had not read the book, so she was in the dark and confused. Nevertheless, no matter what else was stated subsequently, it was clear that it was the "do nothing" advice that had been taken to heart.

Rhan was still seething a couple of hours later as she was getting changed into her Gloucester strip for the last time. She went through the motions in a complete daze, but as she left the college, she noticed Alice and her crew gathering on the hall steps.

'Good luck!' she called to them, but they paid her little attention.

After a few seconds, however, Tom's friend Fiona called back, 'Thanks Rhan!'

As Rhan jogged down to the river, she barely registered the warmth in the spring sunshine. After so many months of running through a stark wasteland, the meadows were showing green buds on the hawthorn, and furry catkins on the willows. She was thinking much more about how spring would change as the earth was roasted alive by apathy, instead of concentrating on the race to come. Her musings were interrupted when she came across a large contingent from her own college ambling down and carrying last-minute additions for an afternoon of partying.

'Hi Anthony,' she breathed, stopping beside one of the rugby crew.

'Rhan, good to see you!' Anthony whirled round in surprise at being addressed by Rhan for the first time out of her role as cox. 'So you row as well?' he added, noticing her tracksuit.

'Yes, this will be my last row with a Novice Eight in another college. It will be sad, as they are a good bunch. Can I ask you a question, Anthony? I believe you are a physics post-grad?'

He was a few years older, and looked it. His broad shoulders, however, were more impressive in the scrum than in a rowing Eight. As Number 4, he provided a good share of the power, but his movements tended to upset the balance of the whole boat.

'Yes, I'm testing wiring for spacecraft and especially for the Martian landings. You're an engineer, is that right? Much of what I do could be considered engineering, if it was crashing onto the earth rather than Mars.'

Rhan smiled and nodded. 'Can I ask you about global warming? How much have you looked into it?' There was a brief pause before he replied.

'My family doesn't believe in anthropological climate change. I'm sure it's not mankind's responsibility.'

'But as a physicist you must have looked at the effect of greenhouse gases and the net solar gain we currently have? Don't you believe in the greenhouse effect at all?'

'Look, I don't see such things as being our concern. If the world does happen to be doomed, then it's God's will and it would be wrong to interfere. So I stay well clear of politics, both at departmental and national level. However, I think it's disgusting that some departments here get so much money, just by going along with the pretence of fighting nature. There are whole departments wasting money that could be spent on useful research rather than chasing icebergs.'

'Oh!' Rhan stuttered. 'That is a really interesting perspective,' she forced the words out. 'I...I have to run. Thanks for that. Bye!'

~

Even as her crew once again lowered the boat into the water, her mind was still fixed on denial, passive acceptance and active avoidance of climate obligations. The reality of the race only partially returned as the boat was manoeuvred against the bank into the starting position with the help of the boatman. Nick was giving them last-minute instructions, yet George was missing.

'Take it easy again this time. One more bump and you'll have a chance to row in the next division. I've watched the boat ahead and they are very vulnerable, so don't mess around, Shrimpy, but don't rush the bump. And...'

The explosion of the starting gun came as a shock once more, and Rhan was jerking backwards before she realised that the race had really begun. She belatedly started to concentrate on rowing.

Think. Stroke. My legs feel like jelly. Take it easy. Blade out, clear of the choppy surface. Ignore the shouting and screaming. Listen out for anything unusual from the cox. Slide, catch, pull. Take it easy. Everyone is following me, so be calm. Alice will not give me permission next term, so this could be my last row with this Gloucester crew. So relax and enjoy.

'Three! Four! Five!' yelled the cox. They were halfway through ten firm, hard strokes and were doing well. Rhan lifted her head and looked over the cox's head to confirm that the boat behind was still not catching them. She caught sight of George, running along the bank behind, shouting support that she could not hear.

'Six!' All they had to do was catch the boat in front and they would be in the third division. George was there; she only had to row.

'Seven!' Shrimpy shouted.

We will be into the normal strokes soon, Rhan planned in her head. *Keep them calm and deliberate – give the crew an easy lead, so the slides don't jamb again.*

'Eight!'

Pull up, slide, straighten the legs, pull. The muscles started to hurt, but that was ridiculous – they had only just started. Rhan had great pride in her strength; now stamina and fitness were needed. She was not going to mess it up in front of George on the towpath above.

'Nine! Come on, pull, last one!' promised the cox. 'Then it'll be easier. We're already ahead and are leaving the trailing boat well behind.'

A few moments later, Shrimpy changed her mind and yelled, 'Ten! We only need five more good strokes and you are there! Don't ease off. One!'

Could she be right? Rhan pondered, while doing as she was told on the effort but reducing the rate of strokes. She knew that they had put effort into the first ten strokes, and asking for more was dangerous. She couldn't believe that the boat ahead was within reach so soon.

'Two! Three! Keep going! Three more!'

Rhan could hear screaming from behind and from the bank ahead. She noticed that they were now rowing through very choppy and disturbed water, so the boat was close ahead.

'Four!' Shrimpy's hand shot up. 'Hold hard!'

Rhan was digging her oar into the water and was pushing instead of pulling to apply the brakes. She felt slightly cheated, sitting in the rear of the boat facing down the river; she had missed the excitement of catching the boat ahead. Now it was all over – they had made a bump. The bow pair took a couple of strokes, which tucked the boat against the bank so that the race could continue around them. It was marvellous sitting and watching as the other boats raced past.

'Well done Gloucester Hall!' Nick's familiar voice came down from the embankment above. You did what you came for. You'll have to hang around for ten minutes and race again. You're in the same division as the Gloucester First so I won't see you at the start, but good luck.' He was gone and would not be coming back.

They hung around waiting and chatting awkwardly over their shoulders about the ease of their success and the surprise at leaping up a whole division. George stood some way off. Rhan wondered whether he and Nick had exchanged a word.

Before they turned around and headed back to the start at the bottom of the next division, some of the new competition rowed past them. Elizabeth led a big cheer for the Gloucester main boat, who had clearly not expected to see them, but were delighted once they realised the significance of the second boat still being on the river.

'Go Claire!' Rhan called out.

'Well done! See! You didn't need me!' Claire called back.

Glancing at the next boat, Rhan dropped her head as the gaudy colours of her own college flashed on the ends of the dipping blades, wielded by her college contemporaries with Alice in the bow. She braced herself, expecting Alice's annoying and patronising remarks. But with other things on their minds, none of the crew noticed her. Rhan had taken no great interest in the divisions and had not realised that this league was so interesting – things were getting awkward.

Instructions from the cox soon saw the boat gently spin around, and it was their turn to glide past all the other boats to the bottom position in the starting grid. The first boat they passed was from Rhan's own college, but the crew were busy reversing into their position at the head of the division so no one even glanced at Rhan. Their position as top boat, however, indicated that they must have dropped out of the second division the day before.

A few boats further down, there was a great cheer from their fellow Gloucester boat who were all set up and ready. Claire's voice could be heard again.

'See you at the finishing line Gloucester Two! Don't bump us!'

At last, they reached bottom position and turned into their slot against the bank at the downstream end of the division. It felt relatively stress-free having no boat behind them at the start; as bottom boat they were no one's target.

As they waited, it was pleasant not to be frightened. They all felt relaxed after their victory. There were no cheering fans, there was no Nick giving them last-minute instructions. They chatted about how much they had achieved already that week, climbing from fifth to third division. The celebratory bumps dinner that the college owed them was the major topic of conversation. There were also quiet whispers about their "fit" guardian angel, who yet again hovered in the background, watching them silently.

Without the advice and pep talk from Nick, the start felt like a rather sluggish affair compared with their previous frantic thrashes and without someone steaming up behind them. There was no great impetus in the first ten strokes. For the crew looking down the river as they rowed, it was rather a surreal experience. There was little real indication that they were in a race apart from isolated boatmen spaced along the bank with their long poles, looking upriver after their racing boats in the manner of pigeon fanciers. After a hundred metres or so, they had still not reached any competing boats. It was several minutes of steady rowing before they swung wide into the river to try and pass a couple of eights with tangled oars, and either sobbing or exuberant girls.

'Gangway!' shouted Shrimpy angrily as none of them had felt at all inclined to tidy up the waterway for the tail-end boat. 'Slow rowing, Gloucester!' she ordered. They ended up having to almost stop and it seemed to take ages before they were underway, relieved yet again that there was no boat behind to bump them as they waited.

They passed two more pairs, who were slowly heading back to base, but it was clear that in this higher division, boats had to work much harder for their bumps. There were cheers ahead and the shouts were for Gloucester.

'Well done!' Rhan heard both Jenny and Elizabeth shout back breathlessly. Rhan was the last one in her boat to be able to see the Gloucester First boat, well entrenched into the tail of another boat.

'Enjoy your last row together!' Claire's voice rang out yet again. 'That looks great!'

Elizabeth caught up the theme and called out, 'Yes, this is our last row together. Come on, let's show them! We've been the best. Let's show how we can race the whole course in style.'

The balance was true, the strokes were smooth; it was delightful – a real controlled effort. Rhan could switch into semi-trance and let half her mind wander to other subjects, leaving the cox to take charge and mark the timing.

'Pull!'

It was so strange that anyone could suggest that global warming was not urgent, if it meant almost certain conflict and misery to come.

'Pull!'

The Establishment was effectively going to ridiculous and illogical lengths to ensure that there was no safe path to a low-carbon future. Why did leaders feel empowered to be so reckless?

'Pull! Right up!'

The stupid, brash and dangerous assumptions would utterly shock the next generation.

'Pull! Balance up and continue with the stroke!'

Yet it would soon be too late. The future was looking pretty fixed already.

'Pull!'

She took her anger out on the water, forcing it away. Those with an interest in the future would have absolutely no chance to recapture all the carbon dioxide that was being released now, never mind from the last year, the last decade or the last century.

'Pull!'

George knew all this. He was prepared to see nothing done. He had, however, made the effort to come down each day to support her. He was following them on his bike somewhere.

'Pull!'

She smiled, slightly annoyed that she had eased up on the last stroke.

'Pull!'

That was better. The others seemed to be coping. She checked the stroke side, glancing over her shoulder.

'Pull!'

Not all strokes were the same length, but still.

'Pull!'

She checked the bow side, throwing just a slight glance for fear of perturbing the precious balance.

'Pull!'

There is no way that she could ignore climate change. That was obviously the reason why God had chosen her to escape the vast number of continuous snares that could have befallen a girl from Aleppo.

'Pull!'

It explained how she had passed the entrance into Oxford when so many better students had failed.

'Pull!'

It is up to me.

They passed more pairs of boats who had rowed almost half the course before getting their bump. Some crews just lay there, clearly exhausted, but others were slowly returning to the boathouses. A familiar voice in a strangely subdued tone cut through the afternoon's exercise.

'Gloucester Hall Two, I have some news for you!'

There on the steep bank on the inside of a sharp bend was Nick on his bike – popping up when they least expected him, yet again. He was talking to their crew in the water and they could tell by his manner that there was something exciting about his behaviour.

'There's another eight just around the corner. They don't know you're on their tail, so no shouting Shrimpy! They're a long way ahead, but they were forced to sprint up here and are shattered, while you are rowing beautifully.' He was pedalling slowly to keep up with their progress up the river.

'The other news is that there are VIPs waiting to watch you row from our clubhouse. Give them something worth watching – a bump right in front of the boathouse!'

Rhan knew straight away that the remaining eight must be her own college. They had done well to escape being bumped. Nevertheless, they were doomed. The hunt was on.

'Power ten?' the cox asked Rhan quietly.

'No! Check our strength first. We must have a kilometre or so to go.'

'Plenty of time Gloucester – just pick it up slightly!' Nick endorsed the policy without having heard what Rhan had just said.

'Anyone struggling? Just shake your head if you don't want to up the pace yet!' The cox asked.

'Go for it!' Suzie called.

'Yeah!' several voices responded.

Rhan actually slowed the pace slightly, and exaggerated the care in each stroke, while she extended the reach and pulled up with extra leg power. In that manner, each rower could contribute what she could. The boat felt as though it was shooting forward. Rhan now thought of little else but her technique, the strokes, the capacity of the crew, how fast Alice and her crew could manage once the chase started and where they would bump. A bit of her mind was, however, wondering whether the college rector might be watching this last day. It also crossed her mind to show George what they could do, although he would hardly be happy about her bumping her own college.

'Let's go for it!' Rhan told the cox. 'Don't worry any more about them seeing us...just go for the best course.'

They now had quite a few followers running along the towpath. Nick had been joined by the ever-present George and then by others from Gloucester, who had previously been supporting their First Eight. Viewed across the flood plain, supporters of the boat ahead would now be informing their crew. Down in the river Alice and crew would see nothing beyond the twists of the river bank, so news that they were being pursued and had yet another race to run would be a harsh blow. Meanwhile, Nick was growing hoarse with excitement.

'OK. This is it, the big moment. Just follow the stroke. Keep to that rate, gradually picking it up. They'll panic when they see us flying along. If so, we'll have them. If they don't panic then we'll catch them right in front of the boathouse. Now start picking up the power! Pull! – Pull! – Pull!'

Rhan did not change the pace, but Nick's encouragement improved the power for a short while. Ahead of them, they could now hear a speaker, presumably announcing the arrival of the first boat, now in sight of the boathouses. A few minutes later there was more noise, which she guessed meant that the Gloucester boat was also now visible to the nearer boathouses as they came clear of the meandering "gut" section of the river. The spectators would not appreciate the relative speeds of the boats, but Rhan could imagine the horror in the leading boat to find that they were being pursued, with still several hundred metres to go. They could also hear, from closer to hand over the water, the sounds of a screaming cox, driving her crew to power strokes. The noise of support grew. It was the Saturday of Torpids and this was the first race to reach the boathouses for the well-oiled tongues to give vent.

She could now make out the sound from the loudspeakers. It was indistinct, but was clearly trying to build up excitement as the commentator realised there was going to be a real race to the finish. On the other hand, words of encouragement and advice could no longer be heard from Nick and other supporters on the towpath, which was now some distance away on the wider, almost straight reach of the river past the boathouses to the finishing line.

Rhan was suffering, and ruefully wishing that she had selected an easier sport. She was exhausted and it was getting harder to row, as the balance of the boat was becoming erratic. Her breath was tight and her wrists were suffering from the constant pulling and twisting. Sometimes she had to fight to get her oar clear of the water as the boat lurched over. She looked at the whirlpool puddles left by the blades of the rowers. There were only two or three of any size: hers on the stroke side and Suzie with Elisha on the bow side. Suzie had proved a great replacement for Claire at Number 7, although she was as shy and self-effacing as Claire was ebullient.

'Stay with me, Suzie,' Rhan yelled. 'That…is…brilliant… rowing!'

'Thanks.' The words came back from behind her and Rhan had the satisfaction of seeing the size of Suzie's pool increase significantly for a while.

The boat continued to rock, and Rhan knew that even her own rowing was becoming scraggy. 'Concentrate!' Rhan instructed the cox. 'Don't mess up now!'

Shrimpy could see the problem and relayed the message. They had set too high a target. Rhan could not even hear the boat ahead; they must still have a good lead.

'Slowing! It's too much!' Rhan called out to the cox, who nodded and took action.

'Keep control and slow the pace. They are now just thirty metres ahead, so no hurry. Just take your time; we've got two hundred metres past the boathouses to the finish line, so we'll get them at some point. They're wrecked. Just keep going, we'll get them...I think we're still gaining, even after we slowed. They're completely done in.'

'Shorten the strokes...but pull through...balance the boat at all costs,' Rhan gasped at Shrimpy, who willingly passed on the message.

The boat became stable again, but it had also slowed down. Yet Rhan could now see rough water to their port side; they were still gaining on their prey.

The gap stopped closing as they passed Rhan's college boathouse. Rhan did not look over, but she could imagine her friends going mad to encourage the girls to their first victory of the week. They were so near the finish line. Just a few more good strokes and they would be safe.

A short distance later, the dynamics reverted to Gloucester's favour, as they could now distinctly hear the Gloucester Hall boathouse on the other side of the river, closer to the course that Shrimpy was steering. The sound provided the boost that the tired crew needed. The whirlpools increased in size again and the boat took off. Rhan shook her head, amused that Nick had understood the race so correctly.

'Come on Bar!' Rhan heard a familiar and commanding voice boom across the water from the Gloucester boathouse. She sprang erect in surprise, instantly recognising the voice of Dumas. She straightened her shoulders, sat up and used her legs to spring down the slide on the next stroke, full of energy. She had no idea that the male university president had such a loud voice. It was very compelling.

Now listening, a few strokes later, Rhan could hear the even more familiar voice of Roger, who had exhorted Rhan so many times before from the riverbank. Despite her dire need for concentration, she could not resist looking towards the home boathouse, close at hand. There was a mass of people shouting and waving on the crowded balcony of the Gloucester Hall roof, yet there was a group of figures who had been given their own space. She spotted the tall, recognisable figure of Roger wearing his usual flat cap, and the broad shoulders of Dumas, beside him. In front of them leaning over the rail was Esther, and others she could not recognise.

'Pull!'

Why were they there? Rhan wondered.

Her eyes welled with tears of gratitude; three people she so respected were in the boathouse, shouting for her. She shook her head again, the only part of her body not rigidly locked into powering the boat. She had been told all she needed to know by Nick – all she needed to do was concentrate on clean, strong strokes. With all their friends watching, the rest of the boat followed her crisp movements.

Rowing was easy again. Rhan could feel real force being applied to the water from the rest of the crew. Rhan concentrated on improving the strokes rather than increasing the rate; they were almost back to exhibition rowing. Shrimpy, however, did not look altogether satisfied with their improved performance; she was peering ahead anxiously. Rhan watched her, wondering what it meant. After just a few more strokes, she found out.

'OK, half pace!' the cox announced in a cool voice. 'Slow rowing for the bump please! Steady – they've conceded. We're finished here. Just hold the oars clear of the water! Sit up straight and balance. Sit up, 3! Let's finish with style.'

CHAPTER TWENTY

Endings and Beginnings

'Three cheers for that boat!' Elizabeth, their boat captain called, not interested in its identity, while Shrimpy used their momentum along with the river current to turn away, towards their boathouse. Rhan hated Shrimpy for not allowing them to collapse or release their oars; she just wanted to flop. Yet with so many people watching, and anxious to get away, Rhan made do with wiping the sweat from her eyes as they left the defeated boat. Without having to turn her head, Rhan could now look back to see the utter exhaustion of her crushed college adversaries, many now crying and with no interest in her or anyone but themselves. The race had been far too personal and Rhan's conflicting emotions quickly subsided, leaving no elation at crushing her own college. The rest of her boat were recovered sufficiently to congratulate themselves on their achievement. She only felt relief that she had not been recognised by Alice and her crew.

Rhan looked across at her own boathouse and wondered how long it would be before Alice and her crew discovered the dire implications of being bumped by the sandwich boat from the bottom of the division. In a wave of anguish, it occurred to Rhan that next year, she would probably make the women's boat and be involved in the long, slow climb to recover from that drastic fall.

In just a few well-executed strokes, they glided towards their landing pontoon in front of an exuberant Gloucester Hall crowd. The hall's Women's First Eight had followed them up the river after their own bump, so both boats arrived together from opposite directions, amid much shouting and screaming at the exciting double victory.

As the crews climbed out of the boats, Rhan was forced to concentrate on the celebrations that she needed to enjoy. Nick arrived wearing bicycle clips and was almost thrown into the river, until he pleaded that he soon had a race to row himself. He gave all the girls a quick congratulatory hug, but the hug with Rhan was accompanied with a loud 'Ooo!' from her teasing crewmates, much to everyone's amusement. George was standing slightly to the side of the boathouse with a group of tourists, unnoticed by all but Rhan. While the crews returned their oars, Rhan slipped off, slightly unsteady on her feet after the two consecutive races and grasped him gratefully around the chest.

'Having you there each day has been great, partner. Thanks for coming,' she said stiffly, but then added a more personal touch. 'I am so glad that we are meeting up in the holidays,' she confided and had the satisfaction of feeling him hugging her back, while he affectionately and repeatedly kissed her forehead.

'Rhan! Where are you? Everyone's waiting,' a girl's voice came from above.

'Oh God, I'm hardly presentable.' Rhan pulled away from George, suddenly self-conscious as she wiped beads of sweat off her head and adjusted her outfit.

Here, quick, use my handkerchief and you can borrow this top.' Rhan knew that he would need his warm jersey as soon as he stopped moving, but it didn't stop her accepting his offer.

'That was Claire who was calling. She will be with me at rowing camp next weekend – she's also coming to tea to meet you on Tuesday, so I will have to buy some extra mugs and stuff.' She watched the expected disappointment spread across his face.

'Well we can keep the single set for the maths tutorial day lunches, if you like – now go!' she ordered.

He looked at her closely, laughed, and walked away smiling, but then called back, 'Enjoy the celebrations! You deserve them.'

She raced up the stairs to join the last of the rowers. There were catcalls and the sound of clapping from above as the two crews entered the bar ahead of her. She was glad to be wearing George's comforting jersey. It crossed her mind that she appeared to have remarkable control over his happiness.

The clapping had almost died down as Rhan entered, slightly late. To most in the room, she was one of the unknown strangers, borrowed from another college to make up the numbers, but the onlookers were soon asking about the identity of the tall, imposing girl who was attracting so much attention.

'Where were you?' exclaimed Claire as she gave Rhan a hug. 'I can't believe what you lot did! You completely leapt over us in the tables!'

'Well you should have stayed with us, Claire,' Rhan responded, smiling broadly. 'We were taking the express lift to the top.'

'Well you've really messed it up for Claire, if she's captain of boats next year.' Nick came over from the balcony to grab Rhan. 'A Hall Second Eight, which is half a division above the Hall's First Eight – it's ridiculous for a college with so few girls! Anyway, that's next year's problem. Right now you have guests who've been waiting for you.' He ushered her to the balcony position that Rhan had previously spotted from the river.

'Whey hey! We have royalty here!' Claire declared, spotting the guests for the first time and waving a half-empty bottle of lager around. 'Two presidents and a university coach! We are honoured.'

Esther gave Claire a hug and congratulated her on the bump. Claire insisted on hugging Roger, but then she glanced around her friends to whip up enthusiasm as she presented herself for a hug from Dumas, to another chorus of 'Ooo!' from the thirty of forty watching spectators and crews. The rest of the party smiled indulgently, but then almost ignored her, so Claire theatrically bit her lip without actually looking at all abashed before heading back to her friends. Nick guided Rhan forward and spectator interest in the guests rapidly dropped.

'This is such a surprise. What are you doing here? How are the university crews shaping up?' Rhan unashamedly fell into the arms of Roger, then Dumas and then Esther. Rhan noticed Esther's friendly smile, which contrasted to the almost aloof attitude at the cocktail party the previous week in front of other members of her crew. The change confirmed Rhan's expectation that Esther still needed to dissociate herself from accusations that Rhan, or Bar, had helped her excessively at the seat trials.

'Extremely well, thanks to you,' Esther murmured meaningfully.

'Yes, very well,' echoed Dumas.

Roger started speaking for them as soon as the hugging abated. 'We came to see you after the last race, but as sandwich boat, you failed to come in. Fortunately, and despite our schedule, we took notice of the text from Nick, which promised an exciting finish in the second race and hung around to witness that bump right in front of us. Ted, this is Bar. Bar, this is Ted Scott from the Sports Faculty.' Rhan shook hands with the middle-aged man who had the build of a rower, and who carried a camcorder and a laptop bag.

'Bar, did we really just see your crew bump the top boat in the third division, after starting from the bottom position as sandwich boat?' asked Esther, laughing. 'You had presumably just bumped the top boat in the fourth division in the previous race just half an hour ago?' Rhan nodded a couple of times, smiling sheepishly, aware that Esther probably knew the score. 'That is mad! No boat ever climbs like that. It must be a record,' Esther suggested.

'I'm not sure if I should mention this, Bar, but was that your own college First team that you just bumped?' Dumas asked in a more pompous manner. Rhan sighed and nodded again while shrugging with her arms, indicating that it was true, but unfortunate.

'OMG!' Claire exclaimed dramatically from behind them, with her hand over her mouth. 'That was your college First you just bumped!' she dashed off to tell Elizabeth and the others.

'That's not meant to happen.' Dumas seemed to be following Esther in an attempt to build up Rhan's achievement. 'Novices hardly leave the fifth division, never mind climb to the top of the third. Nick obviously deserves full credit for coaching and for recognising talent.' Nick said nothing but nodded his appreciation. Rhan was pleased to note that the two presidents seemed to be acting in unity, but still wondered what they all wanted.

'Actually, Ted,' Roger chipped in. 'Going back to that discussion over Bar's very short experience, she has rowed in challenging conditions but I don't think she's had any experience at anything other than winning. That may be just luck, because outwardly she appears extremely uncompetitive. However, after just six months from picking up a blade, Bar and Esther put almost a whole crew of international rowers in their place, so I'm not sure it is luck. She has much to learn, but she certainly matches your specification as a rising star.'

The stranger finally addressed Rhan himself. 'An impressive start to your career, young lady! I've heard that you specialise in rough-water rowing, which is hardly my thing, yet after the Rio sinking, the weather can clearly make fools of the most ardent favourites. However, I've just reviewed my footage…' Ted paused to indicate his camera rather pompously. 'It confirms that I have just seen you dragging an eight through calm water – almost single-handedly when you first came in sight. The others managed to pick up in time to help you with the bump in front of their friends. What are you doing at Oxford and for how long?'

'Engineering Science – I am in the first of a four-year course,' Rhan answered in a formal manner, aware that both presidents were allowing this stranger to dominate the conversation after their strange build-up of Rhan's attributes. This was obviously not a social call and appeared to be a repeat of the previous term's meeting with Roger.

'On the recommendation of your friends here, and from what I have just witnessed, I would like to invite you to attend trials for the National rowing squad.'

Olympics! flashed into Rhan's head. She wondered what her family would say, then realised that she should be paying attention as he had continued speaking.

'…we pay expenses and a small living allowance. Your friend Esther here will also be joining us and has already given me your contact details. So, if you don't mind, we must rush off. I hope to see you soon.'

Nick moved aside to help usher the guests out as they began discussing the next candidate.

'Now, we are behind programme. Dumas, you wanted me to meet another up-and-coming rower from the men's squad?'

Esther gave Rhan another quick and excited hug as she passed, but at the entrance to the bar she gave Claire a hug too, right in front of the whole Hall, cleverly compensating for being so rude earlier. Roger patted both his protégés on the shoulder with a few words before they disappeared down the stairs. The crowded room fell silent for a few seconds, and then there were hoots of excitement as the celebrations started up again once the door had closed on the interlopers.

~

On his return to the bar, Nick announced that he wanted to say a few words about the women's events before anyone dispersed. He had obviously been preparing for some time and it all went down brilliantly with the exuberant crowd, who cheered and heckled nearly every sentence.

'How am I meant to get in the mood to row in the men's division after the excitement of those races? I can hardly talk! My boathouse has been invaded by the top dogs from the university and even the National squad. The women's rowing is clearly in a complete mess! What are we going to do next year with a Second Eight, which is a division above the First Eight? It's ludicrous!

'There are a few things that we need to sort out. To celebrate gaining bumps on each day of the racing, Elizabeth's team of heroes are entitled to the traditional bump dinner in college tomorrow night. They will need a massive wall to chalk up their achievements.

'Bar-the-oar-breaker, you are expelled from Gloucester Hall. Four bumps would have been adequate – you were not meant to be aiming for four divisions! You can push off to your own college, even if they don't know they need you – there would be a justified objection to you rowing for us beyond this point. You've gained much from us, and you have repaid our faith in you. However, did I hear you're

Olympics-bound now? The only proviso is that when you become president of the Blues, you take Claire and the rest of these Gloucester heroes with you.

'In the meantime, and to help the Hall build on our successes today, Gloucester Hall will be appointing Claire as the first female captain of boats next year. She will be helping out as my vice-captain with immediate effect.'

Even when showered and changed, Rhan did not leave, but hung around to watch and cheer as Nick's eight rowed-over without being bumped. On the way to return George's jersey, a voice over the speaker system announced that Richard and her college Men's First team had been bumped in the last race of the day. Keeping a low profile, she hung around and caught George as he was heading away from the river.

~

The end of term was much more fun, knowing of her long-awaited trip to George's family home after rowing camp. With the countryside now alive to spring, George and Rhan cycled out to explore country pubs, canals, woods and walks. They enjoyed hunting down The Trout Inn, the adjacent Godstone Priory and the upper reaches of Port Meadow as featured in Philip Pullman's *Book of Dust*. They also planned weekend trips for the summer term where they could camp in woods, removed from their normal college life.

Rhan enjoyed having no boat to row over the last few days of term, but she was kept surprisingly busy as a cox. She found it interesting to see and judge the quality and strengths of the various crew members, especially as she was press-ganged into coxing Richard's First Eight the day after their cox, Kim, went home. As the college emptied, Rhan hung around the eerily quiet buildings with Claire, reading their choice of papers in the common room, waiting for the minibus to transfer them to rowing camp.

The days with the junior squad flew past. Rhan and Claire worked with other coaches and saw relatively little of Roger who was helping Peter with Esther's First and Second crews in the last days before the big boat race. The whole junior squad travelled down to London and celebrated the success of Esther's crew in the Blues' race the first weekend after the end of term. This was marred somewhat by Cambridge's victories with the Women's Second boat and later in both of the men's races.

Rhan had hardly seen the capital before, and had no problems being patronised by her crews who enjoyed spending hours showing her round before heading back to their riverside dormitories. They wandered around streets with names familiar to Rhan from so many Monopoly games with her cousins. They took her to the National Gallery, where Rhan was happy to be dragged off by each of the squad to see their favourite room or painting. By far the best fun was to be had from jumping on and off buses where the gang were relieved to rest their aching feet from sight-seeing fatigue.

Once the annual boat race was over, Rhan and the junior squad suddenly had the facilities and their coach, Roger, to themselves. It was relaxing and enjoyable. Claire gave much credit to Bar for the continuing ultra-friendly atmosphere, reporting that everyone was very much in awe of the good-natured and quiet first-choice stroke. The competitive rowers quickly learnt to cloak their ambitions with generosity and kindness. Even after Roger's return, Rhan continued to be tasked with selecting the crews and she patently placed the team above individuals, who risked spending a day on the fitness machines or sculling alone.

Rhan herself missed two days of training with the junior squad to join the first National trials. She enjoyed the second day when she was joined by Esther, now carefree and relaxed. Rhan immediately noticed the difference in Esther's mood now that seven months of physical and psychological pressure as president had been lifted after the successful completion of the boat race.

On the return journey to Oxford from the camp, Roger mentioned a bit of news that Rhan and Claire, who were sitting next to him at the front of the team minibus, found extremely interesting.

'I'm afraid that training over the summer term will be rather ad-hoc. Not only will we have to fit around all your various college training events, but also my college coaching. I've been offered a job by a college. I think Bar destroyed their Women's First Eight in front of the boathouses at Torpids. I have the unenviable task of trying to stop their college men's eight plummeting from the first division at the summer bumps. I couldn't turn down the money, but it may wreck my credibility as a coach. The men didn't do too well at Torpids, so I have just a few weeks to turn them around somehow.'

'Oh that'll stop you getting bored, Roger!' Claire declared, suddenly wide awake and interested, over-emphasising her words. 'Rhan, isn't that your friend Alice's college?' she asked mischievously. 'I reckon it might not be the impossible task it appears, Roger. That college has hidden depths!'

'Really?' Roger replied, now distracted and concentrating on driving the minibus and long-boat trailer behind them. 'Claire, can you just check the boats as we drive around this roundabout? See if anything has moved, will you?'

PART TWO

Prologue

The wind was blowing relentlessly over the coarse heather, reeds and occasional scraggy grasses on the moor tops. Yet after an almost complete absence of two thousand years, the young branches of both deciduous and fir trees were starting to offer some resistance to the wind. Sapling trees were seizing the opportunity of the milder climate to once again spread across the empty slopes of the North York Moors, despite the efforts of mankind.

The bells in the Norman church proudly announced the quarter hour on the side of a somewhat sheltered valley. The double-bell chimes managed to reverberate around the stone-constructed village houses, cobbled footways, and asphalt roads with neatly mowed verges devoid of mud and banks of weeds to attenuate the sound. Without modern insulation and double glazing, two or three hundred of the residents could have heard the chime, just as they had for centuries past. Yet in the years of the third millennium, only one person happened to notice the marking of time: a teenager waiting at the chunky oak bus stop. Despite the Kings of Leon wailing directly into her ears, a quiet lull in the music allowed the first external clang to pass through her headphones.

She frowned at the intrusion to her music and checked the village clock against her phone. She sighed at the confirmation, hoping that her bus had not gone early and was just late, wondering whether to panic or wait. She looked around, but she was alone. She stared wistfully at her phone screen, willing a way for her to track the flow of rural transport.

As the student stood undecided whether or not to wait longer, the mid-morning light noticeably faded to a murky haze. Where there had been clear air and clouds last time she had looked up, the air above the rows of cottages on either side were now filled with dark foreboding. A touch of puzzlement and worry crossed her face as she tried to explain this sudden, unexpected darkening. Her diagnosis was soon confirmed, as a few high-energy splats of rain hit her hand and face, flung by gusts of wind that were channelled around the natural and man-made valley features. She stepped back into the cover of the shelter, deciding to give the bus a few more minutes after all.

From the vantage of a gritstone boulder perched on the hillside above the village, time and whether the bus was early or late had a different perspective. The squall of dark cloud that was just passing over the village had been visible for some time above the horizon as it cleared the distant Pennine Dales and had rapidly traversed the upper Vale Of York on its quest to deliver its load of rain as far as it could. From the timeframe of the boulder however, the thousand years or so of comings and goings in the cluster of village dwellings halfway down the hillside was just a fraction of mankind's history.

The gritstone boulder was created by a rare storm in the arid desert at the heart of the supercontinent of Pangea, trapped far from the nearest ocean by the North American continental plate to the west, the Europe plate to the east and Africa to the south. The storm washed desiccated rock and salts down the future River Rhine, passed dinosaurs fleeing the flood, and out into a delta in a shallow tropical sea that would become the future North Yorkshire, adjacent to where the Atlantic Ocean was just starting to form as America headed west. The thick layer of almost cementitious course sand and grit settled and was compressed, sandwiched between other layers of mud shale and sands.

The strata of the low-lying delta were later squeezed upward to form the moors, becoming rippling foothills to the Alps, as Africa decided against dispersal and crunched back into Europe.

The boulder, therefore, found very different conditions when it was plucked from its birthing place by a massive glacier. A river of ice was streaming down from the Scottish and Norwegian mountains to the north, but encountered the rock block of the North York Moors, which refused to be bulldozed aside. The obstinate hills forced the flow of ice to divide and go round the moors; down the Vale on one side and down the North Sea on the other. Yet the thickness of the ice almost matched the height of the moors, so stepping from one to the other may have been relatively easy for a mammoth on a mission. But at a pace much slower than any mammoth, the vengeful ice ripped at the flanks of the moors, creating vertical walls of rock.

From the top of such a rock face, the boulder was snatched into the turbulent world of ice and was ground against adjacent rocks. Yet it wasn't dragged far. Light reached the boulder and on the ice surface it was pushed sideways, out of the flow into a water-filled valley. As the ice continued to lose its grip, the boulder, now in the backwater, was dumped and partially buried with other ground-up fragments, marooned high on a ridge between a valley and the Vale.

The barren land evolved, following temperature and climate changes from ice to heat and back to ice again. In the warm interglacial period, trees that covered the hillside where the boulder had come to rest struggled with the heat and had to give way to scrubland as fires swept through the forests. The hills became home to hyenas, looking down on the grassy vales of Yorkshire, watching hippopotamus, rhino, bison and elephants. Yet the sheets of ice gradually returned as the earth wobbled on its axis and voyage round the sun, making tiny but significant adjustments to the warmth received in the northern hemisphere. However, this time the boulder stood safe just clear of the new glacier and the ensuing perched lakes of water trapped against the north bulwark of the moors. These lakes of meltwater gradually, then in spectacular torrents, carved through the hills as the landscape returned to yet another interglacial period.

Yet things were different this time. The occasional group of Neanderthal humans were now replaced by tribes of Mesolithic hunters, carrying yet more of their tools. One group started assembling each year on the patch of rocky high ground, elevated above the fearsome, forested and boggy plain below. They gathered hazel nuts on the hillside, but also started to use their timber and stone tools with sharp-edged flint to clear competing rowan trees and to spread the hazel shoots. They met up with others who were hunting and fishing in the valley beck, flowing between ponds still trapped by dams of glacial debris. One year, the tribe examined the top of the boulder and dug it free from the surrounding debris with antler picks and dragged it over, proudly setting it as a mark on the observation point.

These Mesolithic Stone Age nomadic tribes, and later Neolithic Stone Age people, along with their Bronze Age successors who invaded as mounted hoards from the east, set up and settled in villages on the moors. It was easy for them to clear tree roots and plant seeds in the thin soils of the moor tops above the cloying clays left by the ice. They dug the turf and turned it over to form ordered lines of ridges with deeper soils between drainage furrows. They set up industries to provide flints, salt and axe heads for their well-ordered communities. They buried their dead in cists then tumuli. But the thin soils were doomed. The cooling weather and lack of glacial clays and silts meant the crops and rain soon drained the soil of nourishment, until it was washed or blown away, exposing underlying stones. The process could not be reversed by piling the exposed stones into clearance cairns, so the settlements gradually moved from the hills down the valley and into the vale beyond.

However, the slow cooling as the climate headed gradually back towards the next ice age came to a sudden halt. These humans had learnt to transfer matter from one time zone to another, which started to change the planet. They dug up pockets of exposed coal to feed their fires and kilns. Bigger coal, oil and gas fields were developed, which exploited carbon captured and stored in hot climates, hundreds of million years ago, and released it into the atmosphere of their temperate era as greenhouse gases, with obvious consequences. The usual minute changes in temperatures rapidly became exponential heating. The humans knew that they were lazily harvesting forbidden fruit that would transform and overheat their world, but that did not stop them. The almost free supply of energy was just too good to resist, regardless of the consequences to others.

So the meta-stable conditions meant that the African grasslands could be rapidly returning to North Yorkshire. Winter droughts when verdant protection was absent had already allowed the dried soils to simply blow away, and unheard-of winter forest and moorland fires had already started. The wet peatlands were already doomed by the forecast temperatures, with the released methane expected to join the already excessive greenhouse gases. This was no minor adjustment of radiation from north to south, and this time the temperatures would soar throughout the world, making much of the surface uninhabitable. With no will to even slow down the rate of increase and no conceivable method to reverse what they were doing, these humans were creating truly interesting times. Only the rocks would be able to see the future.

CHAPTER TWENTY ONE

Yorkshire

The start of Rhan's next adventure was fitted in as a stop-off on her return north to Sunderland. She grabbed her belongings from the porters' lodge, but had trouble deciding what to wear for her Yorkshire trip. She worried that George's house would be more formal than her uncle's, and anxiety about introductions drove her to retreat into her traditional black attire. The long train journey provided a useful opportunity to sit and consider all that had been happening over the past term – the unreality of her rowing successes only seemed more extreme when she was removed from the Oxford bubble.

She read George's detailed instructions with a smile, marvelling over his uncharacteristic attention to detail for her visit. It certainly made her feel appreciated and calmed her nerves at the prospect of staying with his family. As directed, Rhan prepared to get off the train a bit beyond York, when she could see the Pennines to the west and the Moors to the east side of the train. In the manner almost of a stranger or cousin, he gave her a kiss on both cheeks on the platform and led her to a green MG with its top down. As Rhan got closer she noted that one wing of the car was black and was evidently still a work-in-progress.

The chrome bumpers were hardly shining bright, but the prospect of a fun ride was exciting. She could tell he was very proud as he stowed her bags in the car, even if he came over as grumpy.

'Getting texts from you while you've been in that rowing camp of yours was like getting blood from a stone,' he complained. 'What've you been doing? Who did you watch the boat race with? Did y'ever think of me?' he demanded.

'Well I had plenty to distract me, but if you must know, you were never really forgotten. I spent most of my time watching the race with Claire – who you know – but I had a fascinating time. Was it good to see your girlfriend again?' Rhan went on the attack. She decided not to point out that George's Oxford accent had slipped somewhat after just a few days back up north.

'It's been good – we're quite good friends now and she wanted to know all about you.'

He smiled at her as they stood either side of the low, open-top car and added, 'But talking hasn't stopped me missing you every few minutes.'

'I'm pleased to hear that you are suffering as well,' Rhan laughed, lowering herself into the sports car as gracefully as she could. 'But apart from help with your maths, your practicals and other aspects of your university life, which aspects of me do you miss?'

'Oh God, what a question!' he replied, looking straight at the road ahead as they drove through the town. 'Well, the thing I'm still missing most in this open car is the scent of your breath; it's like summer heather. You look fantastic from every angle, you taste better than chocolate ice-cream, the sound of your voice calms me down...what's left? Oh, touch, well that's great whether we are fighting, sitting close on a lecture hall bench or cuddling or whatever. Is that enough for you?' She nodded, smiling.

After over-indulging in such personal conversation, talk was then dominated by the car and whether she needed an extra scarf or hat. It was indeed freezing once they started to move faster in the cool spring air. As they drove down winding back roads, Rhan was delighted to be able to look up and search the trees for the signs of spring that she had noted in the south. The blackthorns had a sprinkling of tiny flower buds, which stood white against the dark hedges and other trees that were still starkly dormant. Hanging catkins decorated the hazels, which suggested that not all the trees were as dead to the awakening world as they appeared.

'I have to say, it is relaxing to be here,' Rhan admitted, loudly enough to be heard once they were clear of the town. 'I find it mentally exhausting being away from you.'

George threw back his head and laughed at Rhan's confession. He then kept up an excited commentary on the scenery, the car, his home, his family and his hopes for the next few days. At each viewpoint, the moors loomed closer, rising dramatically from the vale. His village sat on the side of a nibble taken out of the hills, where two valleys met. As they drove up into the centre of the village, George waved a greeting at almost everyone.

They mounted a steep drive, and Rhan could again see the hills, which were now close; they appeared to rise sharply just beyond a short-cropped green field, framing the village houses on three sides. Her study was interrupted by the appearance of George's sister, Grace, who had reddish long hair; and their mother June, whose hair was shorter and dark. They came to greet her through a heavy oak front door. Rhan was delighted at how enthusiastic they were to meet her, despite the circumstances of George bringing home a rather strange female university colleague – but their welcome was nothing compared with Hamish's. The terrier was ecstatic to meet a visitor who already knew his name and what he liked most. After a few seconds of being fussed over, the dog started sprinting around in excited circles, to the amusement of all.

The house felt both airy and homely, with views that looked up at the moors from every room. This was further captured on the walls by large, realistic oil paintings of surrounding villages and landscapes of the moorland in a range of seasons, many blanketed in snow, which Grace proudly presented as her mother's work.

June plied Rhan with many questions about life at university, her rowing and her tutorials, obviously keen to hear aspects of her son's life from a new source. George had clearly told his mother that Rhan was a distinguished rower who was not recognised by her own college, so Rhan described the rowing camp, and her first trip to London for the boat race. She decided not to brag about the two days she had spent with hopefuls for the National squad, who wanted her back for further trials and were offering to pay all rowing expenses. She knew enough about George's home life to be able to strike up easy conversations with June and Grace, while George fetched Rhan's various bags that were stashed in the car.

'Your father's down the garth,' June informed George as he wandered into the kitchen from his tasks. You can take him down a cup of tea and introduce Rhan. He needs help topping the ash trees before they drop heavy branches onto the sheds.' With some reluctance, Rhan moved away from the log-burning cooker in the kitchen, which had only just started to warm her after the chilly journey. She made the mistake of rejecting offers of drab but warmer clothing that George then cheerfully claimed.

On their way down the long, narrow garden, George showed off the various apple, plum and cherry trees of various ages, which were only starting to consider blossoming. The nut trees were heavy with long catkins on hazels, chestnuts bore round husks, but there was nothing yet on the young walnut trees. Rhan was most interested in the views of the bleak moors, visible beyond the garden hedges. She briefly shook the hand of George's father, William, and exchanged pleasantries as he stood sipping his coffee at the foot of a tall ladder.

After a few minutes, Rhan watched while George, strapped into a safety harness, wielded a handsaw from the top of the ladder. George was dressed up in insulated Muck boots, an old coat that had belonged to his grandfather, leather gauntlets and a cap. Rhan was still wearing her presentable dark coat, scarf and thin shoes, so she was relieved when, after a short stint, George came down again and thoughtfully pointed out her condition. 'Poor Rhan is still freezing after the MG. Look, we'd better go in.'

'OK, that's fine. It's good to meet you, Rhan.' George's father reluctantly admitted defeat.

Even with a mug of tea in front of the stove, Rhan still felt chilled to the bone. Accustomed to rowing with river ice on her oar, and braving the North Sea over Christmas, she felt ashamed that she was so cold in George's house.

'Can I borrow your boots, George?' she enquired politely.

'Of course, there are several pairs you could try on out there.' He indicated the porch.

Wearing padded boots, coat and hat, she felt ready for the challenge of helping with the sawing. Despite confessing her inexperience at both sawing and heights, her offer to don the safety harness and have a go up the ladder was gratefully accepted by William, who yielded the saw and the tied ladder.

Rhan started to feel warm blood circulating again after just a few minutes of sawing above her head, while George's father held the ladder below. The fear of falling was receding rapidly too, as she concentrated on branches at a higher level. She soon grew tired and hot and threw down the furry hat that had been perched ridiculously on top of her headscarf to allow the heat to escape. She was getting complaints from muscles in her body that were neither employed in rowing or in gym machines. She was glad to follow advice as the blade started to jam, and she rotated the saw around the branch for different angles of attack, changing arms as the opportunity allowed. Her skill in sawing had to be learnt from scratch, so using her left arm was no great problem.

'Goodness Rhan! You're doing an amazing job,' George's father complimented her as she lowered down a length of the central trunk on a rope. 'Is that what rowing does for you? You've obviously been exercising hard at that camp of yours. So does this mean that you stand a chance of a Blue in your second year, despite your late start?'

'Yes, but I have also benefited from two days' coaching this week with the National coaches. It's not likely to come to much, but I had fun with my friend Esther in the trials.'

'Blimey! George never mentioned that.'

'No, none of my college knows. There will be problems ahead, but so far keeping a secret of my strange ability to row has been a major advantage, especially as the National coaches will drop most of us after the next sessions in a few weeks' time.'

'What are you two up to?' George was calling from halfway to the house. 'Dad, you need to let her go; you can't enslave an unsuspecting friend. She's hardly spoken to Mum, or me.'

'I'm fine George! This is fun and I am warming up at last,' Rhan called back from the top of the ladder. George retreated into the house.

'You've done well, but I think you need to come down from up there!' George's father affirmed after a while. 'You must be shattered and will soon start to let go of things that need to be held, and vice versa, if you get my drift. Don't forget to unclip. OK, I have the ladder.'

'Yes, one does lose perspective of safety after a while. I was terrified and clung onto everything when I came up. Climbing down now!'

'You are full of surprises, Rhan. I gather that you're a Syrian Christian – are you very religious?'

'Actually, I generally go to the Catholic chaplaincy with George and others from the college, and occasionally to the Greek Orthodox on St Giles. It is mainly a cultural thing I suppose. My aunt and uncle are relatively strict Muslims, and as a small compromise, I agreed to carry on wearing traditional Syrian Christian dress and to keep my head covered around the college. I have taken that in rather a literal sense, so I use western styles for sport outside of college life. It must all seem so petty.'

'I don't fully understand. George mentioned that some of your family came from Sunderland before Syria?'

'Well my grandmother came from County Durham, so the family links enabled my uncle to return; he now has a small engineering business in Sunderland. He became a Muslim, while his sister, my mother, remained a Christian. I suppose that my sister and I have followed that lead; she has become very interested in Islam, largely through the influence of the man she intends to marry. I must be a disappointment to my Sunderland family.'

'From what I have heard of you, I bet they are very proud,' William reassured her before continuing. 'Is there any chance you can hold the ladder, while I climb up and saw those last lower branches? I'm afraid there will be plenty of sawdust coming your way. Let me know if you start to get too cold.'

'I will enjoy cooling off! Will this ash tree definitely die?' she asked from the base of the shortened ladder.

'Well, I'm not certain,' he responded between struggles with branches. 'As you see, it's close to the shed and some branches are dead and others are already a problem as they damage the felt roof. Keeping trees to a manageable height is almost a full-time job here. Watch out for this coming down!' He paused his answer as Rhan pushed the lowered branch to the side, but then continued.

'Ash was called "the widow maker" because ash branches and trunks can snap at any provocation, leaving the tree surgeons in real danger! That is a serious problem with dieback so trees need to be felled while safe. Can you manage to pull that branch out of the way please?'

He went on. 'We try to use timber for structural engineering to store the carbon. Ash is as strong as green oak, according to some engineering research carried out in the 1960s, backed up by tests my office carried out with a full-scale test rig. We like to use local hardwoods in buildings as a low-carbon alternative to steel. It's stupid to let the timber rot away or burn it. That simply releases all the carbon stored in trees. We've learnt nothing since Dutch Elm disease.'

'Are you suggesting that these logs that we have cut from this tree could be used as structural members?' Rhan asked in surprise. 'We never discuss anything like that at university.'

'Yes, that trunk there…what, three metres long and 250 millimetres in diameter, could support a two or three-storey building as a post. Those curved bits would make excellent knee bracing between posts and beams to stabilise the posts and to provide wind bracing. But ash needs to be sawn correctly because it doesn't half shrink, twist and split! Like most timbers ash has many contradictions that we haven't worked out yet!' William kept up his lecture from the top of the ladder, stopping occasionally to clear the lighter branches.

'The portable test rig at work can test real beams up to six metres long. Would you believe that the correct orthodox method to assess the quality and capacity of the timber is by a simple visual inspection? So if you took a large section like the one you lowered down, one would never know about the defects hidden inside until it failed and you found that it had grown around a poly bag or something stupid.

'We have only covered the simple concepts, so far,' Rhan said, expressing interest while trying to clear branches and holding the ladder at the same time.

'We need to know so much more about the engineering properties of our natural resources if we want to cut carbon emissions,' William continued. 'The trouble is that we don't even know what we don't know, and little or no research is being carried out. There is no commercial body to push the use of British hardwoods, yet country estates could make fortunes. Without any proper research, both the British Standards and the recent Eurocodes totally neglect most local hardwood timber. It illustrates nicely how any move for engineers to cut carbon is blocked!'

'Blocked by whom?' Rhan was fascinated to hear this.

'Well anyone who wants to stand against green engineering, I suppose – especially anyone related to steel and concrete. I have noted that the steel and carbon industries never attack each other but they both denounce timber. The high-carbon industries have control of funding, research, committees and the status quo. As relatively few people believe we need to tackle climate change, any committee will inevitably include climate sceptics.'

She looked at him to check he was being serious, but let him continue.

'The timbers that I find best, in terms of looks and properties, are sycamore and beech. They don't split too badly if one relieves the stresses with a saw cut, and they both have a tight grain with a lovely honey colour, once waxed. Branch coming down! Such hardwoods dry in months, while oak dries in years. Another coming down!

'So I would prefer to save oak for external use, where it's ideal and the only durable timber around here. Using green oak beams to support masonry is a real problem as large beams shrink over a decade or so. Unfortunately, high-carbon materials such as steel or concrete are usually specified, so we just burn this brilliant timber and make more steel beams. It's all crazy!'

Rhan had been surprised to find that she didn't need to speak; she could just listen to new areas of engineering that would never be covered at university. She was, however, shocked into responding.

'So after so much talk about climate change over the decades, there are still no moves to allow low-carbon design by engineers. That sounds worse than I thought possible!'

'Yes it's shocking, especially as the UK's treaty obligations are only met if the carbon stored in trees is stored for the foreseeable future. In the case of ash like this tree, it decays from the pith and starts to have a hollow core once it's more than just forty years old – just a bit older than this tree. There's no chance of saving that carbon, particularly with ash die-back, if we don't prepare to use the bulk of the timber. It was the same for Dutch elm disease; the vernacular barns and some houses around here used beams from ash or elm branches until the 20th century. The elm timber decays quickly if wet, but often lasted a couple of hundred years in the dry, despite beetle attack. In a modern, dry, centrally heated house, these local hardwoods would last forever. More branches coming down! I'll climb down now and give you a hand to clear the mess.' While they carried and sawed the branches, she returned to the subject.

'What about the relative costs of timber or steel beams? Is timber expensive?'

'Dirt cheap at firewood prices. Ash and sycamore are cut down as weeds around here, so unless it's top-quality furniture or violin grade, the cost of green timber is not an issue. Timber dried for a year or so in barns goes for three times the price and can cost more than steel, but it's still cheaper than buying a steel beam and spending time trying to clad it to look like wood. There are still too many clients and architects who are stuck in the 1990s' antiseptic style of the Ikea era and want to avoid the natural look of timber. Most of my clients are very reluctant to use anything other than steel. Architects and owners can be horrified by the idea of posts in rooms to reduce spans, yet on the next project the interior designer can introduce fake columns and partitions,' he laughed. 'That's even true when restoring historic castles! The conservation establishment effectively vetoed reinserting timber on one project and insisted on steel and concrete that had been labelled the previous year as "inappropriate" for that monument.'

'Why?' Rhan asked, perplexed and wanting to show interest. William stopped working while he recalled the phrase.

'They said timber would be pastiche! It goes to show how far we have to move with such attitudes.'

As they were piling the branches for burning and storing the structural timber to dry, an old-fashioned bell rang from the house and the two of them tramped to supper through the gloom of the evening, feeling very content with their labours. Rhan also felt very satisfied that she had learnt of so many engineering and sustainability issues with such little effort.

CHAPTER TWENTY TWO

Licence to Kill

The atmosphere at supper was light-hearted and fun. Although this was her first meal there, Rhan quickly gained the impression that the family knew about her and she soon relaxed, feeling like an honoured guest. June had prepared a lovely meal for them which included homemade bread straight from the oven. They talked about their college and the characters that George had previously described. George's family were keen to get more views of the Marxist, the rough Cornishman, the sophisticated chemist and some of the girls they had heard about from George. George's father, William, was interested in the engineering course. Grace, who was still at sixth-form college, wanted to hear about the life her brother was leading and the various pubs and drinking exploits.

Although George and Rhan were excused from clearing up at the end of the meal, Rhan insisted on staying to help, on the grounds that it would make George help too. Grace was delighted to find a comrade in arms against her brother.

The evening was not yet fully dark when George and Rhan wandered back down the garth through the orchard to the old agricultural sheds where George's father was siphoning cider from one jar to another. He was pleased to have help with holding the tubes in place and extracting them at the right moment to avoid transferring the sediment. This time Rhan had grabbed the tatty old nylon gardening coat; she was very glad of its insulating qualities on her shoulders.

'This is one of the few relatively consistent harvests that we manage to produce in this garden,' William explained, pointing at the cider. 'We've just finished off last year's eating apples but still have cooking apples. Yet in some years I have had to beg for apples to keep up cider production when we've had a poor crop. It must be really difficult being an agricultural producer, particularly with bees and weather-sensitive crops. Global warming has not sorted out the spring frosts that kill our blossom. Our hazel and walnuts are probably the most consistent products here.'

'He's not joking!' Grace announced as she entered the shed behind them. 'We plant three bags of spuds and harvest two! After Dad prunes an apple tree, it takes nine years to recover!' she laughed.

'Yes I'm afraid there is so much more to this "grow your own" than I imagined,' conceded her father. 'God help us if, or when, we have a shortage of food, as our vegetable patch only provides food for a couple of weeks a year, so we'd be doomed without the nuts. My concern is that in the near future, the Gross National Produce, which we as a country can eat, may be much more important than the Gross National Product that we currently hear about so much.'

'Absolutely!' Rhan exclaimed. 'Our economics friends at college spend their lives discussing GNP, yet it will have little relevance when food runs short. The people of Syria simply seek security and food and hardly have a nation, never mind a GNP.'

There was a short pause after this surprising outflow; George and Grace said nothing.

'It's so refreshing to hear of a youngster taking an interest,' their father responded encouragingly with a laugh.

'Well, George may have told you that I am particularly interested in climate change,' Rhan continued awkwardly, yet pleased to be discussing the subject. 'We never learn anything useful about changing climate on our engineering course. In the Middle East, my family have, over the generations, experienced the terror of social and political collapse several times. They – and most recently my parents – needed to face the possibility that all normal life was over and that we had to make the hardest decision of all: when to run. My fear is that environmental change could mean even worse social upheaval and that everyone will need to run, yet there may be few places to go.'

'There's Scotland,' piped up George, yet Rhan gave him a look which she hoped was withering, knowing that he was being facetious. Grace added a slap on his arm for good measure.

'Hmm, yes,' his father responded, ignoring the squabbling. 'I'm afraid there are few places as good as the British Isles, and Scotland has the best potential. It seems unfair on the rest of the world, considering how Britain started climate change with industrialisation.'

'It is so strange to hear your father saying the same as me,' said Rhan as she shot another reproachful look at George.

'I know, I know,' George sighed. 'Climate change was *made in Britain.*'

'Can I just ask?' Rhan paused before plunging into her question. 'Do you still have some hope that something can be done?'

George's eyebrows shot upward in surprise, but he said nothing. Grace quietly slipped away.

'Well it's a brave question which I have never heard anyone ask!' The older man stopped clearing away the siphoning paraphernalia and sat down on one of the massive timber beams that were stacked around the sides of the long agricultural shed. 'Oh, by the way Rhan, this is one of those ash timber beams we were talking about,' he added before addressing her question. 'This one is around six metres long. Lovely aren't they, compared with a steel section?'

With a slight change in tone, William turned to the matter of interest.

'Well, if our planet was the Titanic after it hit the iceberg, we've not only been re-arranging the deckchairs, but are still planning the following week's menus and events. And now we are continuing to stoke the boilers while heading into more ice fields. We may have cut some of our coal burning, but we've done little else and have no plans to prepare for the bad years that are to come.'

William patted the beam contemplatively.

'There's no way now to avoid major warming. I was told over twenty years ago, in 1996 – by a climate scientist from Oxford University as it happens – that we had ten years to change our ways if we were to avoid a major disaster. By 2006, it was clear that we had missed the chance of avoiding that disaster, and since then we have just been banging nails into our children's coffins,' he laughed without mirth. 'After two or three decades, nearly all the powerful politicians are more interested in avoiding rather than taking effective action. No voters call for action.'

Rhan was heartened to hear statements from William that were not shielded by polite fudging. She found it refreshing that someone other than David was arguing against denial and unwarranted optimism, or was not suggesting that it was all a waste of time, as in George's case.

'The next couple of decades will be "interesting times" regardless,' William continued. 'It might be totally demoralising once society realises that everything will only get worse. Almost everything will suddenly be seen to be vulnerable, judged by today's standards. There will be massive breakdowns in lifestyles, morality and stability. I presume that you know this better than any of us, Rhan?'

At this bidding, pictures of warfare in Aleppo from the web and imagined images of her bombed house were conjured.

'Dad, that's not the issue,' drawled George, bringing her back to the present. 'Rhan asked what can be done. She knows how doomed we are – we discussed that, literally to death, last term. Tell her whether or not you have any ideas that will help, then we can go somewhere warmer.'

'Ah. OK – my approach. Well I would start by simply rationing the use of dangerous fossil fuels that eventually produce greenhouse gases. Each person would have an allowance for emissions and anything beyond that would need to be purchased from those willing to sell, after payment of tax, of course. Carbon ration would allow our society to face the issue of dangerous greenhouse emissions from the bottom up; from people's demand, rather than the top-down taxation approach attempted so far.'

'Come on Dad. You sound like our friend Tom with such communist-like diktats. No peacetime democratic government would be allowed to intervene like that. There is no war to justify rationing.'

'Well, people are already dying because we have not waged war against those who want to destroy the planet. Why should we be allowed to burn as much carbon as we want, knowing it will kill others in time?' There was no response, so William carried on.

'The sooner we exchange our persecution of developing countries and the younger generation for a war against climate change, the better. We'll be fighting for land and food soon enough.'

Rhan was gazing at George, recalling their previous extraordinary conversation in the pub with David so many weeks before, and wondering just how bad the future was going to get. However, William was suggesting a much more palatable line.

'I personally would much prefer to see the beginning of defined rationing than the main alternative approach, which involves taxing carbon at its sale, at the border or within the companies that supply it. I just never thought it would work...and it hasn't. Any government that imposes high tax on fuels tends to meet opposition soon enough.

And besides, I'm not sure that meddling with the costs will be at all effective at cutting the quantity of fossil fuel extracted to zero. As the infrastructure is in place, there will still be suppliers who can pump oil, bleed off gas or dig up coal for next to nothing.' William shrugged with a wan smile. Rhan had not fully understood the taxation approach but she let it pass, allowing him to continue.

'We need a bold fix rather than a minor short-term adjustment, so I don't see any option that leaves out rationing. As George inadvertently implies, it will engender a war spirit.'

George snorted.

'I am glad you're here, Rhan, as it's forcing George, for the first time, to listen.'

Rhan adjusted the coat around her shoulders and sat down on the low bench opposite, which she guessed was a chunky beam that had been set aside to dry. It had a smooth, rich grain with a deep honey colour. She glanced at the still-standing George, who stifled his arguments so that his father could continue.

'That's one of the sycamore beams. It's a real surprise – strong and beautiful, yet normally chopped down as a weed and burnt. It's similar to beech but slightly richer in colour in my opinion.

'Anyway, as George points out, no one is prepared to vote to save the planet. I kept thinking that voters would care,' he sighed, 'but I agree I was wrong! Even the most religious or caring people have other causes to fight. Safeguarding the future of the earth can always be postponed to another day!'

Rhan nodded, encouraging William to continue.

'Political leaders realise that people may be prepared to vote for self-sacrificing financial restraint or even war, but won't vote at all for carbon restraint or climate balance. The reasons are extraordinary, but not really understood.'

'So you agree that nothing will happen?' George pounced.

'I'm afraid that I have recently come round to that possibility, George. But for myself, I'll never accept the "do nothing" approach. We must keep fighting. I can't accept that turkeys would actually vote for Christmas – that our generation would prefer to destroy the future for both our children and ourselves, just so we can enjoy the pampering for a few more years. Is our whole morality so superficial that we are happy to kill people indirectly? Any good we do now will reduce the severity of what is to come.'

'Yet you think people would accept carbon rationing?' Rhan asked, trying hard to concentrate on the positive aspects. 'Is this worldwide or just in Britain? I thought it had been tried but it failed?'

'Well I can't speak for anyone, never mind other countries,' George's father said emphatically, 'but I think a system that is just and relatively equitable for all would go down very well, and it could and should start here in the UK.' He pointed down at the ground with a short stab.

'At present, it is difficult to ask anyone to give up on, say, a flight to the Caribbean or Turkey on moral grounds, when colleagues or neighbours will burn that saved carbon. We all think *"we're worth it"*. If there was moral stigma, supported by knowledge that such a flight would involve subsequent cutting of car mileage or reducing central heating to avoid paying through the nose for the extra carbon credits, then there would be every reason for people to cut carbon emissions.'

'Rationing has been tried. It failed.' George sighed in a derisory manner. He moved across and sat down next to Rhan on the sycamore beam.

'You're dead right about the European business rationing system,' his father persisted, talking enthusiastically to Rhan. 'It was set up for businesses within the EU to trade companies' carbon emissions. Unfortunately, it was initially sabotaged at the outset by politicians and technocrats who had no interest in penalising their leading companies for a greater good that few believed in. Anyway, that top-down system only affected the senior management of the largest companies and was of no interest to their shareholders or customers.' William waved his hands in exasperation before expressing his new hope. 'Actually I hear it's starting to work, so it might be useful for the major producers, but it's of no interest to most mortals.

'I want to see a bottom-up approach, with each and every individual having a personal interest, and rationing would create that. If the UK, the country that started the industrial revolution, led the way on this, others would follow.' William looked up at Rhan to see what impression he was making. It was his son however, who responded.

'Just think how much legislation would be needed, Dad,' George pointed out, shaking his head.

'Well we introduced many laws and convoluted incentives and tax measures around the millennium for business to cut carbon. We then subsequently just changed our minds to please politicians, voters, consumers or industries, yet there was a will and some action for a short while.'

'But since then, this country voted to leave Europe to avoid such a direction. It's just not going to happen!' George said exasperatedly. 'The people who voted for Brexit to recreate an island state – they won't be bothered about the rest of the world, will they?'

There was a sudden silence while they considered this and its implication.

'There will be opposition, I agree,' William conceded at last. 'But there needs to be something to ration the number of fellow human beings we will each indirectly kill, just because we can afford the petrol or whatever.'

Rhan examined the sycamore grain in the beam beneath her, while George held his tongue so she could hear the arguments.

'The main problem is that capitalism has broken down. It costs so little to dig up coal or release gas or oil from the ground where the carbon has been trapped for hundreds of millions of years. We are happy to pay for extraction but no one ever pays for clearing up the problem by re-storing the carbon for even the short or medium term.

'The value of carbon emissions needs to swing up from 30 pounds per tonne or whatever meaningless value it currently has, towards the true cost of recapturing a tonne of carbon – probably around £300 per tonne or perhaps £1,000?'

William raised his eyebrows to invite bids on a more realistic value.

'Well there is no price,' George affirmed. 'It's currently an infinite sum because there is no real market. No one's putting carbon back after burning oil, gas or whatever.'

'A bit like the waste from nuclear fuels,' Rhan added.

'Hopefully a price to store spent nuclear products and contaminated material would follow suit. We could then compare the whole-life processes of burning and subsequent storage of both nuclear fission, and the burning and capture of fossil fuels. The economic data would appear very different from our current defective system.'

'Sounds expensive for both,' George retorted.

'Rationing would provide an incentive to develop capturing and storing carbon. The government could ease off its half-hearted attempts to plan and subsidise the green economy and let new developments take over to avoid the greenhouse gas ration. Rationing would ease the shock to individuals and their suppliers in the transitional period to a no-emission economy.'

'How would it work?' Rhan asked politely.

'Well, let's just think what would happen if any government announced that it wanted to act on global warming by rationing carbon emissions,' William said eagerly. 'It could start at say five tonnes of CO_2 per adult for the first year, which I think is around the average current emission level that people can individually control, excluding several tonnes of CO_2 emissions outside their immediate control. A fraction of that would be allocated for children.'

'Sounds reasonable,' Rhan said, glancing at George.

'There would a warning of subsequent annual cuts in the ration, so people could prepare. Such cuts could be, say, as much as a tonne per year, given the precarious condition of the world. Alternatively, other aspects of our total carbon footprint could also be added to bring down other high-carbon elements. Meat for example could be added to reduce agricultural greenhouse emissions, along with other products containing plastics, cement or metals.'

'There would need to be a referendum or an election,' George got in. 'And who would vote for rationing?'

'It's too cold in here to debate that,' William suggested, rubbing his hands together. 'Let's just imagine that people realised they were voting for or against the younger generation, or that it followed the lines of the argument for and against slavery and was eventually passed. But, once rationing was foreseeable, then there would be a sudden economic rush.'

'From the rush to spend?' asked Rhan.

'Well a bit of that,' William agreed. 'Mostly it would be preparations. The point is that each person, each voter, will immediately demand that their politicians should supply low-carbon electricity, buses, trains and insulation to keep their constituents' carbon expenditure down in both winter and summer heatwaves.

'They'll demand that their heating and other power is low carbon, not just low cost. Investment capital will flood into the low-carbon economy. The power of the grid will be loosened so it will be delivery of low-carbon power that is important. You young engineers will be rushing round installing pumped storage schemes to regulate the peaks and troughs of electricity supply and to save wasted overproduction. Each community will want their local wind turbines and solar panels on their roof to be able to operate off-grid so life can continue in a sustainable manner.'

Both youngsters were now listening intently at the new ideas, which continued to flow as William expounded his solution for the planet.

'Once rationing starts, those with a prolific lifestyle will see that they are fighting public opinion and are letting down their neighbourhood. They'll feel the cost and the shame of driving past the queue for the bus. People will be ashamed to admit they're jetting off on holiday. Carbon credits, just like cigarettes, will need to carry a death warning.

'The poorest in society would benefit enormously from rationing as they'd be most likely to have unused emission allowances to sell, especially if they had no car and tended not to fly. The richest would like it because with land they could make use of their capacity to produce green energy and to produce low-carbon products. I still don't think the rich should be allowed to use negative-carbon products to offset their private jets, however. That would give a very bad impression.'

William patted the beam he was sitting on to indicate the new currency and looked up from delivering his message, clearly expecting a hail of abuse from George.

Taking advantage of the silence, he continued in a slightly rushed manner as he collected stuff to take back to the house.

'If we adopted a ration system, then everyone would have a vested interest, and it would become self-policing in a manner surpassing smoking bans and recycling of waste. As happened in the war years, money would become almost secondary to the carbon rations. Employment would be good, as projects would employ people, rather than carbon-consuming machines – a bit of a step backwards in industrial terms. Everything would slow down because, while time currently means money, time would then be allocated for the most low-carbon approach. As long as the speed of the dentists' drill was not restricted, then life could improve – well, in my opinion anyway.'

'Mmm,' Rhan sounded thoughtfully.

George was less reserved. 'Well I can see it might be fun to try, but it won't happen, will it?'

'Probably not. My hope rested on the saying, "cometh the hour, cometh the man"…oh, or woman…but no one stepped forward. Climate deleted from every agenda! All we needed was one politician in this country, one Churchillian leader, or one William Wilberforce with the backing of a few moral assistants and we might've had a tiny chance to save our society. It might have been possible to change the future of the world. The key aspect is that a fair rationing system would allow us to enter the new era in a positive manner.'

'You totally ignore the selfish nature of humans,' George argued, raising his voice slightly.

'Yes, but you don't appreciate how the mood of society can suddenly change, if the need arises, and I think this is relevant both worldwide and in the UK. Going back to what you know – just look at how the most selfish individuals have become fastidious with sorting their rubbish and recycling. And no one thought that smokers would be prepared to simply stop smoking in pubs and public places. Yet those major changes to lifestyles were adopted with little compunction for marginal gains. Imagine what we would do if we knew that giving up hydrocarbons might just save our nephews, nieces, children and grandchildren.'

'But how long would it take to set up such a system for rationing if a government wanted to act?' Rhan asked doubtfully, in an effort to keep George out of the argument.

'I think that the fossil fuel retailers and airline ticket sales operators could set something up very easily, in just a few weeks if there was no choice. Collecting carbon credits would be just like collecting Tesco vouchers or whatever, and would be hardly different from managing and transferring VAT.' William was grinning now, enjoying the conversation. 'It could start simply with government stamps, as in the last war, but records of allocation would be easy in the digital age.'

With the conversation in a more relaxed mode, Rhan returned to absentmindedly tracing the grain on the honey-coloured sycamore beam, glancing sporadically at George and William as he developed his concept.

'There would be a real buzz that would shrug off all thought of negative inflation and recession. There would be a boom in construction and the housing market as people prepared and swapped properties so they could work from home or be near the office or a bus route. There would be real demand for solar panels, electric cars and the like. Town property would need to be adapted back to residences to cut commuting. But in London there would be demand for the release of all those empty properties, owned by the rich of the world as a one-way bet in the only capital city with a climate change flood barrier. Squatters' rights could be thrust into the spotlight!'

'So you think the selfish attitude would just melt away?' George asked, eventually exasperated into breaking his silence. 'You think we could or would want to just take such unilateral action regardless of trade arrangements? You think that the oil industry would just accept a curtailment of their trade?'

'Nothing is as fixed as you think,' replied William, apparently unsurprised by George's harsh questions. 'Ask Rhan whether such issues were considered in Syria once the crisis came. Under the right conditions, and with the right leadership, the selfish spirit would disappear and be replaced by a national sense of purpose. You'd be amazed. The invasion of the Falkland Islands and the death of Princess Di both illustrated just an inkling of what could be possible. Even the most self-centred climate sceptic wouldn't dare step out of line or be caught cheating on their carbon credits once they were seen to be harming the next generation, and once "greenhush" was denounced.'

Rhan smiled and nodded at the obvious point. She was now gazing at the various bikes scattered around the shed while William continued.

'The essential ingredient would be fairness,' William explained. 'It would be very different from previous initiatives – knowing that equitable measures were being taken by all, for the good of all. Rationing could be a great leveller. Of course, the landed rich would have more room for wind turbines or whatever, but just look at who benefits from solar panels now – it's not the poor.'

The older man was enjoying the chance to preach his message.

'With the first post-industrial economy, the UK would have the opportunity to build a whole new series of industries. Of course, there would be big losers: the airlines would mourn the loss of jobs as Britain gave up the race to remain a hub airport for Europe and the southern holiday destinations would miss our trade. Coal is dead and buried but the chemical industries and almost every business I can think of could adapt to new approaches and still make money. Scrap metal merchants would continue to flourish with the new demand for reuse rather than recycled materials.'

George winked at Rhan to indicate he could see the conjuror's trick, but that he was still enjoying the show.

'My industry, construction, has done next to nothing to reduce the carbon footprint of structures. Yet we would face boom times. There is so much to do to prepare for a new hot planet and to cut carbon. We would be constructing pumped air or water power plants to store offshore energy, opening new railway lines remote from rising seas, creating new flood bunds with tax-free inert dumping to protect huge tracts of the country from those rising seas, setting up new industries and housing in places that would minimise emissions of works and industry.'

Rhan was nodding now as he spoke, hearing what she expected.

'The northern powerhouse would revert to its roots. If the northern streams once powered manufacturing with dozens of mills and then hydroelectric turbines, then all we need is engineers with the correct skills to reinstate the power source that every village and every valley once provided. We can't perhaps match the generation of the power we currently have, but we can use technology to fit the solution to the problem.

'Once materials are required to be low carbon…well, human input becomes a secondary rather than a prime consideration.' William pointed dramatically to the beams they were sitting on. 'No one wants my air-dried beech, sycamore and ash beams, simply because we are accustomed to steel beams and have misguided views on risks. We need to make the risk or certainty of killing someone far away in place and time simply unacceptable. We also need to change the architectural fashion to fit resources.' He sighed, aware that George was dying to vent his opposing views. 'In my office we could design buildings around the available timber or whatever second-hand steel beams the client can salvage. It's essential that we stop using high-carbon newly-made steel throughout, just because our economy is set up that way. Carbon-free would mean jobs for all and horror at the current CO_2 throw-away society.' He slapped the chunky timber beam he was sitting on.

'You're so deluded Dad,' George blurted at last. 'You've been proved wrong for decades now – no one's going to even start giving up carbon. There are too many vested interests and far too much apathy. Cutting high-carbon industry wouldn't seem viable. Just look at the steel industry. Would any government allow all high-carbon industry to simply flow to China or wherever?'

'No, that's just my point. We could find a way if we wanted! Steel works are usually near hills and above deep mines, so local supplies of tidal or wind power could be stored and regulated by the pumped storage, in a simple, proven approach to provide peak power to regulate supplies while we wait for the expected batteries to be developed. With power from the Dogger Bank wind farm out in the North Sea, we'll need clever solutions to regulate the power.'

Rhan saw the conversation starting to veer off, and wanted to prevent the father-son dispute she felt she was creating.

'I can see that, as George points out, politicians have no mandate to introduce green measures. If rationing was introduced...there would be an incentive to catch up on the ingenuity from a century ago, before the apparent ease and simplicity of fossil fuels removed incentives. Shall we go in?' she added unexpectedly.

With nods all round, they shut out the lights and headed into the dark garden, where George, bringing up the rear, grabbed Rhan's hand. She was pleased by the gesture and glad of a guiding arm. She wanted reassurance and affection from George and the sudden transition into the dark had left her bewildered.

'George may scoff,' William persisted in the darkness. 'And it may already be too late, but I'm convinced that rationing's the only way to control carbon emissions in an equitable manner. Another key benefit, though, is that it will help society get ready and prepare for the shock and stress once things get awkward.'

'Well that was really interesting.' Rhan expressed her thanks while squeezing George's hand as he steered her around the apple trees towards the lights of the house.

'I'm afraid that you two are almost the first to listen to my cranky ideas!' William said, a faint silhouette ahead of them. 'Others have advocated the rationing of course…but not many. It's one of around a hundred measures I would introduce to soften the impact of what lies ahead.'

'Well that's fine then,' George's sarcasm cut in. 'No one is going to accept even step one, never mind the rest!'

'What are the other measures?' asked Rhan, releasing George's hand in both annoyance and because their way was now lit from the house windows.

'Well most are relatively minor, but we may have just seven good years left to get ready for seventy years of absolute hell. Almost any preparations might have a big impact and would cost little if started early. For example, I would ensure that every property with a garden and any village green or park or highway verge had to have a fixed number of productive fruit or nut trees depending on its size, unless the owner gets planning consent to avoid the regulation. Bigger gardens will need more on a ratio basis. The point is that the resilience of the country needs to be enhanced, and the sooner that process starts, the better. My walnut trees take fifteen years to produce, so laws are needed urgently if we can just get past sceptics like George.'

'Hang on! I believe in global warming!' George exclaimed as he followed Rhan through the garden door. 'It's people

I don't believe in. I actually think it would be fun to start getting ready.'

CHAPTER TWENTY THREE

A Walk Back to the Bronze Age

The next morning after breakfast, George and Rhan pulled on boots again. They stood outside waiting for Grace in the bright early-morning sunshine, looking across the fields at the elongated shadows cast by the spring sunrise climbing over the hills. Looking in the other direction, they gazed with fascination at a grey sea of cloud that isolated them from the plain below. Even as they watched, they could make out the sun beating back the mist and revealing more trees in the valley, yet Rhan felt relieved not to be taking the open-top car back down into the cold mass of fog. Up here, under a blue sky, they were the lucky ones.

Once assembled, they set off with the Cairn terrier leading the way – or at least the way he wanted them to go. 'No Hamish, not that way today,' or 'Wait for us!' were much-repeated phrases at the start of the walk.

They walked along an alleyway between high sandstone walls and dived into a covered passageway, cut like a tunnel through a terrace of houses. They found themselves at the village centre, to be met again by patches of bright, warm sunshine between long, cold shadows cast by the buildings. The cheerful light glistened and sparkled in ice coatings to the side of a flow of water running down the verge of the road.

'There used to be a village stream,' George explained. 'It was confined in Victorian times to a stone culvert, but it keeps fighting to run free again on the surface.'

At the village centre, two roads from the moors met the road down into the fog-covered vale below. A stone pillar surrounded by three layers of stone plinths made up a village cross, but Rhan's younger guide rushed ahead, keen to show her a more primitive uncarved stone predecessor that stood sadly across the road, next to a closed-up shop. Both the lonely pagan stone and the once upmarket general store spoke of past eras for the staid village centre. Grace made Rhan peer through the grimy glass shop window to inspect the massive brass cash till and the rows of haberdashery drawers, which could have belonged in some museum or costume-drama film set. George tugged Rhan's coat sleeve and they were soon pursuing the dog up through the village.

'So how many of these are second homes or holiday lets?' Rhan asked her guides. George replied with a laugh.

'It's more like third or even fourth homes, never mind second homes. They're only visited for a week or so a year, if that. Thank God, there're not too many so far – probably around one in twenty, but still crazy!'

They left the tightly packed terraced houses and the more spread-out recent developments as they climbed towards the bright moors. On most sides, they were accompanied by clear winter sunlight, with a crystal blue backdrop that picked out the woods and hills above in sharp focus. Yet the sun, whose slanting rays had vanquished most of the early frost, still had a fight on its hands. An intimidating bank of fog appeared intent on smothering the low-lying world below, forcing the walkers to quicken their steps even as they discussed which fields and sections of the village behind them had been enveloped since their start.

~

Leaving the road, they followed a stream, splashing through the gurgling ice-rimmed shallows or walking beside deeper pools. They climbed the slope of a large dam and were soon walking beside a reservoir, lined along the far shore by larch and pine trees, with immaculate symmetrical reflections in the still water.

'It's very full,' observed Rhan, looking at the water disappearing into the overflow beneath the mock-gothic tower beside the dam.

'Well this isn't used,' George answered before his sister could respond. 'Our water now comes from cleaner boreholes miles away and is pumped to the village. What you see here is only for people to walk round. It's the last modern reservoir above the village. We wonder how long before it'll be scrapped.'

'But I thought that upland storage was the big thing to cut flooding of lowlands?' Rhan asked in surprise.

'Yeah, but the owners, the water authorities, want to destroy dams,' George explained, looking at the water, whose surface was now steaming under the influence of strong sunlight. 'It cuts down on maintenance and responsibility. The trouble is they allow water levels to stay permanently full – much higher than when the water was being used, so there's no bloody storage capacity.' He rolled his eyes. 'Then the dams overtop when we get hit by the new storm cells that liven up our weather nowadays. They then demolish. That's engineering for you!'

He pointed to the hillside opposite. 'See that valley with the mist halfway up it? It once had two other reservoirs, but the second one is being bulldozed this year.'

Grace took over again. 'Yup, Dad rants that the reservoirs could've made electricity for us, and a dam above another nearby village saved a farmer's life by slowing a flash flood – before they demolished it. Whatever…the main drag is that we lose our best swimming lake! Hamish, where are you? Hamish, here!'

'That makes no sense,' Rhan responded, shocked. 'I used to visit precious water supplies with my father. Did you know that he was a water engineer, Grace?'

'No, I didn't.' Grace ignored the dog and fell into step by Rhan. 'So your father – that's why you're an engineer? All that Maths and Physics, ugh!'

'I was the only girl in school to study those subjects!' laughed Rhan.

'Oh my God! That sounds lonely…or did you have someone special?'

There was a slight pause while Rhan worked out what she was being asked.

'No, I was just really quiet. The thought of having a boyfriend never bothered me.'

'You must be a really nerdy swot, like bro.'

'He is no swot now. I have to nag and bribe him to get practicals and tutorials done; we only just scrape through. Everything and everyone is relative I suppose,' Rhan mused as she waited for her study partner, who kept stopping to look and poke at things beside the stream, much to the annoyance of his sister. The stream passed through a gap between steep hillocks that stood sentinel either side of the beck.

'Um, this was from an older generation of dams – one of several,' George announced, flicking a look at Rhan, which suggested this was not just a stopping point on the tour, but a useful diversion to break up the girls' discussion. 'The village was a typical early-industrial Yorkshire town. There was alum mining and linen weaving, which then moved from cottages or large shared attics into mills powered by waterwheels. This was one of three historic dams. They powered two or three waterwheels – another linen factory down there in the fog had another three wheels. Then there was a flour mill between them.'

'Don't forget the bottom flour mill with all the stones, which still has a real living miller in the house next door!' his sister prompted. 'And the two hydro generators.'

'What?' Rhan's flagging interest was suddenly piqued again.

'Oh, the big houses reused old alum dams or made new ones for electricity,' George explained. 'They owned the streams and could afford dynamos to light their houses before the National Grid arrived. But as the big modern dams are redundant, this beck produces nothing. When the power fails, the pumps close off, and so does our water.'

'Welcome to the real unsustainable world,' Rhan said, cutting across his musings. 'In Iraq, we only had electricity and water for an hour or so a day, if things were going well.

Most of my friends from Syria will have forgotten what electricity can do!'

'And then you come to the UK,' George took over. 'And we can't think of life without such comforts. The latest problem is that we even need it to open our electric doors and gates. Without power, we can't even find out what's going on once the local phone masts, the internet and our digital radios fail.'

'So?' Grace said.

Smiling, Rhan responded, deflating the family tension. 'Well it's heaven here with or without power. Just the sound of water – it's so peaceful! Which way now?'

~

Saving their breath for the walk, they climbed through a steeply sloping wood of Scots Pines and a field of rough grass before clambering over a final drystone wall. Jumping down, they were suddenly on the open moor, and were wading through a blanket of calf-high bush that Rhan was informed was called heather.

'In August the whole lot turns shocking pink and purple,' Grace called out, sweeping her arm to the horizon and breaking into a run. Rhan bounded after, laughing at both the exhilaration of being part of a rolling hillside that went on and on into the sunlight, but also laughing at the short-legged dog who was bouncing his way through the heather. They headed towards a collection of five or six stones, grouped together on a slight rise. One of the stones was standing, while the rest were inclined at varying angles or laid flat.

'What are these?' Rhan asked as they slowed their run.

'Stones!' George responded unhelpfully, arriving from behind.

'How do you put up with him, Rhan?' Grace took a symbolic swipe at her brother, but continued in an authoritative manner. 'There are lots of stones peeking out of the heather if you look. On this side of the valley, every stone must have meant something. They were dug up and dragged into position, some just a metre or so but others much further. Well,' she paused, giving herself time to look at the stones before them and then rushed on through her description. 'These are standing stones and along with all those along the edge of the ridge – they're probably Neolithic, which means late Stone Age. They were here to impress, I think. If we had time to look in the heather, we would see the pits they came from – they usually look like they were dug yesterday. Let's see, the stones are sometimes decorated – well those,' she pointed doubtfully at some worn dimples in the top side of a rock, 'could be old cup holders, as George used to call them, but then they could just be natural.

'Oh, look at this!' Grace exclaimed after a few moments from the far side of one of the stones. 'Even George couldn't say so many chiselled marks were natural; there's twenty or so orientated in – what? – three different directions.'

'Yup, man-made! Not a bad find, sis.'

'But what does it mean? Why has someone done this?' Rhan asked, shaking her head in puzzlement.

'It's conceptual art, from thousands of years ago,' Grace explained.

'Unfortunately the instructions to the concepts have been lost,' George added smugly. 'It's not art. I think it was for counting; over on that sunny hill beyond that arm of new fog, I know of a stone where there are six pairs of cup holders. It was obviously a calculator, used back in the pre-metric days, when everything was by the dozen.'

'That fog is definitely getting closer,' Rhan remarked with unease, cutting off George's hypotheses. 'It is amazing, but what happens if it keeps rising?' She watched the ill-defined shadows of white-grey, with wispy outriders, march into the valley below them, flowing in from the ocean of fluff in the plain below. Ahead, a white army used a different route to infiltrate across and below them, cutting them off from the highest moors.

'We lose the sunshine, unless the sun wins and burns it all away,' George replied flippantly. 'It's only cloud without the will to fly, to quote Bill Bryson.'

Rhan turned and started in surprise. From their high position looking out over the fog towards distant hills, she saw something massive in the clear sunlight above the dense ocean of fog. 'What was that?' she called.

The three of them stood, rooted to the spot, while something large and heavy rose lazily up out of the mist a few miles away, leant over and sank back down, like a jumping whale or a badly tossed caber at a Scottish Highland Games. A few seconds later, it happened again.

'It's the top of one of the wind turbines!' Grace burst out, laughing. 'We can only see the blade that's raised!'

'My God, that's cool!' George studied the process a few more times. 'It's great to see them on clear days, right up into County Durham.'

'That is amazing,' Rhan murmured, still watching until urged into action by George.

'Come on! I want to show you some of the Bronze Age roundhouses we think we've found while you've been wasting your time at rowing camp.'

A rapid stride across the flat upland took them to a shelf of land where grass and moss grew beneath a bank of heather. George and Grace dragged their visitor around an unimposing circle of stones edging a low-lying patch of dark green grass, set slightly lower than the surrounding moss and sparse bracken stalks.

'This is one of five or six houses in this settlement,' George reported as Rhan counted seven paces across the diameter and checked it again in another direction. 'They are really spread out, so there could be others in the bracken and heather. They usually have this diameter but some are up to twelve metres. They have a varying number of stones around the edge, every metre or so, and usually a central collection of stones. We don't have the earth bank walls they have in Scotland, or the upright stones they have on Bodmin Moor in Cornwall. We can only see these low stones now because soil levels have dropped.' George walked into the middle where he could reconstruct the building by drawing in the air.

'The edge stones must have been bearing pads for the timber rafters, spanning into the middle,' suggested the trainee engineer. 'If the stones took the axial thrust, they could've done without a central post – but it would have been easier to build, and more sturdy if there was a post in the middle here, on that central stone. I presume the door would be on the low east side, so they could have coffee on the terrace in the morning.'

After a pause, George lightened his tone slightly to indicate a joke. 'Oh I'm wrong there! The Parisi tribe were from the Iron Age, so these residents, if they were from the Bronze Age, would have had to wait a thousand years for their coffee and Gauloises cigarettes. Besides, in the Iron Age, the Parisi tribe were just south of this area when the Romans arrived and this bit of Yorkshire was part of the rival Northumbrian Briganti tribe. That's their military road coming out of the mist on the far side, taken over from the Bronze Age. On a good day, we reckon we can see its route across the flat valley, right to where it crossed the River Tees at Yarm.'

'OK,' Rhan responded suspiciously as she wandered around. 'I agree there is a bit of a circle here, but there are more impressive stones aligned just outside the circle. They appear to enclose a more rectangular shape. What does that mean?'

'Our theory is that...' George started, but Grace interrupted with an answer she had waiting.

'I think they're stables or pens to keep the animals at night.'

'I'm not so sure,' her brother suggested uncertainly. 'Those other stones could be in two lines down there. They look like they could be the beginning of our Bronze Age double wall rather than another building.' George indicated other aligned stones in the heather below the house. 'We haven't tried to join the dots yet. It's all like a Sudoku... any guesses are just that, pencilled ideas, until we have a complete row. Even then it's only our creation, but it makes dog walking more fun finding this stuff.'

'Well, the stones across there are on a curve rather than a straight line.' Grace continued the argument, leaving Rhan in the dark. 'And they're much too far apart, so they're not the double wall. They may be earlier Neolithic.'

'Let's keep going,' George suggested, breaking into a run again. 'We need to show Rhan some sections of that double wall. It's just across here and down.'

The two girls followed George across the flat, slowing over the lip of the moor top through broken areas of hillside, where George paused to continue the guided tour. 'What do you think of these little quarries, Rhan? We used to think they could be Bronze Age, along with the roundhouses scattered all over, and the double wall you'll see soon. There are little quarries all along the escarpment and there are extraordinary knitting-needle-like chisel marks on some.'

They dropped down below the quarries on the lip of the escarpment, slithering down a rough and steep slope, pock-marked by holes. George stopped at the edge of two holes divided by a ridge or short wall of rock.

'The quarries here could be older though, from the Neolithic,' he said, pointing at the dividing rock. 'Look at that partially hacked-out stone! It was intended to be a standing stone around two metres long. It still needs trimming on this side and it's still attached to the outcrop of rock along the bottom. There are others down there. I bet the quarrymen were pissed off when they heard no one wanted these massive stones, after all that work! *"Sorry* mate, haven't you heard? *The Stone Age is over so our time's up and we're done for. At seven o'clock this morning we started the Bronze Age. So no one wants your massive stone monuments any more – they are just too inconveniently heavy.'"*

'That is amazing,' Rhan remarked, appraising the wasted effort. 'It was quite an industry!'

'That's a point,' George said thoughtfully. 'No one thinks of stone quarrying in the Stone Age as an industry, apart from all the flint that was imported from Lincolnshire or somewhere to here. Yet even in the Bronze Age, hacking stones, or even nicking them from the Neolithic sites, must've been the major industry, besides farming.' There was a pause as Rhan considered what life must have been like until George tore off again. 'Come on, you have to see our wall. Run before the mist arrives! Hamish, come on boy!'

'This wall we're going to see – it isn't just ours, Rhan,' Grace explained breathlessly as they bounced down the steep hill through the spongy heather and into beds of dead and brittle bracken. 'The biggest stones, the Seven Sisters and bits of dyke were well known…but we're still claiming most of it…where we've found extra sections…and pushed the bracken down for the first time.'

Rhan made no response, waiting until they stopped their reckless descent near the base of the steep slope amid another jumble of worn and venerable standing stones. She immediately started to examine the large relics.

George was delighted by Rhan's evident interest.

'Just stand here on this bracken mound, Rhan! You'll see how the best-known and tallest Seven Sister stones actually align themselves into two rows of vertical standing stones, two metres apart – you can see another five brothers on one side and seven or eight sisters on the other. It's flipping obvious now, but it took Linda, an archaeologist who Dad used to chat with on the bus commute to town, to point it out.'

'Oh yes!' Rhan exclaimed enthusiastically, holding his shoulder for balance. 'I can see smaller ones as well, peeking out of the reeds and that bracken stuff.'

'You've got it. The stones aren't quite touching – they're spaced at around half-metre centres,' George told her quietly while Grace took no notice. 'OK, now follow the lines of stones down and you'll see more on the same alignments. There's a stretch towards the bottom where many stones were robbed for that square Viking building area to the right, but see how the two lines tie into that dyke beneath the hawthorn tree.' Rhan leant against his back, following his arm pointing across the hillside, waiting for him to continue. 'Archaeologists say stone and gravel were piled up between the standing stones, dug from ditches on each side – typical of Bronze Age cross-ridge dykes.' She nodded, listening in silence, not wanting to interrupt his description. 'Except this wall crosses the side of a valley, not a ridge, and it crosses earlier hollow ways and cuts through much earlier-looking stuff!

'We've found the two lines extend into that bog, but the stones are now coming out of it each year as the swamp dries out. You may be able to see more stones where the walls pop up on the far side of the bog, just by that group of hawthorn trees and that rough area of boulders.' There was a pause until Rhan nodded slowly again, holding on to his pointing arm.

'The alignment is less clear-cut beyond, along that steep slope where the bracken is still deep, but we think the double walls drop into that foggy valley, almost a kilometre away.'

'This is fantastic!' Rhan enthused. 'It's the stuff of goose bumps!'

'It's even weirder when you think of the effort they needed to construct this wall,' George suggested. 'It could've taken many gangs of workers decades upon decades to cut out the stone, fetch it down from up there, and to build this, all without even a JCB. If each stone took a team two or three weeks to quarry, fetch, and place, they may have managed, say, twenty a year. And how many stones? One kilometre, two, four thousand stones,' he calculated using his fingers. 'This double wall could have taken two hundred years for one team of say four people to construct – or perhaps forty people twenty years – about one generation!'

'You're right – it is weird,' Rhan agreed. 'The cost on the community looking after forty workers not producing food or anything useful must have been amazing.'

'Or, I could be wrong,' George admitted. 'If they just took the stones that had been quarried by someone else, it would have only taken a year or so.' Rhan ignored this throwaway comment.

Grace called over to provide more useful background data. 'That's the ancient track George mentioned. It was a motorway, before the Romans marched along it and long before it became the "Drover's Road". So all of this wall might've been security or even advertising for pubs, burger bars or pizza huts selling stuff at a service station down in the valley by the stream. The people up here may have been pretty well off if commuters had to pay tolls. So that may have funded the wall, or maybe they had an EU grant!'

Rhan laughed at her young guide's portrayal of history.

'Or an army of slaves,' George added ominously.

'But what was this double wall for?' Rhan asked them both. 'Where does it go? And why? And how come you know so much?'

Grace had wandered off below again, so George, still standing close to Rhan, was pleased to answer her.

'Well, we revealed most of it over many years of taking Hamish for a walk. See that mound of bracken on the line of the stones on this side?' He pointed at the nearest of many humps of bracken. 'If you stomp that down, I bet you'll expose another stone. Then within a few weeks of letting the air into the old bracken leaf, it'll dry up and just blow away, leaving the stone on display. We know so much because we're currently top experts in the world on this site, so it's easy – we can just make it up!' he shrugged. 'We soon find something else that shows whether we're right or wrong.'

Rhan struggled to grasp the flood of information as George continued his sporadic narration.

'That's the fascinating thing about this hidden valley: we can see who did what and when, relatively speaking, give or take the missing Iron Age. Ground levels are back to their ancient positions so word of mouth, history books and common sense allow us to guess the date of recent excavations, and ancient dykes or tracks. We have First World War practice trenches from the early 1900s, Victorian and Georgian quarries and dams from the 1800s and late 1700s, a couple of farm footprints on the edge of the moor from God knows when and that Viking longhouse from the first millennium. Before that we have little in the valley from the Iron Age, but loads of recognised Bronze Age dykes, roundhouses and burials. So older stuff with bigger and more stone must be from the Neolithic Stone Age. Simple!

'That footprint of a "Viking" building area to the right down there for example.' George indicated with a nod of the head. 'It's been looked at by several archaeologists in previous decades, but another archaeologist family friend, Richard, visited recently and says it's just the right shape for a Saxon or Viking longhouse. It would be old anywhere, but it's modern around here and fits with missing stone from the double wall! Cool eh? It must have felt a bit isolated having a house up here, as we think the valley was otherwise deserted, but all that third-hand Bronze Age stone must've been just too convenient and tempting not to use. Oh, and it was able to make use of a water channel from four thousand years earlier to save having to wait a thousand years for someone to invent running water!'

'Besides, Rhan, George was a nerd who read all those *Horrible Histories* books.' Grace built up the picture from ten paces away. 'He spent years fighting Assyrians,

Babylonians and whatever in one of those Empire Earth computer games! Our parents still laugh at his cataloguing of events when he was little – he used to bring his history picture books to them to complain about errors on early civilisations.'

Rhan put her hand to her mouth, chuckling and gazing at her tutorial partner in surprise, while Grace continued.

'Mum publishes books on archaeology, and dad is a conservation engineer, so they know some stuff, but we think most of this would blow the minds of archaeologists. We have no reputation, so we can come up with wild ideas.' Grace was gradually walking closer while still searching the ground. 'We knew we needed to find the Bronze Age roundhouses up there sooner. They had to live somewhere if they built all of this wall. It just took us longer to find than expected. Now we know what to look for, we find new ones most weekends, dotted around wherever the ground levels out. If you think it would be a good place to camp, there's almost always a house nearby, or so we think.'

Rhan looked between brother and sister, wondering who provided the more compelling story as Grace continued their apparent competition to drag their guest back into prehistory. Grace started pointing at new features that Rhan would never have noticed.

'As George mentioned, our latest idea is to work out whether water channels you can see there, with a line of reeds crossing the slope diagonally, were used by the roundhouses, or whether it was just the Neolithic Stone Age people who bothered to construct elaborate cold-and-cold running water systems. Those green areas above us seem to be well-watered paddocks, which we guess the Bronze Age animals carried on using after they took over.'

Grace's tone changed briefly as she pointed at a smudge of grey near the ridge.

'Oh Rhan, have you seen the herd of cattle over there? They have really woolly coats – you should see the calves, they are so sweet…anyway, we're hoping that there are too many crazy coincidences for us to be completely wrong all the time. But just wait 'til you see the really freaky stuff from the Neolithic.'

'Stop talking and come and see!' George was again very keen to continue his guided tour and strode off, talking as he walked, leading the girls up and across the hillside towards the cattle, which were lowing loudly.

'This is where the double wall crossed an older "hollow way" that links to what we call the Neolithic ceremonial walk, going straight up the hillside through that green paddock area with bits of old walls and Grace's water channels. You can see the bigger two-metre-long fallen Neolithic stones spaced out every five or six metres, although it's still a bit uncertain. At the top though, near those cows, most of the Neolithic stones are still standing. They run next to a long-known Bronze Age "cross ridge dyke". We've found another dyke, which goes back along the ridge towards those first roundhouses we saw!'

Rhan began to laugh at the enthusiastic outpouring of extraordinary data, punctuated by more ridiculous sketches in the air as George painted a picture of the ancient landscape. She bit her lip and kept her questions until she had a chance.

'What is a dyke for and what is a hollow way?'

'A hollow way's just an ancient track, worn down by use, with large stones shifted to the side,' came the enthusiastic reply from Grace. 'The tracks had dual carriageways or even three lanes for the steep bits and they seem to have been used like railway tracks, so one or two people could direct a whole herd. And a dyke is a mound with a ditch on one side. Up there the ditch was on the inside, presumably to keep their animals from wandering away.'

'We've got monuments here that could span two, three or four thousand years before Rome was founded,' George boasted to Rhan, who was now exploring as she listened. 'We have cist graves for hundreds of common people. But, we do the finding, not the digging, so we could be wrong. Mind you, even removal of the bracken was like excavating…you should've seen it when the live bracken was higher than your head and the dead bracken leaf more than your knee height. It took some stomping. Stones used to be found then lost for months. But now the level of most of the ground has dropped all by itself…you can see the exposed roots of dead or dying trees left on the surface. Look, the biggest tree over there fell down last winter. The bases to the standing stones and even the bottom of pits appear to be at the same level as they were five thousand years ago on the sides of the hills. We see different things each time we come up, as the landscape changes from month to month and year to year.'

'Anyway Rhan,' George continued with a mischievous grin. 'I know you'll be interested to hear that one of the main reasons we're finding so much stuff so easily is because of climate change…that and those shaggy-haired cattle over there and because much of the bracken has been poisoned.' George now had Rhan's full attention as they climbed slowly, and his sister had wandered off still further.

'And…they say it was climate cooling that drove people off the high moors.' George played a trump card again. 'It was half a degree warmer when people lived up here.'

'Hang on! Warmer than when?' Rhan immediately took the bait. 'We now have more than a degree of warming from pre-industrial times, so it will be much warmer this year than when these hills were occupied!'

'Yup,' conceded George, nodding. 'Most Bronze Age civilisations collapsed when it got cooler. Same as in the Iron Age when the Roman Empire started to collapse. Now we've the opposite problem with mega global warming, so there'll be unstoppable demand to move back up here!'

'Cool! So if Rhan's right,' Grace said as she wandered near to them again, searching the ground, 'it might explain why the bogs are disappearing and we can see more of this old stuff again.'

'Live peat bogs like cool wet zones,' George continued. 'So we're seeing the moors change to shrubland…or do I mean scrubland? But I'm afraid it's more likely that we'll see all the peat burnt away sooner or later. It gets really dry now, even in winter. And once lit, up'll go the moor tops and all that stored carbon. If it doesn't burn it just blows away. Grace isn't kidding – we've lost half a metre or so of soggy bracken soil in the last year or so.'

'But isn't peat on moors one of the biggest stores of carbon in the country?' Rhan asked. 'So is anything being done to fix the peat bogs and stop the release of methane?'

'Well, the short-term solution is to re-soak the ground, which may last a few years. But for the long term...' George put his hands on his hips, considering the problem. 'I suppose rewilding with trees might just help fix the peat bogs and stop the release of methane. Old peat beds can survive at depth and are one of the more difficult soils for us to engineer, according to Dr Graham. But others think trees would exacerbate the problem. No one seems to know.'

His study partner smiled at references to a bit of their geotechnical engineering lectures, which had meant little to her at the time. She hadn't really known what peat had meant, but she now had a peaty-black leg to show there was at least one patch where the drying process had been held up.

'I'll go with the trees!' Grace declared. 'Getting lost in a gigantic forest would be fun.' She had a more romantic take on events, until she had a second thought. 'But the gamekeepers burn the trees anyway – they make money from shooting grouse, so they don't want to see trees... or other wildlife. You should see the lines of wire snares they leave, to throttle foxes, badgers and Hamishes.' Grace wrapped her hands around her own throat to indicate the process, and then rushed over to stroke the dog.

'Could they make money from tourism?' Rhan asked, shocked at the negative publicity for the open landscape.

'Well, these ruins are hardly as grand as the reconstructed Stonehenge, and the biggest stuff here has been pushed over and never reset,' George pointed out. 'And there are other moors with better rock carvings. You're seeing stuff in transition but next year there'll be grass turf on most of this area.'

Rhan looked puzzled at George's explanation, so he carried on.

'Well the biggest Neolithic stones have been allowed to fall over or have been pushed over. The builders of a Christian chapel on the other side of that hill would hardly want to see this pagan extravaganza, would they? But the Bronze Age people may also have had it in for their Neolithic predecessors. They probably wanted to obliterate the splendid works of the ancients with their massive walls, tightly-packed stone towns and stone-lined procession routes, not to mention their bloodline.' He looked around at the remaining landscape, hemmed in by the encroaching fog. 'It's uncomfortable knowing about previous civilisations that lasted for thousands of years. So all their messages to the future – to now – with their indecipherable artwork and major monuments, have simply been ignored or…'

'I thought people are writing books about the Bronze Age like never before?' Grace interrupted from her search above them.

'Yes,' her brother conceded reluctantly, drawing out the word. 'I'm not sure how much interest there'd be in all our roundhouses here, but there'll be even less interest now our society is on the slide. We should've been planting the moors so we can move back up here in a couple of decades' time, but the planning laws will insist we try to resist the inevitable heating world. It'll be cooler and damper for crops like wheat up here when things really heat up, but without preparation, the soil will still be rubbish, so the sooner trees return the better. I'm not sure the adders will like it.'

'Are there many snakes?' Rhan enquired.

'They're intimidating,' George replied. 'They sunbathe at waist-height on the mounds of moss or on rocks. Ma doesn't let us bring Hamish up here in the summer, so we tend to keep to the moor tops once the frogs and toads come out of hibernation.'

'Hey, come and look at this!' Grace demanded excitedly. 'I think it's another roundhouse.'

George and Rhan strode across and were soon assessing the stones that Grace pointed out in a rough circle, where the mossy ground was replaced by dark, green grass.

'Grace House!' Grace claimed.

'Well if that is a hut, what about those?' Rhan asked, looking at an adjacent set of stones. 'Actually, do you think there may be two more circles? The grass extends under them both.'

'Yup,' George confirmed, pulling a yellow box out of his pocket. 'Grace House and Rhan Houses. See I brought the GPS. I knew we'd find something.'

'I am honoured,' Rhan laughed, glowing with pride. 'Is this how you find stuff?'

'Sure is,' called Grace. 'But we've never found three roundhouses close together before, have we George?'

Her brother became business-like, ignoring the question. 'I'll record their coordinates, if you could take pictures of each other in your houses from different angles. We could call these 1 to 3 Wall View Crescent!' he suggested, typing into the GPS box. 'At last, we seem to be starting to find the houses for those that lived and worked up here. They used to say that ancient people didn't live up here and only visited to bury their dead, but…well, you've seen the massive works.' George concentrated on the GPS before continuing. 'We're starting to balance the number of tumuli, where they buried their dead, with the number of huts we think the Bronze Age people lived in.' He waved his hand down below them and up ahead. 'We can start by showing you a few of the best tumuli or barrows. Some are marked on the maps but we've found many more recently – the 'rents and us. What we don't get is that the experts say the tumuli were also built before Bronze Age people arrived, which messes thing up. Anyway, let's go before we get smothered. That bank of mist is winning out.'

~

Hamish had been sitting patiently and obediently to mark one of Grace's house stones for the photographs, but bounded off with the three who were now glad to be climbing again as the cool fog started closing in on their heels. The air was no longer bright and sunny and they were glad of the warming exercise. It was some time before Rhan worked out who the "rents" were, but she was glad she had not asked once she'd worked out the answer.

Once they regained the top plateau, they ran across the very short heather to two circular mounds, and George showed Rhan a hidden third, all with different forms of construction. The hidden one was almost flat, surrounded by a stone kerb and a water-filled ditch. Another had a hollow, circled by two ditches and mound walls, while the third was a stone-covered mound around five paces across.

'It's strange how each tumulus is so different. You would think that Uncle Bob would get the same as Grandpa?' Rhan mused.

'Very odd,' George agreed. 'From the twenty five or so in this valley, hardly any two are the same. Some tumuli still have the borrow pits nearby where they dug out the stone – they rarely got round to backfilling, the messy bastards! Down there's an almost square one, which might have had stone side walls. We only have one tumulus that's a textbook classic; the rest must've been made or designed to measure, just like the graves for the lesser members of the family we might see later.'

'They certainly liked great views from their tumuli,' Grace commented in a low voice, obviously talking about the interned chiefs, before continuing in a more flippant tone. 'But we've found lots of new ones all down the hillside and in the valley bottom just by the car park, so perhaps some preferred ice cream vans to a good view! These mounds up here would be a great place to be buried, but perhaps not today. We've been caught by the fog at last.'

'It's going to be cold,' George said. 'We seem to be back into yesterday's weather. Are you going to be warm enough Rhan? Let me.'

Rhan was happy to let George wrap the borrowed woollen scarf around her head and tuck it into her jacket, as though she was a little girl again. From the corner of her eye, she noticed Grace smiling at her brother's mollycoddling.

As Rhan studied the ancient burial mounds, it became possible to look up directly at the fading sun. It turned orange, then a ghostly red before the silhouette of the great disc disappeared into the roof of fog over their heads.

'So this is what "Fog on the Barrow Downs" was all about,' Rhan exclaimed, standing on top of the largest tumulus.

'Was that *The Hobbit* or *Fellowship of the Ring*?' enquired Grace.

'Fellowship!' Rhan and George chimed.

'Can I just check: you know your way back, don't you?' Rhan asked uneasily as they started to walk downhill into an unyielding wall of fog. 'The swirls of mist are spooky... Oh God, what was that?'

She stopped dead. A disembodied yet distinct voice from the mist called out.

'Go back – go back!'

It was answered by another on their other side.

'Go back – go back!'

Hamish dashed off to investigate. There was a whirring noise followed by a third warning, further off. Rhan stood still, shocked, peering into the mist for at least one of the voices. She then thought to look at the brother and sister and relaxed as she realised they were struggling to repress their laughter.

'It's just grouse. This whole moor's protected so they can be shot,' Grace explained, adding, 'Their call's really eerie, isn't it?'

'You two are enjoying my unease and are showing off,' Rhan chided them. 'OK, it is scary, but it is also exhilarating and it's a totally new experience for me.'

'Sorry, but it was fun.' George linked her arm in his and a few seconds later Grace had grabbed her other arm. Walking three abreast made it difficult to wade through the heather over the rough terrain, but it was cosy, until they had to split up to navigate a descent. They were now walking in swirling, dense cloud of drizzle that numbed the senses and made it hard to keep balance, leading to frequent stumbles. Rhan concentrated on looking at her feet and tried to ignore the inhuman calls of the grouse to "go back". She even enjoyed the bickering of her guides, as the two constantly debated their best route or even where they were. In this featureless world without paths, encircled by just a few metres of grey, the slope of the ground was the only clue to their location.

CHAPTER TWENTY FOUR

The Neolithic Community

It was Grace who was the first to fall as they descended from the tumuli-decorated ridge, carving a tunnel through the impenetrable blanket of wet grey mist. She tripped over a stone buried in the heather, but managed to keep her balance as she half fell, half jumped to land on her feet in a little squared pit. The knee-deep reeds and grassy bottom contrasted with the enveloping heather. George chuckled as he looked about in the mist. 'Great! Grace appears to have found the necropolis we were looking for!'

Rhan peered at the depression in the ground, which she thought looked recent. She then noted that it had stone sides and a leaning standing stone at one corner. She was horrified as it dawned on her that her new friend had stumbled into a grave, even though Grace seemed in no hurry to get out again.

'You think that's a grave? Why?' Rhan asked.

'Ma says that the burnt remains of commoners where left in cists like this down south,' Grace lectured from the bottom of the pit. 'There's around thirty or so graves on this hillside. They'd have been visible from that ancient motorway we saw earlier, but not today.'

'There are other burial sites of a similar size on that hillside and a much bigger one with hundreds of cists just over that hill.' George directed Rhan with his hand again, which in the mist had absolutely no relevance to anyone. Both Grace and Rhan chuckled at his behaviour.

They went from hollow to hollow, inspecting a good handful of graves, delighted with Rhan's interest, as their guest gave a running commentary on her discoveries.

'So most appear to have been cut into the bedrock on the side of a hill, leaving two or three stone sides which could be the natural bedrock as well. That could suggest quarrying? But then some have a standing stone right beside the hole. On the downhill side, there is sometimes a smaller stone, but it is missing in that one, and that one. Could these graves be just places where stones have been extracted?'

'You have to decide,' George responded, without committing himself.

'Oh, that stone could have been a lid! I see your point. This one is big, yet that one is tiny.'

'Come on, Rhan, we've got something more to show you.' With renewed purpose and a definite direction in the reduced mist, Rhan was led down a hill, up the far side and across a plateau, where George restarted the grand tour.

'We've circled round and are just above the double wall again. Look first at all these quarries just below the crest.' They picked their way between quarry pits some three or four metres wide and a metre deep, similar to those they had seen earlier in the walk. 'We used to think these quarries were for the double wall, but it appears they're not.

'Are you sure these are old?' Rhan asked, deciding to question the wisdom of her guide.

'Just look at some of the stones that've been left by the pits,' George suggested. 'OK, the pits could've been dug last year, but look there – that stone's fallen over, yet it's weathered both on its tip where it stood, and also on its side after it fell or was pushed over. It's been there for many centuries. No one has suggested that they did much up here in medieval times, which would mean it was quarried in ancient times. Anyway, come down here and see where most of the stones went.'

They walked down the drop, which was strewn with boulders or partially shaped stones and pits to a flatter area. The mist allowed Rhan to see that it was just above the bottom of the slope.

'Stand on that stone there!' George ordered. 'You on that corner Grace, and I'll take this one.'

'I see your point,' Rhan declared with some relief after a few moments of feeling stupid. 'We are at the corners of walls, presumably to a house. That unoccupied corner is built up with several courses. It's…' She stopped, left her perch on the lowest stone corner and paced to each of the others. It's six metres by seven. Quite big! Is that an internal wall and a small room in that corner??'

'Yeah, we haven't figured that out yet,' Grace responded shaking her head. 'We call this East House. Just look. Those stones below this wall that we're stood on make a curve, which we think could've made a yard. Shall we carry on down?'

'Look around you now, Rhan!' George said enigmatically after just a few careful paces. The ground sloped gently and Rhan peered into the mist, which was more consistent and less confusing than it had been on the plateau they had just crossed.

'There are stones everywhere!' Rhan exclaimed as she obligingly and energetically scampered around in the mist, through a landscape of craters and boulders, while making sure she kept within sight of her guides. She felt relieved that the dog decided to join her and was sniffing around while the others stood watching. 'Some stones are piled in mounds, but others are in lines.'

She paused now and then to kick piles of dead bracken away, which were either soggy or dry enough to turn to powder and revealed yet more underlying stones. Keen not to be alone, she continued to report her findings, aware that the brother and sister seemed to be waiting on her observations. She began to think that everything she had seen previously on the walk had just been preparation for a test at this site.

'Large-faced stones…shaped…some with chisel marks. Some of these line walkways or hollows in the ground… sunken areas, similar to those grave hollows. What did you call them? Oh yes, cists. Except the low bits…they are larger and longer, like passageways, formed with massive stone sunken kerbs. The heaps, and the gaps between hollows, have smaller, partly shaped stones. What a waste of good stone! How strange! Are these more graves or is this a quarry, or a stone dressing area for your double wall?'

There was no reply from the two watching guides.

'Well, I know you are waiting for me to say it's a town or something, but you two are presumably keeping something from me,' Rhan complained eventually.

'No, we don't know anything,' George laughed while Grace shrugged her shoulders. 'This stonework was only revealed when the bracken started to die off a few years ago and it's still emerging, so we just wanted to hear your views without influence. We've probed the ground and there is usually soil rather than rock underneath, so your guess of a quarry is no good. These stones were presumably from those quarries just up there, so were dragged down here for a purpose.'

There was a long pause before Rhan spoke again.

'If these lines were the foundations to walls of ancient houses like that East House you showed me, and the hollows were the gaps between them, then …that would mean that all the rest of these stones, as far as I can see in this fog, are also probably ruins of stone houses. How unusual would a town be? How many houses are there?'

Rhan paused. 'I remember my mother saying that in Syria, the rectangular houses were older than the round houses.' She looked up to see George raise his eyebrows at his sister.

'My mother used to translate for tours sometimes,' she continued, aware that she had spoken so rarely about her mother. 'So is this a wrecked version of Skara what's-it in Scotland? Surely someone would know if this was an ancient town or village?' She was waving her arm as she spoke, amazing herself at what she was suggesting.

'Skara Brae is in Orkney on the top of Scotland,' George helped. 'We visited a few years ago and there are spooky similarities that could be just coincidences in the layout of the passages, if that's what they are. Skara Brae has eight surviving buildings and was Neolithic, say five thousand years ago, before the Bronze Age. They weren't meant to have stone towns like this around here in Neolithic times, just timber settlements. Then the Bronze Age had the roundhouses that we've found.

'But that could be all wrong. Someone spent decades quarrying all the stone for this town, temple or whatever. And except at East House, where you've just seen up to three or four courses of stone in one corner, not much has survived above the foundations. Anyway we've started to call this settlement Scarth. We thought at first it was a necropolis, didn't we Gracie? But we wanted to see if you thought it was a village as well. We've plotted around ten roughly rectangular houses like East House, along with their attached curved walls that could be outside yards, but we keep finding new outlying houses. I think there are at least sixteen, maybe twenty houses. You won't appreciate it now Rhan, but this was a great place to live. It gets sun from dawn to dusk but is sheltered by that hill we've just come down. It's a pretty dry spot so they just had to be inventive to get water here.'

'How come you have never mentioned this to me before?' Rhan demanded of George. 'Who knows of this site?'

'Well,' Grace intervened, defending her brother at first but then dumping him in it. 'The hillside is known to be of interest for its archaeology, but the site was covered with bracken. No one seems to have explored this place as much as us. You've had the up-to-date tour – except for the stuff George told me not to tell you 'til the end. It was in *New Scientist* a few months ago.'

Rhan looked from one to the other and back again, waiting for an explanation. Grace looked at her brother who just smiled, so she began.

'It's beginning to make *Game of Thrones* look like a picnic compared with what may have happened here.' Grace had obviously planned a theatrical beginning. 'The Neolithic people, who built the later bits of Stonehenge and who we reckon lived in these houses and put up the biggest and best lines of standing stones and water channels around here – they may have been wiped out really quickly, or at least the men. There was a version of the Black Death and then a vicious tribe from the east who swept right through Europe and brought the Bronze Age, and all that. They say that genetic tests show they had few of their own women, but took the local women. The men's genes seem to have stopped dead.'

'That's dreadful,' Rhan said, looking at the mist all around the stones, as though it hid a host of eastern riders. 'All the men killed?'

'It was Genghis Khan, minus three thousand years,' George confirmed. 'They probably invented cavalry, and I guess had bronze swords and survived the Black Death by living in isolated circular huts, like those we saw earlier. This cheek-to-cheek community, if it was a Neolithic town, would have been a death trap during a Black Death outbreak. It might explain why this township could have been systematically destroyed and left with hardly any stone on another. It all sounds a bit far-fetched, but…it's more likely they just had timber walls and we only see the foundations. We'll have to wait for an archaeological dig.'

'It's freezing. Let's go!' Grace had clearly had enough and led them down the slope.

'I've been looking forward to showing you this ever since our second day together, Rhan,' George confessed as they started to follow his sister. 'A couple of years ago, Pa brought some engineers and the landowner up here, but you're one of just a handful to see this place…you're the first outside the family who we've shown East House since the bracken died back. So that makes you the first to be relatively sure of what you saw!'

'Well I have no knowledge,' said Rhan, defensively. 'It seems strange to be at the forefront of a major find that no one else knows about. One always thinks that the experts know everything already – it's a bit like climate change. Even admitting we are in trouble feels like a step beyond sanity.

'So this sunken bit between walls…' Rhan stopped walking, taking in her surroundings as best she could in the mist. 'We are now walking the streets of an ancient town! You think you may have your very own metropolis, which…'

'Oh you need to look at these lines of reeds,' George interrupted as they crossed a nondescript patch of short turf, bare of stones but with a few scraggy clumps of dark green stems marching diagonally across the slope. 'Grace has mentioned water courses. This one collects water from three tiny streams and takes it to the two bottom houses of the Scarth village just below us – those stones there. We haven't worked out whether it was clean running water, or a flush system like they had in the toilets in the medieval monastery at the bottom of the hill.'

'My father would have loved the water system. But how come this area is almost paved?' Rhan asked, realising she was not likely to see much more of the water channel.

'It's that Bronze Age double wall again,' he repeated, and stuck both arms out at right angles indicating where the wall traversed the hillside. 'They had more stone than they knew what to do with here where the wall passed through the Scarth town. So they appear to have done something new – we don't know what.' He shrugged. 'But as you say, it's almost a paved area that links the truncated bottom of the Scarth community site – cut off by the Bronze Age wall.'

Rhan became distracted as she looked into the mist. 'Hang on Grace, wait for us! Where are you?'

The walk down was hazardous on the rock-strewn hillside, and the swirling mist appeared to be thicker again as they descended. After a while, the lack of visual references made Rhan feel dizzy, and peering at the heather beneath her feet was no real solution. She and George were happy to use the excuse to hold hands, while Grace still walked slightly ahead, often discussing, or arguing, over the best direction with George. They walked much further than they had expected and Rhan detected satisfaction in both of them when they reached a series of three steep dykes, with deep ditches between, almost as high as a person.

'So what are these?' Rhan demanded yet again of George, as they stopped on the ridge between two deep ruts. Only Grace's head could be seen in the trough just below them.

'Well they could be defensive dykes,' he replied. 'But they're the "railway tracks" that Grace described earlier. They divide and cross just over there, where that extra track comes up from the valley, so they're probably just ancient hollow ways, formed by repeatedly driving animals from the moor to the beck for a drink over many centuries. There must've been a hell of a lot of traffic to warrant a down track, a fast up track and a crawler lane! Or perhaps they kept changing track when a previous route became too muddy? We've had a large herd of those woolly-coated cattle on this moor for a decade or so and their tracks have made no impression at all, so it would've taken centuries or thousands of year to cut tracks this deep. Come on, let's keep moving, we're nearly down.'

CHAPTER TWENTY FIVE

A Mesolithic Hotspot

They took the downward hollow way at the junction, which led them to a modern, stony track. It was with some relief that they stepped from that onto the smooth asphalt surface of a narrow road. A little way along the narrow winding road, the teasing mist lifted for a few seconds to reveal a gravel parking area beside the road. There were only two remaining cars from several that they had seen earlier from the moor. They walked across the car park to inspect the beck that ran cheerfully along the other edge of the stony area.

'Guess what archaeologists found when they laid down this car park?' George asked.

'I don't think I know of this,' Grace complained.

'A Neolithic shopping centre?' Rhan responded, laughing.

'An Iron Age chariot park?' Grace joined in.

'No and no,' George replied, also laughing. 'Nothing from the Iron Age, except a few bumps that may have been a Celtic mill right against the beck, just over there. We know of tumuli and Bronze Age hut circles on nearly every mound that climbs clear of the bog and the stream, but the archaeologists only looked under the car park. Their trial pits found rakes of Mesolithic stuff.'

'Who were they again?' Rhan asked, starting to feel overwhelmed again.

'The Mesolithic were Stone Age before the Neolithic Stone Age,' George explained, and Rhan noticed that Grace was for once listening keenly to her brother. 'The Mesolithic were hunter-gatherers who had no fixed homes, but they were clearly pretty rooted here, especially on the side of the beck. The only other people who were interested in this area were the early industrialists who just flooded the area with that dam we saw earlier to feed the waterwheels. The archaeologists reckon the area is littered with thousands of worked flints, or microliths – some were formed into knives and arrowheads. One of our neighbours in the village used to say the whole moor is also strewn with flints. We've not found any, but I can show you one we were given. This valley was clearly a popular place for them. They could've been here longer than all the subsequent periods of mankind since then, so no wonder they dropped so many tools.'

'So come on you two,' Rhan teased. 'You have shown me Bronze Age and Neolithic houses. Don't tell me you haven't found a Messy…a cosy Mesolithic settlement where I could grab a coffee?'

Grace smirked but said nothing.

'Well…' George was clearly thinking on his feet and trying to remember. 'The trial pits found lots of placed stones, usually inclined rather than flat. They didn't say they were houses, but now I think about it, I bet they could've been elements of dwellings. Reconstructions from Ireland show wigwams made of sticks.'

'So no "show houses" from the Mesolithic?' Rhan joked.

'Not sure,' he smiled in reply, but furrowed his brow. 'Their houses looked similar to the Bronze Age hut circles, but were less substantial with weedier rafters. I wonder if some of our circles just over there could've been Mesolithic rather than Bronze Age.' He paused to consider this, before continuing.

'There are also loads of small standing boulders in and around this valley, which we always assumed were Neolithic, as they seemed earlier than the Bronze Age-shaped works.' He pointed at some mounds raised above the bog beside the road where occasional stones stood proud of the bare grassy hillock in a forbidding manner, framed against a misty backdrop. 'But as they're not the Neolithic's two-metre best efforts, they could be older. Who knows? Shall we go?'

'It feels even more desolate here than up on the moor!' Grace declared once they were walking back down towards the village. 'This is a real honey trap – and might have been a few thousand years ago, as well. Kids used to come from all over in the summer to play in the stream, try to catch minnows, build dams and climb the rock slopes and quarries. We used to love it and Dad claims he used to cycle up here most days when he was a kid. Nowadays you don't see so many children up here.'

'Computer games?' Rhan asked.

George laughed, but his sister continued.

'Maybe, but the biggest downer must be the parking tickets that hit families the most. The authorities only allow parking in the car parks, which take a fraction of the demand. They're empty today, but in good weather places are grabbed early by walkers and cyclists. Unsuspecting latecomers tend to park on the road verges and then get slapped with a parking ticket. No one expects fines without double white lines!'

'You have to feel sorry for the poor bastards,' George said, endorsing his sister. 'They get the message that they're not welcome in the countryside.'

'Careful you two!' Rhan warned. 'You are talking to someone who was largely restricted to playing in a back yard in Sunderland. We made the most of it with obstacle courses, and I used to love the monkey bars or the "spikes of doom", as we called them. If you touched the ground under the monkey bars,' she explained to Grace, 'we pretended you were impaled on spikes like on that *Prince of Persia* video game. It was a real treat to visit somewhere as exciting as this. But being fined would certainly have killed the fun and cut further trips, I suppose.'

They returned down the road through the tunnel of fog at a sharper pace to keep warm.

'Tell you what Rhan,' George confided as he linked her arm. 'I learnt a lot today showing you round.'

'What! How come?' Rhan felt puzzled and suspicious.

'It gave me perspective. Until we started to talk about the earlier hunter-gather civilisation, I had never put the archaeological report I'd read several years ago in context with what we've found in the last year or so.'

'Yeah,' his younger sister called over her shoulder as she walked along the empty road ahead of them. 'We started looking for the Bronze Age double wall. And that led us to the earlier Neolithic stone village and more water channels, more tumuli...ploughing, cist, whatever. It sort of made sense. But I didn't know about that earlier hunter stuff George was telling you about.'

'That's what I was trying to say,' George agreed. 'If you add the even earlier few thousand years, then we have a complete picture that sort of fits together.'

'Quite a representation,' Rhan suggested in a mocking tone. 'If your theories are correct, you have a complete record of prehistory and its associated climate, right here in this valley and hillside. The question is, are you two geniuses or just over-imaginative kids?'

'Probably both,' George admitted. 'We have the pluck to be imaginative but without scraping around we don't have the evidence from findings. They looked for stuff before building the car parks, but then just buried the evidence. It's not like it's exciting Roman or medieval remains.'

'Following your theories though,' Rhan mused, 'there were hunter-gathers here, living in simple wooden tents. Then a village or town that had fixed stone bases for large rectangular house walls, yards and streets between the houses. So the Neolithic really invested in their future to justify quarrying the stone and constructing a system for running water. It's just like now.'

'Not quite!' Grace responded smugly. 'There's a big difference between running water and hot running water.'

Rhan ignored the interruption as she tried to concentrate. 'Then there was something dreadful – plague and war you say, with genocide? But the new people stepped backwards and were happy to live in simple huts again with no facilities at all, whether hot or cold, apart from bronze knives. So how come no one is interested?'

'I suppose it's just too long ago,' George suggested. 'People can't or don't want to relate to prehistory.'

'That makes no sense.' Rhan pulled her arm away in annoyance. 'We are rapidly heading into a major extinction, so we should know how things used to be, and may be again, before rather than after we hit the destruct button. We spend money and carbon exploring the solar system looking for a Planet B, but don't explore the ground beneath our feet.'

'George!' Rhan's step faltered and Grace glanced round. 'You did mention your interest in ancient history and the Neolithic after all. I just remembered. It was in our first term in Danny and Tom's room when Chris was talking about the collapse of civilisations and Bede from Northumberland.'

'Oh yeah, but I can't remember exactly what I said,' he replied. 'The point is I agree with you. The anthropology needs…'

'The study of mankind!' Rhan interpreted for Grace who had looked round, puzzled.

'Yeah,' George continued. 'So if ever the history of civilisation is useful it would be now when everything is going to change. The history of development would be so much more relevant than the dates and doings of kings and queens and the big battles that history teaches. The Mesolithic lasted several thousand years, longer than the rest of our time combined. But for us, it's only in the last few years, and even in our lifetime, that we've been really determined to ruin our civilisation.'

Grace had put on headphones and was walking ahead in her own world. After a few minutes of walking in silence, Rhan asked the question that was on her mind.

'George, how can you be both apathetic and pessimistic? You are so much more sceptical about the climate than anything else. How come?'

'I suppose it's because there's no way forward. So few people believe that we even have a problem. It's only nutters like my father who say anything. You know that everybody else just pretends there's nothing to worry about. If they do know then they pretend we're already doing something.'

'Well I have to agree,' said Rhan thoughtfully. 'But your approach is so different from someone like David's, say. Why don't you think it's worth my while getting involved?'

There was a pause again while they marched past a noisy stream gushing down the hillside through the coarse grass above them. It splashed into a culvert beneath the road, and Rhan could hear it issue on the far side to continue its exuberant cascade down the hillside into the valley below.

'I'll tell you my first example,' George began. 'At school in the sixth form, we entered a national competition – I think it was called "Solutions to the Planet" or something like that. We had to invent something or investigate something that would help. Our team constructed a tubular screw that was similar to one we'd seen in a science museum, one that pumped water. A bit like an Archimedes screw, but we had three parallel sets of plastic pipe in a wooden frame fixed around old bike wheels at each end. Water from a stream entered at one end, and went down the screw which then rotated, driving a small generator taken from a computer printer. It stood clear of the stream, and was held by the bike wheel hubs.

'We made videos of us in the construction process, with it turning with water taken from that mill down there. One of us put together a cool PowerPoint showing how it could be used on about twenty or so streams around here. It cost less than thirty quid to build. We even had an REM soundtrack to the last video at the end of the presentation.'

He started to sing to Rhan, which came as light relief to her after his previous descriptions.

'*It's the end of the world as we know it. It's the end of the world as we know it. It's the end of the world as we know it and I feel fine.*'

He continued his story. 'So our team did really well and we got to the finals, which was in the House of Commons at Westminster. It was brilliant. We got a guided tour of the palace. We met MPs and former Ministers. We had to present in the Grand Committee room with four or five other teams. The judging panel was made up of two older men – London university professors from the Royal Academy, and a young female engineer.'

Rhan glanced at George, impressed. 'God, that must have been frightening!'

'It was great! Being down in London on a school day with three mates was good fun. Anyway, we soon realised there wasn't much competition from the other schools. Their efforts, concepts and presentations were rubbish. But then we got a surprise and realised things were not going to go well.

'One younger group of kids were proposing to write a children's book about a group of penguins and how the penguins' lives were changed by the global warming. It was then that the two professors each stood up and told the school team that there was no justification or proof for suggesting that climate change was real. Can you imagine that? The whole competition was meant to be about climate change, or so we'd thought. It was a vicious attack. We felt really sorry for the poor kids.'

'You're joking!' Rhan muttered. 'Did no one say anything?'

'No. The MPs, who'd spoken all about climate change at the introductions, had left and only returned for the award, so probably were left unaware of the direction of the competition. The organisers said nothing. We decided to try to avoid mentioning climate in our talk and to pass quickly over slides that covered it, but our project set out to save carbon, so we had no chance.

'The winning team came from a Catholic girls' school. They proposed creating charity boxes for mums and babies suffering poverty in the developing world. There was already a similar scheme up and running, so the girls just decided which items to put in or leave out of their boxes – stuff to increase the chances of their babies surviving the first few weeks – I can't remember much.

'We should've won just with our multimedia presentation, never mind all the work we'd put in to developing our idea. It could have been a great new low-tech power source, but anything to do with stopping climate change faces massive opposition. You know it Rhan.'

'So was there no feedback or anything?' she asked, ignoring his accusation.

'Well, while having tea afterwards, Don from our team started seeing someone from the girl's team, and that seemed the most important achievement. We didn't mind, but the female engineering judge came up and apologised. She said she didn't understand how we didn't win.'

The conversation stalled.

'So,' Rhan suggested after a while. 'If your invention had won, would all the farmers now be making money day and night from the little streams running through their land?'

'Maybe.' George laughed and sang, *'and I feel fine...'*

Rhan laughed uneasily.

~

The sight of houses at the roadside materialising from the fog and their return to civilisation was as welcome to them as their escape had been on the outward trip earlier that morning.

Grace and George threw off their boots and vanished into the house, mumbling something about a treat for the dog and coffee. Rhan listened to tapping sounds from the mist, which she decided must be a woodpecker, as well as the mournful cry of a bird that she had learnt was a curlew.

She was struggling to pull off her boots at the back door when she almost felt the air around her lighten and change. Looking up she saw the jaded reappearance of the sun, piercing the thinning fog. Wisps of mist were evaporating from the field in front of her, steadily revealing surrounding hills, already basking in the warm sunlight. The curlew glided almost overhead along the edge of the fog – a relatively large brown bird with its wings curved and angled backwards, its long beak bent downward – still calling out a melancholy *welcome back to the sunny side*.

Rhan gratefully peeled off the scarf and coat that George had wrapped around her. The bright surroundings started to weaken memories of the shadowy morning, leaving Rhan wondering how much of the ghostly remains from long-forgotten civilisations had been real.

CHAPTER TWENTY SIX

Progenicide

'So why do you have this interest in climate change?' June asked in the kitchen after Rhan had offered to help prepare a salad. George had been dispatched to the shed to see if any of the stored cooking apples were still usable.

'It is like an unwanted religious vocation,' Rhan answered in her usual formal English. 'I cannot ignore the way we hardly dare even discuss global warming. The less we acknowledge the problem, the worse it will be. It was George who pointed this out to me, but he is dreadfully fatalistic. He was suggesting this morning that the moors would burn away soon, now that they are no longer cold and wet. That would release huge quantities of carbon dioxide with dreadful consequences to the planet and the lives of many. I find it hard to accept that we should do nothing.'

'Yes, I can see that,' June acknowledged.

Rhan concentrated on cutting lettuce leaves into the sink but then continued talking to June, much to her own surprise.

'I suppose I also feel as if I owe it to my parents. For the sake of our safety they sent my sister and me away, sacrificing our last months together. I suppose I feel that God must have saved me from a life in a refugee tent for a purpose. Through some miracle, I am at one of the world's most prestigious universities at the heart of the Western establishment...Do you have a drainer? Oh...I mean a colander.' She paused while June handed her one, and they exchanged smiles. 'I feel that I have a calling – and it will not involve being a merchant banker, or getting married like my younger sister. Still, working for the environment will be a much less drastic vocation than becoming a nun, or working in a refugee camp like my grandmother.'

'Well that's a tragic and dramatic answer!' June responded. 'How do you get on with your uncle and aunt in Sunderland?'

'They are great, and so kind. It's very good of them to look after us – but both my sister and I realise that we need to be moving on so they can have their house back.'

'I'm pleased they let you visit us,' June said uncertainly, obviously wondering how Rhan could be allowed to stay with a male friend.

'Mmm,' Rhan mumbled while she decided what to say. 'I have not let them know how short our university terms are. They don't know about the rowing camp, never mind my visit here. I hope you are not too shocked? I tell myself that my parents would take a very different line from my uncle and aunt.'

'Well, I can see your logic, but please consider this as another home. It's been very reassuring having you look after George. We started to hear about you from George's first call home, so we feel we know you pretty well.'

Well that's strange, thought Rhan, furrowing her brow as she considered this silently. *It was almost a week before he spoke to me!* Then she said aloud, 'I think he mostly looks after me rather than the other way around; he introduced me to friends, he looked after me when I was ill, and he...' Rhan faltered, deciding not to mention that George did most of their washing. 'He is so much more domesticated than me, as you are probably noticing.'

June smiled, looking at the lettuce Rhan had dumped into a wooden bowl. 'You could slice up some of the eating apples to decorate the top. There are some walnuts from our tree in that bowl if you'd like to crack a few and add them.

'Anyway, we're pleased he's found someone to care about, but I get the impression that he leans on you to get him through the workload. After his initial excitement, he was pretty depressed by the work until you helped him out. We're not sure that he's a natural engineer, but it's a good degree as far as I can make out. So are you are looking for an engineering career that relates to climate change?'

'Probably, but my graduation is still more than three years away. I worry that each year is critical with climate change; Syria had its first drought from 2008, so things will be desperate by the time I graduate, even without wars to make things so much worse. Our friends in Oxford are getting fed up with me always talking about global warming, but I believe that I will need to do something sooner rather than later. I fear that George is hardly going to be enthusiastic if I become a green campaigner, yet he knows more than me about the subject.'

'Well George likes to absorb information. But would you be the sort of campaigner who chains themselves to an oil rig or would you join a university climate group? You seem to have had something to do with George going vegetarian, although he claims it's just incidental. There are plenty of other green things you could do too.'

'I am not that brave! Deceiving my aunt, uncle and sister and coming here to find out more was a big step for me. The carbon footprint of an engineer will be vast compared with any domestic saving I could make, so I hope to save the planet by working from within my profession, rather than through major demonstrations.'

'Oh yeh?' Grace stood in the doorway. 'Joining a major demo sounds more fun – it'd be cool to know an eco-criminal. Ma, have you seen my phone?'

~

While the lost mobile was tracked down, Rhan hurried upstairs to fetch a few printouts from her bag. Guessing their content, George and Grace teased Rhan for still wanting to talk to their father about climate change.

'Look, rather her than us, Gracie,' George took Rhan's side, if somewhat lamely. 'All we ask, Rhan, is that you try not to encourage him!'

Leaving the banter in the kitchen, a gentle reminder from June alerted William that he needed to help Rhan with her questions.

'I presume George told you that I wanted to ask you more about global warming?' Rhan asked as she gingerly entered the living room. The moors outside were now a black silhouette against a darkening sky. 'Would you mind?'

'Ah yes, carry on. Take a seat,' he beckoned. 'It's not often – no in fact, after twenty-five or so years, you are probably the first person I've come across who has actually volunteered to discuss climate change. It's even rarer to find a young person with interest!'

'Yes, I am afraid I need to realise that few wish to discuss the climate,' Rhan responded, smiling. 'George tries to tell me that global warming is a taboo subject that is only suitable for discussion between consenting adults.'

George's father chuckled, laid his laptop down and pressed the remote, which silenced the early evening weather forecast. There was the sound of wheezing from logs on the fire and the soft murmur of voices from George, Grace and their mother next door. Rhan sat on a well-worn leather sofa, leaning forward and studying the patterns on the Turkish carpet. The older man sat in an armchair, resting his feet on a footstool, which was also covered in part of an old Persian carpet.

It feels like Bag End, and the conversation between Gandalf and Frodo, Rhan thought. *Yet there is no magic power here to set evil to right.*

'Oh, congratulations!' her host said, making Rhan wonder what was coming next. 'I gather you and Grace bagged three new roundhouses on your visit to the moors today. That's impressive – I'm looking forward to seeing them. There's certainly plenty to discover about the ancient civilisations up there.'

'It was absolutely fascinating.' Rhan smiled as she recalled the morning's walk, which still seemed unreal. 'George said the Bronze Age people came off the moors when the temperatures dropped. Yet we are now soaring past those high temperatures again. It was fascinating to imagine how their landscape might have looked, through George and Grace's eyes.'

'Yes,' he replied. 'It hasn't taken us long to move into uncharted history up there. You will have noticed that the older civilisation – the Neolithic – appears to have the architectural and civil engineering attributes most similar to our own period.' Rhan nodded slowly while he continued.

'Time clearly does not offer a progression of improvement, so it is easy to imagine someone, in another five thousand years, looking at one of our towns or villages and wondering what happened to cause massive and drastic regression in our civilisation.'

He looked around the room at the walls, imagining what the house would look like as an ancient ruin.

'I understand you think it will get much hotter – and that you believe we will have a tipping point upon us – in the next few years?' Rhan asked uncertainly, hoping to get away from the archaeology.

'Well, tipping points appear to be really unfashionable at present,' William started in a light-hearted manner. 'We are told we need to take the fear out of climate change, which I think means ignoring the risks. Yet that's against a backdrop where global warming, as we know it, tends to be either simply denied, or set aside to be dealt with by negotiation at some future point, currently set at 2030 or 2050.' Before continuing, he smiled briefly at his own joke – the concept of negotiating with the climate.

'Tipping points have been considered to be an unknown and unacceptable hypothesis that need only concern troublemakers. Those troublemakers, on the other hand, have started to talk of "cascades" of tipping points, now that CO_2 levels and temperatures are already going up by leaps and bounds.' He stroked his chin, contemplating the future. 'I suppose tipping points were more of a worry when it was hoped that we had a chance to keep warming to a reasonable level. Cascades suggest the prospect of jumping from crisis to crisis without any ability for mankind to regain control.'

'Is it that bad?' Rhan murmured, shocked – despite her expectations – by the implication of what he was saying.

'It's not good,' he responded. 'I think we are standing on a cliff edge. From all the various scenarios produced by the IPCC, ranging from what – 0.5° to 5°C of warming or more?' He glanced at Rhan, who made no response, so he went on. 'I collected opinions from world experts, who have written briefing papers for my civil engineering journal. They seemed to confirm that there are just so many dangers. It means we have little chance of achieving anything but the worst possible outcomes rather than the official predictions that have been hopelessly optimistic and never stood a realistic chance of coming true. Dangers that were not well defined have been simply ignored.' He sighed and leaned back, raising his eyes and shaking his head.

'I suspected the news was not going to be good,' Rhan acknowledged, adjusting her headscarf as though she could protect herself from their discussion. 'I printed these out and wondered if I could discuss them with you.' She held up the papers. 'I looked at the PIOMAS graphs for the Arctic ice, following a tip from George.'

She smoothed out two sheets before passing them to William.

'There's my version of a simple graph showing two downward curves: the percentage volume and the percentage area of summer Arctic ice against time. It uses the 1980 figure as 100%.'

'Ah yes, interesting,' he responded. 'These cover the timeframe of my working life since starting on the Thames Barrier in 1980. It's probably coincidental that changes in the ice are assumed to have started around then, as sea levels were already rising. The plunge in the volume curve is most alarming isn't it?'

'Yes!' Rhan agreed emphatically. 'It appears to me very unlikely that the downward dive towards zero could ever recover. I find it hard to believe that the summer ice can survive for more than a decade.'

'Quite! And once the ice goes, we will then see the irrefutable evidence that we have irreversibly changed the planet. But what amazes and frightens me is that even the committees at the IPCC prepared the ground in 2014 for failure, suggesting that loss of the Arctic ice over a few months of the year will not be too significant. For a few years many scientists believed and assured us that the IPCC warnings were too pessimistic and alarmist. They suggested that as the planet was heating only slowly, the earth could shrug off the laws of thermodynamics. Once again everyone could believe there was no problem, the ice would not melt, the depths of the oceans would postpone the need for action. Now recent temperatures are shooting up again, so....'

He leaned forward, rubbing his forehead with one hand, before continuing.

'I'm afraid that both your generation, and even mine, are likely to see amazing and dreadful things. As you are no doubt aware, almost everyone, including scientists and engineers, have convinced themselves that there is no immediate danger. Nothing is meant to happen for decades, but the majority are wrong – we have woken the giant. Every land between the Arctic and the Antarctic have all the signs of climate change, so the whole world population is being stupidly suicidal.'

'You don't have hope for the Paris Accord then?' Rhan asked, pulling back into the recess of the sofa.

'Reluctant proposals from Paris to cut carbon emissions by 2030 or 2050 will seem almost irrelevant by the time the deadlines arrive. All current talk of having ten years to start going in the correct direction has no basis. We needed to have started ten or twenty years ago, not in a few years' or decades' time when my generation have all retired. We are the feckless post-war generation who only look after ourselves. As George pointed out, my hopes for action soon are pure folly. To use another saying, here we are, not even aware that the horse essential for the next generation has bolted, and we have absolutely no intention of closing the stable door.'

William turned his palms upwards. 'The laws of physics will drag us down. We think mankind does not need nature. We think we can put everything right again, given enough money. But that's just not going to be possible. The science just isn't there, never mind the engineering to change the planet back to previous normality. We can only save pockets like London for a few decades.'

He stopped, looking at Rhan and waiting to see if he had said enough or too much. After a few seconds of silence, she took the initiative again.

'A real question that I am trying to answer is what might happen in the next decade, at the start of my working life. For example, what do you think will happen once the Arctic sea ice goes? We – George and I, when I could get him in a serious mood – talked about it being like losing an efficient cooling sunhat. I could find no real predictions of what is in store for us on the other side of that tipping point, other than more tipping points. How did we get here?'

'Your working life will be different from mine,' he acknowledged, contemplating what she had asked. 'It's going to be a shock once people realise that we are now on a constant slide to disaster.

'As an engineer I see big differences between the risks…I mean probabilities, stated in the IPCC reports and the probabilities that engineers routinely address when trying to avoid dangers. The IPCC scientists assume that probabilities of less than 1 percent for dangers to the planet are deemed unworthy of worrying about. Engineers go to great lengths to avoid risks such as 0.01 percent if several lives are at stake. Where major loss of life is possible, engineers aim for probabilities of less than one in a million. The trouble is that the IPCC are only criticised by the media when they overestimate the dangers, yet nothing is mentioned when their "worst credible" predictions are exceeded within weeks of publication. It should have been alarming.'

'But surely the scientists carried out the research on what will happen?' Rhan persisted. 'The technical papers must be out there?'

William considered the issues for a few moments. 'Well, in the early years I believe that climate models tended to avoid the incredible scenarios and had the excuse not to spend time analysing conditions that were considered just too dangerous and stupid to contemplate. Then I suppose they avoided items with too many parameters that would be difficult to justify against attacks from sceptics. Greenland and the Arctic just felt too big to melt except over thousands of years, even though there were clear signs in the rocks that they were wrong. We keep seeing the mechanisms for change only when they are upon us: we know sea levels can rise quickly, yet we have done nothing when it would cost little.

'I'm afraid, Rhan, that the future will be a very frightening and depressing place. Our civilisation and society will alter with remarkable speed. There are too many calamities waiting to pile in and make global heating worse, as nature starts to add to our greenhouse gases. Once we have totally lost control, we'll have the obvious excuse to stop even trying to cut the emissions we can control.'

Rhan nodded, her chin on her hand, recalling what she knew of the impacts of removing the reflective ice sun hat that would no longer cool the Arctic; the decaying permafrost in the surrounding tundra; and the unstable clathrate compounds lying frozen on seabeds. She said nothing and let him continue.

'So returning to your question about conditions beyond the summer Arctic tipping point once we first have zero ice – I think that the loss of reflective surface will affect us all in the northern hemisphere much, much more than current models predict. With so much summer ice being lost each year and no effective buffer of latent cooling, the autumn, spring and winter ice will then be on a downward plummet too. My guess is that by around 2035, the Arctic Ocean will be almost ice-free throughout the year; I could be very wrong but the risk is far from negligible. Yet I have no proof – it's just my opinion.

'There are, of course, plenty of experts who also believe that current predictions appear farcically optimistic. Then beyond that, there's no way the Greenland ice sheet will take hundreds or thousands of years to melt once it's surrounded by an almost tropical sea.'

'So the current predictions of just a few hundred millimetres of sea rise within my lifetime are also likely to be just stupidly dangerous?' Rhan suggested.

'Absolutely! Sea-level rises and land sink at those rates were predicted for the Thames Barrier four decades ago. By the time you're my age, you could be looking at sea level rises of a metre every twenty years, like in previous geological periods when climatic conditions flipped around.'

'I hope you are wrong. Articles that I have read still talk in terms of a fraction of a metre this century. But if you are right, then what? Will people take it all in their stride?

How will they react?' She tried to keep him on the track she wanted. 'What will it feel like, or what will we see as the Arctic ice is replaced by water?'

'I'm not sure that I'm the person to ask about people's reactions,' he replied, smiling and shaking his head. 'I've been alarmingly correct at predicting the physical realities of global warming over the past twenty years, but I warn you that my predictions of society's reactions have been utterly incorrect at every turn so far.'

'I appreciate that the issue will continue to be waved aside as someone else's problem,' Rhan said. 'Yet without an ice cap on the world, as you say, everything could start to feel different very quickly. I suppose I am worried that attitudes to death and immigration will harden even faster.'

William nodded and carried on. 'Without the cooling ice, the deep oceans and shallow seas will start to act very strangely. I'm pretty confident that no one knows with any certainty at all what will actually happen to the weather once the ice is gone – we will clearly face a completely new set of rules. Our weather and farming patterns will be in a real dither within a rapidly heating process overall.

'I mean, we've only just started to understand how the high-level jet streams in the skies above are behaving in the new warm-Arctic conditions. The oceanic drifts are just as complicated so I doubt we have any idea what will happen to world weather. I mean, who would've predicted a few years ago that the British Isles could be affected by something as unlikely as low pressure in the sea off the Russian north coast? I don't think there was even much of a coastline just a few years ago. The science and predictions are all too recent. I have a feeling that the weather here in Britain will change as drastically as elsewhere in the world.'

Rhan nodded. 'Yes, isn't it the case that temperature differences between the equator and the North Poles tend to power the south-to-north wind in our hemisphere? With gravitational acceleration, that creates the jet stream with the Coriolis Effect.' She held out her thumb and first two fingers at right angles to work out the directions, amazed to find that she had learnt something relevant in her unfathomable theoretical maths that year. 'Rapid warming at the North Pole means that the jet stream is now sluggish and lackadaisical – more like a lowland river, prone to big meanders and oxbow lakes that leave stranded pockets of hot or cold air in strange places.'

He laughed admiringly at her knowledge and enthusiasm, just as there was a fumble at the door, which opened to Grace's call of 'Gin and tonic!' She entered, bearing two glass tumblers with fizzing ice. She handed them to her father and their visitor.

'Brilliant! Thank you,' William enthused.

'Having fun?' Grace asked Rhan.

'Yes, thank you,' Rhan replied rather stiffly, then chuckled as she realised that she had continued to hold her hand with fingers and thumb extended at right angles.

'Well, I'll leave you to it then.'

There was a pause as Grace left before Rhan started up again.

'A balmy north Arctic Ocean is still difficult to imagine,' she said. 'I can see how a lack of mixing air and water will create massive hotspots that will bring the threatened hurricanes to Europe and surges of water levels up or down the North Sea. But what will happen when the slowed north Atlantic drift hits the Pacific equivalent coming up from the other side of the Arctic Ocean, when there is no ice barrier?'

'I have no idea!' William admitted straight away. 'Good question. All I know is that there will be plenty of work for engineers fighting the new weather conditions and sea levels.'

'So what about countries without resources to construct barriers for rising sea levels?' Rhan asked in a forced neutral tone.

'I suppose that flooded cities and water taxis will become much more common,' he suggested, sipping from his drink. 'Some of the best land will be lost, so farming will have a dreadful time, resulting in food being a major issue again.'

'You mentioned 5° or more. Just how hot do you think it will get, and what will that mean? You think our whole society is at risk? She glanced doubtfully at the dark, cold evening through a gap in the curtains. 'Actually, I suppose I also want to know what it will mean to us, to Syria…and what we need to do to survive here in the UK?'

'Well, I wouldn't start from here,' was his immediate, flippant answer. 'Your generation have been very unlucky to follow my generation.'

After a couple of seconds' contemplation, William got up, threw a couple of logs on the fire and then grabbed the discarded computer again, searching as he spoke.

'Comparing relative temperatures in one region for a given mean temperature rise is well illustrated and readily available from the IPCC; I presume you've seen those coloured graphs of the world? Gaining understandings of just how hot, or when the heat will reach those temperatures and the resulting dangers, are difficult subjects to grasp. A few good books try to fill in the gaps, such as *Six Degrees* and *The Last Generation*. However, I have a different slant here that may interest you. There it is!'

After a bit of tinkering with his laptop and pleased with his find, he showed a table to Rhan on the screen.

'This will not answer your questions directly, but it gives an engineer's perspective on what we face. These are sets of opinions, mostly from engineers, that I've collected in surveys. You'll see that they date from…ah yes, 2008 up to 2015. It may seem strange, but I think that the responses from these very small samples might be as close as you will get to answers for your questions.'

Rhan sat on the edge of her seat again, looking at a column of questions on one side of the table, with columns of percentage values next to the questions. The headers at the top of the table indicated different types of average and quartiles. It dawned on her that William had actually asked engineers to provide percentages as answers for around twenty different questions. She decided to concentrate on the most frequent responses while William started to explain what she was looking at.

'The first questions just cover general issues, effectively asking whether they believe in global warming – around a third considered it a serious issue. That's much higher than a random sample, but still lower than might be expected at a special lecture on the subject.'

Rhan grinned, wondering over the implications, but not interrupting.

'The last set of questions deal with professional approaches on what engineers should do about it. It's the middle subjects that cover aspects of your areas of interest: temperature rise and the impact. For example, on migration…Question 4 covered displacement for a two-degree rise in temperature…the averaged answers indicate that between 10 and 20 percent of the world population will have to move – that's around eight hundred million to one, and a half billion people. Does that sound plausible to you? I gather it's a similar percentage to the migration from the Irish famine in the nineteenth century, when around 10 percent of the population moved, and just as many died.'

'Ah yes, George sent me that figure last holiday,' she replied. 'The results seemed reasonable, even just considering the populations that will be affected by inundation from rising sea levels. Yet the numbers were provided by engineers who know nothing special?'

'Absolutely, but engineers are used to assessing risks by plucking data from the air. The inundation of coastal areas will certainly be significant. Just look at the vulnerability of East Yorkshire and York itself once we have a few metres of rise. Yet even with such relatively obvious risks, there are again no moves to prepare slowly at negligible cost. Anyway engineers aren't alone in having such concerns. I've done larger surveys among non-engineers – school kids and adults – and they produced similar results. The strange thing is that where we've been able to benchmark the engineers' predictions – well, on ice melt – they turned out to be more accurate than the IPCC official consensus of expert advice!'

'Really?' Rhan asked, still not giving the results much credence. 'Ah, these subjects cover engineers' expected outcomes from temperature rises.' She pointed at rows on the table.

'You've got it! That question indicates that around a third of the world's population would be at risk from 3° rise – that's around three billion deaths!'

'The same fraction as from the Black Death?' Rhan suggested quickly. He nodded before continuing, pointing to the next relevant question.

'But if you look at that question, once we get to 3°C, there is almost an even chance that temperatures will shoot up further to a 5° rise.' He looked up to conclude. 'Some scientists are only now, a decade or so later, starting to acknowledge that 4°C or more is now a very real possibility by 2100. Yet I sat on an engineering task force that recommended engineers should at least assess risks for 4° by 2040! As you point out, these are just engineering opinions, with or without positive feedback and tipping points, but...' He paused, shrugging. 'I've no data above 5°C, but the engineers thought that once we reach that temperature, less than half the population would survive.'

He pointed to the last outstanding question. Rhan responded immediately, as she had already been staring at that result on the screen.

'These are not good odds!' she declared, as she moved her drink to one side to focus on the future prospects. 'We are already set for rises of 2° or 3°C unless we find a magical cure for the atmosphere.' Rhan sat forward, studying the data on the screen. 'Once there, we could expect one in three people to die? Yet these survey results suggest there are groups of engineers who would give no better odds than the toss of a coin that we can stop global warming at 3°C of warming before we reach 5°. Then half of everyone will die.'

'That's what the opinions showed,' William confirmed. 'On the projections that I've read for 3° of warming, you wouldn't want to see how much worse everything will get. The Amazon rainforest would be doomed, so further disaster there. The rains would move northward into Canada and that would be repeated all over the world. The productive land would be too hot to grow wheat, and the new moderate zones wouldn't have adequate soils! Starvation would haunt most lands. Huge populations would be looking for food. Technology would have no chance against such changes in both nature and society. I think that things will be at least as bad as those opinions.'

'My God!' she muttered, going through the table slowly. 'I suppose, if I was asked…I would suggest even worse figures! Many people, if not most, probably live in coastal cities around the world, or in regions that will be hit by severe drought, so I can see how most of the world would need to move. A death rate of half the world for 5° seems possible then, or perhaps probable. That leaves the question of when? When will this happen?'

She looked up, hoping for a simple answer. William answered indirectly.

'Well, all I know is that 5° is now likely by 2100, and with the tipping points we discussed earlier, I think it'll be sooner than that.' He looked up, ready to answer Rhan's next question.

'So what did the engineers want to do?' Rhan asked, looking expectantly at the laptop.

'Well from my surveys – everything and nothing!' He laughed suddenly and hollowly. 'On the face of it they wanted engineers to be fully engaged and taking a lead, yet only a small percentage were prepared to take any meaningful measures!

'As I mentioned, the earlier results suggested that around a third of respondents could actually be considered sceptics, as they denied that mankind was responsible for global warming! In the more recent surveys, the predicted timescales for the first Arctic ice melt moved into the distant future, even though they had almost the same evidence as you; so a significant portion was convinced that it wasn't their problem and that we'll have plenty of time to act, despite the evidence.' He pointed at the screen. 'That larger group of opinions was from a wider group of 650 non-engineers, with a high percentage of under-eighteens, and they gave similar results. The results weren't that different – few actually advocated taking any action! Most climate events I've attended say the same – we just need to improve efficiency! Otherwise just carry on as before!'

There was a pause in the discussions while Rhan chewed her lip before continuing on a different resigned tack.

'So your data shows that half the world will kill the other half off, unless something extraordinary happens?' she demanded bluntly. 'Genocide, on an unprecedented scale!'

'Well I think of it as *progenicide*,' he suggested quietly, looking at her askance.

'What?' she asked, looking at him with a furrowed brow.

'Progenicide. I am afraid I decided we needed a new word. My generation, and yours to a lesser extent, inherited a wonderful, vibrant planet, yet we are quite prepared to pass on a doomed world to our children and grandchildren – our progeny. The gist of all these excuses is that our progeny is not deemed worth any effort by our generation. It is perhaps the first case of genocide against our own progeny. Progenicide is what I call it.'

'Does that have any meaning?' She smiled weakly, unsure of the direction of the conversation.

'I suggest progenicide involves...' He had to stop and think before continuing. 'Acceptance or active, complicit participation in a lifestyle that will mean the death of our progeny. Even when either poor or rich people are aware of the implications of both overpopulation and global warming, or both, they are prepared to contribute to carbon emissions and add extra mouths to feed and let others in poor countries die for their short-term benefit. We know the lifespan of carbon dioxide in the atmosphere, so we know that, in the longer term, it will of course result in the death of our own children and grandchildren. Overwhelmingly throughout the world, we have chosen to carry on, regardless of the relatively modest changes that we need to adopt.'

Rhan nodded her recollection of William's main suggestion of rationing on the previous day, while he continued in a slightly aggrieved voice.

'Progenicide means that we've lost every shred of decency and morality, which used to be taken for granted in most societies. I think it's the ultimate sin. We would happily kill others and let our own family suffer, just to avoid walking to work, catching a public bus or missing out on a flight to a different part of the world.'

'Yes,' she spoke slowly in her old-fashioned and slightly dramatic accent. 'We discussed the possibility of an intergenerational conflict last term. It may be related to your idea of progenicide. Our friend, David, thought there would need to be wars to prevent people continuing to pump out greenhouse gases, regardless of the impact.'

'Well I hadn't conceived of anything quite as drastic as that,' he conceded. 'But I have no idea what stopping progenicide would involve. Bombing oil wells and pipelines might come eventually, but too late.'

'Well in science-fiction worlds, like *Alien* or *Avatar*, there are always baddies,' she responded semi-seriously. 'They tend to place profit before the future of civilisation. George told me this morning of two scientists who wrecked a school initiative, but are there many engineers who would actively stand against action to reduce global warming?'

'Oh yes – there are plenty of those in my industry!' William asserted. 'After all, we think we have a vested interest in using concrete and steel and very few want to change back to low-carbon techniques and architecture from a hundred years ago, no matter what danger we bring to the next generation.

'Every other year I stand for election to my engineering committee to act for the climate – I generally get less than 5 percent of votes and come almost last. Yet when I joined, civil engineers claimed to control the natural environment!' He grimaced.

'I was told there were massive procedures on sustainability,' the student suggested.

'Sorry,' William responded sadly. 'The idea of making structures low carbon in the critical short term never caught on! Instead, codes have been developed to allow projects to have big carbon footprints, yet gain sustainability awards based on future promised efficiencies and sustainable demolition in a century or so. As I said, even on projects such as the restoration of ancient buildings, no one wants to put back the low-carbon timber beams in the original sockets in case it could be mistaken for pastiche. They prefer to rip out the foundations and install brand-new concrete piles, pile caps, slabs and steel columns. On every project I have ever worked on there's always someone to insist on steel or concrete. After decades of trying, I've still to construct a negative-carbon structure.'

'I had wanted to ask about that,' Rhan said. 'Our lecturers continue to teach the old steel-and-concrete approaches. Only George notices.'

He nodded curtly. 'I'm afraid that in recent years I have also been really disappointed by the way young engineers, just a few years older than you, vote against their own future.'

Rhan glanced at William, before confirming his fears.

'I have had real trouble trying to find young people who would accept the concept of warming, never mind accept that they needed to take action. I suppose we are still strongly grounded in greenhush.'

William grunted his agreement just as George's voice called out for supper.

'Greenhush allows us to pretend that everything is fine,' he continued. 'People's actions suggest that progenicide is a price worth paying if it allows everyone to just carry on as before, even if it's just for just a few more years.'

He called to George through the closed door as he started to rise. 'OK, we're on our way!'

As he bent down to tend the fire, Rhan quietly brought up the critical question.

'What about my family here in the UK?' she asked. 'Will there be war here, and if so, when? Do you think Britain will become somewhere that everyone will fight in and over, if we are going to be less affected than most? Or can we just sit back and watch the rest of the world suffer?'

He looked up, only slightly surprised before answering after a short delay. He was leaning on the mantelpiece, enjoying the heat from the fire whose flames he had just dampened. 'Well, in both the First and Second World Wars, the UK was said to be on the edge of starvation as supply ships had trouble getting through the submarine blockade. Since then, farmers produce more per hectare, but have then lost good land to developers, and the population has increased of course. I believe we produce around 60 percent of our food, so shortages could be expected within a few years, as previously productive regions such as California and South Australia have started to suffer already – more quickly than the UK.

'It's easy to imagine that even Britain would face hunger as soon as there's a breakdown in the shipping-in of spare food from other countries, unless we start to prepare in the available time. Much of the best land in East Anglia and East Yorkshire are very vulnerable to sea-level rises, yet vast tracts of land that would enjoy a warmer climate, like on the moors here, are still stuck by feudal systems and the enclosures from two or three hundred years ago. There is no investment in land or in low-carbon food or products in the remaining proverbial "seven years of plenty", so we will go hungry when the seven hundred years of famine hit us.' He started putting his laptop away.

'So!' Rhan concluded, biting the inside of her cheek. 'My sister and young cousins are almost certainly going to witness this turmoil.'

'Well, four by 40 is possible – that is, 4°C by 2040 – it would mean things could get very unpleasant soon, but it could be slightly later. All discussions like this tend to end on a high note. It's so much easier and nicer. But it's also wrong to just hope for the best. It would be sensible to at least acknowledge that the worst could happen.'

'At least I know,' she added with a faint smile. 'My parents would have been grateful to you for warning me. Thank you.'

'Yes, I'm afraid that compassion and humanitarian help will fade quickly once the scale of the problem sinks in.'

'And the danger looks like half the world population for 5° of warming?' She tried to nail down their conservation as she grabbed her neglected glass and took a sip.

'Yes but the danger is that 5° is still just a figure. Temperatures appear more likely to rise further and quicker if we repeatedly underestimate the problem.'

'And 4° by 40! That is the scary possibility,' Rhan declared, finally standing up.

'Yup, we could save a lot of lives if we started to get ready for that,' William responded positively. 'And on that note,' he turned and opened the door, 'time for supper, don't you think?' He smiled as he let Rhan pass.

CHAPTER TWENTY SEVEN

Blame Game

Rhan, speaking in a sombre tone with brow furrowed, continued the conversation as she and William left the room.

'You have confirmed much of what I expected about warming, but I have no clear understanding of how we reached this dreadful situation. I just cannot understand how we can be almost irreversibly set on the way to 2°C of warming and several metres of sea-level rise, with all that entails for nearly everyone. Yet I have heard or seen so little discussion, and the subject is effectively taboo. How is this possible?'

'Yea!' Grace unexpectedly joined in the conversation as they entered the kitchen. 'Even in *New Scientist* there've been months with hardly any articles on climate.'

Rhan glanced at her, trying to check whether she was being serious or was mocking her. Grace was leaning against the range, behind a place on the long oak kitchen table which was all set for the meal. Learning nothing from Grace, Rhan was pleased to exchange subtle smiles with George, whom she had missed over the past hour.

'Well, perhaps we should settle before discussing that,' her father responded, now also distracted by other things.

'Oh no,' moaned George. 'Don't tell me you still haven't put the world to rights?'

Once everyone was seated around the table and tucking into the meal, June allowed the conversation to drift back to the climate.

'Rhan, it's a shame you're spending your last evening with us discussing such depressing subjects,' she said. 'We're having another round of cards after supper, but in the meantime, did you find out all you need to know?'

'Oh, I am sorry,' Rhan replied, embarrassed. 'I didn't mean to dominate the conversation.'

'Don't be silly, this is obviously important, especially for you,' said June. 'George has explained what happened to your parents. I'm so sorry. I can understand your anxiety over changes in our society and how that could get worse once hard times set in. I think you're right to be concerned.'

'Yes my parents were early victims of the conflict. A shell hit our family home. My sister and I thought our parents had been cruel sending us here to Britain for school. But looking back, I can see how they viewed the dangers of civil war. Their action meant that my sister and I were actually the luckiest from our school in Aleppo. I am sorry to be a bore.' She apologised again, feeling guilty for introducing such a controversial topic, but was pleased with herself for being able to talk about her parents' death.

'Well you needn't try to solve everything on your last evening here. I hope this is only your first visit,' June continued, glancing at her son. 'Please come at least every holiday and treat this place as another home.'

'Great idea!' Grace exclaimed.

'Well, I would love to try my skills at that card game we played last night. I will enjoy playing it with my cousins.' Rhan couldn't help smiling. 'I have had kind offers to visit friends from other colleges – Claire, Esther and Chandra – but you have all made me feel very at home here and I would love to return. Perhaps I should plan ahead, and write all the engineering practicals in Arabic so George has to get me here to translate.'

'You make me sound shallow!' George protested. 'I think you should take a full-time job sorting out stuff for next term.'

'There is always something more immediately urgent than climate change.' Rhan forced herself to bring the conversation back to the issue that was worrying her. 'It's usually something like writing up an overdue practical or packing to go away. Petty things get in the way so we simply ignore the big picture, even when we know it will effectively kill us. The strange thing is – those on the receiving end, those affected by drought and flooding – I bet they see even less of the underlying problems of climate and population.'

'You know how it works,' George reminded her. 'It's worse than that – the subject is taboo! No one wants to know.' Then, glancing at his sister, he added, 'Even Grace is pointing out the lack of media attention, as soon as moorland and forest fires are no longer headlines. We're happy surviving one day at a time.'

'It involves a "metaphysical disregard for reality", or something like that,' George's father argued emphatically but with a self-critical laugh. 'That was the phrase used in the book *Wild Swans* to describe how the Chinese followed Chairman Mao in the Cultural Revolution, regardless of logic and the laws of nature, with the result that millions quietly starved to death.'

'Yup,' George said, engaging with his specialist subject. 'When I was in China, I saw the modern equivalent: miles upon miles of smoking blast furnaces that have now flooded the world with excess, high-carbon steel. But I think other countries, like Australia, are even more reckless by providing coal. They've sold their soul in a crazy dash to ruin both their country and the planet for short-term gains; same with the US and Canada and their dash for tar sands and shale gas. So, I'm sorry Rhan, but democracies are happy to elect leaders like Donald Trump just so they don't have to listen to the likes of my old man.'

'Rhan and I were just discussing this madness,' his father carried on. 'Despite warnings, we continue to stoke up global warming, which will now almost certainly create the perfect storm of misery and destruction on a scale that has hardly been seen since the K-T asteroid impact wiped out the dinosaurs.'

'Oh come on, Will! You don't believe that's inevitable?' June argued. 'How come it's only you who sees the danger? We're slowly moving in the right direction, aren't we? And the Paris Agreement targets will kick in at some point, perhaps only as the global warming target of 1.5°C flies past, but still. Did William tell you, Rhan, that he was there, in Paris, speaking for the World Federation of Engineers? It was December…was it 2015? Anyway there were no Christmas lights in Paris after dreadful terrorist massacres.'

'Unfortunately, those climate targets from Paris were for the medium or long-term politics, but avoided any necessity for action in the here and now,' William explained critically. 'Long-term targets will not help Rhan and her generation, especially if those targets are being allowed to lapse.'

'That's my generation too!' Grace chipped in. 'Oh and George's I suppose…'

'The key problem,' George went on with a resigned sigh, 'is that no one intends to cut emissions, so policies are only agreed on that basis. The whole population would vote against any future, especially if a single ignorant voice or newspaper suggested there was the smallest chance that it would be our children rather than us that'll pay the price.'

'That's what Rhan and I have been discussing, along with the power of greenhush,' his father agreed. 'We have no other viable plans, but we continue to reject the obvious advice. Option A is to hope it'll all be fine. Option B is to find an excuse and let others bear the brunt. No one considers Option C, to stop making things worse.'

'You're being alarmist again!' It was Grace this time telling her father off. He shook his head, rejecting her accusation.

'You should have sat with Rhan when we were discussing the alarmist stuff,' he replied.

'Oh, poor Rhan!' June interceded again. 'Don't let William dump responsibility for the whole world on your shoulders. We're meant to be a scientifically aware nation with a questioning media, yet there is widespread apathy, as George points out. You can't blame yourself. There's no government, professional body or world religion that thinks they need to act, except William.' At this, June smiled wryly. 'So you need to keep a sceptical hat on too, Rhan.'

'You mention failure of a questioning media,' her husband added, either ignoring or failing to notice the mild dig. 'I would go further and suggest that the media was, and still is, largely responsible for the news blackout.'

'But why? Scare stories sell newspapers and grab listeners, don't they?' Grace couldn't help querying, saving Rhan from asking a similar question. There were shrugs and exhalations around the table until, after finishing the last food on his plate, William related the story.

'Well, once upon a time, following the 2007 IPCC report, there was widespread shock at what was in store for the planet. Climate scientists had, since the late eighties, been warning that we needed to cut carbon emissions straight away and drastically. Dreadful consequences were threatened, such as one degree of warming by 2035!' he laughed. 'We've had that rise, but in half that time – yet no one has blinked!

'Anyway, as I remember it, there was much research and growing momentum for action on many fronts. It was generally accepted that new industries needed to be set up with grants. High-carbon producers would be made to pay. Nearly all the top politicians of every description acknowledged the danger, even if many of the voters were unconvinced; it was all just an *Inconvenient Truth*, as that film was called.'

He stopped and looked around the table, surprised by the lack of interruption, so he continued.

'As I mentioned to you earlier Rhan, the 2007 UN report was pathetically weak in my opinion. It left out the big tipping point or cascade risks and painted a very rosy picture. I expected the media to condemn the publication as dangerous. But I keep overestimating society's common sense when it comes to climate change.

'Anyway, a few weeks later, as I recall it, a Channel 4 programme called *The Great Green*...no, *The Great Global Warming Swindle,* or something like that, suggested that reducing carbon emissions could be expensive. They claimed that the concerns were not absolutely proven. They blatantly extracted edited sentences from longer statements by climate scientists, so their overall meaning was reversed. There were cries of annoyance over the next few days by their unwilling interviewees – but too late. The TV programme initiated a well-orchestrated and well-funded sceptical backlash, and a vehement campaign of widespread climate denial was unleashed.

'This quickly began to stymie purposeful action. Greenhush was in full bloom. The barrage of criticism against green schemes struck the chord that the public wanted to hear – it suddenly became acceptable to deny the whole concept of global warming. Colleagues, family and friends – even those with scientific training – rejected the whole science. Complete victory to the sceptics. They won. Any meaningful discussion of global warming was effectively silenced in every sphere.'

'But it's mentioned quite often now,' June protested. 'OK, not as often as William wants, and they don't go round telling everyone they're doomed, but it's in the media every week or so. What annoys you most is any suggestion that we have plenty of time, isn't it William? But there used to be complete silence or denial!'

There was an immediate response from her husband.

'God yes, most key presenters on the BBC and especially Radio 4 were influential in the denial of global warming,' William responded, becoming more animated. 'The BBC admitted that the subject of climate change was just too hot to handle, so they peddled the denial message along with everyone else. Even now, there are no real discussions or programmes on it, are there? Some years it has just been nature programmes occasionally mentioning it in passing, but I think even David Attenborough had problems.'

'William, tell Rhan about the *Today* programme on Radio 4,' June explained, although Rhan nodded, indicating her knowledge of it. William grinned before obliging.

'Well they once pulled the plug on a scientist who tried to warn people about the melting of the Arctic ice. They somehow thought that the scientist was going to say the sea ice was growing, and panicked when he said the opposite. I started taking notes whenever I heard global warming discussed, but it was only a few times a year.'

Rhan turned in her seat, her interest piqued. Grace, who was about to say something, decided better of it.

'When forced to discuss climate news, the more usual approach involved the interviewer getting the scientist to admit there was some scope for error in the science,' William continued, pausing to concentrate on passing the vegetarian lasagne around for second helpings. 'The interviewer would then introduce a climate denier with no relevant credentials – often Nigel Lawson, the ex-chancellor, who was prepared to state emphatically that there was absolutely no risk or danger, that the Arctic sea ice would recover, that the IPCC was stupid, and that everyone could ignore the problem. Lawson's book, *An Appeal to Reason,* took the more logical yet terrifying approach. It acknowledged that climate change must be taking place, if that's what the scientists said. But he suggested that the next generation were just not worth any effort by our generation! In other words, the next generation could sort out our mess.'

There was a series of non-appreciative comments from around the table.

'Yet there were no complaints?' asked Rhan, cutting through the noise.

'Well, Nigel Lawson didn't actually say that on the radio, did he?' June explained. 'The usual approach was for presenters to use a special, bored and resentful manner when speaking about climate change, but they have just ignored the subject whenever possible, just to wind William up! Items of news were read without comment. It was all very effective at maintaining the virtual news blackout.'

'Well I have also noticed that the subject is never really covered,' Rhan replied. 'I have never once heard any climate sceptic being questioned about the reliability of their previous predictions.'

'You're right! Isn't that strange?' June agreed. 'No programme has ever considered the former assurances – the sceptics have never had to answer for their brash, negligent statements.'

'There'll be a day when they face the music,' Grace said aggressively. 'No one can make reckless statements, resulting in disaster and get away, scot-free.'

'Well, it would be reassuring to know that every statement that is proved to be inaccurate, and every advocate of inaction that proves to be dangerous, will be called to account one day,' Rhan said emphatically, supporting Grace.

'Any bold idiot betting with lives and misery should pay the cost if they are wrong,' Grace went on. 'I bet the future won't be kind to them. Anyone siding with mass death for future generations will pay, one way or the other.'

'Yes, all rules of current justice might change, once things get nasty,' her father concurred. 'With properties uninsurable, useless twenty-five-year mortgages and maps needing to be redrawn every ten years for the new coastline, yesterday's sceptics won't be able to pretend they knew better. I've read some of their books; they have much to answer for.'

'Well.' William's daughter was now giving vent to the injustice to her generation. 'Just for good measure, both the sceptics and those who listened to them will all be conveniently dumped on an oil baron's low-lying island, without any means of contributing more greenhouse gas emissions, to wait for the tide to rise...or not if they're so confident of their assumptions about sea levels.'

'Bit late by then,' George responded in a fatalistic voice. 'It would be great if climate deniers were declared outcasts, but I don't suppose people can be prosecuted for condemning their grandchildren. Yet how could they claim the next generation can tackle something in a way and on a scale that's currently inconceivable? To stop the disaster, we should've started capturing carbon back in the 1990s, when I was in my cot!'

'You are right!' Rhan stated crossly, putting down both her knife and fork more forcefully than she intended. 'As if we will have the luxury to somehow recapture the huge amounts of carbon released by the previous generation. We will be busy with all hands to the pumps, dealing with droughts, rising seas, mass migration, loss of the best agricultural land, and Mediterranean temperatures – even here. That carbon was stored in fossil fuels over millions of years – does anyone think it can be plucked out of the air and re-stored within a few years?' Rhan stopped, suddenly realising she needed more information. 'Has there been any carbon capture and storage?' she asked, turning to William, who had an answer to hand while Rhan continued to eat.

'I have read the odd article,' he reported. 'I hear that some carbon dioxide captured from a few chemical processes has been pumped into an old saline cavern or an old oil well – I forget the details. There was some good news as the CO_2 was quickly absorbed by the rock. So carbon storage works on a limited scale, but it certainly cannot be plucked out of the air. So the easy answer is no – we have no idea how your generation is expected to capture all that carbon in the atmosphere and store it at a rate faster than it took to release! But as pointed out by sceptics, carbon dioxide is still not even classified as a pollutant. So if there's little or no compunction or incentive, why bother?'

'Daft isn't it!' June added. Grace just tutted.

Seeing that Rhan had now finished, George got up to finish making the custard while his father started collecting the dirty plates. His mother remained seated, keeping their guest company, but Rhan noted that she supervised from a distance.

'I read the other month,' George said over his shoulder, while he stirred the pan, 'that to store carbon, nature utilises quantum physics in the photosynthesis process. The leaves do something that prevents electrons simply reverting to where they came from. Even then, it would take nature thousands of years. We can't do that with our current technology.'

'The more we learn, the more complex we find even the simplest aspects of life on this planet,' his father re-joined. 'We cannot challenge God yet.'

'So you are all confirming what I feared,' Rhan stated in a tone that was both triumphant at the acknowledgment, and exasperated at the injustice. 'We are being given an impossible task, which gets harder every year.'

'Crazy!' exclaimed Grace, which made Rhan wonder how much even George's family had discussed the issues previously.

'It's a ridiculously optimistic pretence,' George complained, once he had dumped a hot dish on the mats in the middle of the table with a heavy thud, anxious to withdraw his hands from the inadequate oven gloves. 'There is no real interest anywhere in controlling temperatures on this planet, so it's just a useful fabrication that the next generation can put things right. Promises, such as Paris 2015, are based on doing nothing when it would have some effect, yet agreeing that someone, sometime, should take action in a few years' time, when it's all too late.' He returned to the custard and muttered something to his mother about a suitable serving jug. William smiled and nodded.

'We are giving our children and grandchildren limited choices,' Rhan said bleakly after a short pause, ticking off the options on her fingers. 'A sentence of an early death; a life of killing; or a life of fleeing and running away, hoping for mercy from others. Just because London feels safe behind the Barrier...' She stopped, suddenly realising that she had no need to talk and because George was now serving up what he called an apple charlotte and custard.

'My, that's magnificent, George!' his father enthused, suggesting that George might be showing off his domestic skills.

Rhan eyed the sugared bread and jug of custard in front of her with interest. However, once the practical details of serving had been resolved, she returned to the serious issue.

'We were talking earlier about how the sceptics managed to win the technical arguments on climate change, without any science basis. Is that still the case? Are all arguments for inaction on a non-technical basis?'

'Yeah, what happened?' Grace was showing interest, despite her previous objections.

There were a few seconds of surprise at the sudden change in direction of the conversation, before William responded thoughtfully.

'Well, I suppose that the next aspect of the battle involved the sceptics moving on to the attack. It's now beginning to look like they had large, secret financial backing. They targeted and ruined the credibility of a few leading climate scientists in cleverly publicised campaigns.'

'Oh yes. It was the University of East Anglia, wasn't it?' June filled in more detail to William's recollections. 'An academic was accused of not keeping adequate records, yet his predictions proved correct within months.'

'The attacks were so successful that they resulted in scientists quickly learning to keep their heads down.'

'All the publicity was one-way, which suited the media,' June added.

'Would you believe that even the Church of England, back in 2012, asked me not to rock the boat?' William said. 'I was collecting data for that Christian Census on Climate Change event – Rhan and I discussed it earlier.'

'Oh, was that when George and I distributed service sheets in York Minster?' Grace enquired. 'That was fun.'

'Yes, that's right,' her father replied. 'A quarter of responses wanted all-out action by Christian churches, a quarter were sceptical and wanted half measures, and the rest fell between. Anyway, one of the Church's top climate change advisors was so scared that sceptics would make use of any publicity or data we produced, he actually asked me to stop the ecumenical initiative!' William shook his head and opened his hands in frustration. 'So the person responsible for publicising the evils of global warming was actively suppressing discussion of the moral issues. That is probably the best example of definite greenhush – the Church's guardian angels turned to stone.'

'Or evil?' Grace suggested. William nodded and laughed.

'Didn't the archbishop then give a sermon that attacked your efforts?' June asked, recklessly priming her husband.

'Yes, it was shocking,' William replied, smiling ruefully. 'He said that as Christians we shouldn't look ahead, or measure the height of the mountain until we reach its summit. It might not be as high as we thought. It was God's problem, not ours!'

'Oh yes, that was it. Awful!' June was now more cross than her husband.

George joined in the attack. 'I know it was a Catholic-led event, but don't many of the top bishops, and other denominations or religions, effectively have the same utterly destructive approach? As long as we stick to policies such as no birth control, it's no great sin to ruin the planet and cause the death of billions of poor people and species that we are meant to look after. Overpopulation is a complete no-go area for discussion, yet goes hand-in-glove with climate change to ruin creation.'

'I have friends who have extreme Christian faiths – and they refuse to worry about climate change,' Grace confirmed. 'It's all "God's will".'

'I have come across that approach at Oxford,' Rhan agreed. 'They seem to like the idea that everyone will suffer.

However, I joined a very sympathetic Methodist church in Sunderland, which actively campaigns for climate justice.'

'Oh yes, the Methodists, and the Quakers, seem very progressive, along with some of the Baptists,' June added.

'Absolutely!' her husband endorsed her opinion. 'I attended a brilliant conference put on by the Quakers up here. 'I can claim that I have actually seen a Quaker quake! She was a scientist from Somerset or somewhere in the south and had travelled all this way for the day-long conference in York. She broke into tears as she told our group about the life and choices she foresaw for her young grandchildren growing up in a heated world.

'We Catholics have the Justice and Peace movement, which used to be very focused,' he continued. 'I've lectured on the Pope's 2015 encyclical, which repeated a key question from New Zealand bishops over whether it is a mortal sin to contribute emissions that we know will kill people. I'm afraid the encyclical hardly gave an emphatic answer.'

'Stupid, isn't it,' June sighed. 'If we don't care about how many die from our indifference, is that better or worse than direct murder?'

'Very few individuals are aware or have calculated how many deaths their personal or professional carbon emissions are likely to cause,' William declared. Rhan sat up and looked at him intently, obviously interested in this new line.

'Oh come on,' George complained. 'Don't start telling us more bad news!'

'I estimated, back in 2010,' William persevered, 'that emissions of twelve tonnes of carbon dioxide per year would kill one other person. The answer felt about right at the time, but that figure will be much worse now, because the timescales for action are so much shorter and carbon concentrations so much worse.'

'Twelve tonnes per death?' Rhan repeated.

'Well if I recalculated it now, few of us would be innocent of murder or manslaughter. Catching an aeroplane, using coal, or – if you're an engineer, architect or developer – by choosing to use concrete or steel instead of a low-carbon timber alternative. It would all be considered criminal in a just world. I have heard that structural engineers have a carbon footprint of around a thousand tonnes each per year, which could easily be the case. I can save tens of thousands of tonnes if I can prove and persuade a client that a building doesn't need to be knocked down and reconstructed, but can just be altered instead.'

'Maybe, but it's just too socially unacceptable to even notice,' George suggested. 'As I keep saying, it's impossible to think that anyone but a complete nutter would stop flying, no matter what the cost to others.'

'Yes – I am starting to see that!' Rhan murmured. 'I had already heard that it would need five hundred dedicated vegans to offset each structural engineer! It's so wrong.'

'Of course it is.' George hammered home his point. 'We will convince ourselves that it's inevitable and normal for the climate to get worse and worse, but that it's nothing to do with us. Just look at the way we destroy other bits of the environment such as the fish stocks. I mean, did anyone take the blame when overfishing wrecked the nineteenth-century annual North Sea herring run, with its whole industry and way of life for families around the British Isles? I presume it was just regarded as a temporary poor harvest that never recovered – just one of those things. Dealing with changing weather and stopping refugees from fleeing are becoming everyday parts of life. People will never admit that we have a problem because that would involve admission of guilt. It's just not going to happen.'

'No way!' Grace was horror-struck. 'Sooner or later it will be taken seriously! Then the sceptics will be in trouble.'

'I wonder if we can only start to address issues when we have someone else that we can personally blame,' her father suggested. 'So far it has worked the wrong way round; we blame the Australians, the Chinese and the Americans, but they refuse to even acknowledge the problem. We can't punish them, so the process doesn't work.'

'And they presumably blame Britain for starting and enforcing the industrial revolution in the nineteenth century.' Rhan finished off the sentence, recalling several conversations with her friends. 'We discussed this at college, didn't we George?'

George nodded, playing with the spoon in his empty bowl.

'This is a scandal that will have a major effect on everyone,' June pointed out. 'It's not going to be just superficial to the majority, is it?'

'Yeah well, child abuse, phone-hacking and such scandals, all took time to "blow up" as the scale of the problem was gradually exposed,' George acknowledged. 'Maybe it would help if the media had someone definite to blame so they can then see the problem!'

'Then it'll be far more vicious than anything previously seen,' Grace suggested. When no one else spoke, she continued. 'It's science-fiction stuff! I wonder if our civilisation will survive. A disaster like this and the scale of the scandal should send ripples forward and backward in time.' She smiled and added, 'I'm joking!'

Rhan looked at the girl and nodded, appreciating Grace's point.

'Well, I think you're right,' William said, also taking it seriously. 'It should be possible to see this looming in the future from our past stupidity.'

'Well the blame will be easy,' Grace blurted out more confidently. 'The records will all be there! Articles by bullying and uncaring journalists, high spenders on fuels and designers of Dad's hated high-carbon buildings... whatever. The culprits can't escape the jaws of time.'

'Each flight ticket,' George suggested, 'should have a warning: *"This flight may be used in evidence against you."* It'll be impossible for anyone, or any company, to claim "not guilty", won't it?'

'A vengeful generation!' June said, surprised. 'I suppose it makes a change from apathetic social media watchers,' she added, smiling. 'The legal issues could involve things like, *"Who should have known what and when?"* I suppose that no one capable of booking a flight could claim they knew nothing about climate change, just because they chose to ignore the warnings.'

'Yeh, they'll pay for it!' Grace was now very gung-ho.

George could not resist joining his sister. 'Agree. The crime could easily be considered too awful to be allowed to go unpunished. There've been plenty of examples of retrospective laws in the international courts. Today's respected leaders of society will be in real trouble.'

'Well you two have changed your mocking tune!' June accused her children as she thrust some of the pudding bowls at George to load into the dishwasher.

'No. Just because we think it right that polluters pay, it doesn't mean we have to listen to Pa going on about it all the time,' Grace responded drily.

'Hang on!' her father retaliated. 'I detect some major hypocrisy here. Your generation is much more interested in adding to carbon levels than cutting them. I give annual lectures to undergraduates and each year I'm amazed at the apathy. I just wish your generation would learn to engage effectively! You need to sort them out Rhan!'

'Well, sorry Dad, but your generation is going to get all the blame,' Grace argued with new vitriol.

'Well, I concede that there are few in my generation who are blameless,' William continued as he went to fill the kettle. 'Even the most ardent advocates for action to save the world pull their punches when it matters to avoid being considered alarmist.'

You can't blame scientists for being sensitive to attacks by sceptics,' June intervened.

'But many are now stupidly optimistic!' There was much clattering as William stopped talking while he loaded a cafetiere with coffee. 'Grace, can you pass the coffee cups?'

'The most surprising aspect to me,' Rhan said, pausing while a cup was placed in front of her, 'has been how many individual scientists, engineers and academics deny the issue. In a lecture attended by many from all four year groups of our Engineering course, only George had the courage to stand up and point out the obvious. Did you hear that he got into trouble with the Engineering Department, who had brought in a concrete expert to tell us about sustainability?'

Rhan looked around the table and saw blank looks and shaking heads, so continued with her acclaim.

'He pointed out that the use of concrete could not be sustainable and was only going to make the problem of global warming worse. It was clear that he was the only one in the whole department, including the staff and fourth-year students, who knew what he was talking about.'

'Good for you, George!' his mother praised.

'My God, George – you stood up against climate change!' his sister was shocked.

'Well I never!' George's father rubbed his hands. 'After all your abuse about me being a foolish crank!'

'Yeah well, it was a big mistake,' George said, deflating his built-up status. 'It was just the blatant lies and hypocrisy that wound me up.'

'Looking back, I can see why you thought, or still think, that our generation are quite happy to be witless, ignorant victims,' Rhan mused.

'I suppose the fantasy computer games generation would hardly be the obvious candidates to think that the environment beyond the window has any relevance,' June joined the sad considerations. 'But George, you clearly influenced at least one person!' She glanced at Rhan, who blushed and took the opportunity to stand up to help clear the table.

As she helped load the dishwasher, Rhan asked something she had not entirely understood.

'Our tutor told George off, because the university was following approaches at the professional intuitions. So what did that mean, do you think?'

Rhan realised that a new dispute about taking out the dustbin and fetching logs for the fire was occupying George, Grace and June, which meant that little attention was now being given to their conversation.

'Cards in five minutes!' Grace called out over the clatter of cutlery and crockery as she left the kitchen to prepare the game.

'Oxford engineers probably just follow the take-no-action stance of the main institutions,' William suggested, ignoring the summons.

'So it has nothing to do with George's explanation, that Oxford is stuck in the past?'

'Not in that instance,' he replied with a hollow laugh. 'Oxford has many leading climate departments and institutions, as it happens. I'm afraid that engineers also convince themselves that global warming isn't real and is no threat to the way they operate.'

'Could engineers be persuaded to save the world?' Rhan asked, quickly receiving a hearty laugh in response from the old engineer, who was struggling to clean a large baking tray.

'No. It would only happen if there was genuine money to pay them, together with threats of harsh lawsuits for any emissions that will kill people in the future. On the Thames Barrier project to stop London flooding, we were paid three times the going rate as an incentive to get it finished before the water arrived!'

'Oh, he's not telling you about his time working from boats and tower cranes on the Thames, is he Rhan?' George was back in disruptive mode. 'Dad saved London, don't you know?'

'But only just in time, I was trying to say,' William retorted from his station at the sink. Then, ignoring his son, he added, 'Would you mind passing that last pan Rhan?

'I've had no doubts about climate change after first seeing glacier melt in New Zealand in 1985. Yet, after more than thirty years of clear evidence, I'm afraid that engineers show absolutely no signs of even slowing down contributions to greenhouse gases. We use ever-increasing carbon emissions, in bigger, more imposing buildings, construction of airports for more aircraft, and rail tracks for trains to travel faster. The glass-fronted building designs will be unsuitable in the expected heatwaves, and recent new flood defences will be far too low within a couple of decades.

'As I said earlier, I'm afraid there'll be an infinite amount of work for you to save the planet if you go into civil engineering, Rhan!'

The door flew open; Grace was standing there, obviously no longer prepared to join the conversation.

'Come on, time for cards! You must've worked out how the whole world will be ruined by now.'

'Good timing!' her father responded. 'We clearly live in interesting times, so let's finish on that.'

'Come on Rhan.' George grabbed Rhan round the waist and lifted her away from the drying up. 'Grace is right,' he proclaimed. 'If you can't fix the world in two hours of conversation, it's not worth saving.'

Rhan glanced at the worried face of June, and decided not to struggle. Laughing, she passed the damp tea towel to the now smiling June as she was carried from the room.

'Well that was a lovely and most interesting meal.' Rhan thanked her hosts as she pushed her hair back into place under her headscarf as soon she was dropped outside the kitchen. 'It is disappointing to have it confirmed that nowhere is going to be safe, but it puts my anger at universities into perspective.'

'Well, I think we need more anger if we are to save anything and anyone!' William suggested.

'Rubbish!' Grace responded emphatically, suddenly thrusting a box of chocolates into Rhan's arms. 'Anger's an emotion caused by lack of chocolate. Luckily, Mum told me to bring these to have with the cards.'

CHAPTER TWENTY EIGHT

Sunderland Star

'Try pulling the third stroke slightly further but get that blade out fast, Number 3…yes that's good. Well done to everyone though, that is really coming together. We have some impressive acceleration.'

The college rugby boat was practising the first few strokes of a race. Rhan was teaching them a new technique that she had learnt just a few days before in Roger's coaching with the junior Oxford crews. It involved the initial short strokes required to accelerate the boat from standstill to movement before the normal full strokes could be effective. The start of the race was particularly crucial, as Rhan had discovered in the previous term in the chaotic bump races at the lower divisions. She saw no reason to teach the traditional approach if Roger's technique was better.

'OK. Hold water. Let's see three more starts. Take a stroke, bow. Fine. Ready. Steady. Go!'

It was pleasant in the boat. It was Rhan's first day back at her college – and also her first day of ease after a week of strenuous rowing, both at the university junior squad camp, and in two days of trials with the National team. Before that, she'd started to make friends and had enjoyed training with the Sunderland club, where she jumped from boat to boat wherever there was a slot.

She smiled to herself at the recollection of her reception back at the Sunderland club. Two days after leaving George in Yorkshire, she had presented herself at a summer open day. She hadn't seen any of the veterans she knew, but guessed the identity of the treasurer, Bob, to whom she handed her sponsorship letter. It had offered to pay club fees and expenses up to £500 for the next three months.

'OK luv. Ah'll just get me glasses, but talk to oor Becky at that table first, will yu?'

Rhan had duly approached a woman who was sorting through lists.

'Rowed afore?' Becky asked, glancing up at the unusually tall girl, who nodded. 'How much?' was Becky's obvious response.

Rhan gave a convoluted answer about previous experience.

'So yu've nay more 'n six month of rowing!' Becky announced triumphantly. 'Fine. We'll find a place for you in a novice boat if yu pass y' fitness and the like.'

'My coach...ergometer results...' Rhan had quailed pathetically at the prospect of arguing with the officious Becky about her experience and the sets of fitness statistics she had logged. With a defeated sigh, she had turned away and sat down.

'Fuckin 'ell!' shouted the treasurer a few minutes later, waving Rhan's letter and startling the five other young people who were either signing up or helping with the novices. 'Excuse me French, but does this say what I think it says? Are you in the National squad? And yu ganna muck in wi' us?'

'No, I'm only in trials for the squad.' Rhan had felt very aware that she was the centre of attention, but found it better than being ignored and dismissed. 'And I suppose I actually joined your club last December, the day you broke your foot. I replaced you in the veteran's four. Can you take what I owe from the sponsorship?'

'Orr, watch out Becky!' Bob had warned in good humour. 'She's trouble! I 'avn't 'ad nowt but gobshite from mi old crew since she upped off back to college! They want 'er back in my place!'

~

'Hold water! Ready. Stroke, bow. Hold. Right – ready, steady, go!' Rhan, huddled in her dark coat, spoke only quietly into the microphone.

Oxford on the first Saturday before term was warm, especially after Sunderland. It was fun to be lazily coxing and coaching the Rugby Eight again, although the river was ridiculously busy on this first weekend. Finding a quiet spot to practise the starts had been difficult with so many college crews training for the Summer Eights.

Rhan was beginning to take a measure of pride in the eight burly blokes in front of her. They would be in a relatively lowly division, but they had strength and were starting to gain enough skill to apply their energy effectively. With a new lightweight cox they should do very well.

'Last try, then carry on with a slow and measured "power ten". Ready. Steady. Go!'

A familiar voice, amplified, drifted only slowly into her consciousness before she sat bolt upright in alarm. There in front of them lay the college First Eight, close to the bank, receiving the same instructions from the towpath above that she had just passed on to her crew. The First Eight were being instructed by their new professional coach, and Rhan's university trainer, Roger. He was standing just off the towpath, holding his bike in one hand, megaphone in the other, cap tilted back off his head as usual. Rhan pulled her headscarf forward, thanking her luck that he'd never seen her covered up, and adjusted the boat's course to pass by at a distance.

Roger, however, had other ideas once he spotted the matching college blades. He laid his bike down. 'Hold on a minute – you must be the Second Eight are you? I saw you practising starts back there – so let's see how the two boats compare, shall we?'

'Ease the oars!' Rhan breathed quietly into the microphone, while Richard, the captain of the First, explained to Roger that they were just the Fourth – the recently assembled rugby crew – rather than the Second Eight. Nevertheless, Roger soon had them manoeuvring alongside the First Eight for a competitive racing start. Rhan found it easy to keep her back to Roger while the crew looked up with interest at the man who was being paid to work miracles over the next few weeks.

She kept a steely silence as Roger shouted, 'Ready, steady, go!'

Kim, the First Eight cox, screamed encouragement at her crew. The Fourth Eight knew what was wanted and needed no encouragement to show off.

The First Eight had obviously just made the transition to the new starting technique under Roger's instruction, while most of Rhan's rugby crew had learned it from scratch that morning and had become relatively proficient at the short, sharp, choppy pulling of the oars. She felt herself flush with both pride and embarrassment to see how quickly they kicked their boat into motion. It got worse – Rhan's heart sank; this was not meant to happen!

'OK, hold! Let's try that again,' Roger ordered, none too pleased with the result.

After three starts, it was apparent that it was no fluke, and that the First Eight were still the slower boat. On the third attempt, there was no order to hold, and Rhan quietly directed the first power-ten strokes. It was only after five or six strokes that the more proficient First boat started to close the gap.

'OK, hold it, hold it!' Roger called. He'd clearly meant to stop them much earlier, and he had to collect his bike and catch up the twenty or so metres while the two crews hugged the bank to let other boats pass. 'What's going on here?' he asked, dismounting and letting his bike fall into the long grass again, his cap now pulled well down against the glare of the water.

'We're just getting used to your new technique,' explained Richard, trying to justify the First Eight's performance. 'We just need a bit more practice at it. It doesn't seem as good as the old method of starting.'

'Mind you,' Gareth goaded Richard in his sing-song Welsh accent, 'it was only half an hour ago that we learnt how to start!'

'Sorry Richard. I just think I'm missing something important here. You see, the Fourth are already using that new technique...which you suggest is not as fast. They're beating me at my own brand-new game! So, either it's not so new...or there's something going on...this Rugby Eight with a heavier boat...and you've said only a few weeks on the water for most of them...with little coaching...yet, they've just mastered it.'

His rambling musings subsided, while both crews listened in a silence only broken by the occasional lap of water against the two boats. All felt uneasy under the judgement and incoherent statements of this strange new coach.

Roger was now peering hard at Rhan below him – she could tell by his stance, even though from beneath her scarf she only cast the occasional sideways glance and looked up no higher than his feet. He usually kept his thoughts well hidden, but he evidently had other intentions today as he continued his outspoken review.

'Yet this Fourth Eight...must have had superior training... and from my squad...Bar?' Rhan could almost hear his mind working it out. 'Claire said "this college had hidden depths", didn't she?'

Everyone was looking up at the coach, talking to himself, using names no one knew. It worked. Rhan gave in and also glanced back up into his face on the towpath behind; she could not suppress a slight smile.

'Glory be! Thank you Lord!' Roger exclaimed. He actually pulled off his cap at this point and hit it against his leg in excitement. He rotated on the spot, rubbing his forehead as he turned, so he was ready to address the college captain, his effective employer. He was back to his usual semi-secretive manner.

'Right Richard! I'm beginning to see a way that your college can avoid humiliation. As you saw, the Fourth, after just a week or so on the water, can beat the First, with a heavier boat, heavier oars, and while dragging a rather overgrown cox as extra useless ballast.' Rhan watched as several of her crew raised their heads at the abusive language, but the coach continued without much pause. 'So Captain, if you want me to produce an eight that won't get bumped down the river, it can be done, but it needs the cooperation of the whole boat club. I need the very best available crew. Is that agreed?'

There were one or two sad nods from Richard and others in the First Eight.

'No, I'm sorry, but this needs to be agreed by all of you here!' Roger demanded forcibly, no longer the bumbling academic. There were more nods and calls of agreement this time. The First Eight calls were reluctant, while members of the Rugby Eight suddenly fancied their chances.

'I'll try again. This time, please raise your arm if you agree with your captain that I can select the crew that I want. Sorry, we have a mountain to climb, so it's all or nothing for me. Raise your arm if you agree!' This time Rhan saw universal assent, including from Kim, the other cox. Rhan's arms were down, grasping the sides of the boat, but no one noticed her.

All were now looking impatiently up at Roger, who was still waiting. Only Rhan knew why he waited. There was silence, which was getting very awkward again, but still they waited. There was a slight roaring in Rhan's ears. What would happen if she agreed? Everything would change. She would lose control. Her two or three separate lives would clash, and she would be exposed. Yet, she could become someone of influence. She felt that she was on the edge of a long drop. Now was her chance. She looked up, feeling slightly sick, looking at the trees beyond Roger. Everyone's eyes were fixed on the coach. She nodded just a fraction and glanced at the coach to see if that was enough.

'Good. See you back at the boathouse,' Roger proclaimed immediately.

Rhan mechanically gave the instructions that set them off behind the First team. The slight breeze started to clear her head. Feeling a bit emotional, she addressed the microphone.

'Come on; let's have some gentle but firm and steady rowing. This is the last time that you will row together, so let's see what you have learnt.'

On the edge of tears, she recalled Roger's comments about her being useless ballast and started laughing. Her laughter was perhaps not so silent, because George, most of the way down the boat, and despite the risk to the balance, peered round the rowers between them.

'Don't take it personally about the ballast, Rhan; that weird coach doesn't know how much we owe you, it wasn't personal.'

'It certainly was personal!' she muttered to herself, forgetting again that it would be picked up through the microphone.

There was growing chaos back at the boathouse. The Second Eight had been about to set off in their boat and the Schools' Eight was waiting to take over the rugby team's shell for the afternoon. The two crews leaving the water waited to hear their fate after stacking their oars and stowing all but the First Eight boat. Most of the crews were crowded around their captain, Richard. Roger was standing alone, talking on his mobile, which gave him a chance to wander past Rhan and speak to her without much attention.

'Right, Bar. Sorry to mess up your secret, but can you slip upstairs and prepare your ideal crew? I'll select the stroke.'

She gave him an ironic smile. 'OK, but we need members of the Second Eight and Schools' Eight too. The Schools' Eight will need to be persuaded.'

'Good, leave them to me,' he said as she walked towards the boathouse, and he exchanged a few words with Pat, the boatman, before making an announcement.

'Right! Schools' Eight and Second Eight, upstairs if you don't mind! I need a word with you.'

Rhan noted that George had been watching her from the other side of the large boathouse door. She gave him a short smile as she retreated inside, where she found a blunt pencil, an old envelope and a quiet corner in the empty bar above the boathouse to start working out her ideal crew. She couldn't help listening to Roger through the lightweight timber partition as he addressed the other two Eights and their coxes, sitting on benches in the adjacent changing room. She presumed everyone else was hanging around downstairs or on the riverbank.

'Thanks for letting me speak to you.' Roger's diffident yet persuasive voice sounded ideal, Rhan thought. 'I don't know any of you, and you may not have heard about me. I'm Roger Potts. I've been a senior assistant coach to the university, and over the next two months, I've been employed by your college to get your First Eight through the Eights Week bumps. A list of the best available crew is being prepared, and I believe that some of you will be selected.

There was scuffling and murmurs, while Roger presumably drew breath.

'Well done to members of the Second, but I need to address the Schools' Eight crew. I appreciate that your priority in your last year has been to get the best degree you can this summer. I have also seen why you haven't thought it worthwhile to row in the First Eight! There was nothing to gain and, let's face it, a strong chance that the First Eight would be bumped four times in a humiliating plummet out of the top division.'

Roger's voice paused, but there was no dissent, so he continued.

'The news is just about to break, and you are the first to hear it. The college has a secret superstar.'

Rhan could not help smiling and blushing at Roger's statements.

'I can assure you that anyone in our new First Eight will be rowing behind next year's current first choice as stroke for a Blue, and the university's most promising contender as an Olympic squad rower. So there! That's going to be a surprise for your whole college. The new crew will look nothing like last term's Torpids team – few will survive.' Roger ceased talking to allow a babble of questions to be flung at him.

'Who?'

'How come no one knows?'

'Why's he not already in the crew?'

After a few seconds of ignoring the questions, Roger's voice cut through the clamour.

'Well I'm afraid the terms "thoroughbred" and "farmer's cart" come to mind. You may or may not know that international rowers have no great enthusiasm to row for their college. My arrival here has now sorted that. However, I need your experience too. I can promise you that the new Eight that goes on the water in ten minutes' time will go down in history. This is a pivotal moment for...'

'What are you doing up here?' George's voice from the open stairs cut through her eavesdropping.

'Hi,' she responded in little more than a whisper. As soon as George heard the subject being discussed, he also stopped to listen.

'...a list of the college's best rowers, and no one should judge who will or will not be on that list. If your name is included, I promise you will have something to brag about on your CV for the rest of your life. If you decline, you will be giving up being in the crew behind someone who is clearly destined to be a household name in the manner of Steve Redgrave and Matthew Pinsent. However, I need to know now, this instant, whether there is anyone who wants to rule themselves out of that new First Eight. The press will be awaiting your decision this very afternoon.'

Rhan had raised her eyes at the way Roger missed out female celebrities such as Helen Glover or Heather Stanning, but then smiled as she perceived Roger's cunning half-truth and the arguments for more details started again.

'It's chaos down in the boathouse below as well,' George informed Rhan in a low voice, once he had also given up listening. 'The two Eights are all hanging around squabbling, and the Women's Eight have started to arrive and are delaying their session to see the action. Poor Richard is trying to get everyone to be patient. Are you all right? What're you doing with that list?' Rhan had drawn arrows on an envelope; she now ripped it in two, and started copying her scribbles into a second list while George returned to eavesdropping.

'I can't believe the college has a celebrity rower and no one knew!' A strident voice could be heard in the background. 'How come? Does even the college captain know?' George and Rhan couldn't help but wait for the reply from Roger. George's brow was furrowed in confusion. Rhan held her breath.

'Modesty is one answer, but I'm afraid that your college is the butt of much humour in rowing circles – to have an outstanding asset that you don't even know about. I have a text here from Dumas, the university president. He says…'

Rhan drew breath as she heard Roger gain control again. She grabbed George by the tracksuit bottoms, which he was wearing with his rugby top over his rowing vest.

'Come with me!' she ordered him in an imperial yet mysterious whisper that she hardly recognised herself. He followed her obediently and curiously into the empty women's changing room, where she closed and locked the door. 'I need your vest and shorts!' she demanded, without clarifying the issue to the perplexed young man.

'No way!' he protested. 'I might be selected.' He looked at her unenthusiastic face and added, 'OK, it's only an outside chance, but why not?'

'Look, you are better than some of the current First Eight already.' Rhan made the effort to be positive. 'But I am afraid you will not be in the new First Eight this year. Trust me.' She began undressing, leaving her headscarf in place. He watched in confusion and surprise, but slowly started to copy.

'I don't understand' he gasped distractedly. 'What is going on Rhan? You know the coach...what's his name, Robert?'

'Roger. Yes, he's been my coach at the holiday training camps since before Christmas. Look, I'm sorry that I have not let you know how I got on – it seemed like bragging and you never asked about my progress.'

'Fucking hell! Is this all about you?' George asked, and then answered his own questions without feedback from Rhan. 'They were talking about you! Roger thinks you're going to be a famous rower and in the Men's Eight! My God, is that possible? I suppose...well yes, you will be instantly famous.

'So that paper and the list – is that the crew? And that's how Roger knows who to pick without Richard – you've been coxing them all. This is amazing – and I had no idea. You're bloody amazing! I hope you, or Roger, can carry this off.'

'Oh, Roger always manages to pull off the impossible,' Rhan replied as she wrapped her long coat over singlet and shorts while George pulled his tracksuit back on. 'He enjoys starting with a losing hand.' She slipped out of the changing room, followed at a discreet distance by George, but they could not completely escape back down to the boathouse. Roger was talking to Richard at the top of the stairs and, without looking at her or exchanging a word, Roger held out his hand towards Rhan, who placed the tattered half envelope in it. At the same time, she relieved him of his tweed cap. He looked down at the list, ignoring the loss of hat.

'Richard Dix! Thank God, you're on the list,' the coach affirmed. 'You clearly merit a place. Well done! Here, what do you think of the rest? I'm hoping you'll endorse it.'

Richard looked at Rhan in surprise and embarrassment. Roger was not even pretending to have selected the crew. Richard read quickly through it. He looked at Rhan again and went through the list a second time, shaking or nodding his head.

'Great, but will James and DT cross from the Schools' crew? Are you sure of these chaps? DT's in his fourth year and was in France last year, so I've never even seen him row. James is by far the best rower in the college and was my predecessor as captain last year with two years' experience in the First Eight, but he refused a place this year.'

'Everyone in the Schools' Eight has just agreed,' Roger confirmed.

'God, well done!'

'So, you've taken Danny and Gareth Wright from the rugby crew, allowing me to move to Number 3. It may give us extra strength, but these are new, untested rowers; Danny has only been in a shell a few times, although Gareth rowed last year and perhaps even the year before.' The coach raised an eyebrow, which managed to suggest that he had no desire to mention the surprises from the practice starts of half an hour ago. Richard clearly received the message because he continued on a different tack, in a slightly aggrieved tone.

'It's clear that Rhan here has done a great job coaching the Rugby Eight, and she has coxed all these boats, but she's only coxed us once, so this is a hell of a leap in the dark.' The coach again made no reply, so with a sigh, Richard continued with the list. 'She has brought in one person from the Second Eight, and has left just two of the current First Eight, plus Kim as cox. I presume Jeff Carpenter stays as stroke? His name is missing and the stroke slot is empty. You've worked with us for a week now...I don't understand.'

Roger rubbed the side of his nose and in an apologetic tone finally took some responsibility.

'I've seen your crew on the water three times, and I'm afraid we need this radical shake-up, and you know it too. I asked Rhan here to select the ideal college crew, but the choice of stroke is mine alone.' Roger grabbed the list and added a name. He looked up saying, 'Bar, or Rhan as you call her, will stroke.'

'You're joking? I didn't even know she was a rower. No! No way! This is crazy. Sorry Rhan, you….we will be a laughing stock and we'll be disqualified.'

Roger chose his moment to become serious.

'Sorry Richard, I've just been telling the Schools' Eight that I can't start coaching a whole crew in such a short time, but I may be able to teach seven of you to follow the stroke. Now I've coached Bar here for six months already. I also told the Schools' Eight that you're already a laughing stock for not making use of one of the university's best rowers.'

Rhan at last plucked up the courage to look back at George, who was smiling and soaking up the conversation. He used the slight pause to help Richard with the news.

'Richard, she's bloody good – I saw her race last term. I'm afraid Roger may be right about you being the last university college captain to know about her. I was told to keep it quiet.' While the bemused captain blinked slowly, trying to comprehend the news, Roger, ignoring George's contribution, continued on a more aggressive tack.

'You and your four men's boats have all agreed to my demand for a new crew. If you don't agree to my choice, just because I select a girl, my job is at an end. Bar is far too strong to ever row with your Women's Eight. Rejecting her will mark you as a misogynist, and you can wave goodbye to a normal career in any industry once the press waiting outside get the story. Rhan has a very influential following at both university and national levels. She is without doubt the best person to take control of the boat while it's on the water, and…'

Roger stopped mid-sentence as they heard footsteps on the stairs. Jeff, the lanky ex-stroke, stuck his head around the corner.

'Richard. Alice says there are a load of men and women rowing Blues outside the boathouse, including both presidents! What's going on?' Jeff looked with puzzlement at Rhan and George standing beyond. Roger nodded, acknowledging that he expected the news.

'Good. Thanks for letting me know Jeff,' Richard responded without surprise or encouragement.

The former stroke headed off, obviously disappointed that he was not to be involved with helping Richard select the crew.

'I sent a few texts,' Roger confessed. 'Some of Rhan's friends among the university rowers are dropping by to see her stroke the Men's First Eight. That should prevent any committee from throwing the rulebook at you. Your only real choice now is to take the credit and become a hero. Even if my ploy fails in seven weeks' time, you will still get the credit, with little blame. Otherwise, you can sack me and start again. I think you have only one easy option – just see what happens.'

Richard shook his head and exhaled. 'As you say, I have no choice, so I heartily agree. I can't really take this in, but it's going to be interesting! Shall I go and make the announcements?'

'Yes, good idea,' Roger agreed. 'I suggest that the new First Eight should have a quick half-hour on the water immediately to see how things pan out, if that's OK. I'll wait just outside. You can direct the selected members to join me, but give me ten minutes, if you can.'

Richard walked slowly down the stairs into the boathouse holding the list, and everyone fell silent. Rhan, her hair now just tucked into Roger's cap, sat down in her buttoned-up coat beside George on one of the top stairs to listen to Richard. They were sitting at the rear end of the crowded boathouse. She sent a text while Richard spoke.

'I'd like to start by thanking the First Eight for their hard work over the previous two terms and I apologise in advance for the disappointment that many of you will feel at this revised crew. We didn't do well at Torpids and we need fresh blood to challenge at Summer Eights. Without exception, all of our competitors in the top division boats will field stronger crews than last term's Torpids, with the addition of their university rowers for Summer Eights. So, as I think many of you have already guessed, we are going to take drastic steps and trust our new coach.

'As I call your name, please collect your oar from the boatman, Pat, and wait at the door. We'll have a thirty-minute trial for the new First Eight crew.

'Number 1, in the bow is David Turner, commonly known as DT.' There was stunned silence. Furrowed eyebrows and slight shakes of the head indicated that they had never heard of him.

'Blimey!' gasped DT himself, who in some surprise climbed to his feet from the steps below Rhan and George and rushed through the ranks of the much taller rowers to be handed the Number 1 oar.

'Good choice!' one of the Schools' Eight called out.

'Yes, well spotted!' another voice echoed, which made Rhan nudge George with pride in her unlikely selection. DT collected his oar from the boatman and stood by the large doors, watching to see who would join him.

'A light bowman to match a light stroke. Seems clever,' was George's response. 'Who are you texting at such a time?'

'My friend Claire from Gloucester Hall, and Esther,' Rhan replied in a whisper as the captain prepared to make the next announcement. 'Claire sort of predicted that Roger would find a use for me, so I had to let her know.' Rhan decided not to namedrop about Esther, the lady president.

'Number 2 is Danny the mad Cornishman, who strides in from the Rugby Eight,' Richard continued.

'Whoor!' yelled a voice from below that could only have been Danny in surprise and delight, matched by an enormous hearty roar of approval from his former team mates, and a deafening 'Yeah!' from George beside her. There were a few negative murmurs.

'But he's only been in a boat for a few weeks. How can that be right?' was the loudest complaint from someone in the Second Eight. Comments fell away when the captain began to give more details.

'I am very pleased to say that I've been selected to be at Number 3. Kim McMahon, you are retained as cox, so please collect my oar for me.'

During the polite clapping, Rhan showed George her phone with a questioning expression over a reply text from Esther, which read, *"I know x6!"*

'I guess it means you are the sixth person to tell her,' whispered George. 'The news has spread! Is she from Gloucester Hall too?'

Rhan just shook her head slightly.

'Number 4 is Iain Baker, who will transfer from his position as stroke in the Second Eight,' Roger continued. The lanky, self-conscious Iain was also surprised at his call-up as he edged his way through the politely clapping throng.

'Oh bugger, they've nicked our stroke!' a Second Eight crew member below them moaned.

'Well done Iain!' some of his more generous former crew called out.

'Number 5 is another who has kept his First Eight place – Lucas Bamber, who moves forward from his old place at 7.'

There were several exhalations and exclamations at the implications of this major shift in the boat positions for one of the strongest in the old crew. Polite clapping mainly came from his former First Eight colleagues, who now realised how few places were left for them.

'Number 6, in the engine room, we have a second oarsman from the Rugby Eight, Gareth Wright!' Richard was beginning to enjoy his role. Several of the girls, alongside the rugby players, gave the inevitable cries of approval.

'So does that mean Jeff Carpenter or the Schools' chap is stroke?' someone asked at the bottom of the stairs. Rhan glanced down at Jeff, who was leaning confidently against a pillar. Had no one told him of Roger's promise of a new stroke?

'Number 7, returning to the First Eight for the third year running and the second person from the Schools' Eight, is James Nicholson.'

James nodded and moved forward, evidently expecting his recall. No one could argue against his strength and experience.

There was general relaxation as the remaining rowers realised that the selection was all over for them.

'Where's Roger? He's not back!' a surprised and slightly worried George informed Rhan. 'He didn't even stay to watch his new crew being picked.'

'He will be manipulating other people into managing the next scenes,' Rhan explained calmly, before half-murmuring to herself, 'I suppose that means I need to give him more time.'

'Then we come to Number 8, stroke, the key position!' the captain continued, building up the tempo and volume of his voice against fading interest. 'Here we have the biggest surprise yet!'

Jeff Carpenter stopped still, just as he was moving clear of the column. Rhan noted that a shadow seemed to pass over his face as he leant heavily against the steel stanchion again. Perhaps he did know, she thought. There was a long pause. Everyone was looking round trying to think who had been overlooked.

'So who's the Blue international?' one of the exasperated Schools' Eight asked. 'Who is it?'

Rhan retained her position on the step beside George, who murmured, 'Oh my God, Rhan!'

'The name I have from the coach for stroke is Rhan Arken.' There was stunned silence. The exclamations began slowly.

'What the?'

'A girl!'

'And a fresher!'

'Be serious!'

'Fucking hell!'

'Does she even row?'

'It won't be allowed! We'll be thrown off the river!'

All were now looking round for her. Rhan was still sitting at the top of the stairs, but now stood up slowly, her coat still wrapped around her. There were comments, but no clapping or cheers as she descended. She walked, barefoot, down the boathouse towards Pat, the boatman, who stood open-mouthed listening to the mumblings.

'Daft!'

'Rhan? She's just the Rugby cox isn't she?'

'A woman in the men's team!'

'What does she know about stroke?'

'She's that one who's always banging on about climate change!'

Halfway down the boathouse stood Alice. The lady captain's unmistakably shrill voice cut through the noise, aimed at Richard, her fellow captain, who made no attempt to reply. 'This is impossible! She can't row; she wrecked the balance of our boat and used the excuse of a broken oar for pathetic effort.'

James, the former captain, deliberately placed his oar against the wall in protest. 'That's not what we were promised! We were misled,' he complained.

'She's only started to row in the last few months,' Alice continued, arms now crossed. 'She wasn't good enough for our college, so I let her row for another college in Torpids last term. And now, someone's suggested she should row in the Men's Eight instead of Jeff. This is madness!'

There was an awkward silence as Rhan came to a stop in front of Alice.

'And yet, Alice,' George's voice boomed, 'even I didn't know about the training she's been getting. She bumped your boat from top of the division clear to the bottom!' No one was surprised to hear George standing up for his workmate, but his news shocked Alice.

'You were in that boat that bumped us on the last day?' Alice demanded of Rhan, outraged. 'You were meant to be in the novice division.'

'Sorry Alice, we climbed quickly.' Rhan spoke for the first time, smiling slightly. She appeared totally composed and unaffected by Alice's hostility. She nonchalantly slipped off her long black coat, and hung it on a boat rack. Most of her college had never seen her without a coat before, never mind with her hair tucked up into a tweed cap instead of the usual headscarf. Alice's brow furrowed and she fell silent, taking a step backward to look up at Rhan. The "pathetic" rower now stood tall and continued to walk slowly up to the boatman in just her borrowed cap, rowing vest and shorts.

'Just look at those shoulders!' someone blurted.

'You wouldn't want to argue with her!' came another voice.

The stocky boatman, holding the final oar close to his chest, stood gawping up at Rhan. She held out a single arm at a right angle to her body and took the heavy blade in her outstretched hand. There was a flash from a camera, followed by several more from outsiders looking in through the semi-closed sets of bifold doors. Rhan stood, weighing up the beautifully shiny carbon-fibre shaft of the blade. 'Are you sure I won't snap this one as well, Pat?' Rhan asked wryly.

He looked up at her foolishly as she stood still, her arm muscles tense with the weight of the blade.

'Blimey, so you did fracture that ladies' shaft! I only gave it a quick look. Number 1 wasn't it? Well, you won't break this one…I don't think so,' he added less certainly, glancing at Rhan and then resentfully at Alice, before immediately scuttling across the boathouse to look for the broken oar.

Alice's distinctive voice interrupted again with a different accusation.

'God! Are you Bar? They're out there waiting for you! You sometimes stroke for the Women's Blue boat. No wonder you bumped us! We didn't stand a chance. You must've been stroking for that boat which set a ridiculous record for jumping three divisions in one Torpids week!'

Rhan turned, placing the shaft handle of the oar to the ground so she could look back to the ladies' captain. She was still wearing a wry smile, which gave Alice the confidence to move on quickly, without waiting for confirmation.

'Oh my God Rhan! You are Bar!' Alice screamed excitedly. 'And in our college!' Once again, she had an audience hanging on to her every word as she tried to make sense of the baffling revelation.

'They say you passed up a Blue this year, just to help Esther, the president, with a mutiny. Yet you'd already proved that you were the best stroke! And you're training with the National squad! You're going to be a nomination for the university lady president next year – and you're in our college. This is amazing!'

'I am not sure all of that is completely true,' Rhan responded in a bizarre conversational tone. She noted that James had surreptitiously picked up his oar again.

There were several phones out now, taking photos and videos. Alice, however, was still thinking out loud and showing off her knowledge of who's who.

'You're a member of Pinks, the top university sports club, so…oh God, I'm sorry, how embarrassing!' Alice blushed, obviously recalling incidents from the garden party, but she struggled on. 'Hey, this is history. You, stroking a men's crew. Well done Richard – good move. I was chatting to several Blues out there. Esther and Dumas, the presidents, were working on something; it could only have been press releases. This is amazing!'

Rhan lifted her eyebrows and nodded her thanks to Alice for the news. On turning again, she saw a relaxed Roger now waiting by the door.

'Right, crew!' Roger took charge. 'As you may know, there is quite a crowd out there. They include the press, and a TV van is just arriving, so I'm afraid that it's going to be a very public first trial. I told you that you'd be famous.' He aimed the last comment at James, who nodded his acceptance.

'Don't stop for interviews now, but Richard and Rhan, you'll need to say a few words on your return.'

Roger then added a few rowing instructions. Rhan recognised his clever means to boost confidence among the nervous new crew members for their first outing in the frighteningly superior First shell. He also made it clear to all that while they were on the water, Rhan rather than Richard had the lead.

'OK stroke, I want off in twenty-five to the turn, back at thirty-five for a row-past, and I'll see you down the river. Your sharp, snappy, simple style, OK? Everyone else simply has to follow stroke and pull hard, crisp, slow strokes. You must all be good strong rowers – or you wouldn't have been on that list. So be confident and pull through hard! We can sort style out later.

'Now to get to the boat…Richard, I presume that you'll want the cox leading the crew down in ascending order, but I suggest you bring up the rear with Number 8. So, lead on cox, slowly!'

~

When Rhan stepped outside, there were two well-ordered lines of around a dozen men and women forming a corridor from the boathouse down the sloping concrete apron to the steps and the floating pontoon. On either side were puzzled students, along with a large party of Asian tourists who were all milling around, looking for entertainment.

The cox and DT were already waiting by the boat when Rhan and Richard, carrying their oars vertically, started down the human tunnel. Rhan was shocked to realise that the lines were made up entirely from the four sets of crews and reserves of the male and female university crew members. There was a photographer with a huge camera, and she spotted the same reporter who had been down in London on the stormy banks of the Thames for the trials.

Despite Alice's warning about the reception, Rhan was slightly overcome at seeing Dumas close by. She could say nothing – but then neither could he. She simply kissed him on the cheek as he stood at the head of one line. Dumas patted Richard's shoulder, giving himself time to recover sufficiently to say in a hoarse voice, 'Nice try Richard, but even with Bar, there's no way you're going to bump us. We'll leave you standing!'

'Come on Bar, if Dumas gets a kiss, I want one too!' complained Joe, the university stroke at the end of the other line, whom Rhan had started to walk past. 'Sorry Richard, but Pip and I will be in the boat behind you, so if you can't catch Dumas' college – well I'm afraid we'll ruin your historic day by bumping you down!'

Rhan and Richard had to progress down both lines, respectively receiving congratulations and bombastic threats. Richard soon enjoyed rebuffing the threats, once he overcame the surprise that his name was already well known.

Rhan heard one of the male student onlookers ask, 'What's the fuss?'

Another voice answered. 'See that girl, that's Bar. She's going to be stroking a men's eight in the top division at the end of this term.'

'So what? It's hardly a big deal is it?'

'Oh yes it is!' a female voice contradicted him.

The crowd had thickened and Rhan could see that members of her own college had now reinforced the sides of the corridor. With her shrill voice, Alice – now Rhan's biggest fan – was very recognisable. Friends and rivals from neighbouring boathouses wanted to see the transformation of the boat, and the growing weekend crowd distracted crews out on the river and attracted tourists from along the riverside in ever-swelling numbers.

Rhan and Richard had almost reached the floating pontoon when an explosion of noise reached them from the other side of the river. A well-orchestrated group on the far bank were shouting and screaming. Other students were converging on that side as well to see what they were missing. The sound evolved to a chanting of, 'Bar, Bar, go! Bar, Bar, go!' Rhan waved back, not really knowing how many of her old Gloucester crew were over there, but recognising the outline of some her tallest friends.

'God, Claire's got a noisy mob!' Esther complained with a smile at the river end of the line. 'Good luck Rhan, keep it simple. I don't want to make matters worse for you, but they've set up at least one TV camera and I'm due to be interviewed – *"The emergence of women in the historic universities"*. It could make the news, here and abroad.'

'Good, but...'

'Excuse me madam president.' The sports reporter was still wearing the same long raincoat, which had been so essential last time Rhan had seen him. 'Can I have just a few words with the new star?'

'Fine Ben,' Esther yielded as she stepped back so that the reporter could get closer to Rhan, who was sitting low in the water fixing her oar into its gate.

'I've done a bit of research since Esther and everyone else managed to keep you and your role hidden at the mutinous January storms. I'm beginning to appreciate now why none of the experienced international rowers was inclined to mention the contribution of an upstart novice at stroke, even if you did have expertise in rough water. My first question is, are you to be called Bar or Rhan? Please tell me something about yourself.'

Rhan, now fixing her feet into the oversized shoes, glanced up at the man standing over her. A chain of college and university rowers were keeping others back, so only the reporter had been allowed to step down off the concrete steps and onto the timber pontoon while the boat was prepared. There were occasional slaps as waves on the river washed against the floating mooring. She knew that several rowers in the crew would be finding this superior shell an intimidating experience, but she told herself that she had messed around in an even more superior craft during the university seat trials. She could relax. She made herself breathe. This was her show.

'Bar is a nickname,' Rhan responded, noting that several devices were pointing in her direction. She looked around, but returned to the matters in hand once she had spotted George standing nearby. He appeared proud, but mesmerised by the spectacle. 'I was born and live in Sunderland, but was brought up in Aleppo. I am now a student of engineering here in Oxford. I gather that I have the honour of being the first woman to row in a college first eight.'

'Will that be allowed, if it's a men's boat?' the reporter asked, pointing his device towards himself to catch the question, then back at Rhan.

'For the good of the college, I am happy to accept the position. I hope that any rule against women will be quickly set aside. I am keen on the publicity to highlight the impact that global warming will have on my generation. The ...'

'Can I ask about your inclusion in the trials for the National starter team after only a few months of rowing?' the reporter interrupted.

'I can hardly fill the shoes of my predecessor here for the college,' she declared, pointing at her feet and smiling as she thought of an answer. 'Let's say my concern over global warming is driving me as far as I can go, just so I can have interviews such as this. The main issue is that I row against *four by forty*.'

The journalist looked gratifyingly baffled at this new technical term, but his interest allowed Rhan to continue.

'I want to publicise the dreadful risks that my generation face if the older generation do not take real measures to avoid 4° of warming by 2040. I suggest you look at what that would mean to your pension, your family, your mortgage, your retirement and your children and grandchildren.'

She saw his eyes widen.

'This is going to be fun,' she suggested, smiling.

He smiled back uncertainly and muttered, 'Fascinating!' as he retreated up the steps.

~

Rhan was ready, but others were still making adjustments. There was still much sorting out behind her as James was having trouble with adjustments after swapping shoes; he was being helped by Pat, the boatman, and supervised by Roger, who was obviously anxious to be off.

Rhan looked up and spotted the curly head of her friend Tom above the crowd of onlookers and rowers behind George. It was the first time she had seen Tom this term and the first time she had ever seen him down at the river. She flicked her head upwards and smiled. Several on the riverbank turned to see who had the attention of the new star. This gave an opportunity for a striking young lady wearing wire-framed glasses to push forward from beside Tom to the edge of the pontoon near George.

'Hello Miss Rhan,' she said. 'Congratulations! I am Temi from Somerville College.' Her impressive and enthusiastic voice was heard easily across the pontoon, despite the background noise. 'My friend Tom says you might give me an interview. I freelance for several outlets.'

'Definitely!' Rhan called back. 'Just talk to Tom and George to arrange it.' Then, glancing at the reporter and onlookers who were videoing the scene, she called out, 'I would be pleased to give any interviews, so long as climate change gets a mention.'

Temi nodded her thanks, but then added a question that appeared more personal.

'Is it true that Eritrea will be in real trouble?' she asked. 'That is where I am from.'

'Yes! Most likely,' Rhan responded almost straight away. 'Sorry, every country needs to face the fact that we are facing major irreversible heating, and I would think Eritrea will be particularly bad…although some parts of East Africa are due to get heavy monsoons for a while, I believe.'

'So Greta the Scandinavian schoolgirl is right to warn us then?' Temi called back.

'I have not yet heard of any Greta,' Rhan admitted, even as she saw her coach stand clear at last. 'But any warning sounds right.' She nodded to Temi and smiled at Tom before turning her attention to the cox.

The cox, seeing signals from Roger, sat up and took control. Rhan was soon out on the river, removed from reporters, the crowd, and civilisation – connected only by a refreshing, light breeze. She now focused on how fast and far others in the unfamiliar boat should be reaching forward to replicate her movements as they dropped their blades into the calm, cool water.

*We think that mankind
does not need nature*

*After decades of trying,
I've still to construct
a negative-carbon
structure*

*There's always someone
to insist on steel or
concrete*

*Any good we do now will
reduce the severity of
what is to come*

*Why should we be allowed
to burn as much carbon as
we want, knowing it will kill
others in time?*

*We think we've found a Stone Age
village and it appears to be more
civilised than any time since*

*Long-term whole-life
targets will not help
if we keep ignoring
short-term action*

*2050 for removal of greenhouse
gas emissions seems a long way off*

*Carbon rationing would
allow our society to face
the issue of dangerous
greenhouse emissions from
the bottom up, rather than
the top-down taxation
approach attempted so far*

*Many spend their life in
retirement jetting to exotic holiday
locations knowing the irreparable
harm it will do*

*There needs to be something
to ration the number of
fellow human beings we will
each indirectly kill*

*A ration system that
is just and relatively
equitable for all would
go down very well*